Peeping Through the Reeds

A story about living in apartheid South Africa

Musuva

authorHOUSE®

AuthorHouse™ UK Ltd.
500 Avebury Boulevard
Central Milton Keynes, MK9 2BE
www.authorhouse.co.uk
Phone: 08001974150

First published by AuthorHouse   7/9/2010

ISBN: 978-1-4520-2877-4 (sc)

Front cover art work by Amadeus Artworks

This book is printed on acid-free paper.

For Annie

Note to the reader:

Some of the words and sexual descriptions may offend, because this part-fictionalised story of a deeply brutalised people is told in the authenticity of its context, such as the deeply racist language and descriptions, which are thankfully all banned as "hate speech" in the new South Africa today. Sexual violence and the brutalisation of the body are integral to such a story based on true events. All characters and conversations in this book are imaginary and any resemblance to persons living or dead is purely coincidental.

My heartfelt thanks to my sons: Art-el, for compassionately designing the cover and Lance, for advising on the cover and for reminding me daily to get this book published. Thank you for your constant respect and admiration and for never giving up on me no matter what life throws at us.

My sincere thanks to my friends and companions in South Africa, England, France, the USA and Denmark – to Michael, Saul, Shula, Paul, Wayne and Chris for their earlier comments at the very early stages of this work; to Rose and Peter, in Cape Town, who long ago suggested the title for this story; to Bill who read and listened for tireless long hours; to Sonia of the Church of England, who allowed others to listen and to learn in London; to compassionate Terry, who inspired me and gave me the confidence that it was a story worth telling; to Rachel, who constantly reminded me of the importance of the story a year later; to Jack, who opened many doors for me and who believed in me; to David, for his admiration and respect and who remained curious and interested; to Gorm, who gave me the confidence to write about the loss of teeth; to enchanting Colin in London, for providing much needed laughter, space and warmth in the final steps of completing this work at a difficult personal time; to Sis'Lindiwe, Irene, Moira, Roy, John, Chris, Anita, June, Shaheera, Clara, Makeda, Jenny and Sylvester for their many interesting and stimulating conversations; to Margaret, Helen and Richard who made many things possible for me; to my friends, ancestors and close relatives who have passed on and who encouraged me along the way. You all convinced me that this story is worth telling.

This thank you is not complete without mentioning my beloved friend and confidante, Paul, in Paris and my husbands on two continents with whom I've shared part of my life's journey.

Finally, a special thanks to Alison of FirstEditing for her comprehensive comments, professionalism and encouraging feedback that gave me that final push to publish this work with confidence.

Prologue

He pushed the boy's face into the hot brown sand in the veld of colourful spring flowers in the Karoo. He squirted his evil juice deep into the boy's innocence. "Klein *kaffirtjie!*" (Small little *kaffir!*) "Jou *hotnot* gemors!" (You are *hotnot* dirt!) The boy snorted, and tried to breathe as he lay face down under the scorching African sun. The burly White man with the rough sunburnt skin let go of his catch and pulled up his zip. The boy's blood trickled into the hot sand of the Karoo, and fed the bed of purple flowers amongst the proud aloe trees. The young boy remembered as he walked home in shame, with the notorious limp, to his quietly dignified African elders. Nobody will talk about what had happened on that otherwise beautiful spring day. This shame and many others, repeated for generations for over 300 years in the beautiful South African landscape, are little spoken about; the vast blue African sky sometimes the only ancient witness.

****

This is a story of colonialism and apartheid; about the experiences and observations of a girl named Tumelo, which is an African name that means "faith" and "belief". It is also a wider story of her people and their eventual freedom.

Contents

Chapter 1
Ambi and That Thing

Tumelo was born on the slopes of Table Mountain at the Cape of Storms, as one of the people of the wind swept sand plains between the two mountain ranges and the two oceans, one bitterly ice cold, and the other sweet and gently warm. She was of a people caught in the geographical schizophrenia of the Cape's shores; of the two respective worlds of icy indifference, from the Atlantic that stretches vast across the earth to wash up on the shores of the Aztec and Inca peoples in the Americas, and of waters that stretch across the Indian Ocean in unimaginable vastness to the Australian Coast of the dispossessed embattled Aboriginal and Maori nations. These are a people she saw pictures of in *National Geographic* magazines as extinct exotica dressed up in colours, like the people at the Cape that the *boere* (White Afrikaners) called the *"coons"*. They are a festival and dance people, with their notorious missing teeth and painted faces of tears and stars, dancing in every New Year's Celebration since their days of enslavement under the Dutch at the Cape.

When Tumelo was a teenager and a young woman fighting apartheid, she thought of herself as "African woman", "Black woman" – simply sometimes just *woman*. During the times of the transatlantic slave trade at the time of the British Empire, the conquerors of lands and people might have referred to her as *mulatto,* derived from the Spanish for "mule" – suggesting someone who is born of "mixed breed" and "idiotic and stubborn". If she had arrived in England in the 1800s, the English in London may have described her very simply as an "undersized yellow skinned *Hottentot* girl".

1

Her awareness of this *Hottentot* and *mulatto* shame all started with her old childhood friend called *Ambi*. Tumelo was one of six girls in the family, and on Sundays it was "skin lightening day" at her Aunt Freda's house. This was the day Aunt Freda and the family put aside especially for *Ambi*. If you work out the mathematics of *Ambi,* you'll find it to be very special. Because *Ambi* got full attention once per week and four or five times a month in their family, *Ambi* got over forty days a year. That means that about 400 days of Tumelo's childhood were devoted to her life companion, *Ambi*, which is over a full year in her childhood. That is at least six years of her family's time, if we count the time for each girl child and her own personal relationship with *Ambi*. Her Aunt Freda spent even more time with *Ambi*, because *Ambi* preoccupied every Sunday of her life when she was already in her thirties. *Ambi* was Aunt Freda's companion on her off day at the White madam's house, and she was focused on one thing for the day – to lighten the girls up, to help them look a little white. As little girls, they queued desperately every Sunday, hoping they would be light enough in time to get a part in the school's spring concert in *Snow White and the Seven Dwarfs,* or as *Mary* in the annual Christmas play they put up for their family and for the visiting White charity workers who brought them balloons, prize packets, and fizzy drinks of many colours. However, not one of the girls ever made it to qualify as *Mary*. They were disqualified year in and year out, for not being White enough, even though *Ambi* was their most intimate friend and confidante.

However, Tumelo and her sisters never gave up on their friend *Ambi*. They kept on rubbing and rubbing their young skin with their friend *Ambi,* and their faces burnt red and pimply. Aunt Freda would go "Tssk!" as she rubbed in vain Sunday after Sunday, and slapped them out of the frustration that they did not even turn a *little* white when it was time for the annual concert and the Christmas play. Aunt Freda hit them very hard, as if it was their fault that they did *not* turn *even a little white*. "Oh never mind!" She lifted her hands up in frustration for her own anger for her own dark chocolate skin, in which she often felt uncomfortable and in pain; it was something she wanted to peel off her being until her skin was pink, like after human flesh has roasted in a fire. Even if she could burn it off, and she looked like a roasted pig – at least she would be classified "White" and would be able to go swim in the sea, walk in the park, get a good job, get a decent house with a pavement and with electricity – even if her skin was stinging. She would go to the best schools, be buried in a cemetery where there are public toilets, go to the front of a shop to buy bread, not the back, and go for a picnic wherever she wanted. Apartheid did not grant her this. So in her imagination every Sunday, *every day, she* peeled her skin off, burnt it on a funeral pyre, roasted her body, discarded her being like a snake, and pulled out her hair at its roots for new sleek hair to grow. She despised herself and got all the girls in the family, and even the boys, to despise themselves. As her grandfather always told her when she was a child, "It is a *shame* if you are born with *kroes* (kinky) hair and *Black* skin, and it is an even *bigger shame* if you *die* with it! You should at least look a little beautiful in your coffin, with *straight* hair and a lovely *white* skin...While you live as a *Coloured*, you must do everything to get the *gam* (pronounced with a guttural *g*) out of *yous!*"

Hearing this commotion every Sunday about hair, *ordentlikheid* (decency), and skin colour, Tumelo's grandmother would shout from the kitchen in between the sounds of gospel music. "Praise the Lord and all the angels! It is the day of the Lord!" after which, she'd remind the frustrated aunt, "Even though these piccaninnies of mine are supposed to be Coloured, their one uncle is so Black, his gums are even navy blue! You can't *make* them *White!*" Their granny would cut back yet again at her daughter, "And, in any case, you are a *Bushman* yourself! Get a life! They'll look like *khaki Europeans (not the real thing)* when you have finished with them!" As she put the roast chicken and potatoes back in the oven to roast a little more, the old woman in her big starched white apron, with her frank no-nonsense boisterous laughter, and small piercing eyes which underlined her crass style, would continue singing loudly in a high-pitched voice along with the apartheid-managed Springbok Radio station, *"Amazing Grace, how sweeeet thou art that saved a wretch liiiiike meeeee....I once was lost but now I'm found...!"* She liked the feel of the words of being "saved" from being a "wretch".

Tumelo's journey as a fellow wretched person started with a small black spot between her two beautifully white and solid front teeth. She was curious to see what the local White *boere* dentist in Ottery thought of it, so her mother sent her off to the dentist to fix it for her with a filling. Dr. Piet was one of the dentists who looked after the teeth of the poor working class Coloured folk on the Cape Flats. This dentist only did two things, extractions and dentures. The boys fondly called Tumelo "dimples," as they winked at her and whistled when she passed by on the way to buy bread or paraffin at the shop. Dr. Piet had a nameless African Black male assistant dressed also in a white coat, who was trained to restrain cheeky Coloured patients who were scared, or who wanted to run away, or who shouted too loudly during an enforced extraction. Dr. Piet was a huge White man with blue eyes in a white coat with an injection and teeth extraction spanners always ready in his hands, even when he walked down the corridor or when he stood at the door of the waiting room, calling patients one by one in his flat Afrikaner accent. He deliberately spoke to them in their second language, English. Yet, he could speak their first language, Afrikaans. He was known to be a no-nonsense dentist, and the only White doctor in the poor township who cared to greet his patients, who sometimes also called him *"baas"* the Afrikaans for "boss". He knew that the poor, often uneducated, Coloureds feared him – because they'd all get to know his gloved fingers in their mouths at sometime or the other. He was actually like a local undertaker. As a Coloured, you ended up with him one way or the other in the township ruled by apartheid. Teeth don't last. They get rotten, they get old, and they can leave you in excruciating pain.

"And so, little *meisie* (girl), how can the docterrr help you today?" he quipped in his flat Afrikaner accent with his back turned to Tumelo as he washed his hands in the basin. His assistant (whose name nobody knew and never bothered to know), who looked as if he also feared Dr. Piet and his pain-inducing instruments, stepped closer towards Tumelo to pre-empt an escape. It was said that the nameless African man was well trained in catching both Coloured children and adults who ran away from Dr. Piet. With a constant bewildered look in his eyes, the quiet African man with his beautiful white teeth was always ready for the chase. Tumelo's cousin, Patrick, stood up to Dr. Piet when he was brought there by his big brothers one day under much protest to have his teeth extracted. He was a daring little boy. When Dr. Piet and his African helper wanted to pin him down on the big swirling chair, Patrick fought hard and kicked Dr. Piet in his balls and ran away calling him *"jou naaier, trek jou eie fokkieng tande! Jou bek stink!"* "You are a fuck, go extract your own fucking teeth! Your trap smells!" At that moment, Tumelo remembered what Patrick had done so fearlessly, and thought to herself that should Dr. Piet want to do anything nasty with her, then she was going to kick his balls and tell him he is a *naaier*, a fuck. Tumelo's mother put a raw chilli in their mouths if her children swore these ugly words. She feared her mother's punishment. She was a fearsome woman and did not want her children to grow up to become *skollies*, notorious Coloured hooligans and gangsters. Even if she would hear from someone months later that they heard that someone said they heard from someone else they don't know that one of her children had sworn at the boere dentist, she would whack all seven of them for hours in a locked room until they bled and one of them owned up – even just to stop the beatings. So instead, Tumelo smiled and rubbed her hands nervously while she looked up at Dr. Piet's face. She jumped onto the big swirling chair before Dr. Piet's helper laid his hands on her. She wanted to show that she was a big, brave girl that did not fear the boere dentist and his Black helper the way the other children and big Coloured people did. That day, she wanted to show Dr. Piet that she was a good girl, a proud girl who knew how to take care of her body.

Tumelo found pride in her first pink lace size 32A bra that her mom had bought her when she started to menstruate. It was a cheap bra purchased from the local OK Bazaars with crooked wiring that hurt, yet it made her feel special. It was a sort of comfort, one that took her mind away from her swollen tender young belly and the light blue plastic fat pack of *Johnson's Sure* sanitary towels that her mother threw at her every nineteenth day of the month. This mother knew her daughters' monthly cycles, and watched like a hawk to make sure that they did not skip. "And now don't be *ougat!*" (saucy), she shouted at Tumelo every nineteenth of every month. "And stay away from the *skollies!*" She never explained what she meant, and Tumelo and her sisters did not dare to ask, because their mother would give them a *snotklap*, one of those hard, notorious working-class Cape Flats smacks that left your nose running with mucus or blood, depending on the severity of the blow and the sting of the anger directed at the victim.

Now Tumelo was alone with two men on a swirling chair with nasty instruments in trays – one White, one Black – with very clear roles in the initiation of her officially becoming branded as a "Cape Coloured;" a bit like the Star of David, one could say. At that moment, Tumelo became aware of the power of these men over her body; that they could do anything to her in a most intimate part of her body in that little dusty surgery room with the lonely skewed picture of an English countryside town on the wall, with men dressed in black top hats and tuxedo suits, with English ladies at their sides; a little distraction subtly displaying the White dentist's idea of decency. In school, the teacher always read them poems about England. She imagined then the clean White children running across wheat fields in a pristine countryside littered with red apples and wild berries, the white clean snow and the reindeer, the jam, and scones that went with a civilised cup of tea; it was a place where even the sheep were white. For a moment in that chair, Tumelo saw a little glimpse of that world all poor Coloured children imagined as *the ideal world of civilisation.*

"Open your mouth!" Dr. Piet demanded. His tone was no longer friendly, but impatient and hurried. There were many patients waiting and he had to cut time short in case Tumelo, like all other young Coloured children in his chair, caused any drama his helper stood over Tumelo, ready to restrain her. She opened her mouth to show her beautiful white strong teeth. At that moment she had one deep desire, that Dr. Piet would compliment her beautiful teeth, or use her for toothpaste advertisements perhaps. She drank fresh milk from the cow everyday – jugs full. She ate lots of cheese, and she brushed her teeth day and night.

She looked at the extracting silver instruments in the little kidney-shaped silver tray at the side of the swirling chair, and then realised what was coming. Tumelo tried to plead decently, "My mother said Doctor must please fix the little black hole between my two front teeth. "
"Ah, lets see...how old are you?"
"Just turned twelve, Doctor."
Dr. Piet proceeded to put his whole face into Tumelo's mouth. Well, he almost did. He continued in his flat Nazi-like Afrikaner accent, "My child, you must *understand* one thing that this docterrrr is going to tell you *ni-ow.* Very few of *your people* know how to look after their teeth and these are permanent teeth, and already there is a little black spot! Ooh, I don't know...*your people...Where do you people come from?* Where?! God knows..."

He sighed and shrugged his shoulders in despair, gesturing to his anonymous African assistant.

Tumelo started to feel awkward. The words "you people" made her scared and reminded her that he was a *boer*, the people who were in charge of the country who looked down on you and decided what was good for you. She knew that even her fearless robust mother feared the boers. He looked at his helper, gestured him to be ready for any action. The next thing she knew, Tumelo was staring into a huge long needle aiming for her young pink gums.

Dr. Piet made a point of being business-like. He gave her no choice in the matter. "If I take out two, you'd look funny and you won't fit in. I suggest we take out four. The Coloured girls come to me to ask that I take out four. They say it makes them popular with the boys for this thing called a French kiss and other naughty things." He winked at her suggestively and giggled like a dirty old man.

Tumelo froze. Her body went stiff. Her legs went lame from fear and helplessness. This was not what she had wanted! She did not come to have her front teeth taken out!! How was she going to stop this? She wanted to run away, but she knew there was no hope. Tumelo could hear other patients (mothers and fathers, big brothers and big sisters) fearfully coughing and sneezing in the adjacent waiting room. Most of them were adults like her parents, and they all had one thing in common. They feared Dr. Piet. They did not argue with him. You did not argue with a boer in apartheid South Africa. The educated Coloureds and Africans who did that and even argued their case - well, they got locked up, imprisoned, and killed.

Since the days of slavery at the Cape you knew your place. The dentist was like the boere police. You don't argue. Tumelo thought of Patrick and what he had done to Dr. Piet. She must call him a "naaier" and kick him in his balls. She must jump up and run. She did not want to lose her teeth. She did not want to lose her smile. She did not want to lose her dimples, because when your front teeth are out, your dimples look like misplaced wrinkles on a young face. This White big boere man was going to take something away from her forever on that day, and Tumelo knew that. Dr. Piet said they were permanent teeth, which meant that if they were taken out they would be permanently gone! Tumelo was deeply confused. She had seen many Coloured people with gaps in their mouths, in front, like the "coons". Despicable, hapless people, usually gangsters and poor women. She did not want to look like that. She did not want to do French kisses and other things to boys. She came to show Dr. Piet her beautiful teeth and how good she looked after them like the way the teacher said she should. She wanted to come and show him that she did not fear the dentist and his tools. She wanted to show him how much she wanted to keep her teeth and be a nice girl with a nice smile. Tumelo started to sweat. She felt helpless as she stared into the long needle heading for the warm pink softness of her gums. At that torturous moment, she grew more aware of the sanitary towel between her legs, more aware that her body was bleeding. Little balls in her body that she could feel just above her hip bones, and just below the softness of her navel and buried deep in her belly, were throbbing madly, and warm blood was flowing out of her; this was nature's way of telling her that she was now a woman and that she had to look after her body, become aware of its mysterious and profound power, protect it, and be careful what happens to it.

Dr. Piet seemed in charge of poor Coloured people's mouths, teeth, and bodies.

No, the actual truth is that Dr. Piet did not have all the power; he could not control the feisty tongues and caustic humour about the *"dom boere"*, the idiotic boers, of these creolised people. The suppressed voice of an angry fellow patient made out an obviously toothless slur through bloodied cotton wool stuffed in her mouth as she ran down the staircase littered with oil-stained newspaper from the famous "English fish and chips" parcels sold at the cafe next door. She shouted from the pavement up into the window of the surgery, her voice slurred in blood. *"Jou wit poes! Jou boere naai!"* "You are a White cunt! You are a boere fuck!"

The local people knew that every Coloured tooth was bread on the table for Dr. Piet and his family, who resided in the adjacent upmarket White neighbourhood; he made twenty pence a tooth. Extractions were frequently without much consent or discussion, and usually also took place without much anaesthetic.

Dr. Piet sighed as the woman shouted up into his surgery room's window from the littered pavement. "The vulgar Coloured fectorie girls again...", he muttered in a monologue to his speechless helper. Tumelo felt that he spoke as if she was not in the room. "I tell you, we must sort these people out. They don't *know* what is *good* for them. It is a catch-22 with these people. If you leave their teeth in, then they don't know how to look after them. Best thing is to take them out. And let me tell you, they *like* to have their front teeth out for this *pession-thing*. So I do them a favour. When the Coloured girls come to me and they have that shy quiet look on their face and these knowing giggles, I don't wait to ask. *I know what is good for them. I know what they want*, and I do it for them before they ask. You see, they like that *thing*. Then I see them again years later for dentures. Because you see, they can't find decent work without their teeth. So I am always there to help them either way, in case they want to become teachers of the Coloured children. Then they need their teeth to teach the toothless Coloured children to say words properly. Otherwise, they all end up with a lisp and the school inspectors don't like that business. I am a kind of saviour with these Coloured folk, you can say; first with the pair-sion, and then with the work. But the fec-torie girls and servant girls, they are a *different* story. They must have *the look* – toothless with a love bite in the neck, helping to suck their scruffy necks clean. I *know* these people. I have worked with them for *many many* years. There is nothing you can tell me about Coloured people that I don't know. You can say, I am a Coloured people's man...I help them. You can't mix colours, you see. You don't even do it when you do your washing...Hehehe!"

He laughed and looked at his silent and speechless helper. Tumelo noticed that the anonymous man had not lost one tooth to Dr. Piet, and she wondered why not. African people in South Africa don't normally have their teeth extracted; they are known for their beautiful, strong white teeth.

"Right, four to go with this little one. Pass the tray..." Tumelo closed her eyes. She could feel her eyes going misty. She felt a lump in her throat. Her legs felt like nervous wobbly jelly. She felt helpless and scared. Bizarre, confusing thoughts raced through her mind. "That is why my mother sent me to the dentist, to help me with that *thing* with the boys. I was menstruating and I was now ready for that thing. I have heard about the French kiss at school. I have never done it. They say the boys push their tongues into your mouth and it helps when you have a gap to massage his tongue in your mouth. Another friend told me it helps with sucking the boys, with the suction action. But I did not come for that. I want to be a decent girl."

As these thoughts raced through her mind, the needle pierced her gum, travelling into the nerve ends under her nose almost into her nostrils, a cold, long prick into her warm, young, innocent soft mouth. It was a long, thick, cold needle. Her top lip felt instantly huge and numb. Dr. Piet pushed his huge, cold gloved fingers into her mouth, caressing her numb gums. He was an older man, already gray, older than her father. He pinched her top lip while his old blue eyes pierced through her young innocent brown ones. "Feel that?" he queried, almost pervertedly, but gently. There were brown blood stains on his white coat. Tumelo wanted to pee right there and then on his swirling tatty black leather chair. She was bleeding and she wanted to pee all at the same time. Her heart was pouncing. Her head was angry. Her body felt small and helpless. She could feel it all happening to her while the Springbok Radio station played popular Afrikaner songs. Run by the Afrikaners in the 1970s and until the end of apartheid, the all time *Sarie Marais* was playing. A traditional Afrikaans folk song about the forced removal of a young boere mother and children to the English concentration camps at the time of the Anglo Boer War at the end of the nineteenth century. Dr. Piet was a true and proud Afrikaner as he whistled and sang along to the boere all time favourite that was sung around camp fires. A deep loss was about to be forced upon Tumelo, like it had been on many other young, poor Coloured girls and boys before her. Her body was being invaded. She had no say over her body. This huge White man in the white coat wanted to be the master of her body, of her mouth, of her face, of her pride, of her intimate vulnerable parts. Dr. Piet pulled hard and tucked away at Tumelo's new young permanent teeth. She could smell the rubber gloves on his huge claws tucking away in her mouth. One, two, three, four. Excruciating pain shot like electricity through her skull as the roots of each young healthy permanent tooth were dislodged unceremoniously from her gums. Her mouth tasted cold, bitter, and bloody. She did not want to scream like the Coloured factory and servant girls. She wanted to be a decent girl. Be a decent girl. Be a decent girl, have dignity in resistance.

Dr. Piet's mission was accomplished. He asked the wide-eyed African helper to give a tissue to Tumelo. "It is for the tears," he said matter-of-factly. "Happens when you take out the four front teeth; it is the nerve that runs from the eye that causes the tears." Then he proceeded to sing randomly along with the song that followed - Johnny Nash's *I can see clearly now...*, he pushed his old eyes into hers again. "Cheer up now, *meisie (girlie)*...smile for the docterrr!" he whistled. He smiled, showing off his own teeth; he seemed mission-accomplished happy - sort of strangely satisfied that he had branded another Coloured girl. He gestured to his African helper to bring the mirror, while he continued singing with Johnny Nash. "You like that s-a-u-ng, hey? Smile for the docterr."

His accent was even more thick and flat with ancient familiar prejudice as he tried again.

"You like that s-a-u-ng hey? Smile for the docterr."

Dr. Piet teased Tumelo as if he was aware he was making a sick joke. At that moment, Tumelo noticed that he had all his own teeth in his mouth. Shiny, healthy teeth from since the time he was a boy as young as her. She felt cheated. She looked sheepishly and enviously into his mouth.

"A bit of a bloody one, but nice, hey?" he smiled again as he stared at his handy work in her young mouth.

His flat, coarse accent somehow added to the cruelty. He pushed his gloved fingers underneath her top lip to showcase his work of art in her mouth in the mirror, in case she did not appreciate and realise his favour. Tumelo was horrified, but still tried a smile. Her dimples were gone in a flash, replaced with enforced premature wrinkles on a young face. Her beautiful young white teeth were gone. Instead, she stared into four fresh deep holes in her gums filled with fresh, thick, dark maroon blood. She looked like a typical Coloured factory girl of the 1960s. Devastated, she wanted to die right there and then.

Dr. Piet's African helper looked at her as if he felt sorry for her. He did not seem pleased with Tumelo's new look, but he did his job. He was also about Tumelo's father's age. He was ebony dark like her father. He could have been her father, a blood relative. The anonymous helper stuffed cotton wool into Tumelo's mouth. He was used to stuffing cotton wool into the bloodied mouths of poor Coloured people; it was just a job that gave him a little money to buy *pap* (maize meal) and brown bread for his family in the African township. Many local shops did not allow him to buy white bread from them because he was Black. He knew that the Coloureds were more privileged than him; they could buy bread of a colour of their choice, they got better jobs than him, and they were not forced to live in poverty-stricken homelands nor to carry a *dompas*, a stupid pass book, an apartheid identity document for African people only. He carried his in the pocket of

11

his trousers, because if the *boere* caught him without it, he would be beaten up and jailed. When he chased the Coloured patients down the road, it was his *dompas* that he held on to for dear life, because the boere said that "A kaffir without a pass was a dead man" in South Africa. He knew that Coloureds suffered at the hands of the boere, but that his Xhosa and Zulu people suffered even more; Indians were second class, Coloureds were third class, and Africans were fourth class. He had mixed feelings about these people who suffered at the hands of his racist boss, as he often heard them shouting in the street, taunting each other, "You will suffer like a kaffir!" It was most feared to be a suffering "kaffir", like being an "untouchable" in India. The Coloured people rhymed the words in their pronunciation - "suffer" and "kuffer"- and they mocked him everyday on the street on his way home. He was a man who completed all his schooling, who could read and write, who could speak many languages – but who could not get a job because he was Black. The people whispered on the streets that he was a "Swahili", who were noted for their *knopkieries,* walking sticks that doubled up as much feared weapons in street battles.

The sympathetic African man whispered to her gently, "Bite on it, it helps with the bleeding...And here are more tissues for the tears." Tumelo searched for her father's white handkerchief with the brown-striped border in the pocket of her purple and white floral dress. Her mother gave it to her as she left the house, "Here, in case you cry at the dentist..."

Dr. Piet countered his helper's sympathetic gestures, "Don't worry. In two week's time, she is going to be a *hit* with the Coloured boys. They like that *thing*!" he teased, winked, and laughed, his huge fat body shaking in excitement. "He-he-he!"

The African man looked shocked; it was a permanent expression on his face. Tumelo still did not really understand what Dr. Piet meant by the *thing*. He dried his hands, winked, and smiled at her shrewdly, with a deliberately flat and crass *"goo-bye"*.

Chapter 2
Lay Me Down in the Fynbos

"We are from the Griqua people – the people of the desert plant, named *kanniedood,* which means 'cannot die'. These plants have a peeling, papery bark; it does not look just like any tree. It grows on the stony mountainsides along the Orange River, its roots clinging to the rocks. They are like our people – resilient and unique, not just to be found anywhere in the world, and wherever they go, they proudly take root in the hardest of places on Earth. They are strong and resistant, yet they also bear soft delicate fruit, thinly fleshed and often brightly Coloured. Their succulent fruit need very little water and are used to droughts. It is about resilience, child. Prosper even in drought... even during hardship, and your roots will stay strong and undisturbed by the wind storms. Be like myrrh, like the Balm of Gilead, be the medicine of our people, be the incense that can cure our people from our many diseases today. Like the *kanniedood,* thrive in the desert, be persistent in your fight for what is right... "

Aunt Margaret, a self-educated, unmarried bespectacled Griqua Sunday school teacher in her early fifties with a conservative appearance, her hair tied in a bun on top of her head and wearing an ankle length orange and blue floral dress, was comforting Tumelo after her ordeal with Dr. Piet.

She took a photo out of the drawer in the crockery cupboard in the kitchen. It was covered with dust, and she traced her finger in the dust as she spoke with a notable quiet anger in her voice. "Same story. *Geslag na geslag.* Generation after generation. Look at this photo of your great grandpa. See how he poses? See the way he is dressed, like an honourable Englishman, like the Black men in London, there, far away in England. He always wanted to go

13

to England, where he said Coloured gentlemen go to talk politics and to organise for things to be put right in their land. He never had time for riff-raff; these Coloured people who have lost their front teeth and who dance for the Cape coons , the gangsters and *skollies...*" At this, she went quiet, realising her unintended slip of the tongue with her niece who had just lost her teeth.

"What I meant to say is that he fought for the decency of the Coloured people day and night. It was his passion. When Queen Victoria died, he was a very sad man, and died himself a few years after, because he did not know who to go speak to. He thought a lot of her, because the world made so much of her in the newspapers as she ruled England for a long time. Sad story is he never got to England, and he was put to rest in his coffin dressed up like an honourable old-fashioned English gentleman, still waiting in vain to go to London to meet the queen.

"Look at us. We are survivors. We've been through the hardest hardships of slavery under the Dutch. Then the English came with their cruel punishing ways and segregation laws. 'You can't do this; you can't do that.' We fought hard, but in the end, we lost our land first to the Dutch and then to the English. And then we had to help them fight each other in the Anglo Boer War. Then they dropped us just like that and divided the land amongst themselves through the South African Union and the Land Acts that followed soon after."

Tumelo's Aunt Margaret spoke in a long monologue that afternoon. She continued talking while she stirred the huge pot of samp and beans soup in the kitchen of the family's wood and iron cottage in the woods. Tumelo listened in amazement, as she sipped on warm custard to allow her mouth to heal.

"The boers, like Dr. Piet, started in Van Riebeeck's time, and the English joined hands later with them against the natives, after they had made peace to fight off the rest: the Ma'pondo, the Griquas, the Zulus, the Sotho, and the Ndebele. There are many groups of natives in our land; I can't remember all the names now...."

Looking down, trying to remember all the groups and names, she continued with a sigh, "This is what all led to the political stuff amongst natives and our Coloured people today. Your great-great grandfather wanted to be peaceful in his fights for rights, like Gandhi and the others. He admired the people like Dr. Abdullah

Abdurahman who led the Coloureds in a deputation to England to talk about the politics and the vote.

What I'm telling you now you won't be taught at school or at Sunday school. I learned these things through the stories told to me and the political leaflets that we got to read that were handed out by these political people. The old man read many political papers to help him at parliament. I remember one newspaper he always liked, *The Coloured People's Opinion*. It was written in funny English, but many people liked it, as it gave them information on what was going on. There was also another newspaper, *The Torch*. He always spoke about all these people and the things he read. We grew up with these names and conversations in our house. "

She took out another photograph from the stack of old pictures in her hand. "I have another photograph to show you of your uncle's father, who fought in an important battle in the Second World War."

The small old black-and-white photo was stapled onto cardboard. There were four Coloured soldiers in the photo armed with rifles. On the reverse side of the photo, a family member's shaky handwriting in thick pencil read: "Uncle Arthur Peters on active service in Second World War, 1942, Al Alemein, Egypt."

"See this? What did they get in fighting in such a big war? Nothing! Only apartheid in 1948!"

Aunt Margaret cleared her throat and continued.

"But one thing, the old man used to say, the early European travellers were ignorant people because they could not understand the language of his people, the Hottentots. You do learn about them in your history books, don't you?"

Tumelo did not answer her aunt, because her teacher told them at school that it was a shame to be seen as a "Hottentot", as they were described as "lazy crafty cattle thieves" in the history books at school. She could not believe that she and the teachers came from these shameful people. Aunt Margaret seemed oddly proud of being a "Hottentot", though she knew that the boere called her people "the hotnots", the people who came from the Hotnotte and other people, a mixed people without pride, without a culture, the shameless toothless dregs of Cape society. It baffled her that Aunt Margaret was so proud of an otherwise shameful people?

The old man used to laugh, and shout, "Oh, the Whites say we speak from the throat, and we seem to sob, sigh, and hiccup when we speak, like the clucking of hens and turkeys! They never understood us! Poor things... they were ignorant. They did not know much about this part of Africa. They were simply travellers...and always looked down on us, insulting our women's huge backsides and their breasts. What was pretty for us about our women, was ugly to them. Yet many of them secretly slept with our women. Where do you think the hotnots come from? From Whites sleeping with the natives and the Hotnotte..." She grunted at the irony, and started to grab a garment to iron from the laundry bundled on the wooden kitchen table. She continued speaking as she ironed the garments, not looking up much in her pedantic angry monologue.

"When you have lost your name, your place, your language, your family – you hold on to your quiet self. You don't want to lose more. And by being quiet, you keep a lot. Because silence is hard to steal. Silent thoughts cannot be taken away. Some of us Coloured people have learned to be quiet, but it does not mean that we have given up. It is a big thing God would want you to remember; his children never give up. We are all his children. We must pray and ask God to give your teeth back. Dr. Piet stole them from you to feed his White family..." she sighed.

Like most Cape elders, Aunt Margaret did not give Tumelo much space to ask questions or to respond to her stories, "So, no, our family does not trust the White man; not the boere and not the English. The British said he must speak to the boere, and the boere in turn said, go speak to the rooinekke – *hulle is die skelms in Afrika*; go speak to the rednecks – they are the real thieves in Africa. So he got sent from pillar to post in his suit, dressed like an honourable Black Englishman in London.

The old man knew a lot about people in other parts of the world who had similar roots. He used to say, 'But it is the same for native people like us in Australia and the Americas. And like them, we have survived it all, my child. Look at me. I am a decent man. You won't find me without my handkerchief, my bible, my suit, my walking stick, my hat, and without my teeth! I am not a *skollie*. I am not a gangster. From Sunday to Sunday. Everyday of the week he used to speak about his decency. It was important to him.

He complained that the White people pretended that they did not understand his language, or what he was trying to say when he told them that they must return the land to the Hottentots and Griqua people. He was therefore always practising his English for that day to go to London to talk to Her Majesty about giving the land back. London must listen to us, he used to say, because we are the ancient people on this earth, like the Aboriginals in Australia and the Red Indians in America, the people who were here first at the Cape.

We buried him amongst the *fynbos* (meaning fine-leaved trees in Dutch), where he asked to be laid to rest, in the shadow of the small bushes with which our people identify closely."

Chapter 3
The Bitter Fruits of Orchards

But there was more to the old man's pride in being a "Hottentot". Amongst many Coloured people at the Cape today, the sense of shame of being Black or of being called *kaffirs* goes back a long time, since the arrival of the Dutch at the Cape in 1652. Coloured men formed a part of the more than 300,000 Africans from the continent that were recruited in the allied forces to battle against Hitler's racism in Europe. As part of the Cape Corps, Coloured men were used in the nineteenth century wars against the Dutch and the Africans (in the so-called "Kaffir Wars") and against Hitler and the fascists in the 1940s. Then Prime Minister, General Smuts, promised that they would not be discarded after the war, but they were. The African and Coloured soldiers were like today's Ghurkas in Britain, known to be a "used and discarded people"; recruited when needed, and discarded and forgotten once they had served their purpose in times of conflict and war. Yet, this shame is unfortunate, because many Coloured people are indigenous to South Africa, descendants of the oldest and most diverse people with the most diverse DNA in the world, the Khoisan (which gradually replaced the pejorative "Hottentots" for Khoi and "Bushmen" for San) – many of them are to Southern Africa, as noted earlier, what the Aztecs and Incas are to the Americas, what the Maoris are to New Zealand, and what the Aboriginals are to Australia. Others come from enslaved people in the East (Malaysian, Indonesian, and Indian), and others from interracial affairs with other African people and "White" people from Europe (Germans, English, Irish, Scottish, Dutch, Portuguese, French, Jews, people from the Baltic sea, and so on and so on). However, others could have come from the rape of indigenous women by White colonial masters and soldiers, such as those who fled Namibia, then known as German South West Africa, at the turn of the nineteenth century during the genocide of the Herero and Nama people by the Germans. Many Black Africans in South Africa today do not want to be mistaken as "Coloureds" nor do they want to be viewed as "of the Hottentots". Because of its history, the Cape remains a place of deep racial tension and unspoken shame.

This is the background to the next story.

The year was 1939 in South Africa and it was the month of August, when the cold winter changes for spring and when one can see large blankets of yellow, pink, orange, and white blooms of the indigenous *vygies* (Lampranthus) with their perennial succulent silvery stems and leaves covering the sand dunes of the Cape. Eve, a local woman from the Griqua and Khoisan community, was a child then. She was cosily at home with her grandparents when they received a visit from her mother and her mother's husband that morning. Eve felt nervous about going with her mother and this man whom they now told her was her father. Until then, she had felt so safe and cared for in her granny's home where there were regular church gatherings, travelling Griqua singing choirs, visiting gentlemen in black suits, table manners, and regular meals. Her grandparents wanted the best education for her, and taught their granddaughter what the missionaries taught them, to sing hymns in Dutch and to be able to fluently recite the *Our Father* in both English and Afrikaans. She helped her aunts set a table, starch the white tablecloth, and learned how to make Cape Malay curry and sweet beet root salad for Sunday lunch. She liked the security, the systematic organisation of her home, the way she was spoiled by her aunts, the household chores they taught her, the cousins who visited, the men who came to talk politics, the aunts who paraded endlessly for attention from the handsome male visitors, the visits to parliament in Cape Town, the Sunday singing, and the predictions of the numerous visiting Khoisan prophets about the land and droughts and floods and of the succession of chiefs. Her grandfather had status in the Griqua community, and she was treated as a princess. The Griqua prophets called her "the salt of the house", the "princess of Table Mountain", and brought her gifts of rosemary in abalone shells.

She could run to her grandmother when strangers came, hide behind her huge backside, hang on to the bow of her navy blue silk dress, and just find comfort in the familiarity of her quiet, stern, yet warm presence. Her grandmother was like sweet potato and custard to her. She found comfort in the smell of the fresh polish of the wooden floors of the old cottage and in the faint sunshine that filtered through the window of the room where her grandfather recorded the history of the creolised Griqua people who came from the indigenous Khoisan, the African Tswana, the Dutch and French peoples. She tried to stay up with him until the early hours of the morning as he prepared documents for presentation at parliament until the oil in the lamp burnt out. She found comfort in the smell of braised onions as her granny prepared the meals, borrowing from African, Malaysian, Dutch, French, English, and other indigenous cuisine. On Mondays they had *bobotie*, a Malaysian curried minced meat dish with spices of masala, ginger, marjoram and lemon rind, garnished with raisins, chutney, milk and egg. On Tuesdays, they would have Malaysian-Dutch cabbage bredie (stewed lamb and cabbage), followed by Indian curry beans with roti (flat dough). On Wednesdays, they would dig into African samp and beans, or flavour the lasting honey-like tastes of turmeric tripe stew on Thursdays. On Friday nights, her grandpa would buy English fish and chips from the local fisheries and she would have the privilege of licking the delicious vinegar soaked salty batter off the newspaper at the end of the meal. On Saturdays, it would be English braised liver, onions, boiled potatoes, and fresh vegetables, topped with a thick gravy. After dinner, her aunts would prepare the chicken, beef, or pork, and peel a half a bag of giant potatoes for the Sunday roast. Her grandmother would soak sago overnight in a huge ceramic bowl of milk and butter with cinnamon as a desert preparation to go with the Sunday roast.

Eve was the little protected daughter of her grandparents. She would play hide and seek amongst her grandfather's tailor-made coats which hung in the huge wooden wardrobe, which smelled of mothballs. She would hide herself under bales of wool and cotton in the box in the corner where the winter sun found its place in the comfortable Newlands cottage.

This Sunday would change her life forever. The elderly couple were reluctant to give their granddaughter to their daughter.

"Know what? Our daughter married a *kaffir*. Can you believe that? After all our struggles for *decency*...." Eve's grandparents, the Indian woman, Nazurah, and the Griqua Khoisan man, Moses, spoke candidly about "the *kaffir*" their daughter had married. They so easily forgot then their own family tragedy of being called, viewed, and treated as "*kaffirs*" by racist White South Africans. It was a mind boggling phenomenon for any sane onlooker.

"We have not visited our daughter since she married the *kaffir*", they would tell friends who visited on Sunday afternoons for tea.

"But we are all the same...the Hereros, the Namas, the Xhosas, Zulus, the Basuto and the Khoi...?" a political friend dared to question.

"No, Hereros are *klip kaffirs*"

"What does that mean?"

"Kaffirs of the stone..."

"You mean as in *rock*...as in *kanniedood*?"

"No, that is *our* symbol, not *theirs*...we are *not* the same..."

"Ah, yah perhaps you are right."

"See, the Griqua are a mixed people of White, Tswana, and Khoi. The Hereros are not a mixed people."

The Griqua colleagues confirmed to themselves that although they were "born out of generations of shame", and were described by the White racist governors as "bastards of mixed breed", who did not enjoy equality with Whites, they were nonetheless, "better than the *kaffirs*".

"What was she doing with a *kaffir*?" Moses asked Nazurah one day, as if his Indian wife bore some responsibility for their daughter's seemingly unfortunate choice.

"Coloureds are *Coloureds - people!*" Moses reasoned, and shouted at his wife.

"Coloureds are decent, not from the North; they are indigenous to the mountains, seas and *fynbos* of the Cape," he mumbled further.

"That is why there are so many children to feed. The *kaffir* does not know when to stop..."

Her grandmother would protest, "Sweetheart, don't use that word...you know the story of how your grandpa got killed by the White man for trespassing on his own land....they called him a *kaffir and spat on him*...all of us were treated like slaves at the Cape; we should not be calling other people *kaffirs*. Don't talk like that...like the English and the boers..."

"Nazurah, there are *kaffirs* and there are *kaffirs*...they are not all the same. My daughter has married the wrong *type* of *kaffir*! There are decent *kaffirs*, the ones who teach there in kaffirland in Transkei. Some are even lawyers and priests and write for newspapers, and go to England to speak to the queen. I call them the 'clever *kaffirs*'. Why didn't she choose a clever *kaffir*?! You tell me...She married into the stupid *kaffirs* that got murdered out by the Germans because they were weak...they did not resist as they should have..."

"And they saw themselves as superior to the Coloured people of the Cape?"

"Yah, point is they say they are not from the slaves of Jan van Riebeeck's time. They battled with the White man for a long time. They did not just give up their land...battles were still taking place the other day in the last century."

"Yes, the Khoi also lost their land, some were murdered through genocide like the early people of Australia and the Hereros and Namas of South West Africa, and some were enslaved...many were a people without a land...we are all the same really...where are all the diamond fields of the Griqua people today? Gone...the English robbed you of all your wealth...we are no better than the Herero and Nama people..."

"No, some of us were just stupid...to just give up like that..."

"*Liefie* (loved one), he is not that bad. He is *mixed* they say. I think a bit Coloured. They say his mother is Herero and his father is German."

"Yah, I know he is from the *klip kaffirs*. His mother is an illiterate herd-girl, can't even have a proper conversation with us. You can't invite her for tea here. She would not fit in with my Griqua friends from parliament."

"In the eyes of the White man, old man, we are *all kaffirs*, we are all maids, we are all illiterate – no matter how educated you are! You are just a *kaffir* puppet in parliament... they don't take you seriously. Who has the land in this country? Who has the wealth? Who do you call *baas* (boss)? Hey?!" Nazurah often got angry and impatient with Moses.

"Let's leave it there. You always become emotional and sensitive when we talk about *kaffirs*...I don't understand why... are you perhaps one of them?! You are supposed to be a Muslim. I don't know why you are so concerned over *klip kaffirs*. The real problem, Nazurah, is that this *kaffir* is illiterate; he does not know better, does not know how to care for his family, and now the *kaffir* is fetching my daughter to work for him!"
He persisted with his *anti-kaffir* talk relentlessly.

Nazurah never gave up in correcting his prejudice, "We should stand together against the White man...we are all the same...been robbed and mistreated by the White man. Why is it always the-kaffirs-this-and-that?"

Moses usually stared at Nazurah when she had these outbursts with him about colour; in disbelief in her unwavering faith in *kaffirs*. He had a habit of intensely drawing on his pipe with a sarcastic smirk on his face at such times of heated argument about race, "Perhaps *you* are also a *kaffir*...perhaps it is the truth in *you* that is hurting..."

He had pushed Nazurah's emotional buttons, "Don't say that! We are from *White* people and the *Griqua!*"

"So *you* also don't want to be a *kaffir*...he he he!" He laughed loudly, pleased with himself that he had won the debate. Push her in a corner like a rat, he thought to himself, and call her a *kaffir*; she'll soon give up on defending *kaffirs*. He knew that there was one thing Coloured people of his time did not like, and that was any suggestion or evidence that they may be Black or from Africa.

Nazurah, whose people came from the "untouchables" in India, always opted out at the point of being called *kaffir*, to save her the shame and humiliation.

"We brought her up well with good Christian values. That is all that matters – that she carries that over to her children and their children. Marie and Kruger are married now. They are husband and wife. They have children. There is nothing we can do about that. Just pray for things to turn out right for them. They don't live with his *kaffir* family; they live with the Coloureds."

"Yes, but he'll hook up with the other *kaffirs* in the *pondoks* (shanties) and at the shebeen, and before you know it he'll take our daughter far away to the Transkei, to *kaffirland*. You know the story..."

"Have faith...it won't happen..."

"...umph!" Moses sighed, grunted, and puffed, smoking his pipe with anger.

On this day in August, Moses and Nazurah were going to come face to face with their much feared and despised "*kaffir*" son-in-law, who came to fetch their granddaughter.

"Who ever thought that a *kaffir* would one day be in my sitting room opposite me?" Moses thought to himself in shame. He ordered Nazurah not to serve tea, and "not to make the *kaffir* too comfortable".

"He does not know about English cups in any case...don't waste your time...and in any case I'd get rid of that cup once he has put his lips to it...Don't make him comfortable in our home. He must get the message...once and for all...!"

Nazurah protested, "You are darker than him...what are you fussing about? You look *more African* than him...he has blue eyes like his German father...I think it is the *kaffir* in *you* that you fear!"

Moses was not only a racist, but also a snob.

"Just because *your* family comes from *kaffirs* in India, don't think mine comes from *kaffirs* too!"

After some more moments of a loud exchange of harsh words and the inevitable insults about *"kaffirs do this and that; kaffirs look like this and that"*, Nazurah summoned Eve to pack her bags in a suitcase and to go with the visitors, whom she now learned were in fact her parents.

Her grandmother's sobbing made her feel sore inside. Eve knew this was not good and started to weep uncontrollably. Her grandmother pleased her with a piece of sweet dried apple, her favourite comforting snack. She wiped her nose for her in a gentle gesture of reassurance, and lovingly combed and stroked her rosemary-greased hair.

"We'll come visit every Sunday, little one. We promise," Nazurah spoke gently.

Moses interrupted loudly for his guests to hear, "And we'll make sure you are not made to slave and not beaten! Their sort are like the Swahilis and the Arabs who unclothe and beat their women in the streets...!"

Moses was too angry to show affection to his departing granddaughter. He huffed and puffed, marched up and down, as if he had lost control.

"Come here, little Eve. Come to Pa", Kruger Verwerp gave her a warm smile. She looked up at him as he pulled her towards him. His eyes were a grey bluish colour. He was lighter than her racist grandfather, with a spot of freckles over the bridge of his fleshy huge nose.

"And what are these on your cute little red dress?" He pulled at her dress, and traced the white butterfly pattern on her dress with his rough-looking knotty crooked huge index finger.
"Little butterflies, and little white frills?"

"Yep, Uncle..." Eve said shyly.

"And look at this butterfly! It is so huge. I wonder if it can fly away...you think it can fly away and become a happy butterfly?" he joked with her.

Eve giggled. She felt safe and wanted in the new family man's presence.
She stuck her little finger in her mouth, making her mouth hollow, and twisted the finger in the inside of her cheek. She was too shy to talk to this big new man that she had now learned was her father.

"Come with Pa. We are going home. It is a long way to go. Have you ever ridden on a horse cart? Come, Pa will put you on the cart."
He lifted her up onto his shoulders, and from there onto the wooden bench on the horse cart. Eve could smell his sweet comforting tobacco. She curiously listened as he coughed persistently, an irritating yet reassuring familiar cough for a child to hear.

Her mother shifted in next to her, her huge behind taking up most of the space on the narrow wooden bench on the wobbly cart, "Eve, you're a big girl now. We'll come visit and you'll see Grandpa and Grandma again."

Eve swallowed back the silent sore hard cries in her throat. She swallowed each hurtful cry down deep into the deepest cavities of her lungs, burying them forever in her confusion and pain – hoping that they'd never resurface. Her heart was racing. She felt nauseous and avoided looking at the cosy Newlands cottage, the place where she grew up and where the up-market, educated Coloureds lived; the ones who went to the best schools for Coloureds and who spoke English rather than Afrikaans; the ones who had all their teeth in their mouths and showed off their long straight hair – many of them looked like her Indian and Malay relatives.

Her aunts were not outside to greet her on that day of her departure from the educated Coloured world. They stayed in their rooms, crying for the little girl that they dreamed to rear into an "educated and decent Coloured lady". They were always frustrated by her wild, unmanageable, kinky light brown hair that they struggled to comb each morning, but they were in awe of her freckles and her mysteriously inherited fair skin. In spite of her father's efforts to make her feel safe, and her mother's huge presence next to her on the narrow wooden bench, Eve felt alone, exposed, and vulnerable.

This man, now her father, cleared his throat, and casually spat a ball of yellow-tinged sticky mucus to the ground as he settled into his seat on the horse cart. The old people looked away in disgust as they leaned over the wooden gate to wave goodbye to their daughter and grandchild in front of their modest Newlands cottage. Without a goodbye, Kruger Verwerp drew a raw shout and whipped his black stallions into galloping action.

Nobody talked on the way home. They journeyed through dirt roads littered with stone and lined with *fynbos*, to a place called Blouvlei, meaning blue marsh, on the Cape Flats. As they travelled, things started to look starkly different than orderly, quiet, Coloured middle-class Newlands with its brick houses, its teachers, its tailors, its Muslim-Indian traders, and its small shops.

They were travelling towards the beach. Eve breathed in the smell of the ocean in the harsh notorious Cape South easterly wind. The air was moist, washing over her coarse hair, which curled up against her scalp as the salt in the wind from the nearby Indian ocean shores clung to her. The air tasted salty, and she could feel her skin drying and stinging in the wind. Her freckled cheeks turned an angry red, protecting themselves against the notorious harsh sea air and wind of the Cape. She narrowed her eyes, hoping it would help to shield her from the violent wind that tucked at the dress her grandpa had lovingly sewn for her for Sunday school on his Singer sewing machine.

They were travelling towards the mountain, to the place where her grandpa said Autshumao's Goringhaiqua, the strong Hottentot clan who were the first to fight the Dutch at the Cape in the late 1600s, lived. Her grandfather fondly called it "the mountain of the Gora", as known to these ancient inhabitants of the Cape for hundreds of years as passed on through oral tradition. He chose not to call it Muizenberg, as the Dutch called it, referring to the battle over the occupation of the Cape in which the British defeated the Dutch in the late 1700s.

Eve had heard many stories of the battles of her people, of plunders, and even about the crystal healing magic of the majestic Table Mountain. She found comfort in these bedtime stories of heroes and heroines who fought Jan Van Riebeeck, who visited the area of the Cape marshlands to see the much talked about zeekoeie (cows of the sea; hippos) that roamed there in their dozens.

She recalled her grandfather's stories, "These are the shores where those scoundrels landed; the strange White men who came from the sea. This is where the trouble in this land began."

Who will tell her these stories of ancient heroes again? Who will put her to sleep when she becomes scared in the dark of the night, when the owls in the dark bush hoot eerily at full moon?

Eve's parents lived the lives of Cape Flats woodcutters, making their living through cutting firewood and selling it to fellow poor Coloured families who lived in the various informal settlements in the Cape to keep the fires burning for food and warmth. In summer, things were a bit difficult, as not so much wood could be sold. So, it was in time for summer that they fetched Eve.

As they approached the village, her father seemed to become excited and noisy. He became rough as if he was a man who could change like the wind, and become angry like the notorious unpredictable Black southeasterly wind that blew since ancient times at the Cape. The women came out of their colourful painted shacks when they heard him coming, waved at him, and shouted his name as if he was a hero who had returned home from war or battle after a long absence. Young men ran into hiding, fearing that he might promptly summons them to voluntary work in the bush.

As he entered the shack village, he shouted and whipped the horses with an increasing vigour, shouting abuse at all and sundry.

"Hey, all you bastards! Wake up from your sleep! The sun is shining high in the sky. Get your lazy ass hole husbands out of bed!" His loudness was well known in the village; he behaved like a cowboy. Some women locked their doors to block out his noise. Others came running out and waved at him, laughing and enjoying his irresistible pedestrian wildness.

"Hey, you are all whores! Where are your husbands? I am not into screwing married women. And some of you sleep with *kaffirs!*" He laughed loudly as he shouted abuse and whipped his horses. They were charmed by his vulgar style; the way in which he commanded fear amongst the villagers of the *pondoks*. Everybody knew that he was different from the others in the village of shacks. Some whispered that he was a man born from a gang rape by the Germans of a Herero woman, and that he could therefore not help his vulgarity, and they forgave him.

"See, you can see the German in his eyes..." the women would gossip on their way back from the communal taps where they fetched drinking water in their silver tin buckets, balancing and carrying them delicately on their heads on their way back home. "He is the son of a rapist. His mother fled when the Germans put them into concentration camps. After the rape, she ran, because if they caught her pregnant by a German man, they'd hang her high from a tree. So, she fled with her mother to the Cape..."

Nobody spoke about this truth openly; everybody whispered.

Kruger's manner was unsurprisingly obscene with the women. He could change like quicksilver – from a kind, caring father, to a loud vulgar man shouting sexual obscenities. He seemed like someone with multiple personality disorder, and at full moon, everybody avoided him, as everybody believed that he was somehow affected by the energy of the full moon. His mood swings, charm, and unpredictable violent outbursts made him even more feared. He quietly detested his Griqua in-laws who spoke loudly about him as the *"wild kaffir"*. He never told them what he thought of them and their insults. He buried his anger very, very deeply within his being, like lava in a volcano to erupt one day, even when he would not be able to tell when and how. In his loud and vulgar conversations about indulgent sexual escapades with the women of all colours in the shacks, he wanted to prove that he was *not* a *kaffir, because kaffirs knew their place and feared the police and the dompas.*

He shouted at the women frequently, "The *kaffirs* have huge things....get them out of your beds and cupboards where you hide them from your unwitting husbands...I'll show you my big tool and you'll change your mind about falling for the *kaffirs!*" He laughed and teased, pinched their bottoms, and rubbed his intimate anatomy against their large buttocks, as if he was a dog and they were the trunks of trees.

Eve's mother dropped her head in shame from her loud abusive husband and defiantly mumbled throughout the roughness of the ride. "You have no respect for a woman. And you are bringing our child home. I would have expected you to show some respect – at least just for today."

"Ah, shut up woman! Don't be like that snooty Griqua family of yours...this is home...*I rule here*...I am no *kaffir* here...!"

To show his annoyance with his wife, he whipped the horses hard and the horse cart sped over stones and rusted tins and broken bottles that littered the street. Eve and her mother held tight onto the bench, being thrown from one side to the other. The ride was rough. The chickens in the road ran for their lives. Goats escaped, sheep scattered, pigs squealed, and ducks paddled speedily away. He intimidated everybody and everything in sight.

Eve did not understand what he was telling the women. She had never heard those words before – only the ugly word *kaffir*, which her grandfather spoke about each and every day, a hundred times a day. He made sure everybody in the house understood what a *kaffir* was, and why a *kaffir* should be avoided, mistrusted, and mistreated. Everybody was always talking about *kaffirs*. Eve did not even know who and what these people called *kaffirs* were, because all the Coloured people looked different, and many looked like the people they chose to look down on and called *kaffirs*. It was all very odd and confusing. Eve looked around at all the people living in the *pondoks*. There were dark ones with short, dry curly hair, lighter ones with blond hair, and brown ones with long hair. What she did know is that if you want to make someone feel really, really bad, you call that person a *kaffir*. It was the ugliest and most hurtful word to say to someone to make them feel bad about themselves. She had learnt that was when you use it.

In spite of his vulgar manner, Kruger was a well-known and well-liked man in the informal settlement where Coloureds and Africans lived side by side, sharing an abundance of wood, African sorghum beer, *snoek,* (traditional Cape line fish), *pap* (African-style cooked maize cereal), watermelons, figs, pumpkins, and bunches of sunflowers from gardens. Though Kruger spoke and joked about *kaffir* men and their "big equipment", they all lived together and frequently partied, drank, and danced together at the local shebeen. Some were his best friends.

The sun shone relentlessly down on the colourful roofs of the dozens of shacks. The sand was hot. Kruger lifted his daughter off the cart (intermittently coughing, spitting mucus, and swearing obscenities). He placed her roughly down on the sand. The soft pink soles of her feet roasted. Her father's huge hands hurt her young tender flesh on the inside of her upper arms. However, Eve knew instinctively not to complain.

"Come, Eve, quickly now. Get into the house. Don't waste time. Your father has work to do. He is a busy man. Lots of wood to cut. " Marie always seemed fearful of her loud Herero-German husband, and was careful not to upset him.

Their house was a huge shack with pages from magazines pasted to the walls as decoration. It was dark inside. There was no smell of food, no smell of fresh floor polish, no light shining through a window, and no smell of sweet peas and roses in a sunny front garden. The new home smelled cold and stale, like the smell of soiled nappies mixed with the ash of cheap cigarettes. Eve could hear children crying in one of the back rooms. Eve went cold, she became frightful. There was not even a bed for her, and no aunts, no sweets, no grandma, and no grandpa.

In spite of the obvious misery and poverty, Kruger Verwerp whistled merrily. He put on his cap, took his whip, and went off again on the horse cart to do his day's woodcutting business – seemingly undisturbed. Marie seemed quietly miserable and irritable, almost awkward with her new life of poverty. "Where is your suitcase? Come now, pick it up and put it in the room at the back, the one on the far right where the children are with your aunt."

Eve's small frame dragged the heavy brown tattered square leather suitcase with the rusty silver lock into the huge dark room. This was where the children slept. A tall dark woman was sitting on one of the beds. Eve could only see the white of her hollow-looking eyes and the crooked white chipped teeth of her friendly broad smile in the dark.

"Hello, little Eve. Don't be scared. Come inside." She pulled Eve tenderly towards her. She was chewing a sweet smelling tobacco.

"I am Aunty Ella, your father's sister. I am going to look after you and teach you many things."

Eve stuck her finger in her wet mouth again, forming her cheeks to blow them out balloon-shaped, to try and cope with the nervousness of such a strange, new, dark cold home.

Noticing her awkwardness and anxiety, her aunt comforted her, "I am not from here. I come from South West Africa, from the Nama and Herero people, from far north."

Aunt Ella spoke a broken kind of Afrikaans. She spoke in a foreign tongue; she made click sounds with her tongue. Eve instantly felt safe in her spontaneous warmth. Eve's little brothers and sisters were all over her aunt, on her lap and hanging at the end of her white cotton dress that was patterned with stripes and shapes of all colours, their noses and eyes unendingly moist and red.

Over the weeks and months, Eve grew close to Aunty Ella, who believed that children are sacred and should never be shouted at or beaten.

"Your father is my half-brother", she said "I don't know why he is so harsh with children. We come from the Hereros. Your father and his brother are different; they come from the Germans and the Hereros. That is why your brothers and sisters have the light eyes of Germans and the dark skins of the Hereros. My mother used to say that your father and his brother are as cruel as their German father. They have lost the softness of the Hereros. But we just accept them like that; they can't help the mongrel blood in them. When he is harsh and loud with you, you come hide behind Aunty Ella. Promise? "

Eve could not understand why her grandfather hated her father so much. Although he was dark, he called her father that ugly word, a *kaffir*. Aunty Ella told her, "No, he is not a *kaffir*. He is a *mixed breed* man, a Coloured. We are *klip kaffirs – as in kaffirs of the stone* - well, that is what the Coloured people call us. They say the Hereros are *klip kaffirs*. The Coloured people in Cape Town don't like us. The women here don't talk to me. When I go outside to hang the washing on the line, they shout over the fence – 'Ella you are a *klip kaffir*, go back to the Hereros!' That hurts me. But they like your father, because he is not pure Herero. They like him because he is half-German. It is all silly and confusing. You must not worry about this *kaffir*-business. Aunty Ella loves you and will look after you."

"See, you have coarse hair like the Hottentots and the Hereros, but you are fair like the Germans. You are also a mixed breed like the mongrel dogs outside in the yard. Hereros are Black, but pure, like the *kaffirs*. That is why your father is so wild and unpredictable; it is the mixed blood that makes him go mad, especially at full moon. He cannot help the madness in him. He gets as rowdy as a mongrel dog and he howls while the owls hoot at night. Have you noticed he shouts a lot at night after a bout of heavy drinking? We understand that this madness happens when blood mixes. You must not behave like a mongrel. Be like the Hereros – upright and proud. Not loud, and never out of control." The Aunty patted Eve on her head, as a gesture of reassurance that she will not grow up to be wild and untamed.

"The Herero people fought proudly against the Germans when they came to take our land. To get rid of us, they decided to wipe our people out. They poisoned our water holes in the Kalahari Desert. Any Herero person found by the German soldiers was shot on the spot. Some of our people were left to die a slow death in the desert from starvation and thirst. Many women and children were put in these death camps. Many women and young girls, like my mother, were forced to have babies with the German men to breed out the Herero people. Some were made as slaves to work for the Germans. The Germans brought in scientists to do tests and experiments on us. Many thousands of our people were killed. We were lucky. We escaped, and that was how we came here. They say this German man, Hitler, who is now wiping out the Jews, is like them and is doing the same to the Jews as what they did to us. That is why there are many children like that today in South West Africa."

In spite of Aunty Ella's many explanations and frightful tales about Germans, Hereros, mongrels, and *kaffirs*, Eve remained confused about all the names and insults for all the people. It was the main conversation everybody had in the village, yet they all lived together and helped one another.

During winter, Cape Town grew stormy, cold, and miserable. It would rain for weeks, and the damp firewood would not burn. The family would sparingly use the dried wood stacked up during the summer and autumn months, and feed on sweet potatoes baked in coals on an open fire, or on mole from the garden, or on a stew made from water lilies, called a *waterblommetjiebredie*, or on roasted pheasants caught in a trap. On a sunny day, they would be lucky to catch trout from the Vlei nearby. However, preparing wild trout was a big adventure of soaking the big wild-smelling fish in vinegar for days to neutralize the taste of the mud and the polluted water. Sometimes, they would resort to the Khoisan way of surviving, and the children would be sent into the veld to dig out indigenous plant roots such as *bolletjies* (roots) and *eendtjies* (a flowery plant that grows like peas in a pod), or to simply catch tortoise and boil it in a big paraffin tin on the open fire. Tortoise was a great luxurious delicacy, reserved for special occasions. It was quite a feat practised to perfection to boil a monstrous, wild, kicking mountain tortoise until tender and ready to be eaten. One obese woman in the neighbourhood is said to have had the reputation of selfishly devouring the tortoise delicacy, not sharing it with her twelve children, nor with her thin, elderly, and ailing husband who was dying of tuberculosis, the death curse of the poor on the Cape Flats. In such instances, catching a tortoise and fittingly bringing it to boil by poking it down with the broomstick in the large used paraffin tin for one person to indulge in seemed a senseless and cruel act. Eve started to grow used to the regular Khoisan staple food of water lilies, tortoise, and mole and the hard life of poverty on the sandy, wet, windswept Cape Flats.

It was especially also tough during winter, when the wood would not dry and the sales were not too good, as the community relied on the cheap Swedish-made mobile paraffin pressure cookers, primus stoves, instead. They bought spirits in small glass bottles from the local stores. They pumped their little dangerous stoves (designed for use in outdoor camping and expeditions), which would sometimes burst, torching a few dozen homes. Children trapped in the shacks would burn to ash, and the loud banging of a skull and hysterical screams of a distraught mother would wake the neighbours out of their deep winter slumber. This happened often, and surviving relatives and neighbours found themselves in the unenviable position witnessing such a tragedy with hysterical trauma in the dark icy cold of a relentlessly cruel Cape winter's night.

As time went on, the aunts from Newlands did not visit that much. They were carrying on with their own middle-class lives and responsibilities as they got married. They found their sister's working class life a little bit too unbearable – the tortoise and mole cuisine, the slaughter of pigs, the eating of Khoisan roots, the many devastating fires and the vulgar loudness of the foreign man their sister had chosen to marry. Their lives in Newlands were different. They kept tortoises as pets in their garden, bought their meat from the local butcher, and fed pheasants on the nearby field. When they had conversations, they were in soft, discreet whispers.

Aunty Ella taught Eve to speak Otjiherero, the language of the Herero people, and soon the two of them established a strong bond through the indigenous Nama tongue. Eve's mother had worked as a domestic worker during the day and had long ago given up her father's wish that she becomes a qualified teacher, like a "respectable Coloured", as he put it. Aunty Ella taught Eve how to care for the children, how to cook, and how to clean the house. At the insistence of her grandparents, Eve was sent to continue her schooling, but her father promptly took her out after a few months. Aunty Ella was concerned that a young child could be so worried about people being called *kaffirs.*

"Oh, child you are too young to have so many worries. Come sit on Aunty Ella's lap. Be a child." She protectively stroked her legs, with her long slender shiny dark hands, wanting to shelter them from the harshness of South African life.

It was not only the racism that disturbed the young girl. It was also the many babies being born that popped out at home barely a year apart from one another. She wondered about the mystery of creation, of how babies get made – she intuitively did not believe her Newlands aunts' story that they were made by baboons in the mountains from where parents then collect them. It just did not make sense that her poor, miserable parents would so willingly fetch so many babies, one after another, from the baboons. The babies would certainly perhaps have been better off with the baboons in the mountains than with their miserable poverty. It was a mystery that haunted her mind for many nights. When she heard the confusing shifting, rhythmic sounds of a worn-out mattress coupled with the loud sensual sighs of Marie at night that sounded like agonising cries which she did not understand, she secretly hated Kruger Verwerp for beating up her mother behind closed doors once the candle was blown out. However, her mother's happy singing of *"Heaven, I'm in heaven..."* and her non-ending quiet smiles the following morning thoroughly confused her.

Eve's family moved from the informal settlement closer to the bush and the sand dunes to make the search for wood easier. The grandparents were not visiting regularly. "We are furious with the way our grandchild has to work for the *kaffir!* We are not slaves any more. Our family battled for two centuries to be free. He comes here from Namaland and makes our child a slave...just like that!" her grandfather explained to family, friends, and Coloured politicians visiting in middle-class Coloured Newlands.

"I warned my wife that he is a no-good *kaffir.* I don't trust these ones that come from the north, from those Germans. Their mothers were whores. We prefer the Tswana, the Sothos, and the Zulus. We also don't trust the Swahilis. They are too close to the cruel and cunning Arabs. The Zulus are actually the best. They are more royalty than any other African tribe. Remember how they sorted out Piet Retief and his party of thieves in 1838? They worked out a cunning and brilliant plan and lured the culprits to their own deaths. They are not easily cheated, nor fooled. They are a brilliant people. You can't go wrong with a Zulu on your side in this land. They are more pure, more proud, and more resilient. The Coloured people do not mess with the Zulu people; they respect them. Nazurah kept on defending this no-good-kaffir, about the *German-this-and-that*. Point is, his *klip kaffir* blood is stronger in him than his German blood, because his mother is a *klip kaffir*. He drank *her* milk. He did not drink German milk!"

Eve's mother always tried to defend her son-in-law against the tirade of her uncompromising prejudiced Griqua husband. "But maybe it is the cruel German blood in him that makes him so heartless...the *kaffirs* never made Coloured people their slaves? Remember the killing of the Herero people in South West Africa? And his German father raped his Herero mother? Remember? That could be the problem...he is not *pure* any more...he comes from a rape...but we are all not pure...Griqua people come from the Tswana, the Khoi, the Dutch, the French..."

Once out of school, Eve turned into a full-time caregiver of her siblings, but soon there would be another baby. This cycle repeated year after year. So it came that Eve's father took her to work with him for a White family in the nearby fishing village of St. James as a live-in domestic to increase the family's income.

"You are thirteen now. Just the right age to help me work for the White madam in St. James. You are going to start working with me tomorrow as a live-in servant. Dress nicely. The White people like Coloured girls who are tidy and decent. Ask your mother how to dress."

Her mother handed her two floral dresses, one blue and one red, a white apron, and a white cotton headscarf. The dresses were far too long, dropping untidily over her frail shoulders, and too wide at the sides. She looked at herself in the mirror. She felt poor, condemned forever. Her aunts did not look like this; they would die if they could see her, she thought to herself.

Noticing her young daughter's discontent, Marie came up from behind her, tied the apron strings tightly for her, and warned sternly, "Try to look like a decent Coloured lady. Otherwise, the madam won't give you work. And only say 'yes' and 'no'. Never answer back – even when you are right. The White madam does not like cheeky Coloured girls. Understand?"

"And remember one thing about working for the English. Every sentence must end with 'please', and they can never hear enough of the words 'thank you' and 'sorry' from Coloureds – even if you don't mean it, just say it. It makes them feel good and in control. It makes them feel superior to you, and it is a way of reminding you to know your place in their homes. Even if you sound like a stuck record, just do it. Remember quietly that they are the fools, not you. You must always act like the grateful girl in the house of the English madam. Go on. You'll learn quickly."

The next morning Kruger woke Eve up early to make the fire.
"Come, Eve, wake up child. It is five o'clock. We must be at madam's at seven."
Kruger boiled water on the coal stove in the huge battered tin kettle which he picked up from the dump in the bush nearby while Eve got dressed as her mother had shown her the night before. She could not see much of herself in the broken piece of mirror that was leaning against the wall. The candle flickered faintly, creating only a small patch of dim light in the corner of the room. Her shadow against the wall formed tall and lean, much larger than her frame in the dimly lit room. She was not that small after all, she thought. Her distorted image in the shadow made her feel big enough to go out to work for the family.

Kruger poured the Dutch *moerkoffie* (boere ground coffee) into the chipped blue tin mugs. "Come, drink quickly. Leave the bread for the children; the madam will give you jam and bread to eat. We must catch the six ten train at Retreat Station, and it is a long way to walk."

Marie got up to greet them. Still half asleep, barefoot in a creased nightie and with unkempt hair, she rubbed her eyes with her one hand while nursing the youngest at her breast.

"Take these sandals and shoes, and some of my other old *char*-clothes (domestic clothes). And see what else you can collect from the madam to keep you going."

Marie spoke sternly without saying much of a goodbye.

"Quickly now, Eve. The madam does not like you to be late. I'll see you two on Friday night." Kruger and Marie, who never showed affection in public, did not kiss. However, oddly at night, Eve could hear them moaning aloud as they made more babies.

After a long walk to the station, they travelled for a short distance by train to the quaint coastal White town on the warm Indian Ocean. St. James was named in the mid-1800s after the Roman Catholic Church, which was built to service the shipwrecked Filipino fishermen and refugees who made nearby Kalk (lime) Bay their new home; it was a place used by the Dutch settlers for fishing supplies and lime for construction purposes to build and expand Cape Town. These Filipino people became part of the growing Coloured population at the Cape with surnames of de la Cruz, Delcarmey, and Fernandez. The Filipino people were later joined by freed enslaved people from Batavia, Java, and Malaysia. They all came to be classified as "Coloured", and lived in fishermen cottages, separated from the huge mansions of the English and Whites on the mountainside, long before apartheid came to South Africa.

On a sunny day, Kalk Bay and St. James are picturesquely beautiful and enchanting with their cobble stone streets, their white cottages with thatched roofs, the white beach, calm blue waters, and rocking fishing boats. Today, St. James is still known for its abundance of fish and its segregation, even long after the release of Nelson Mandela and the end of apartheid.

Eve and Kruger walked up the steep steps made of cobblestone in St James. Eve dragged a brown paper shopping bag in which her clothes were packed, unlike the day she had left Newlands with a suitcase. Kruger had sold her brown suitcase to a neighbour to earn some extra pennies. She struggled to keep up with him as she tried to find her own pace in Marie's old big leather sandals, which could not be fastened as the buckles had broken off, and the big old bra straps were constantly falling off her thin shoulder frame, which caused her to stop frequently to try and pull them back into place. She was also trying to wipe her constantly cold-ridden runny nose with her sleeve as she ran behind Kruger to keep up with his quick huge steps.

"Eve, we are going to be late. Hurry now, child! It is not a good start."

It seemed like ages before they got to the White madam's house perched high up in the mountain overlooking the beautiful False Bay coast. The smell of the nearby sea and of fresh fish hung over the garden. They could hear the seagulls and the "choo-choo" sound of the train passing by. They knocked on the freshly painted heavy green wooden gate, and it took some time before someone came to answer the door. Though their call was expected by the madam, there was no hurry to receive them. The madam's house had a high white wall, made from mountain rock. The garden was beautifully kept. There were bushes of pink, red, white, and purple roses. There was honeysuckle in the corner where the bees gathered. There was a fish pond with huge red goldfish, and there was a white wooden bench in the shade under a grapevine next to a white, painted, small stone statue of a young girl holding a dove in a water fountain.

Eve noticed that her huge, confident father went quiet in the White suburb, almost burying his real person. She was puzzled by the silence and sudden childlike manner of his otherwise loud and commanding presence.

"Pa, why are you so quiet?" she whispered to him at the madam's gate.

"Shhhh, Eve, we must not make a noise here in the White people's place. Be quiet and upright. Be *decent*. You must *know your place* here. Madam will talk to you about it."

Kruger Verwerp acted like a child in the presence of Mrs. Thunderstorm, a tall, lean, fair woman who wore her blond hair shortly cropped behind her ears. She was dressed in a white crimperline dress, and wore a lot of jewellery: a white pearl necklace, pearl earrings, and huge engraved silver bangles. She covered her breasts with a soft pink shawl, even on a hot summer's day.

"You are a little late..." she looked down at Eve, condescendingly casting her eyes over Eve's awkwardly dressed young frame.

"Is this your daughter? She looks a little young." She played with her pearl necklace as she asked, slightly tilting her head with a gesture of English distance – a body language that Coloured people were so well acquainted with in their dealings with the White masters and madams of the Cape.

Kruger became nervous and terrified. "Yes, Madam... But she has been *house trained* by her mother and aunt, who are native women, to work for White people. They say she is quite good. And she does not back chat. She is also good at saying please and thank you. A well-mannered girl, I promise, madam. I promise..." He was desperate to get his daughter to work for the family.

"Ok then, go around to the back door to meet me there. Oh, before I forget...and what is her name?"

"Eve"

Mrs. did not smile, nor did she stretch out her hand to greet.

"Go around to the back with your father, Eve."

She called her son. "Andrew, love! Where are you? Come meet our new maid!"

A red-haired White boy with freckles, not older than nine years, came rushing down the staircase to the back door.

Breathless, he gasped in surprise and bewilderment, "Mom, we have a new *maid*?!"

"Yes. Come see."

Andrew gave Eve searching, hostile looks. "Hope she does not steal like the other one...!" he shouted Eve's way.

Mrs. was still not smiling as she rubbed Andrew's head to reassure him, "No, love, our boy, Kruger, says she is a *house trained* servant."

"Hello boy!" Andrew turned to greet the middle-aged Kruger.

"Hello - my *master!* How have you been?" Kruger shifted nervously as he talked to the young White bossy bespectacled child.

"Alright." Andrew was still frowning and staring at his new Coloured child servant, who was barely much older than him.

Eve found her father's lack of confidence in the presence of Mrs. Thunderstorm and the nine-year-old Andrew unsettling, especially since he referred to her fifty-year-old father as "boy", and he called Andrew "master" in turn. This was bizarre. This mind-boggling ambivalence was most unsettling to Eve's own confidence, which crumbled in the presence of the madam and her interrogative son, who questioned her father about his lateness, making Eve want to pee in her panties. She trembled, not knowing how to relate to these White persons – a kind of people she had come face to face with for the first time in her life. The adults at home often spoke about the White people for whom they worked and how they feared them.

At the back door, Mrs. Thunderstorm looked down at her young servant, suggesting a greeting. "Have you been taught any manners?"

"Hello..." Eve blurted out nervously to the severe-looking White English woman.

"Hello ....*who*?!" Mrs. Thunderstorm reprimanded gently but firmly.

"Madam..." Kruger nudged Eve quietly. "Eve, say *madam* and *master*...like you were trained. Remember?"

"You said she was *house trained*?" Mrs. Thunderstorm asked sarcastically, with her nose turned up, still not allowing them in at the back door. It was as if they had to earn some decency first. They stood like horses at a stable.

"Eve, say 'Hello *madam* and *master*...'" Kruger nudged Eve again as he whispered loudly, his elbow knocking the side of her head.

"Hello madam and master...thank you...please...sorry..." The words blurted out in a string, as Marie had rehearsed with her in the mirror the night before. Eve trembled as the words barely formed properly in her young mouth. Even if you sound like a stuck record, *always* show the English that you are grateful and also sorry. *Always. All day. Everyday.* Not always sure what you must be grateful about and sorry for? Just repeat it endlessly, and they'll like you forever. This is what her mother was trying to tell her.

"Madam and master, I am sorry...she is perhaps a little nervous today. It is her first day." Kruger seemed ashamed.

"Don't worry, boy, she'll come right as time passes. She needs to be house-trained."

"Right madam..."

This was Eve's first encounter with White people – the families on the Cape Flats often spoke about White people and feared them. They hated the *kaffirs* and feared the White people. They seemed closer in the way they were treated to the people they called *kaffirs* than to the White people who mistreated them, yet they hated them and wanted to be like the White people.

"I have to be with my children's charity meeting in Simonstown within an hour. So I don't have much time."

"Yes, madam"

"Eve, come through to the kitchen."

Kruger disappeared quietly to begin his day's work in the huge garden.

This was the first time that Eve was in a house where White people lived. The house was huge, with shiny wooden floors and shiny brass handles on huge doors. There were a black mahogany grand piano, a huge white vase filled with differently coloured roses, huge mirrors, and a fat white cat was lying lazily on the bottle green couch in the sun. A picture of the Queen of England hung in the hallway. Eve noticed her crisp smile and her necklace of white pearls. The queen gazed down on her. Oh, her grandfather would have liked to see that picture, Eve thought to herself, and this picture also reminded her of the many stories he told the family of wanting to visit the queen in England one day. Mrs. Thunderstorm noticed Eve's preoccupation with the picture.

"Oh, that is Her Majesty, our Queen Mother. England has been good for you people. If it had not been for the English, this place would have been wild and backward. The English brought manners and education." She smiled condescendingly at the young girl servant, reminding her to be grateful, as she stroked her own white pearls of her necklace with her long slender fingers. Then she suddenly became businesslike, "Come now. Time waits for no one. Lots to do. I must still go do my charity work for the poor children – the White children living in the homes with the nuns."

Eve, continued with the ritual, "Sorry madam...Please madam... Thank you madam..."

Mrs. Thunderstorm smiled quietly and seemed instantly pleased with her well-mannered Coloured servant child. She was already learning quickly – saying sorry, please, and thank you in a systematic, well-practised manner – the trademark of a well-groomed Coloured servant. In the coming days and months, Mrs. Thunderstorm made sure Eve noticed her approval as Eve passed the house training programme a little bit at a time, everyday and all day.

"Let me show you your room in the back garden, and then we have some house rules to go through."

Eve has never been in such a huge house. She panicked in her young heart. How was she going to clean such a huge house? Her father had lied. She was never trained as a servant. She wanted to pee even more. Her bladder wanted to be relieved of the nervous tension. It was such a big White people's house, where you don't know how to walk or where to touch, not even how to breathe. Everything seemed so forbidden. However, she somehow intuitively knew she could not ask to use the toilet. So, she squeezed her thighs tightly and kept her pee in. She was now hungry for the piece of bread and the jam her father promised she would get from the White madam. However, in the coming weeks, she would learn that one has to wait patiently to eat in the White madam's house of endless rules, gratitude, apologies, and regulations. Her room in the back garden had a light blue painted door. There were no carpets, only an old grey loose mat on the concrete floor. She looked at the single bed in the corner, covered with a pink, striped, thin, hard blanket. She was happy to have a bed of her own again, such as in the days in Newlands. A hard, light blue, much-used bath towel was folded on the bed. It felt hard, like a floor rag. The room was provided with the bare minimum. On the little old white chipped pedestal next to the bed were a jug of water, a small brown wooden radio, and a white bible. The bible was old and tattered, like it'd been read over and over again by many sad and lonely Coloured and African girl servants before Eve. This is where and how they learnt to pray for God's mercy, and to (in the process) learn to read. There was also a small blue alarm clock, silently ticking away. This clock would become important in her life; it would regulate her life. On the chair was a yellow basin and a bar of cheap *Lifeboy* soap, advertised in magazines for Black people to buy to keep them clean and fresh. There was no bath or shower, only another small room in which there was a toilet and a yellow plastic basin. The toilet was one of those that flushed water. Eve pulled the long chain at the side a few times, and watched in amazement how the water gushed like a waterfall into the white ceramic pot, and then swooshed away into a curved hole. It seemed like magic. The curtains were covered in dust and were made from cheap cotton with unimaginative brown drawings of buildings somewhere in a far away place.

Mrs. Thunderstorm suddenly appeared at the door of her little room. "You like your room?"

"Yes, madam. Thank you madam."

"This is where you will live. It does get a little cold here in winter because we are close to the sea. But then again, it is cool in the summer. At least the roof does not leak when it rains. You'll be fine. It is important that you keep your room tidy at all times.

Come back inside when you are done and we can talk about the house and work rules."

They walked back through the beautiful rose-scented landscaped garden, where the bees sucked indulgently on the yellow honey suckle blooms in the corner.

"Oh, by the way, the garden is for madam's and master's use only. *Never* sit in the garden. Your *place* is in your little room, or you could go for a walk on the beach and do window shopping during your lunch break...usually around one o'clock."

Mrs. Thunderstorm led the way back into the kitchen of her huge house, with Eve following closely behind, setting the pattern for the rest of her life as a Coloured servant in the White English madam's house at the Cape.

"Come sit down at the table. This is your chair and place at the table. *This* chair, not any of the others. Andrew gets very upset if you sit on his chair. So be careful. This is *your* plate. This is *your* fork. This is *your* spoon. This is *your* mug. I'll put them for you in the corner on the shelf in the pantry."

"Please madam. Thank you, madam."

Even though Eve had no reason to say "please", Mrs. Thunderstorm smiled with unashamed satisfaction, and continued.

"*Know* your place at the table. It is important. You'll always eat by yourself at the table, but you must *never* sit on the wrong chair or use the wrong mug, fork, plate, or spoon. Understand?" Mrs. suddenly sounded angry.

"Sorry madam...thank you, madam..."

Mrs. Thunderstorm smiled again with a satisfied smirk on her face, and continued.

"Tea or water?"

"Tea, please... madam. Thank you, madam..."

"Dinnertime tonight will be the first and last time I'll be serving you, Eve. From tomorrow morning, you'll be serving us. *Understand?*"

"Sorry madam...Yes, madam...thank you, madam."

Mrs. Thunderstorm poured the tea into an off-white chipped tea cup for Eve. She poured a cup for herself too, put a teaspoon of Nestle condensed milk from a tin into Eve's tea and poured fresh milk from a glass bottle delivered by the dairy into her own cup. Her cup was white with emerald green painted leaves, and a gold rim with a matching saucer, sugar bowl and milk jug.

She continued with the rules as she sipped delicately from her gold-rimmed cup, her eyes staring over the rim at Eve, watching her every move. The last time Eve held a cup was in the house in Newlands. At home, they drank around the fire outside from handmade tin mugs made from used paraffin tins. Her little hand trembled as it held the cup.

"Master Andrew must be obeyed at all times. He is *always* the boss, and should always be addressed as 'master'. Remember that although Andrew is your age, he is *not* your friend. Understand?"

"Yes, madam...sorry, madam..."

"Fine."

"You get up at six. I'll set your alarm clock in the room for you. Never later than six, come rain or shine. Understand?"

"Yes, madam"

"You wash your face, brush your teeth, get dressed and comb your hair. Here is an old face cloth of Andrew's. This is an old hair brush of mine. All still good."

"Thank you madam..."

"Did you bring a toothbrush?"

"Sorry madam...no madam..."

Mrs. sighed."You can have Andrew's old one. I somehow knew I should not throw it away when I heard you were coming..."

"Please madam...thank you madam...sorry, madam..."

"Always wear your white apron and your head scarf. Your hair must always be straight, flat and down. Neat and decent, not bushy and wild. Understand?"

"Yes, madam"

"I want you in the kitchen dressed and decent by six thirty. The kettle gets switched on at six thirty for my tea, served in bed."

She walked over to the cupboard and showed Eve the electric kettle." This is how you switch it on. Always make sure the kettle has enough water."

"Yes, madam"

"Here is the tray. Here are the cups."

"Yes, madam"

"I'll show you my bedroom later. It is upstairs. You serve me morning tea in bed."

"Yes, madam"

"And always be careful not to spill the tea on the tray. Be careful not to drop things. *Expensive*...I'll have to take money from you when you break my things or when things get stolen... understand?"

"Yes, madam"

"Breakfast for me and Andrew must be ready on the table at seven. Andrew goes to school at seven thirty. Education is important for a child. I don't want you to make him late for school in the mornings."

"Yes, madam...sorry, madam."

"We have oats and hot milk, toast, and jam in the morning. Whatever is left on the table *after* we have eaten, you may have."

"Yes, madam...thank you, madam."

"I cook lunch and dinner. But you set the table and serve us. Understand?"

"Yes, madam"

"Always remember that you only eat *once* we are *done*. You can sit at the table. Your father also eats of the leftovers, but *outside* in the shed. He has his own tin mug, saucer, plate, knife, fork, and spoon in the shed. Understand?" She showed Eve the cutlery and crockery for Kruger – all chipped and stained. The forks, spoons and knives were bent and crooked.

"Yes, madam...thank you, madam"

"Come, let me show you the rest of the house...and by the way, no friends are allowed, no servant friends, no boyfriends, no family. We are quiet and private people, and I want to keep it that way. Understand?"

"Yes, madam"

Andrew came running into the kitchen as he overheard the rules being read to Eve. He gave their servant more searching looks, standing at the opposite side of the huge wooden kitchen table, setting the boundaries from the outset. "And don't you *dare* steal my stuff!" He folded his arms in an intimidating way, and narrowed his eyes, and pulled his lips skew to one side.

"No, master...sorry, master." She feared this child who was a little younger than her and did not even know why she apologised so repeatedly to Mrs. Thunderstorm and Andrew.

"Come now. Tea is finished. Jam sandwiches later. Go to your room now. I'll call you later to go through the rest of the house."

"Yes, madam"

Eve retired to her small cool room in the backyard. Kruger was on his knees weeding the garden in the hot sun. He was concentrating too much to hear her pass down the footpath. She was happy to be in her own little room. A room of her own, like in her grandpa's house. She lay on the bed, feeling the coolness of the spread underneath her, and sighed. It felt good to have a room again, and to have a toilet that could flush, but her bladder was bursting. She lifted the black toilet seat, sat on the cold white toilet, sighed, closed her eyes, and allowed her body to let go. It was a big pee that seemed never ending as the bottled-up tension burst warmly out of her small body and rushed its way out of her frightened being into the big deep white toilet bowl.

In the days that passed, she learned her routine around the madam's house. She escaped into Andrew's room upstairs when he left for school, and often forgot to make his bed or sweep his floor. There were a variety of colourful cars, big ones and small ones, kites and rubber soccer balls, and a library of books. There were huge books with colourful illustrations, of witches riding on broomsticks to the moon, of children going on an adventure in the bush, of frogs and fairies, of sweets and ice cream and colourful candy, of fairytale cities that Eve only dreamed about when she lived with her grandparents in Newlands. She made up her own stories in her head from the pictures because she could not read a single word.

"Eve! What are you up to in Andrew's room? You are not *stealing*, are you?!"

Mrs. Thunderstorm would shout up the staircase.

"No madam...I am reading his books."

"You have work to do, child! Why are you staring into space dreaming of *Alice in Wonderland?* And what do you know about reading! One day when you go to school, you'll be able to read books. For now, you are a servant. You must learn the ways of discipline, child! Your father needs the money to feed all the children at home. I believe there are ten of you...Goodness! When does your mother stop? Does she have nothing better to do?!"

But all this ritual and discipline could not keep Eve away from the mysteries and magic in the books in Andrew's room. It was the closest she could get to the endless tales told by her Khoisan grandfather. The stories were different, but they had the same magic as gained from the colourful illustrations. She often buried her nose in the pages of the books. She loved the smell, the big fat words, the pictures, and the comforting feel of the rough white string that kept the pages together. Her grandfather told her many fascinating stories, but never gave her a storybook to read.

Two years later, when Eve spotted blood on her linen one morning, it was to Mrs. Thunderstorm that she ran, worrying.

"Madam, I think I hurt myself badly. I bled during my sleep last night."

Mrs. Thunderstorm sat her down at the kitchen table and warned, "It is a sign that you are now a woman, that you can have babies. Stay away from the Coloured *skollies* when you go out walking for lunch. Will you? The Coloured boys from Kalk Bay know no better than to make a girl pregnant. They are like dogs in heat. They should go back to the Philippines where they came from. Don't fall for them with their handsome looks and narrow eyes. They are like you people, like the Coloureds; they came here with the boats from the East. Besides, I can't have you as a servant if you get babies."

"Sorry madam..."

"I'll give you some white rags from the old linen bedsheets that you have to soak in bleach when they are stained. Use them every month when it happens. And when you get cramps in your stomach, take an aspirin. It helps. I'll buy you a box of aspirin to keep in your room. "

"Please madam...thank you, madam."

"You can wear some of my old panties if you bleed too much. But always wash your rags in bleach, because they'll turn a smelly unpleasant brown if you don't take care ...."

"Sorry madam...thank you madam..."

"You can have my old bras too. They are a bit worn out now, but they are good bras and panties; I bought them from the best boutiques in the Main Road in Cape Town. I'll give you some elastic to help keep them up."

"Please madam, thank you, madam..."

In the two years that had gone by while Eve was working for Mrs. Thunderstorm in St. James, Aunty Ella had passed away in her sleep, and life was now a little different for Eve when she came home.

It was during this time that Eve grew close to Kruger's brother, Kaiser, who also helped in the garden, when Kruger had to do other handy work around the house. Kaiser seemed a lot like his brother – rough, yet compassionate, as she came to know them both. They had worked together for a long while then as a family team. They had one common enemy, Mrs. Thunderstorm. Eve became used to Kaiser's familiar tobacco smell, his constant coughing and spitting, and his loud shouts like his brother's when White people were not around.

On one of their long walks home over the sand dunes and through the dense bushes, he remarked, "Hey, Eve, you are a *woman* now..."

"Ah, yah, Mrs. Thunderstorm says so too ..." Eve tried to hide her discomfort with the inappropriate remarks by uncle to niece.

"Really? And why is that?" he winked at her suggestively.

"Don't know..."

"Hey, I like that red floral dress with the low cut top that you were wearing the other day. Makes you look beautiful, especially your lovely, slender, smooth legs."

Eve blushed and brushed the comments aside. "Hey, Uncle, look at the beautiful white wild lilies. Mom likes them. Shall we gather some to take home? She can put them in her big orange plastic vase. Don't you think? It will make her happy if we bring some flowers home."

Kaiser grew irritated with Eve's dismissive attitude. "Yah, flowers grow everywhere. I am sick of flowers. I work with them everyday." Then he changed his tactic, "Roses, lilies, dahlias... are just flowers that get devoured by ugly worms ...you are more beautiful than these flowers. You are like a white rose, pure, untouched, and innocent...without the worms...and the thorns..."

She avoided his inappropriate attentions again, and looked up at the blue sky at the flock of white pelicans with their huge yellow beaks that were streaking the sky, in the formation of a jet.

"Look Uncle, see the pelicans... Awesome!"

His mood changed and he snapped at her banging his chest with his balled angry fist, "Flowers, birds!" He sighed. "...is that all you think about on these walks home. What about *me*?!"

She did not understand his anger.

In the days that followed, he withdrew and did and not speak to her for days. How could she reject his advances, his attention, his existence, his being?

Eve felt uncomfortable about his wild impulsive comments about her beauty. He never spoke to her in that way before. It started when she turned sixteen. It was from that time that she always caught her uncle feasting his wild light eyes on her young bosom. She folded her arms over her breasts to cover them discreetly to discourage him. She started to feel unsafe around him, and made sure that her door was tightly locked during lunch hour and at night. She was too scared to tell Mrs. Thunderstorm. She preferred to protect her uncle from the predictable severity of the White madam.

For a while, Kaiser Verwerp never dared to touch the young girl in his care, and Eve grew strangely at ease with his distant sexual attention. She decided not to tell anyone about his unsolicited attentions, not even her Newlands snob aunts – they would just have said that is what *klip kaffirs* do. If Aunty Ella was alive, she would have said, "That is what *mongrels* do – my brothers are *Coloured* men, *not pure respectable Africans*." She remembered how Aunty Ella warned her of the wildness of "mongrel blood". She sometimes wondered about her own innate wildness, because everybody believed that everybody else was wild, and everybody had names for everybody else.

Eve tried to look less of a woman, hoping it would discourage her uncle. She wore men's boots and milked the cows when she was home. She soon became an expert in holding down fierce bulls and boar pigs fighting for their lives against the sharp brutal daggers of Kruger and Kaiser Verwerp.

The brothers boasted around the fire at night about accurately piercing the beasts deep into their hearts, and how they'd stop their hearts beating within minutes. They described with relish how to slit the throats of pigs, cursing the beasts as "bastards", and how to savour their fresh hot blood immediately after a slaughter. The young boys and Eve listened in awe in the black darkness of the African night to these ancient stories of manhood.

However, to Kaiser, every slaughter of a pig was like an act of dirty, raw sex, climaxing in curses, and Eve's participation in the killing ritual was likened in his imagination to an orgy. When the blood squirted, and the animal sunk to the ground with life-ending agonizing grunts and snorts, he saw in it the orgasmic finale. Contrary to her expectations, and unbeknownst to her, Eve grew perversely and intensely more attractive to Kaiser Verwerp – he saw the stories around the fire as a kind of dramatic foreplay. The slaughtering became more frequent as he enjoyed playing out the incestuous sexual theatre in his mind. Eve sensed his increasing desires and lust for her, and kept her distance from him with an uncomfortable coy smile as her only ironic protection.

It was the time of the persecution of the Jews by Hitler in Europe. Mrs. Thunderstorm, who had Jewish family in the East End in London, became visibly more lenient towards Eve and more trusting of her. She sometimes looked at Eve, and watched her quietly as she got flashes of horror stories told by her relatives of the camps of Auschwitz, Belzec, Chelmno, Dachau, Treblinka... disturbing images of barbed wire enclosures, and wooden watch towers. The stories in letters from distant relatives and friends abroad did not escape her mind. They never did. Human abattoirs. The crime of being viewed as "other", as "different", of being a Jew, of being reduced to gold teeth in ash ovens. Mrs. Thunderstorm felt relieved in the fact that she was not a Jew in Europe; that she had lost this identity along the way because of her English father, and that she was therefore better off than the rest of humanity.

Eve frequently caught her madam in deep thought. "Why are you staring at me, madam? Is something *wrong*?"

The images continued to flash in Mrs. Thunderstorm's mind, the slaughter of her distant Jewish relatives, young and old, at the hands of the Nazi psychopaths. There were images of striped uniforms, mass graves, and gas chambers. There were descriptions of the smell of burnt human flesh, of wheelbarrows of ash, and of skulls that burst. These were the horrors of racial prejudice and beliefs in racial purity and superiority.

At such moments when Eve caught Mrs. Thunderstorm in deep thought, her madam looked down, quietly ashamed, and continued stitching her patch of embroidery, still deep in thought. "Oh, no, nothing, dear. Just thinking..."

On such days, Mrs. Thunderstorm would be quiet and compassionate towards Eve, indulging her momentarily in equality around the home. However, on other days, she would forget about the common humanity in all beings, and snap back into the bizarre racial power relations of the White domestic kitchen in South Africa.

At times like these, she would reason in her mind that she was being kind enough to Coloureds; that they were not as *bad* off as the Africans condemned to the bottom of the heap in South Africa, nor the suffering of the Jews in Hitler's killing fields in Europe.

Eve did not know what was going on in the confusing head of Mrs. Thunderstorm. Instead, she tried to cope with the unpredictable mood swings of her White English madam.

Mrs. Thunderstorm was also confused about her feelings towards the German-Herero brothers who worked in her garden. It was the colour of their eyes that bothered her. Kruger had once told her out of the blue of the rape of his Herero mother by the White German soldier. He had also told her how his mother fled to avoid German persecution and death in the concentration camps. Was he perhaps lying? Was he trying to get her to sympathise with him and with Coloureds who fled South West Africa? She never knew that this had happened to the Herero and Nama people well before the killing of the Jews in the gas chambers.

She defensively told him, "Kruger, shut up with your sorry-tales and get working!"

Yes, the brothers looked mixed. Those eyes and freckles could not come from his Herero mother. Then again, she reasoned that Black women were *always* seducing White men. The English women at her croquet club in Fish Hoek had warned her of the seductive ways of the Coloured and Black women. "Don't get too familiar with them, and never leave them *on their own* at home with your husband. Make sure the gardener or children are at home to see that she does not steal his affections when you turn your back."

An English lady at church once told her, "The Coloured women in Kalk Bay all sleep with our husbands. Did you see their children with the light hair and eyes? They say our husbands raped their mothers and we must therefore give them money. All nonsense! Keep them at bay. Make them *know* their *place* in your home. They take advantage very quickly because they are *very* clever, and they know how to seduce our men with their *huge* buttocks and fleshy thighs. Lets face it, Black and Coloured women are fleshy and they somehow enjoy sex more than we do. Well, that is what my foolish husband tells me all the time...*dirty* old man! He is messing around with *dirty* smelly servants...I told him he'll give me *pubic lice*, if he's not careful! I have myself checked often, just in case..."

Mrs. Thunderstorm was always disturbed by these stories from other respectable upper-class White women and wanted to know more. "Then what do you tell your husband when he talks about his lust for these Coloured and Black women?"

"I tell him, now go get yourself a Black whore! You are like a *dog* in heat! *They* can lie down for you. I have too much respect for my body. Point is, I think he actually waits for me to say that and then he disappears during lunch time to see if he can find one walking along the beach in her servant overalls. He likes the overalls..."

"But my mother tells me it is an *ancient* thing between Whites and Blacks, like the joke goes – when you are so busy stoking the coals in the fire, you do not notice the mantelpiece nor the *beautiful white snow* on the mountain... "

Mr. Thunderstorm often worked away and hardly came to know Eve. After hearing all these powerful stories of Black female seduction, and as Eve developed into a young lady, Mrs. Thunderstorm was indeed quietly happy that she was a grass widow!

Andrew was by then a fully grown young man, who had learned to respect Eve, who had grown into a confident, strong woman who now dared to reprimand him for leaving his clothes on the floor in his bedroom. He admired her secretively, watching her sensual movements from behind when no one was looking, and stealthily stroked her underwear on her short washing line made from his mother's worn pantihose that stretched tightly across the door of the small servant quarters in the far corner of the garden. He admired the cherry colour lipstick Eve wore, the penetrating smell of her cheap musk scent, and he fantasized about touching her firm, inviting breasts. His imagination about their attractive servant abandoned him to solo sex trips in his bedroom, masturbating and feeling guilty afterwards, avoiding her eyes for days as if she knew about these lonesome, disgusting episodes he had with his body. If his mother found out, it would drive her to suicide, he concluded. So he prayed to God every night that his mother should never catch him masturbating, calling Eve's name out uncontrollably loudly when he eventually climaxed.

In the meantime, Kaiser's volcano was about to burst. One summer's day out of the blue, he asked Eve to join him on a train trip to visit the South West Africa family in Stellenbosch. Her mother protested that the children had to be looked after, the animals needed to be attended to, and the timing for a visit to Stellenbosch was rather odd, as the family only expected them for Christmas and Easter, not just any time of year. She noised in protest as she washed the dishes. In any case, the train trip was expensive, and one could not visit a rural family empty-handed, she muttered angrily. Kaiser promised to take a slaughtered chicken and some herbs from the *veld*, known as *Hottentots kooigoed* –

literally meaning "Hottentot's stuff for the bed", intended for his aunt's many troubling ailments, which he apparently had promised her some time ago. He also wanted to give Eve a break, he argued, as she was always working so hard every weekend without any reward. More than that, the Stellenbosch family always came to visit them, and they never returned the favour, he tried to convince his feisty sister-in-law. In the end, she agreed reluctantly.

After securing permission to have Eve accompany him on his trip, Kaiser ran excitedly amongst the chickens they kept on the yard; he caught one of the cheeky black cocks that he had been fighting with for a long time on the yard, grabbed it by its feet, and with one mighty swing of the long handle axe, its head was severed. The headless cock did a few rounds of the yard, until it dropped down kicking, its blood dripping in the sand and on the block of wood he used as an impromptu slaughter board. He stored the chicken, feathers and all, in a dusty used maize bag. Eve carried the *Hottentots kooigoed* tied in a tidy bundle with twigs and flowers on her head, and Kaiser slung the maize bag stained with the cock's blood over his shoulder as they set out on their journey to the Boland, the fertile land of vineyards above the blue Cape mountains.

The enchanting beauty of the Boland is often described by Europeans as a "slice of the south of France in Africa". This is especially true for Franschhoek, meaning "French corner" in Afrikaans, established by the French Huguenot refugees of the late 1600s. With its abundance of French wines and variety of cheeses, its old farm names are etched in French place names like *Provence* and *La Dauphine*.

It was a pleasant journey, with the summer breeze gushing through the windows of the train, bringing relief to the unbearable, hot, dry, Boland wind on her skin. It was Eve's first long train journey out of Cape Town. She had heard so much of Franschhoek and of Stellenbosch; of the vineyards, of the fruit trees, of the genuine blue mountains, of the river streams, of the oak trees, and of the Dutch architecture dating from the time of slavery in the close to three hundred years before. She remembered her grandfather's stories about Stellenbosch as he lectured to them at the dinner table, while smoking his pipe after family prayers. He knew so much history, about this town and that town, as told to him by his elders. As they travelled as gypsies from town to town he said, they also learned so much from the people who lived there.

Eve fanned her face with her hankie to relieve the relentless summer heat in the dusty train.

She remembered how her grandfather spoke with much affection of Stellenbosch. "Stellenbosch, the ancient slave town, built by slaves, with streets lined with oak trees, its name going back to the days when the Dutch Governor Simon Van der Stel visited the area in 1679, meaning 'Van der Stel's bush'. The White settlers from Europe liked it there and settled along the river, and used the yellow wood trees and stink wood trees to build houses with huge wooden doors and windows with black thatch roofs. They also made their own furniture with the wood. And my people worked as slaves for them."

She learned about the few hundred slaves that lived in Stellenbosch that came from West Africa, Madagascar, and India, like her grandmother Nazurah's family, and how they were sold at the public slave auctions of the Boland. They did the hard work in the hot sun on the vineyards and amongst the orchards where the train wormed through. Many of these slaves were also skilled builders and artisans who built the beautiful buildings and houses that she could now see from the train. They made the beautiful furniture, the vats, and the wagons for which the Boland became renowned.

Surrounded by magnificent mountains, blue mountains like in France, Stellenbosch is South Africa's second oldest town established by the Dutch on the Eerste River, meaning 'first river' of colonial settlement. The river is the most beautiful in the Cape, flowing out of the mountains into a shallow fertile valley, and nurturing the vineyards with its many springs.

Moses de Swart was a man steeped in history. He also told her how the slaves were punished and executed in public in Stellenbosch, like the Dutch did with slaves in Green Point in Cape Town. Like in Cape Town, many of the slaves rebelled and started fires in Stellenbosch. The punishment for that was public hanging. "Stellenbosch is a beautiful place, but built on violence and blood!" he used to shout as he smoked his pipe and leaned over the back-door watching the chickens feed in his yard. "'The bitter fruit of Stellenbosch!" my grandmother used to say. "It is a beautiful place of shame."

As Eve feasted her eyes on the blue mountains of the Boland, she recalled these little history lessons and her grandfather's many stories of places and people, stories of a slave history hidden deep in the silent echoes of the blue mountains. As the train passed through the valley and orchards, Eve could not believe that she was now seeing with her very own eyes the cottages and vineyards and mountains that her grandfather had told her about. How she missed those days just listening at the dinner table to the affectionate yet feisty old man, so much like his daughter.

The journey took about two hours. From the station, they started the long journey by foot in the hot sun to the family's farm workers' cottage, buried deep in the panoramic blue mountains about which the family often spoke. The white cottages with the dark wooden window frames and heavy doors were nestled in the mountains, as if locked in time. The oak trees patterned the winding, quiet, gravel roads.

While trudging their way through the vineyard lined steep and winding gravel roads, Kaiser and Eve passed the time talking about Mrs. Thunderstorm and her visiting tanned lovers from the upper echelons of Cape society. The scent of roses, lavender, and rosemary hung in the air, and the many colourful Cape birds were singing, adding to the tranquillity of this rare place of heaven on Earth.

Kaiser initiated the uncomfortable conversation. "Hey, Eve, Mr. Thunderstorm stays away far too long from his wife...don't you think?"

"I never think about it....in *that* way..."

"Look, Eve, *a man is a man*...and must keep himself and a woman happy. Mr. Thunderstorm *must* have a woman up north. They say the Coloured and Black servants in Johannesburg are *hot*...you know what I mean?"

She avoided desperately the drift of the conversation. "No, I don't. This heat is unbearable. We must walk quickly to get out of the hot sun."

She turned her mind to the beauty of Stellenbosch, as they walked the gravel road passing the vineyards and orchards of red and green apples, yellow pears, succulent red plums, and large yellow juicy peaches. She marvelled at the hundreds of vineyards, showered with layers of breathtaking maroon and golden coloured vine leaves, black and green bunches of ripened grapes hung heavy in their sweetness of the Cape sun. The singing birds picked on the plums with excitement, noisily flying from tree to tree. The sound of the many colourful birds of various species could be heard a distance away. A bicycle or donkey cart passed every now and then.

It was in this moment of the tranquillity of Stellenbosch and relaxed conversation about this and that, that Kaiser Verwerp could not resist the woman whose virginity he wanted so badly. In mid-conversation, he pushed his niece to the ground, his eyes suddenly cold and wild. Her body reeled with fear and shock. She yelled helplessly in the deserted beautiful surrounds of the valleys of the Cape mountains.

Her shrieking frightened voice echoed loudly, several times, but no one answered back. Kaiser suddenly became monstrous. He was no longer laughing or joking as Eve tried to fight him off. He rolled with her down the riverbed, and they landed in a fighting fit on dry grass next to the tranquil river stream, with him on top of her. He covered her fearful mouth with his strong tobacco-smelling hands and shoved his other hand roughly into her pink cotton panties, bruising her delicate inner thigh. She protested violently, like an animal fighting the slaughter, though his eyes fixed for the kill. She called out loud for the departed soul of Aunty Ella to help her and to her grandfather, Moses – he who had told her so many enchanting stories of this place. Kaiser ignored her desperate screams as the demon-possessed spirit of his rapist German father took over.

Kaiser Verwerp had waited so long for this moment. He bit her virgin tender nipples and pushed his wanting tongue down her resisting throat. He had always dreamed of her maiden blood squirting, perhaps in his face, of her shouting, squealing like a pig, of him grunting and snorting as he breaks her body into womanhood.

They were far away from the haunting spirit-presence of Aunt Ella, and far away from the perceptive stares of Mrs. Thunderstorm. While he tried to conquer her physical being, he reasoned that he would be king of her body, master of her soul, and nobody would ever get to know his sweet secret. With this thought, he thrust his angry large hardness deep into her being as flashes of killing a pig rushed through his mind. As he forcefully sunk his angry, aged flesh into her protesting young body, seemingly unrelated thoughts rushed through his mind; these thoughts were racing with angry words and conversations.

He hated Mrs. Thunderstorm and all her patronising and derogatory questions.

He hated that child, Andrew, for calling him "boy".

"I despise that White English madam – the inquisitive, controlling bitch! No, she is not a madam. She is a bitch. Just a bitch! Always remarking about the colour of my eyes...You don't look Black, *boy*...I heard you were born from a rape by a German man. Is it true? Why did she always have to call me 'boy' when I am *her age*?!"

"Madam, my father is a German, but I am a *kaffir*. Simply a *kaffir*. I know how the Europeans fear the Germans. Now, fear the German in me, bitch! English woman, I prefer to be what you want me to be. Just a *kaffir*, just a plain *kaffir!* In any case, that is what many call me. A *kaffir*. I may as well do what a *kaffir* is *supposed* to do. *Kaffirs* are supposed to be cruel and murderous!"

He played out all his bottled up emotions in sexual theatre. Eve's body became a functional deep dark hole in which to thrust his bottomless anger. It became many things. It became the prejudice of the African gypsies that he despised so much. Eve became the White "bitch" that his father would have sent to the furnaces. She also became the hurtful tongue of his Herero half-sister who called him *a mongrel*, "not a pure Herero", "not a pure African".

"You are a mongrel. Not a pure Herero. Not a pure Herero. Not a pure German. Not pure. Not pure. A *mongrel*."

Words and labels played over and over again in his head as he sunk himself further in and out of Eve's vulnerable body. With every thrust he became angrier. The blood rushed to his angry bottom, making him harder and more brutal in the act of assault. He felt intense anger with every violent thrust, building up to a climax. He also felt relief. The body became the theatre of deep racial hatred, of painful ambivalence and of soul-wrenching confusion. What mattered were not the names he was called, but that people feared him, that he could command in the village, and that he had power.

At this point, he lost his body in bitterness and anger. He lost control. Eve did not exist. Her body did not exist. She was simply a hole. Why did Mrs. Thunderstorm like him only as a *gardener*? Why did she like him for his "loyalty and honesty" only? She kept him in the garden and out of her kitchen. He had to eat *outside* in the makeshift storeroom, yet Eve could eat inside. In any case, she was looking for this. She *wanted* it; he had to *give* it to his niece, before any other man did it. She was wearing the dress that showed her young virgin breasts. Yes, she wanted it; he knew because he is a man, and a man *knows* a woman's needs.

Eve felt cold and numb with pain and shock. It felt as if she had lost her life; her body felt like a huge gaping wound. She drifted away from the relentless assault on her body and fixed her eyes on the cloud formations against the vast blue sky. She imagined that the bottom part of her body was amputated, that only her head existed. She imagined that she was a feather, flying lightly in the wind. She wished for death. She prayed that at that moment there were angels that would fly with trumpets down from the sky that would pick her up and whisk her away on a flight with the singing birds into the blue heavens of serenity.

Dramatic shouts of Kaiser's beastly anger echoed through the valleys of the Stellenbosch mountains. Her uncle's body contorted violently; his face turned a little blue, and angry sweat pearled on his forehead. His eyes stood still and glassy in his head, and suddenly he fell down limp and heavy on her body, his face buried between her violently bitten breasts; his unpleasant weight and piggish smell burdening her frailness She felt a warm, wet rush of fluid down her thigh. She hurt deep inside; a raw, deep hurt.

Kaiser started to sob uncontrollably on the violated breasts of his niece. His body shook heavily and violently on hers. In his sudden and perplexing weakness, she pushed him off her and wriggled her way out from underneath his smothering heaviness. She rolled over on to her stomach on the dry pine needles and leaves. At that moment, she silently begged God for death. Because how does one live after this brutal confusing act of the flesh? She kicked him away from her, cursing and crying in confusion. She was bruised and her back hurt where he had pushed her down on a rock at the stream. No bicycle or horse cart passed by. It felt like a conspiracy, like a dirty, evil trick. Her orange cotton dress was stained with her virginal blood and her uncle's semen. Her hair was peppered with dry thorns and pine needles and twigs. She felt wild and dirty, like a "mongrel". She felt ice cold and numb, even in the heat of the relentless Boland afternoon sun. She tried to run away from the grown-up family man with whom she had lived and worked, to find her own way home back to the familiar sand dunes of the Cape.

"You know your grandfather will kill me...!" he shouted after her as he pulled up his zip and tucked in his creased, soaked, sweaty, red-checkered shirt.

The birds were singing in the trees as if nothing evil had happened in their territory. Crickets were noising in the long dry grass, enjoying the heat.

Kaiser caught up with her, pulled her at the shoulder, begging forgiveness and understanding. "Don't tell on me...please I beg you, Eve, to forgive me...you don't understand, child, this *devil* in me - maybe it is the German in me, maybe it is the *kaffir* in me, maybe it is the *Herero* in me...or maybe it is just me...the *mongrel*... whatever people choose to call me..."

She pushed him away in painful anger as they walked the rest of the journey in stony silence, Eve sobbing. They stopped at a nearby waterfall where she walked into the fast flowing brown water of the mountain stream. Steadying herself on a rock in the gushing stream, she rinsed her blood–soaked dress and cleaned her thighs and breasts.

Eve avoided looking at her uncle as they continued the walk on their journey to deliver the *Hottentots kooigoed* and the black feathered headless cock to the waiting relatives. Instead of conversing with him, she focused her eyes on the overripe spoiled red plums strewn on the ground in the orchard; some were rotten and some were hollow, devoured to the core by worms.

Chapter 4
A Branch of Honeysuckle for Our Love

By the time apartheid was introduced in South Africa in 1948, society was already rotten from segregation and racism introduced previously by the Dutch and the English. The Afrikaners (who emerged from the Dutch and others) perfected the madness, and made it a political institution, a big *mad house.*

Now, apartheid South African laws were bizarre. You could find yourself entangled in a range of bizarre laws that prohibited "interracial sex and marriage", and that dictated where people could live, or move. There were the following laws: Prohibition of Mixed Marriages Act, the Immorality Act, the Pass Laws Act, the Reservation of Separate Amenities Act, Act no 49 of 1953, and so and so on. The list was endless. Through the Population Registration Act, Act no 30 of 1950, you could change from White to Cape Coloured; Cape Coloured to White; Cape Coloured to Chinese; White to Chinese; White to Malay; Malay to White; White to Indian; Indian to Cape Coloured; Cape Coloured to Indian; Indian to Malay; Malay to Indian; Other Asian to Cape Coloured; Black to Cape Coloured; Cape Coloured to Black; Black to Griqua; and Cape Coloured to Griqua. To be reclassified White from "Coloured", you had to be fair-skinned and had to also pass the pencil-in-the hair test. They would then be first class, not third class. This was therefore a popular choice.

Even some African people with fair skin or long hair got themselves classified "Coloured" in the process, and pretended that they could not speak Xhosa or Zulu, or any of the African languages. They made sure they were fluent in Afrikaans, as this qualified you also as a "Coloured", and they chose not to visit their families in the homelands. They also changed the pronunciation and spelling of their surnames as to not sound "African". They would then be third class, not fourth class.

Kaiser and Kruger's mother also ended up in domestic service with a White family in the White coastal town on the Atlantic Ocean, Sea Point, and later gave birth to a number of children younger than Kruger, Kaiser, and Ella. Some looked like the Hereros, and the others looked like the White English master, Mr. Swain. Their younger brother, Robert, chose the life of a play-White. During the apartheid 1950s when hundreds of apartheid laws were passed to regulate the lives of South Africans around privileges and segregation, the family split right down the middle - the dark ones living their lives as Coloureds, and some of the fair ones had themselves reclassified as White. To be reclassified as "White" from "Coloured", some people said they paid £100 for a "White" or "European" identity card, and had to sign up with the racist ruling National Party, giving them their vote in every election. They also had to promise that they'd cut all contact with Coloured and Black people, including their relatives, after which, they disappeared into the maze of Cape Town's White ghettos, never to make contact with their Coloured siblings again. The newly re-registered "White" brothers never bothered to look again for one another, choosing to live a life of privilege with better housing, well-paid jobs, the ability to go to the best beaches, restaurants, decent theatres, and cinemas.

The White-Black pattern remained to haunt Kruger's family for generations, and became the dinner table conversation over and over again in painful memories at Christmas and Easter time.

How could brothers and sisters just disappear like that, never to look for each other again?

This was all very confusing, as Kruger and others knew that before apartheid (though there was segregation introduced by the British) many people used to mix, living together and having children. Some ended up looking like the White mother, and some like the Black father. Therefore, it was also the case that many Coloureds looked like "the Aryan race" that Hitler described – fair, blond, and with blue eyes. While some of these people chose to be classified White and never made contact with family again – even in small Cape Town, others preferred to stay with their families and kept their race classification as "Coloured". An inevitable mental madness and emotional brutality and confusion emerged in apartheid South Africa amongst Coloured people, more so than amongst African people, especially in Cape Town. Many looked like Kruger Verwerp, and were too Black to be White, but also too White to be Black. The diverse beauty of the Capetonian people (Coloured and African) turned into a type of Holocaust mental concentration camp – a psychiatric institution in itself, in hospitals, in kindergartens, in streets, in families, in schools, in churches, in mortuaries, in cemeteries, in coffins, and in graves.

In Sunday school, the Coloured children were taught to sing, "*Lord Jesus, I long to be perfectly whole; ...Now wash me and I shall be whiter than snow. Whiter than snow, oh whiter than snow...*" Children with "kinky" hair covered their hair with woollen caps and scarves in shame at school, and those with long straight hair and fair skin showed their hair and colour off and got special treatment and privileges. These fair children with the straight hair won prizes at school, sat in front in the class, got chosen to play Mary, Jesus, Joseph, and the Three Wise Men in Christmas plays. Many Muslim children with sleek hair and fair skin landed these roles. Such children got the best clothes and treats in their families, and never got hidings. The Black children took hidings on behalf of their White-looking siblings. It was just the way things worked. White equalled Jesus, God, purity, and goodness. Black equalled ugliness, evil, and darkness – the seedy underground.

Christmas and Easter were times of great festivities, but also of silent deep sadness and unspoken shame for many Coloured Cape Flats families. It was a time to gather around to share in slaughtered pig, duck, sheep, chicken, and turkey, and in jokes about hair and looks (usually about those with flat noses and big buttocks and kinky hair in the family). However, it was also a time to be silently reminded of the empty places at the dining table of those who cut ties with the Coloured family to be classified as "White". This was often done with typical tragic wit and Cape humour.

Christmas and Easter were "the big days", a time to make sure your hair was straightened and to rub *Ambi* in your skin to boast a fair complexion. It made the awareness of the empty chairs in the family less painful. Every Sunday and at Christmas time and even at Eid, families would be reminded of the missing play-White relatives; the ever-present ghosts at Cape family gatherings. They would speak of them with sympathy and longing, but also with bitterness; of how play-White aunty and uncle this and that would be missing listening to Jimmy Hendrix, playing dominoes, sharing in the loud laughter of jokes and traditional English fish and chips on a Friday night.

If you were a play-White, you had to change all of this. This was a complicated procedure in itself. First you had to get reclassified through the pencil-in the-hair test which involved the White race classification officials pushing a pencil through your hair once you have made your application to be White through the Population Registration Act of 1950. If the pencil fell out, and you were fair enough, then you were re-classified as White. When it got stuck, then you were in danger of failing the test and returning to your Coloured life, like a dog with your tail between your legs. However, if you did pass the test, then you had to make some crucial lifestyle adjustments.

Tumelo heard of Eve's story through local gossip. She had many aunts, and she learnt much more about how apartheid worked through their various coping methods, behaviours and stories. As Tumelo grew up, she learnt that your mental antenna had to be razor sharp, picking up every little thing that may betray your Coloured-ness. If you had four front teeth missing, then you went to the dentist and had the entire mouthful of teeth removed and had them replaced with a full set of dentures. Then, you bought yourself some pearl earrings and a necklace from the second-hand shop in middle class White Claremont with two crimperline dresses (the colours pink and powder blue were good choices) to match your imitation pearls that looked like the string Queen Elizabeth wears on the photograph on your front room's wall. Her Majesty's visit to Cape Town in 1947 as a twenty-one-year old with her father, King George VI and her mother and sister Margaret, is still a talking point amongst many Coloured elders who were always in awe of the queen and her empire.

The little inspection at the time of a Coloured child's birth determined how she would be treated in the family for the rest of her life. The story of Sandra Laing is well known. Born in the apartheid 60s to White racist Afrikaner parents, nature had played a trick and Sandra got the pigmentation of a Black great-great grandparent. She was reclassified twice, first to "Coloured" and then back to "White". She was thrown out of school with the help of two policemen, and refused ice cream at the shop and the company of White children. She became a lonely, rejected child, prone to bed wetting.

Tumelo learnt that it was torture to keep up a play-White life. Her play-White Aunt Maggie got herself some dark sunglasses to hide her shame, and to make sure her Coloured relatives did not recognise her in Main Road, Wynberg. Aunt Maggie walked like a peacock; she made sure she never looked down. She practised in the mirror to never laugh that raw, uninhibited, loud Coloured *gam* laugh again, which was always a dead give-away. Instead, she suppressed her laughter, and allowed faint noises to escape at the sides of her pressed lips, while she elegantly covered her mouth with her dainty starched white embroidered hanky. She never went out without her white gloves, always displayed to be visible in her hand clutching the bag, or on the table. People had to see those white gloves! She had black ones for winter; white ones for summer. In public, Aunt Maggie watched the world from the side of her eyes; picking up any little movement from a Coloured mortal who may have wanted to shout "Aunty so and so!" Her husband, Uncle Jack, got himself a golf set and a straw hat, even though he could hardly afford it. They learned the White symbols quickly. The couple regularly hunted the second-hand shops for "White life" memorabilia to help them along. Uncle Jack bought cigars, not cigarettes, and also a pair of dark sunglasses. Aunt Maggie and Uncle Jack spoke nasally, mimicking the White voices on Springbok Radio. They also avoided having children, in case they gave birth to a dark child with "kinky" hair. When they reached their mid-thirties, they adopted a White baby with no tell-tale traces of a tan at the bottom rims of her finger nails, or on the edges of her ear lobes or on her behind. Aunt Maggie was well-trained to check the notorious spots on a fair-skinned baby's body – the blue spot on the back or buttocks that was in fact the real colour that would eventually spread to cover the child's entire body as she grew older. She knew to avoid a baby born with a bush of curly sleek hair, as that turned into "kinky" African hair when she turned a little older. Aunt Maggie adopted a baby with a bald head, a sign of sleek hair to come.

As a play-White, when people asked about Uncle Jack's dark shade in summer, he explained that he spent many holidays in the Mediterranean or that he was a distant relative of the film actor Omar Sharif who acted in *Doctor Zhivago* and *Lawrence Of Arabia*. (Egyptians were traditionally not viewed as part of the African continent or people.) Another safer option was to tell them about his distant link to the Western movie actor Yul Brynner. In spite of their mixed heritage, both of these world-famous actors conveyed some sense of Whiteness and decency. If people asked the couple about their families at Christmas time and Easter, then they said they were "foster children or orphans". In such uncomfortable conversations, Uncle Jack always made sure he was the first to start the conversation about the "dirty, lazy no-good Coloureds". In that way, he figured, no one ever would have guessed who he really was. The couple consciously changed the way they talked, gestured, and laughed. They ensured themselves a quiet, private life together. Uncle Jack took photos of Aunty Maggie with a pedigree dog on her lap, a parrot on her shoulder, and while she was having afternoon tea with cucumber sandwiches. These photos were sent to their carefully selected White pen pals in London, Durban, and Johannesburg. They kept a stiff upper lip when friends were around and contained their natural laughter. They enjoyed sand bathing on the beach, studying the minute details of nature with their binoculars, and they indulged in plenty of bird watching. Aunt Maggie entertained her guests with platters of cheese, raw carrots and celery sticks. They avoided "Coloured" entertainment food like deep fried chicken drumsticks, French cold meats, cream crackers with cheese and sardines, and cheap white wine called "lurk" - a poisonous rotten drink that haunted many poor and unemployed Coloured people for days and nights, as it turned them into violent self-loathing beasts. This was the wine said to have been handed out to slaves at the Cape by Dutch settler Jan Van Riebeeck in the 1600s, a practice called the "tot system", to keep them in a trance. They listened to soft classical music, and when they had a White Afrikaner visitor, they even played *orkes-musiek* (Afrikaner classical music).

Aunt Maggie learned to play croquet and ate cucumber sandwiches in uppity White Rondebosch. She practised her pronunciation of words for hours in the mirror: *crew—cay;* not *craw - kett*. She also learned to practise the sound *shhhhhh* in the mirror with her index finger gently placed on her lips. Words like "private", "quiet", and "routine" became part of their daily conversation, their standard White dictionary, and their new carefully crafted regimented existence.

Uncle Jack dumped their vinyl records on the dirt heap in the neighbouring Coloured township; single hits of Nat King Cole, Louis Armstrong, and Jimmy Hendrix. He replaced them with singles of Dean Martin, Frank Sinatra, Judy Garland, Vera Lynn, and Marlene Dietrich.

Aunt Maggie and Uncle Jack lived a calculated, ordered life of schizophrenia. Aunt Maggie, for instance, knew that she also needed essential life long provisions from the Coloured world for her parachute into and her life jacket in the White world. She had a little secret closet in which she stored *Wella* hair straightener for those rainy foggy days when her "hair went home", as in the local expression *(gaan huis toe)* – meaning *frizzy*. By this they meant that it becomes natural, like the way you were born, figuratively meaning "going home to your roots". The roots of your hair as a "Coloured" person come out when the mist, fog, and rain turn your hair into an indigenous shrub, like *fynbos,* the endangered Cape shrub vegetation meaning "fine bush". The temperamental Cape climate with its seasonal wetness and fog as in Ireland put play-Whites under tremendous pressure and in mental agony. Aunt Maggie knew that if her hair went home, it was a dead give-away that she was definitely Coloured! On foggy days when she saw the tablecloth of mist forming over Table Mountain, she and the play-Whites did not venture out. On such days, she made sure she was alone at home and booked no visitors, to take care of the straightening job that made the house smell as if someone had emptied a dry toilet in there. This smell clung to the walls of their modest home in the poor White area, hanging there for some hours, and the vapour made her eyes burn as she kept the windows tightly closed so that the well-known whiff could not travel to the noses of her unsuspecting White neighbours. After her hair had been straightened, she did the delicate swirl-job.

Now, how did she do this? She flattened her hair by combing it to one side, holding it down with the palm of her hand. Then she took a brush to press it down more flat. Then she held it with one hand – the part where the hair ends. Then she took a tight stocking (part of the legging which includes the foot, because it must form a cap) with the other free hand, and she put it over her head. She pulled it tight to the side to which she swirled the hair. The tricky part was when she went to sleep with her swirl, lying in bed besides Uncle Jack. She had to try to lie still on her back and only try to roll her eyes to the left or right – and only if she really, really had to. *Really,* only if she was forced to! No movement of the head was allowed, and Uncle Jack knew no lovemaking and even snoring was allowed on swirl nights. Otherwise, he'd fuck up her swirl during the passionate commotion of copulation, and the vibration of his snores could also possibly cause havoc. If they both behaved themselves during the night, then Aunt Maggie's hair would be straight in the morning, like the White people's hair – but only when there was no fog or rain. The good hair seasons were from January to March. April was known to be risky, as the wet autumn wind that blew from the sea made her hair sticky and knotty. Aunt Maggie ordered her straightener through a private post office letter delivery system, and stocked up volumes of tubes for May to August, which were "bad hair months" in Cape Town. During these months, she only ventured out for work (where she wore a scarf as a chemist's assistant) and to the doctor. She skipped unnecessarily risky outdoor gatherings such as funerals.

She had unpleasant memories of big weddings and parties in civic halls in Coloured townships when there were distressing hair encounters as everybody was obsessed with straight hair. Guests would arrive with tight scarves and woollen caps and form long lines in the ladies' toilets for the mirrors, not the toilets – to carefully first remove all the layers of stocking from their hair, and then to comb the hair out straight before facing the other guests. Fights often broke out in the ladies' toilets at functions because of hair. She remembered a feisty young woman shouting at her for spending too much time in front of the mirror, *"Teef!'n Hond kak ook hare!"* *"Bitch! A dog also shits hair!"* This was a favourite battle cry amongst Coloured women with "kinky" hair and indigenous looks as they pulled the hair and bit into the flesh of an unsuspecting woman with slightly sleek hair and Whitish or Asian looks. She remembered on such foggy days in Cape Town, how the girls already fought in primary school over hair; they would corner their sleek hair victims after school. The whole hair-drama would start with a whispering campaign a few days before for an audience to back the "kinky"-haired group taking on the "play-White" children. Dozens of children gathered in the sand pit to witness the attack on Aunt Maggie on a scheduled Friday afternoon, to "sort out the *sturvy* (snooty) bitch". These little girls would also enjoy the backing of their mothers who themselves also had "kinky" hair in the local townships, and who fought with the mothers with the sleek hair in the public toilets. Endless narcissistic grooming in front of the mirrors and monopolies of the public spaces of imaging and at schools and churches by women and girls with sleek hair usually triggered the wrath in their African, indigenous-looking counterparts. Not to mention, hairdressers were under immense pressure to create sleek hair, and to make magic with "kinky" hair. A hairdresser who failed to do the magic, would meet with the wrath of a gang of women in the family, hitting the hairdresser and swearing her *"poes"! (cunt!)*

Like Aunty Maggie, Uncle Jack also lived with the daily overwhelming fear that his hair would "go home". He found the swirl procedure uncomfortable and painful. Once, as a teenager, he stole his mother's new pair of stockings for church and slept with the sharp edged strong stocking on his head, and it cut through his skin on his forehead. He not only suffered a huge smack from his unimpressed mother in the morning, but had to also endure the laughter at school in the morning at his "swirl line". He envied his Muslim friends who were mostly from Malaysia and India and who did not have to worry about their hair "going home". Quietly, he wished that he could be like the African women and men in the township magazines who took pride in their Afros. They looked like famous pop singers and local African musicians like Hot Stix Mabuza and Sipho Gumede - and like Miriam Makeba with her beautiful hair dress in African beads. Africans did not have the play-White pressure in the township.

For Aunt Maggie and Uncle Jack, life was a little more complicated and brutal. On a bad swirl day, when Aunty Maggie had overdone the swirl job, she looked like a nocturnal rodent, like a porcupine with its black spiky pens. Like the porcupine, she'd have night wakes as she jumped up regularly during the night to swirl her hair from one side to the other. Even Uncle Jack would sometimes end up with a bad swirl job, looking like *Lovelace Watkins*, the popular Las Vegas Black singer of the ironical *The Way I Am* with the straightened hair who had amongst his fans the most ardent apartheid government leaders at the time!

Uncle Jack and Aunt Maggie reasoned that it was all worth the effort, though. By being play-White, they could exchange a life of poverty and misery in the township to a life in a White suburb with parks and pools, pavements to walk on, big houses with huge landscaped gardens. They could even hire African and Coloured servants and gardeners for cheap, even get a good job and earn a good salary. They could go to the Whites-only beach on hot summer days. They could go to restaurants. They could go see films and theatre. They could use clean and regularly serviced Whites-only public toilets. It was a tempting choice. For those who never made it, they tried to imagine they were White in the Coloured township and played White in the family and neighbourhood, demanding the seats in front in the local church, the biggest plates of food, and so on.

Aunt Maggie and Uncle Jack also knew that if they chose the play-White life that there was no return. They had to come to terms with the fact that they made a sad and painful choice as they lost family, laughter, joy, and togetherness. Before Aunt Maggie met Jack, she was married to an Englishman, and the people gossiped, "Yes, she met this bloke, a new arrival from the council estates in England. After she got together with him, she did not want to know us. She said we were Black, and that he did not want any of her Coloured family on his doorstep. He beat her up every weekend and swore at her about her Black family. He treated her as if he was doing her a favour, saving her from misery and giving her opportunities such as living in a White area and not in the township. They came from England in their thousands in the 1960s to benefit from apartheid. Did you ever go to see how they lived in England, and then they come to South Africa to play madam and master? They get better pay here, also inconvenience pay when they teach at Coloured and African schools, and they live in big houses with swimming pools. Aunty Maggie must be regretting turning White. She is the only one who is fair in her family with light eyes. I saw her once in the street carrying heavy grocery bags, and she embarrassingly turned away when she saw me. She was wearing dark sunglasses to hide a black eye."

The gossip continued ruthlessly in the township, "Heard she told a friend he can't get it up! He flies at half-mast, so to speak. So he has this damp, limp piece of flesh dripping with pee between his legs that he tries to force into her when she has desires. What some Coloured women would sacrifice to have a White man...!"

"He needed someone to sponsor his drinking habit. So, Aunty Maggie was a good catch."

"That is not a life of dignity, I tell you. And now she can't come back – the shame of returning to your Coloured family after you disowned them as your family as not good enough for you!"

The table was stacked with English Christmas mince pies and home-made ginger beer – and everybody quietly knew that Aunty Maggie would give the world to be reunited with her family again to taste the warmth of a family Christmas. After this frantic festive gossip, her family held hands and pulled the words as they sang and closed their eyes like a congregation singing gospel hymns in a charismatic church.

"*...I am dreaming of a white Christmas...!!!*"

Nostalgia filled the air, and in the bitter sweetness of a Coloured family Christmas at the time of apartheid, wine and tears flowed, disrupted by spontaneous sweet infectious laughter of an endearing brave people.

There were also tales about notorious play-White Uncle Robert.

Uncle Robert wanted to be White, but only to live in a White suburb, pay cheap rent, and get a good job at the council without much education. The funny thing about Uncle Robert - he only screwed with Coloured women. Not *any* Coloured woman—he was quite picky—she had to be from the indigenous Northern Cape desert people, from the Bushmen. He said he liked them "closer to the bone", that Coloured women of mixed "race" were "untamed" because they came from too many people in the world – the North, the South, the East, and the West. Because they came from the foreigners who landed over the centuries at the Cape, he therefore found them "quick tempered".

Uncle Robert did not know his Coloured family during the year, but he visited them the weekend before Christmas, when everybody was very generous and sentimental about "family". Every Christmas Eve, he arrived like royalty, dressed in a suit and a hat, and he only spoke English with an affected European accent as if he had a hot potato stuck in his mouth. He then expected to be treated like a king, nothing less. "Hey, you!" he would say, to a cousin of his, "When last did you comb your hair – that despicable steel wool mattress on your head? You don't have to buy steel wool to do the dishes, use your hair!" He insulted his Coloured relatives one by one on such occasions. Worse, they were all nervous because "White Uncle Robert" came to visit. No, the family did not chase him away in disgust. It was all bizarre. They hated and despised him when he was away living his White life, and adored and worshipped him when he visited them; colour betrayals were easily forgotten and forgiven. They knew that he was born from the *same* parents and he grew up with a snotty nose like everybody else.

Uncle Robert would phone at a time well ahead of his visit to order that the family cooked his favourite dish, - curry sugar beans - and he liked custard and jelly with sago pudding. When he arrived, he sat alone at the table, and then everybody had to serve him until he had finished his meal. Everybody in that family feared his volatile temper, which they said he inherited from his German father. Small things could annoy him easily - the bark of a dog, the innocent giggles of children, even the unexpected banging of a door in the wind. It was like walking on eggshells around him. He also was known for head butting family members who annoyed him. He insulted the food while he ate. He burped rudely in-between eating, talking about this and that, usually about the "vagrant no-good toothless *Coloureds*" with whom he worked as a supervisor of labourers at the local municipality.

One family member had a rude awakening when she returned home and bumped into him on the station after such a visit. "Hello Uncle Robert. It was nice to see you after all these years", she said. "Who are you? I don't know you..." he replied rudely, straightened his tie, and pulled up his trousers up to his ribs while fisting his hands in his pockets, lifting himself up on his toes to show off his polished shoes bought at *Top Shoes* in a gesture of superiority.

They say he looked down at her, staring pointedly. With a hazy, bewildered gaze in his eyes, he said to her, "I do not know any *hotnot* people, lady! I am a *White* man. The name is *Robert William Constance Daniels, born in 1925 in Tewkesbury, Gloucestershire, England*. Ever been there, lady? From your looks, I guess not!" On that note, he turned up his nose and walked away, a completely different man from the Uncle Robert who had just enjoyed a plate of curried sugar beans with this same family member. The startled family member protested in embarrassment at the station, "But, Uncle Robert, we just sat together an hour ago eating at Aunt Margie's place this afternoon. You could not have forgotten...It is me...look...me, Anne. I served you some nice curried beans and yellow rice. You are my *uncle*. My mother's brother. Remember? I am Aunty Marta's daughter...the Herero aunt!" At this revelation, they said he turned around angrily and said, "Don't talk *kak* (shit) to me, lady! I don't know you. Know your *place*! You are a forward Coloured. You people are always *voorbarig* (forward); you never know your place! *Gam maniere*, Coloured manners. Give you a finger and you take the whole bloody hand! Do I have to repeat, *meid!*? (Coloured street girl). I'm an Englishman from *T-e-w-k-e-*

s-b-u-r-y, G-l-o-u-c-e-s-t-e-r-s-h-i-r-e. ' He pulled the words, with his mouth pulled askew as he stood on his toes, his nose turned up, and he stared down at her in a condescending pose with his spectacles balancing over the tip of his nose. "I *don't* know you *Coloured* folk!" He lifted his head up, shifted his spectacles in place, and turned his back on her. She still persisted in a state of dismay; she found the slithering change in his behaviour bizarre and shocking. It was as if a poisonous chemical change happened in his mind and soul within one day, within a few hours, within minutes, within seconds. Just like that, from one personality to the other, it was like observing quicksilver in a laboratory tube.

In response, he stormed off. "In any case, I'm in a hurry to catch the train. Don't know what you are talking about. I don't have a sister. I *don't* have a Black mother. I'm a *White* man. Can't you see?! Can't you see?! *Gaan kak man* (go shit man)!" Then, he paused to catch his breath, "Listen, here, this is all a big mistake, *meisie* (little girl)!"

He had suddenly lost his aristocratic English pretence and turned into a self-made *boer,* crass in accent and manner. In his play-White persona, he became like a chameleon, changing colours as it blends into different environments, and vigilantly rolling its eyes 360 degrees to spot any targets and threats.

Uncle Robert became very angry. "I have just returned from a church meeting. *Fuck off* to your Coloured trap! You are not right in your head. Go look for your Coloured *whore-family* somewhere else. Goo-bye!"

After which, he promptly turned his back on Anne and proceeded to board the Whites-only carriage, walking quick escapist steps, as he suddenly slipped back into English aristocracy mode. The family told of his uncanny well-rehearsed ability to change from a loud, swearing, uninhibited working-class Coloured to a snooty aristocratic Englishman, to a Calvinist racist Afrikaner Nationalist – within a matter of minutes. It was like well rehearsed roles in theatre, like a one-man act.

Uncle Robert had the working-class Coloured street in his blood. He could not hide it. Probably read about Tewkesbury, Gloucestershire in a storybook, or heard it over the radio in some show of some sort, or perhaps in a movie.

The interesting thing is, Uncle Robert lived a double life. He lived with a woman of Khoisan descent, Lena, whom he called with proprietorial audacity, "*my* Bushman". However, Lena could not accompany him in public, not even to the Coloured relatives in Heathfield. They were forbidden by the Mixed Marriages Act to marry, though Uncle Robert was originally Coloured like Lena. She was secretly his common-law wife when the two of them were alone at home in the poor White council estate. Now, yes, he seemed to have loved her. Well, they say they had a passionate romance going in spite of their apartheid problem. She told how he would chase her around the table, grab her, kiss her, and drag her playfully to bed. He would make love to her, until the sweat soaked their bodies. At such moments of ecstasy, she would shout, pleading to have his baby. Visions of a beautiful bronze-skinned child with a bush of curly dry hair would momentarily appear before her eyes. However, this never happened. God did not want them to conceive, Robert explained to her; it was nature's way of punishing people who broke the rules of mating. You must sleep with your "own kind". He made her feel guilty about living and sleeping with him as if the problems and damage in South Africa were all her fault. Weeks after every penetration, he'd stand over her with the syringe and the bottled concoction of fluids and chemicals he collected monthly from the notorious Afrikaner *moeder* (mother) in the seedy back streets of Salt River.

But they say that Uncle Robert could sadly never tame the wild animal in him who preferred women like Lena for the raw sexuality he believed they oozed. He convinced himself that he loved her and would play Jim Reeves' *I love you because you understand me* for her. He danced slowly and passionately with her and reassured her that nothing would ever come between them. He would suck her tender small breasts in the privacy of their bedroom in their cottage in the Afrikaner northern suburbs town of Belville where they lived together in hiding. To his White neighbours, she was simply his Coloured *meit*. When they knocked on the door, she hurriedly put on her apron and her *doek* (headscarf), and opened the door. Then she would proceed to call the *baas* (boss).

Uncle Robert was perhaps not even sure if it was jealousy, fear, shame, or perhaps even love that drove him to order her to hide in the wardrobe (so that he could leave the doors of the bedrooms open as to not cause suspicion that he may be hiding a "kaffir" or a "hotnot") when his White friends and colleagues came to visit. He did not even want them to think she was the servant.

Lena recalled how he spoke with her, "Come, honey, there they are, knocking at the door. Get into the wardrobe, love. I promise not to keep them here for long. We are only going to have a few drinks, hey. You don't mind, hey, love? Should only be an hour or so..."

At such times of madness, she doubted his love and wondered how a man who loved her so passionately one minute could slip so madly into insanity at the drop of a hat.

She challenged him, even though she feared him, "Robert, I know the truth deep inside of me...God is going to punish you for living such a lie! You are a fraud! You are a common bastard!"

And he always had his way of working things out, "'Lena, *patience....patience*...you don't want to make me cross, *girl*...just understand these *difficult* things, *pleaaase....*"

He would pour a glass of neat whiskey and withdraw into his shell, smoking his cigar on his badly stained sofa in the lounge and go silent. He knew that his father's Coloured family, who moved to live in the Eastern Cape and had farms, called themselves "pure Afrikaners", and would shoot Lena at first sight if she should ever claim to be his common-law wife. They hated *kaffirs* and *hotnotte* – and also *kaffir boeties,* people like him who were friends or lovers of such "races".

She would hesitate a bit, talk calmly as she feared his temper while he was drinking. He once smacked her in the face for being cheeky and her nose bled and she could not even call for help, because he was her White boss and she was a Coloured servant. The police would have put her in jail and beaten her up even more for daring to stand up to a White man. It was not done in apartheid South Africa. She knew that the police were not on her side, not as a woman, and not as the common-law wife of an Afrikaner White man – their union was illegal in any case, as it was against the Immorality Act. So she learned over the years to do what he said even if she did not like it. She would rather cry quietly in the wardrobe. "Robert, I am sorry...I don't want to make you cross...just tell them I'm your *meit*. I'll serve the tea and call you *baas*. They won't know. I'll behave myself", and he'd turn the guilt on her, like a serpent. "No, dear...you know I don't like to hurt you...it is *always* your fault...you make me angry and then I can't help it...you *piss me off* sometimes..."

Lena knew what this meant. She knew the pattern too well. Days of silent anger often erupted into a violent rage with Robert hitting her face into a purple, swollen disfigured pulp. His days of silent rage were days of deep self-loathing and confusion that knew no other way out – like the uncontrollable pressure of lava in a volcano that has reached eruption point.

Somehow, Lena always backed off in the end as she nursed her wounds with the indigenous Giant Honey Flower herb with the maroon flower and large green milky leaves, *kruidjie-roer-my-nie (meaning "herb-touch-me-not")*, "Robert, I am so sorry...I won't back chat again..."

He delighted in his small victories with her, patting her on the head as if she was his dog, "Good, Lena. We understand each other then. *Good girl...*"

Her childlike obedience calmed his rage, and made him a happy man that she knew her place. If she could only always know her place - be quiet, be obedient, be grateful, be nice to him, not say when she is unhappy or sad or upset, not disagree with him, not wake the demons in him – then things would be alright, and the angry lava in him would perhaps turn into calm blue tranquil waters. However, the pattern of their unnatural life together was compulsively violent, almost necessarily so, as they tried to be normal human beings in the huge asylum of apartheid.

In the short bursts of peacefulness, he would playfully and suggestively pinch her tight buttocks and wink, "Be ready when they leave...my *liefie*, (little love)."

Lena would sit quietly in the huge empty oak antique wardrobe, listening in amusement to Robert's conversation with his White Afrikaner comrades about how great Prime Minister Verwoerd was, who masterminded apartheid, about how the *kaffirs* should be sorted out to make sure South Africa does not turn into another deplorable African state ruled by a Black man, and about how it was in the best interest of the country that everyone should keep to his own type. *Soort by soort!* Funnily, Robert would be the instigator of all the conversations about Coloureds-this-and-that and kaffirs-this-and-that, while the woman he wanted to believe he sincerely loved sat in the wardrobe. Then, he sounded like an Afrikaner boer of the northern suburbs (the equivalent of the American Deep South of Cape Town), and not like the Englishman from Tewkesbury. He played different roles with such ease and an uncanny skill. These were moments of entertainment for Lena; the dark wardrobe turned into a theatre – she as the audience, and Robert and his unwitting Afrikaner guests as the actors; a tragic comedy.

When his guests had left, he would release her and he would talk with an unaffected Coloured accent and with Coloured gestures to relate to his Lena. *"Jy tjy, klim uit die kas uit!"* "Hey, you, get out of the wardrobe!" He'd laugh with the spontaneity and crudeness of a working-class Cape Flats Coloured man.

She would watch in amazement his relief that his White friends had left, how the sweat pearled on his brow; his hankie wet with distress. She would feel sorry for him, yet also quietly hate him deeply for his play-White weakness.

Lena would not let him know what she really thought of him and his boere friends, and would retreat to the bedroom in stony silence, visibly angry and humiliated for days after, refusing intimacy. Robert would try to win her back, begging her to understand the dilemma of being half-White in South Africa. *"Jirre, ek is so jammer, Lena...God, glo my vrou...God is my getuie!"* "I am really so sorry about this Lena, God, really believe me, wife...Really, believe me. God is my witness!" He would make the sign of the cross in a very dramatic swinging of his arms. *"Ek weet dis moeilik, liefie – maar dis die boere wat die ding aan ons doen!"* "I know it is hard, love...but it is the *boere that are doing this thing to us!*...you know they'll jail us if we get caught..."

Lena would forgive him eventually after a few nights of heated arguments and beatings from him, shouting in tears. "You bastard! You fetched me as a young innocent girl working on a farm and you promised my parents that you'd treat me well, but you have turned out to be a play-White wife beater and a common hooligan! You change from a Coloured *skollie (hooligan)*, to a snobbish English gentleman, to an Afrikaner baas. How do you think I must cope with this madness?!" She thought of him as a weak-willed fool then, a confused and pathetic alcoholic.

"Lena moenie kak praat nie, man! Lena don't talk shit, man! It was your own choice to come and live with me far away from your family. I give you a plate of food every night. You are better off than on the farm with the boere! You ungrateful Bushman farm bitch!"

Still, she protested, trying to plead for decency with him, "I work for you every day. Clean the house. Do the washing. I can't even have friends. I have not even been out to see the city...and I don't get paid! You treat me like a common prostitute...*Ek is jou Boesman hoer!* I am nothing more than your Bushman-whore!"

However, this only provoked more anger, "Lena, remember to be *nice* to me. I am only good to women who are nice to me. It all depends on how well you treat me. What value do you bring me? *Tjy is 'n las, meit*! You are a liability, slut! Your own fault lady... who said you should come live with me so far away from your family? Where do you think you'll get a job? Who is going to give you a place to stay? At least you are now living with a *White man* in a brick house...think about it!"

Lena still believed she could somehow rescue the true human being in him, "Robert, please stay like a gentleman. Don't be a White rude boer. Be the gentleman, even the one from Tewkesbury... Don't switch. Promise me you are not going to *switch* again. God help me..."

She'd sob for his forgiveness, her hands trembling, clutching the collar of her cotton shirt to hopefully prevent another beating. He would turn his back on her, walk away, ignore her with a deliberate swing in his violent quick steps towards the cheap pine wine cabinet he bought to impress his White boere friends. A deep sinking feeling would flow over her heart as she watched him open another bottle of alcohol. On such nights, he did not share a drink with her. On such nights, she was evil incarnate; she was everything he hated about himself and his family. He would deliberately ignore her, to push her to the emotional edge to help him release his own lava. He desperately longed for her to push him, so that the volcano could erupt justifiably. She knew this dysfunctional pattern too well. However, she wanted to push the boundaries with him, as if she depended on his violent eruptions too, with her own tsunami brewing, waiting to flood in gigantic unmanageable proportions of pent-up emotional anger. Her sympathy for him would turn into violent emotional anger.

When Lena got angry, it all just burst out uncontrollably, "Play-White! Liar! You are not even White! *Jou ma is 'n Herero-hoer!* Your mother is a Herero whore!"

When this happened, Robert felt strangely relieved. This was the moment he had waited for, that she should insult his *mother*; it was the button he needed her to push so that he could justify beating her to a pulp. She played time and again into his hands; she fell for the trap again and again. He would push her over and throttle her; justify in his mind why she deserved to be beaten until she could no longer breathe nor stand. She, the evil demon and whore in his life. "You deserve to be fucked up, Lena! It is all your fault! You are not *nice* to me...I warned you what happens to women who are not *nice* to me...I am a nice man; my behaviour is *impeccable.*" Just repeating his niceness to himself made him feel good about himself again. "I am the perfect man with no flaws or faults, but nasty, evil women like you bring out this side of me. Just fucking learn to be *nice*! You are an *irredeemable asshole*! You are not a decent human being! You have *fuck-all* and you brought *fuck-all* into my life! Whore! Bushman *Poes*! Cunt!"

Every time, Lena had nowhere to run.

After such brutal beatings of Lena, he would beg for forgiveness and drown himself in remorse. He nursed her wounds with kruidjie-roer-my-nie like a father with a little girl that fell off a swing through recklessness, or through not listening to him. He would remind her how bad she was for herself, how she brought these things upon herself. He would bring her coffee in bed and in spring pick a red rose for her from their pretty garden. In winter, he'd pick her a pure white lily. In summer, he'd bring her rosemary twigs, and in autumn, he'd pick her a branch of yellow blooms from the honeysuckle creeper that grew over the fence and watched her lovingly from the kitchen window as she endearingly sucked the sweet nectar from the blooms. How one can hate and love a person all at once, he'd wonder to himself, while he watched her as she hanged his laundry on the line in their wine-bottle littered unkempt back yard. They would make up through intense, angry, confusing sex in bed that drove them both to tears and overwhelming depression for days after. She would drown herself in his icy blue eyes, stroke his dry straightened hair as he succumbed to her sweet, firm, inviting flesh, kissing her pouting lips and sucking the saliva between her protruding healthy white teeth. He liked the taste of the sweet comforting natural juices in her soft mouth. He loved the clean smell of the rosemary herbs and olive oil with which she massaged her body every night without fail. He loved her short, coarse hair, which she combed neatly out of her face to show off her red beautiful bony cheeks, and her striking, small, narrow Chinese-like eyes. He was mesmerised by the indigenous, unblemished beauty of "his Bushman woman" as she proudly called herself. He would curl up against her familiar smallness at night, and bury himself in her pulsating warm flesh in his quest to seek refuge and comfort from the hard, confusing, and relentless South African life of a play-White male. They would both savour this short moment of sanity, because they both knew it never lasted long enough. She would stroke his hair and intuitively hum the American minstrel slave song that pretended happiness on the slave plantations, *Way Down Upon the Swanee River*, which had been sung for generations by Coloured families at the Cape around the fires at night - until he fell asleep – silently assuring him that she understood his dilemma and the ambivalent confused demon within him. Like the confusion in this slave song of longing for the plantation, she intuited that he did not know what he wanted and for what he longed. She knew he did not know who he was. He just knew he was sad, almost suicidal with his confusion. He was simply roaming, living a lie from day to day and changing his personality from this to that depending on the script for the moment.

In these tender drunken moments, when their souls touched deeply, he would promise her, "Lena, I tell you if those White friends of mine ever visit again, I am going to be a *m-a-a-a-n-n*. A real *m-a-a-a-n-n!* " *"Jy is my vrou, my Boesman vrou.* You are *my* woman. *My* Bushman woman." He'd push his chest out like a fantail dove and he would shout with his arms swinging wildly in the air, "I am going to say, meet *my* beautiful wife Lena – only for the other men to look at, but not to touch! And if any one of them says you are a hotnot-Bushman-Coloured girl and asks what am I doing with a hotnot-hoer then I am going to hit him so hard, even if I have to go to jail!"

But in his confusion of trying to be White, Robert chased his own tail, in a never-ending nauseating vicious cycle of confusion and humiliation. When the boere friends from the municipality in the Northern suburbs phoned again to fix another visit, his spine shrunk. His neck sank into his shoulders. His eyes twitched nervously. His mouth dropped, and he left sheepishly after the phone call through the back door and returned with bottles of sherry, brandy, and whiskey in a plastic bag from the local off-sales. Mr. Tewkesbury's personality had escaped then. The arrogant confident Afrikaner boer had escaped then. He became, for some hours after, someone else – the one personality only Lena came to know in his moments of deep vulnerability, an almost spineless being – he was then like an amoeba, who could also constantly change its shape and even burst into tears.

His voice slurred, "Lena, my sweetheart, come drink with *your man.*"

She would snuggle up to him. She would feel special and safe in his vulnerable embrace and they'd drink glass after glass, bottle after bottle. When he was vulnerable, she was no Bushman, no hotnot – *just a woman*, a confidante, and a friend. They would rub their heads together like two cats on a sofa soaking up the faint winter sun.

"What is life without a *good drink, my girl?*"

She would nod in agreement to please him, to help him believe his own deceptions. They would drown their shame and sorrows, numb their emotional pain, their helplessness, his emotional impotence, and their deep confusion. They would sober up only at noon the next day, sprawled on the lounge floor. Everything reeked of the sadness of alcoholism and their loneliness – the toilet bowl, the walls, their clothes, the sofa, their skin, even their breath. He knew that only Lena understood his deep yearning for humanness, like many of her ancestral Khoisan sisters before her who slept with the confused and pretentious French, the Dutch, the Germans, and the English at the Cape since the 1600s.

When he awoke, he would drink again, eventually pissing himself and collapsing into a hopeless bundle on the kitchen floor. On such hangover mornings, Lena would stare into the mirror to look at her face. She knew she was beautiful and sober before she moved to Cape Town to live with him. She would sob uncontrollably, staring at her own sadness. "I am a drunk... *Ek is 'n gemors!* I am a mess...I miss my people...my little place in the Karoo where I knew myself...my God-fearing family...my proud people...I am a prisoner, a cupboard woman...a play-White's whore!...I want to go home to my people...*my mense* ...*my mense* ...my people my people; just ordinary honest desert people of the Karoo ...*Bushmen* ...proud people ...*trotse mense!*"

He never heard her cries, or rather perhaps pretended he did not. He avoided her red, swollen eyes for days. They'd be silent and cold with each other for weeks on end.

Robert had a fatal and sudden heart attack at the age of 45 years at the height of apartheid, a few years after the architect of apartheid, Dr. Verwoerd, was assassinated.

While looking for his papers, after his death, Lena found a collection of brown and white creased photographs in Robert's wardrobe, secretly hidden under a stack of trousers. There was a faint ink stamp at the back of one of the photographs which read that they were taken by the popular Jewish photographer, Mr.

Shapiro in Whites-only Wynberg - of Edith, Robert, and their Coloured siblings, including Kruger, happily posing together with their proud and loving Herero mother. In one photo, five-year-old Robert and ten-year-old Kruger are holding hands and their mother is standing next to them, with her arm lovingly wrapped around them both. At the back of this photograph, his mother's struggling blotchy handwriting listed each child's full name and date of birth, such as *Robert William Constance Verwerp born 1910.* The photographs had been tied together affectionately with his mother's purple hair ribbon, which someone must have managed to give to him after her funeral in the Coloured cemetery, which he obviously could not attend.

Kruger's regular boere friends organised his funeral with Lena's assistance as his Coloured servant who gave them his papers. Lena decided to paste the photograph of Kruger and his siblings on the inside of the lid of his coffin as a decoration for everyone to see, including his shocked White friends. She lied to them, *"Meester wou did so gehad het. Hy het my gevra.* Master wanted it this way; he did ask me."

The boere mourners were furious with Lena, *"Dis 'n lieg!'* It is a lie!" they told her. *"Jy is dronk!"* You are drunk!"

Robert was buried in the local Whites-only Dutch reformed church on a wet Cape Town August day. In his will, he left some cash for his servant, Lena, to go back home to her family in the Northern Cape. The house was left for his play-White siblings, because only they could live there, yet they did not pay their last respects at his funeral, most likely because they knew of Lena and feared her possible revealing sobs and hysteria.

At the funeral service in the church, Lena stood outside in the sun wearing her white servant *doek.* She was not allowed to sit in the tiny white church, which was for Whites only. She tried to catch the words of the sermon as she leaned against the black hearse parked outside in the churchyard underneath the open church window. She smoked the last cigarette from Kruger's packet of *Lucky Strikes,* which she had found in one of the pockets of the pair of trousers he wore the day of his sudden death. She tried to calm her nerves as a lone mourner.

After the church service, Lena begged for a lift to the cemetery. *"Baas gee vir my 'n rytjie, toe. Ek wil graag by wees as meneer begrawe word."* "Boss, give me a ride, please. I should like to be at my master's graveside when he is laid to rest."

His boere friend was predictably unkind to her. "*Kyk, ek is hier met 'n kar en jy kan nie saam met ons in 'n kar ry nie. Jy weet hoe dinge werk in die land. Vra vir die ander baas. Hy het 'n bakkie en jy kan agterop sit. En moet nie by die graf staan nie, want dis by die blanke kant.*" "Listen, I am here with my car and you can't drive in the car with us. You should know how things work in this country. Ask the other master. He is here with his van; you can sit at the back on his van. And do not come to the grave side; it is in the Whites-only section of the cemetery."

Lena obeyed the rules of Robert's Whites-only funeral. She stood amongst the graves in the non-Whites section of the cemetery where she could catch a glimpse of his grave and his coffin, about two hundred metres away. The Whites-only section was separated from the non-Whites section by a hedge, like the first one planted by Dutch settler Jan Van Riebeeck in the 1600s to separate the White colonists from the indigenous people. The funeral service was short and businesslike. There were only a few mourners – his friends from the municipality and some neighbours. The mourners were mostly White Afrikaner men dressed in black suits and hats with their somber looking wives dressed also in black and holding black umbrellas above their heads. His friend who visited regularly said a few parting words for Robert. His words were short, and sharp like a razor, and calculatingly targeted, loud enough for Lena to hear, "*Hierdie man was nie 'n man vir Sodom en Gomorrah nie! Hy was 'n opregte blanke man; 'n man vir soort by soort! Soos dit hoort te wees.* This was not a man for Sodom and Gomorrah! He was an upright White man; a man for sorts with sorts, types with types. As things ought to be! He was Verwoerd's man."

Bizarre memories of her dramatic life with Robert flashed before her that day in the cemetery as his coffin lowered into the grave. The nights he'd shove his angry being into her, when he pushed her angrily down on her hands and knees like a dog - when he would not beat her, but still leave her in unbearable physical pain and psychological torment. On such nights, he would not speak much. It would simply be a cold, cruel act of punishment that left him relieved afterwards. He would drown himself in drink for days after such acts on her body without her consent.

It was a cold early autumn day of white clouds and brown leaves. She mumbled in deep bereavement along as they sang the hymn of sin, forgiveness, and mercy as the coffin lowered slowly into the damp wet Cape soil of a dark cold grave, *Just as I am without a plea...take me Lord, precious Lord, take me home...*

Her days in the wardrobe were over, but she sobbed quietly as she knew she would miss him; she would miss comforting his tormented confused soul and his bottomless loneliness. She prayed quietly to herself in her cusped hands that God would grant him peace in heaven; that he would have only one personality in heaven, at least just for a day. *"Ja, Robert, vandag begrawe hulle al die spoke in jou.* Yes, Robert today they bury all the ghosts in you." Then again, she also felt happy for him; he got what he wanted – a White priest, White mourners, White undertakers, and a grave in a White cemetery. As the coffin hit the bottom of the grave with a loud thud, her heart tore to pieces and she sobbed with rawness from deep within her. She sobbed for his Herero mother and his siblings. She also sobbed for him and for their bizarre love relationship ruled by apartheid and the play-White madness. She was clutching the photograph that the White undertaker had removed from the coffin's lid and told her, *"Brand die ding of gooi dit in die vuilisblik; dit hoort nie hier nie! Dis lieg en dronk stories!* Burn this thing or throw it in the bin. It has no place here! It is a lie, a drunk story."

However, then she stopped crying. She realised that she was free and that she was out of the Whites-only madhouse where he controlled her and kept her like a dog on a leash. The rain poured down heavily as the mourners filled the grave hurriedly with the wet dark soil. Lena struck a lone figure soaked in the storm, clutching a branch of honeysuckle and holding it close to her breasts. She placed it on his grave in her mind as she watched the White mourners hurriedly arranging the wreaths of plastic flowers in their round plastic covers on his fresh grave.

Chapter 5
The Trance of the Orange Blooms
of Wild Cannabis

After his geyser had erupted on that sunny day on the pine needles in Stellenbosch, Kaiser Verwerp turned into an alcoholic. The neighbours somehow detected his crime and quietly isolated him without ever questioning him. Nobody reported him to the police. Instead, the women boycotted him and treated him like an outcast, keeping young women away from him. There was no charge or trial for him; only a lifetime sentence of isolation in a small community. Everybody retreated to their homes and shut their doors and called their young girls inside whenever he was around. He died a lonely death at a full moon at the relatively young age of 52 years. His funeral was short with no wake. He was buried very hurriedly with not too much fuss, and his photograph was removed from the walls of the family's shack shortly after his death.

However, Eve did not survive psychologically, either. Nobody asked her about the rape, nor spoke with her about it. Instead, everybody in the village offered to take Eve to Valkenberg Psychiatric Hospital in the city of Cape Town for her monthly visits to collect her tablets.

To get to Valkenberg, the family had to travel by bus to the banks of the Liesbeeck and Black Rivers, where the first White arrivals at the Cape settled in the 1600s. The name Valkenberg derives from the Dutch farmer Cornelius Valk, who established a farm there on the same land in 1720. In 1881, a lunatic asylum (as it was called then) was established there for patients transferred from Robben Island, where Nelson Mandela would almost a century later be incarcerated for speaking his mind against apartheid.

Already in the early days then, Black patients were separated from White patients at the "asylum". Later in the nineteenth century, the hospital became part of the University of Cape Town for the training of White psychiatrists. Many of the patients were mentally disturbed and confused Coloureds and Africans. It also became the place of mental incarceration for White freedom fighters like the Afrikaner freedom fighter woman, Ingrid Jonker, who fought the madness of apartheid through her resistance poetry on racism. It was also perhaps a place for Coloured play-Whites who lost their minds.

Kaiser's mother did not escape the wrath of the community either. Everybody seemed determined to make her pay for the sins of the German soldier and for the sins of her son born of rape during the Herero genocide. She often was found wandering in the bushes of the Cape, talking in Nama and acting in a childlike manner. She seemed fixated in the age when she was first raped and gave birth to Kruger. She spent her last days chasing sheep in her mind, as the young innocent Herero shepherdess in South West Africa. She had erased from her memory the encounter with the German rapists and what had happened afterwards in her life. She quietly passed away as a senile and confused woman talking and gesturing on her deathbed like a young teenage herd girl. Nobody could get the news of her death and dying to Robert. The family did not know where her play-White children were and where they had started a new White life in apartheid South Africa. Even if he did come to know about his mother's death, the family knew that he would clearly have chosen not to attend the funeral, as this would have been the end of his privileged White life. He did not want to get caught out. The Afrikaner Nazi police were everywhere.

From early on, Tumelo got to know this world ruled by colour madness and race hate, self-loathing and trauma. She got to know such experiences and moments herself, and she got to know them her entire life, from birth.

When she was very young, before she went to school, she had a caregiver, Uncle Thaba, a Xhosa–speaking African man, who gave her her African name. He was a relative of her Coloured family, who through the bizarre laws of apartheid, ended up being classified "Bantu", and like millions of others in South Africa, he did not escape the pass laws. He taught her right from wrong and he was her earliest experience of pure love as a child. Uncle Thaba was close to her father, who protected him from the police after his return from Robben Island as a convict. Because of what he had been through there, Uncle Thaba feared this notorious island that was cut off from the mainland, far away from his family's wood and iron cottage hidden in the bush of the Cape Flats. Nelson Mandela would be jailed there for 18 years, and it was also the place of incarceration for Pan Africanist liberation fighter Robert Subokwe, and for women leaders such Krotoa in the 1600s. However, it was also a prison for African men who served a sentence for criminal offences, and for lepers. Uncle Thaba remembered very clearly the day in 1964 when Nelson Mandela, Sobukwe, Walter Sisulu, and all the other political prisoners of the infamous Rivonia Trials were brought to the island. However, Uncle Thaba was not imprisoned for political reasons; he was charged for murder and locked away on the island as a criminal. In this sense, he was also a political criminal, because he was Black and everybody in the family spoke of his innocence. The family explained often, "The boere had locked him up because Uncle Thaba was just *a kaffir in the wrong place at the wrong time.*" Uncle Thaba worked as a gardener to earn some money to go home to visit the African side of the family in the Transkei, the homeland of the Xhosa people, which was established in 1959 through the Homeland Act that pushed African people into reserves and the men as migrant labourers. Nelson Mandela was born there in 1918 in Qunu – referring to the area beyond the Kei River in the Eastern Cape.

There was great respect for Uncle Thaba in the family; his presence was quiet yet commanding. When he entered the house, all had to be quiet, get up to greet him respectfully with a handshake, and cast their eyes down to show respect for their elder. If anyone in the village dared to call Uncle Thaba "*kaffir*", the males in the family would violently attack them with whichever weapon they could lay there hands on. Yet, there was something bizarre and surreal about all the drama around Uncle Thaba.

The children in the neighbourhood taunted Tumelo and said to her, "Your Uncle Thaba is a *kaffir*. When he goes home to *kaffirland*, he is going to take you away with him!"

Tumelo once asked him, while sitting on his knee in the sun, "Uncle Thaba, what is a *kaffir*?" He did not reply; he laughed, shook his head, and simply hugged her tightly with warmth and affection.

After such conversations, she would snuggle under his coat and hide her head in his sweaty armpit, breathing in the comforting mixture of odour of his skin and of the sweet tobacco in his shirt pocket. Then Uncle Thaba would rub her head gently and kiss her forehead reassuringly. Tumelo would climb on his shoulders, ask him to swing her until her head would spin, and ask him to tell her stories of ants, tortoises, hippos, and crocodiles.

However, there was one thing about strong, warm, formidable Uncle Thaba that Tumelo never quite understood as a child. It was his fear of the White police in the gray vans. The police visited the village regularly, commanding with whips and Alsation dogs, *"Waar is die kaffirs? Waar steek julle hotnotte vir hulle weg? Ons donner sommer die hele spul van julle!* Where are the kaffirs? Where are you hotnots hiding them? We'll damn fuck up the whole lot of you!"

The police were regularly on the scout for the "kaffirs without passes", and Uncle Thaba would grow scared like a child when their vans pulled up with brakes screeching. It confused Tumelo when her otherwise strong and highly-respected uncle became scared like a child. The tender, warm, protective man with the black duffel-coat feared the White police so much that he sometimes wet himself after a raid in the village.

"I am a Bantu, my child. I must have my passbook wherever I go. I don't want to be locked away on the island. I was there for ten years doing hard labour. If they catch me, they'll do anything to me, and I may not see you and the family ever again."

One day, Tumelo witnessed a neighbour calling Uncle Thaba a *kaffir*. Uncle Thaba went wild that day; he picked up the spade he used in the garden, his eyes grew big with anger, and he aimed to beat the neighbour's head in. This was the start of many such taunting from this neighbour who deliberately and often popped his head over the fence while Uncle Thaba was working in the garden, "Hey, *kaffir*, what are you doing in *our* place? Go home to *kaffirland*! You rape our little girls and you steal our chickens at night. The police know all about this Coloured family of yours keeping a *kaffir* in hiding! You are a Robben Island convict! You are a murderer!"

Uncle Thaba snapped back with deserved retort at the abuser, "You are a *gonga*, a *malow*, a mixed-breed man without ancestors, without a God, without roots!"

Tumelo could not understand why Uncle Thaba had to carry a pass and why he had a homeland and family so far away, yet he was also part of her family. Why was it so damn difficult for Uncle Thaba to go home?

Uncle Thaba tried to describe the situation, "Our family is all apart, some are Bantus, and some are Coloureds. The Bantus moved to Transkei, the land for natives. The Coloureds in the family stayed in Cape Town. However, we are all family. It is all stupid. If I go to Transkei, I'll need money and I can't go home empty-handed. Plus, it is far away; at least a day's drive by bus. There is no work there, my child. The boere put me in jail for a long time, and I must save money all over again. That is why I came to live with my family here in Cape Town to help me to work again and to maybe earn money to go home. Your father does not have a passbook, because he is Coloured. Indians and Coloureds have identity books. Natives and Bantus have passbooks. Indians and Coloureds can walk without their identity books, but African people like me get jailed if we don't have our passbooks."

Uncle Thaba sighed, "My child, it is very difficult to understand – even for adults. When you are big one day, perhaps you'll understand this madness. Don't worry about the boere things now. They will come to pass."

Tumelo rested her head on Uncle Thaba's chest. She wanted to help him, wanted to throw stones at the tormenting police who wanted this book called a pass from the man who protected her daily from harm. She could not understand where the native land for Bantus was. In her mind's eye, she saw a foreign country that one had to reach by boat to visit. Perhaps, she thought, the natives lived somewhere near from where the Vikings came. Her father told her many stories about the Vikings. What a far way for a native to travel to work in South Africa. She twisted these mysteries around and around in her mind, hoping for a simple and satisfying answer.

When the police van came with breaks screeching and dust clouding down the dirt road where they lived, Tumelo ran in fear to find Uncle Thaba to warn him to hide in the broken old bus stacked with maize bags that parked in their backyard. There she would lie on the ground next to him flat on his stomach, underneath stacks of old rags and bags of feed, listening to the thumping noise that such a big heart of a man can make when it fears police in apartheid South Africa. She would close her eyes, fearing that the monsters would find Uncle Thaba. She would wish that things were different in South Africa, that adults would be free to be adults. She would wish that children would not have to protect adults against evil White men in vans.

Her biggest fear was that the monstrous vans would take Uncle Thaba away from her, that she would lose him to cruel White men who would take him back to that notorious island from which people were said never to return. She did not understand why Uncle Thaba was a "native", and why her relatives who looked "African" like Uncle Thaba, but who did not speak Xhosa, were *not* natives. What was this madness about of labelling and mistreating people? Was it about his language?

"Hide your husbands!" the women shouted to their neighbours when they spotted the police vans coming over the hill. Coloured women and their Xhosa husbands ran for their lives, hiding in outside toilet shacks and underneath beds. Even though there was often the taunting neighbour and general loose talk about the "wild kaffirs", when the notorious vans arrived, nobody told on the Xhosa lovers, husbands, friends, and relatives. At such times, almost everyone in the community stood together. On some Friday nights they were all invited to have a Xhosa traditional party of sorghum beer and red meat stew with samp and beans and African jazz drumming at one of the shacks where the lover, husband, family, or friends were leaving to go to "kaffirland" - as everyone, including the Xhosa neighbours, called this far away "home". Everyone would both laugh and cry as they greeted the travelling ones. The closeness of Coloureds and Africans at these parties, in the dark candlelit shacks with the black-and-white Drum magazine pages of Black models with afros, and of African jazz players pasted to the walls, was undeniable. Tumelo would cling to Uncle Thaba's leg in the dark at these parties in the 1960s, hold tight on to his strength, and wish that she would never have to say goodbye to him at sunrise. Sounds of a happy and colourful spontaneous mixture of Afrikaans, Xhosa, and English would entertain her young ears. The women and the men would dance, embrace, and love openly, singing and playing Miriam Makeba's click song, *Qongqothwane*. It would also be *stokvel* night, the local traditional African night of sharing the savings. On such an occasion, the savings would go to the family leaving for the "homeland". Nobody would then speak about *kaffirs*. The shame of "kaffirs" and "Coloureds" did not exist then; there were only happy, joyful people bonded in rhythm and hope, singing together and dancing as humans.

The women chuckled and shouted rhythmically "ooh ooh!" while they stamped their feet and shook their generous bottoms. The smell of the sweet earthy sweat of about thirty people in a small, crammed shack hung in the air. The dancing caused the sounds of thunder; it felt like the small shack was about to fall over. Tumelo clung through it all onto the safety of Uncle Thaba's strong legs, swaying with him as he danced and laughed. She saw Uncle Thaba at his happiest then, as he slumped himself after such thunderous dancing exhausted in a chair, lifted her onto his lap, and fed her a sip of his homemade beer from his mug, the foam of the bitter beer dripping down her chin. He kissed her on her forehead and smiled at her and said, "Aish, my child! Uncle Thaba is a happy man!"

Tumelo's teacher spoke of people like Uncle Thaba as "the natives, the Naturellas, the Bantus". When Tumelo asked about natives and their problems with the police vans, the teacher explained, "You would never understand the story of natives. It is just the way things are. It was just a fact of life that for some reason or the other, natives *always -and always* - land up in trouble." Why this was so, she could not explain and just shrugged her shoulders in despair, defending, "But you are not in school to ask questions about these things. You are here to learn about numbers and colours and to learn to read."

In apartheid South Africa, "natives" were always somehow always invariably in trouble, and therefore they were always on the run and living in hiding from the White people. They were always treated like children. They were always thrown into jail, and they worked in gardens and kitchens. They were called "boys" and "girls", and they got beaten up in the street when found by the police, even when they had a pass document on them, or when they were found walking in White areas. The White police reasoned that they may as well beat them, because they were in any case up to mischief wherever they were and wherever they were going. It was a situation very much like Britain at the time in its "stop and search" approach to Black men.

In the minds of many Coloured people during segregation and apartheid, there were "natives", and even if they themselves were indigenous and therefore also "natives", they did not see themselves like that. Coloured people, you see, even though many of them come from the Bushmen and Khoikhoi, never saw themselves as indigenous – as in the case of the native Americans (whom they knew as "Red Indians"), or the Inuit people of Alaska (whom they knew as "Eskimos"), or the Aztecs or the Incas. They never made the connections of these peoples' lives and battles against colonialism over the land and racism amongst themselves. Most of the teachers, due to lack of education and the enforced apartheid education, did not make these important global connections either.

The first movie Tumelo saw was a Western movie organised by the school in the local community hall on a Friday afternoon. Within five minutes into the movie, the Coloured children and the teachers were all hysterically backing the *roeketjie*, (the chief White cowboy) who sorted out the "bloodthirsty wicked" Red Indians. The teachers never made the connections for the screaming children that once they themselves were like the "Red Indians" at the Cape, fighting off the White cowboys, the Dutch, and the English. Instead, the Coloured teachers encouraged the Coloured children to admire the White semi-nomadic wanderers, like John Wayne. The children shouted and encouraged the White cowboy as they watched. *"Skiet die fokkieng Indian vark!"* "Shoot the fucking Indian pig!" Many of these children came from Indian enslaved people. During break, the children played cowboys and crooks – the fair children chosen as the heroes, and the darker children as the villains, the "bloodthirsty Indians". To Tumelo, her teachers' stories about the troublesome native sounded like the stories of the "Red Indians" in the Western movies – for like them, the natives were portrayed as wild and untamed with an unreasonable angriness and bloodthirstiness that they could not help and for which they had to be persistently punished without question.

On Saturday nights, Tumelo's father read the stories in a book called *Uncle Tom's Cabin* to her. She thought of Uncle Thaba as one of the characters in the book. She thought of him as a Black slave on a plantation on the Cape Flats. Sometimes, her Uncle Thaba was like Uncle Tom, eager to please. Other times, Uncle

Thaba was angry like a Robben Island convict – when he ran berserk with a spade, chasing anybody who called him a *kaffir*.

In the classroom, Tumelo found amongst the small stack of about five torn books that her teacher encouraged them to read a colourful book about *The Three Golliwogs*. The three golliwogs were always up to mischief, and the Black doll wanted to be pink. That afternoon after school, she looked at herself in the mirror. She pulled at her dry, "kinky", bushy hair. Another book was called *The Adventures of Two Dutch Dolls and a Golliwog*.

A child at school told Tumelo that her mother said that she should not go home with her, because her mother did not trust Uncle Thaba, "My mother said that people like your Uncle Thaba cannot help themselves. They get hungry and then they eat anything in sight. They are people eaters, cannibals. They like to eat children because their bones are young, sweet, and tender. They cook them in the three-legged black iron cast pots over a huge open fire in the veld like in the storybooks."

Tumelo's blood boiled that day, but the nasty little girl persisted, "*How* can he be your uncle? He is a Golliwog! My mother said you are like his Pickaninnie! " Tumelo wished that she and Uncle Thaba could run away to heaven, away from the children and their horror tales of "natives" and cannibals. She wished they could run away from the vans, to the places on the pictures of heaven on the walls inside the houses that showed angels watching over little children. In these pictures, the angels had huge protective wings. However, she worried whether they would be so kind as to watch over Uncle Thaba. It bothered her, though, that all the angels that she saw in these framed pictures in all the shacks were fair skinned with blond hair. Even Jesus was. The angels looked like the policemen in the vans, they were just friendlier and softer. She started to doubt that the same angels and Jesus would actually watch over Uncle Thaba. However, she still hoped that they would, in any case. If the slaves were free and no longer whipped by White men, why was Uncle Thaba still not yet free? With these thoughts night after night, she would drowse off to sleep – distressed, worried and tormented.

Noticing Tumelo's increasing withdrawal from the world, her granny suggested to her mother, Lizzy, "Take the child to the wise man, not to these White doctors at the Red Cross Hospital. They don't understand our people's illnesses. They just know about tablets, injections, and syrup medicine. This child needs something special for the confusion in the head. We have seen this confusion before in many of our people. It is an old thing at the Cape with our people. They say it came at the time of slavery, this confusion sickness, and only our wise doctors can heal it. I am telling you no White doctor can help. If you don't get help in time, she'll be like the rest of our people...*mad with the confusion.* Look, she is already talking to the ants. What do the *ants* know about life?!"

Tumelo's granny spoke of the mysterious Cape *kwaai wind,* the angry wind. "It is the evil wind of the restless spirits of the people who long to go back where they came from. Just listen carefully to the moaning sound in the wind at the Cape...that is the moaning of the slaves that want to go home...their souls are lost in the wind, trying to find their way home, because they are buried in a place they don't know. The wise man will warn you about this *kwaai wind.* If it catches a child, it possesses her mind and soul. Because these souls are lost and they want to return. Their spirit is in the wind and has been there for 300 years. When the child plays alone outside with the ants in the wind, it possesses the child. You'll notice that the child starts to ask many questions about this and that, and when you don't have answers, then the child withdraws into confusion and madness. That is why she is asking you questions about golliwogs, pickaninnies, and wooden dolls, and that is why she has been staring into the mirror a lot lately, touching her hair and talking to herself. Tell the wise man everything. I think she has the evil wind in her. Our people know that wind too well... That is why she must see a *Muslim* wise man. Only he knows how to get rid of the evil wind that comes with the Black southeasterly wind. He'll help the lost spirit in her to find its way home to the East, where the slave boat came from. He understands and knows more about the confusion than the White man will ever know. Leave the child in the hands of the White man, and she'll be even madder, or she'll die mysteriously within days...because the White man has no clue of what is wrong with *our people.* He'll put her on tablets for the rest of her life. The old people say madness in our people is a simple thing to understand; it is the longing of the departed slave ancestors within us...they want to go home. That is why our people roam there in that place, Valkenberg..."

Lizzy did not waste time after this advice from her wise mother. She hurriedly dressed her daughter and marched her off to the wise man's makeshift "surgery", which was a few miles away. It was their first visit to "the people's surgery", which was a green painted shack with a wooden bench outside for waiting patients. Nobody spoke as they waited patiently on the bench; they coughed and sighed, each wrapped in their own psychological torment and apartheid trauma. Tumelo noted there was no apartheid on this bench; there were Whites, Blacks, Coloureds, Indians – every colour. Two wicked smelling incense sticks burnt fiercely at the entrance of the shack to welcome the patients. They waited for about a half an hour before the wise man called their turn. "Next!" Tumelo clutched her mother's hand tightly. She choked on the strong smell of incense as they entered the dark, sparsely furnished shack that only had one small window.

The wise man was in his sixties, and dressed in a white djellaba. He had thick eyebrows that crossed the bridge of his nose, and baggy eyes. He sported a beard and wore a purple embroidered fez with a gold tassel. Her mother seemed nervous. The shack, small and tidy, had dozens of empty wine bottles on a table. Filled with clear water and little floating pieces of paper in them, the bottles were arranged on the table at which they were invited to sit down. The wise man pointed to the three wooden folding chairs at the table. He sat on the third.

"Don't worry, missus. All *Holy* water", the wise man reassured her mother, who looked suspiciously at the bottles. Pointing at the bottles, he spoke, "I don't charge for this service. It is spiritual work. You know *spirit*? I work with spirit. Sit down...make yourselves comfortable."

He looked at Tumelo, focusing his gaze on her and not on Lizzy. He studied her face carefully while he gently tapped his fingers on the table. Then he stared into the incense smoke, as it curled mysteriously up into the roof of the shack, and eventually escaping out of the small high window. He spoke slowly, but with much emphasis, "I am a *wise* man. I heal people. They come to me with many ailments that the White doctors don't understand and can't cure – cancer, asthma, tuberculosis, high blood pressure... any sickness. What is wrong with the child? Is it asthma...?"

"No, doctor, she is *confused*..." Lizzy half-whispered.

He cleared his throat. "Uh, one of *those*...this child sees people from the spirit world? She sees S*pirit*? "

"No, doctor,...she speaks to herself in the mirror and to the *ants* about golliwogs." Lizzy was herself very confused.

"Uh...serious then...have you heard of the *kwaai* wind?"

"Yes, my mother sent us. She says you know how to get rid of the evil wind from the East...She was also a patient of yours. You bathed her for the confusion in the seventh wave of the sea on the False Bay coast from where her ancestors came when they were brought to the Cape as slaves. She said it really helped her to connect with her ancestors. Since the bathing in the seventh wave, she has felt whole again. She wants the same for her granddaughter, whom she thinks may have the same disease. "

"Yes,...it is a *s--a--d* wind that will haunt this coast until there is freedom for our people. This wind that haunts our people have a long story. Do you know about the *kramats*, the holy Muslim burial places, at the Cape?"

"No, doctor."

"Well, you should...They are also known as *Mazaars,* the holy shrines of Islam which mark the graves of the holy men and women of the Muslim faith. There are many *kramats* in Cape Town. This is a holy place! Our problem is, few people at the Cape know this. This is part of the problem and the cause of the confusion. The holy people who lie here in the kramats are from India, Ceylon, Java, and Malaysia who were sold into slavery from the 1600s through the Dutch East India Company. Have you heard of Sheikh Adburahman Matebe Shah, who lies at Constantia where the Coloureds were moved from and thrown into Grassy Park on the Cape Flats by the boere? Now, Sheikh Abdurahman was the last of the Malaccan Sultans and arrived here as a captive in 1667. There is also Tuan Guru, who lies in the Malay Quarters in the Bo Kaap. He was a Prince from the Trinate Islands. There is also a *kramat* on Robben Island. Now, you should understand that we live in a sacred place, and we'll all feel the *dis-ease* of these spiritual leaders who died in captivity. "

He cleared his throat and lit another incense stick placed in an empty Old Brown Sherry bottle on the table. He noticed Lizzy's bemusement. "Don't worry, I've cleansed the bottle of its sins. Many Coloured people are caught like wandering spirits in wine bottles, in alcoholism. This place will not come right until all these things get settled. Not many people know just how *sacred* this place is...part of my mission is to teach them this history...to make them aware of their *spiritual* surroundings..."

The wise man folded his hands and closed his eyes. He seemed to be concentrating. After a few moments, he opened his eyes and stared intensely into the smoke of the incense. The room was filled with an eerie presence. Tumelo clutched her mother's hand even tighter.

"Don't be afraid, child. *Spirit of the East* is here...Spirit says that you come from our people in the East...Muslim slaves that arrived at the Cape in the 1600s...right?"

Tumelo could feel her mother's sense of shock with his uncanny accuracy about her great-grandmother. Her hand felt cold, stiff, and tense.

"Yes, Doctor...my mother and grandmother come from Muslim and Indian slaves...from Malaysia and Madras, they say..."

"Now, you must understand...they wanted to go *home*...their souls are *lost* in the Cape wind..."

"Yes, so my mother says..."

"Why did your family convert to Christianity?"

"Don't know...through marriage to the Griquas I think..."

His voice turned firm and low. "That is part of the *problem*... this child will never have peace...will always be confused...part of the madness at the Cape...she is possessed with loss...loss of name, loss of country, loss of faith, loss of family, loss of soul... loss of God. We must pray together for this child to find herself... for all of us..."

He proceeded to pray.

"In the name of Allah, The Most Compassionate, the Most Merciful. All praise belongs to Allah, the Lord Who is the Creator, Sustainer, and Guide of all the worlds...Amen."

Lizzy echoed respectfully. "Amen, Doctor..."

"Good...now we have welcomed our Muslim spirit guides from whom your family comes...we are protected by our spirit leaders from the East. Our people who live in Cape Town are protected by the kramats, the shrines of the Muslim leaders' graves. You'll see one day that the natives like Nelson Mandela will be freed from Robben Island, and we'll be able to go back to live in what is now White areas, where we were born. People must remember, our Muslim people are still imprisoned there today on Robben Island... not just the natives...it is an old story this..."

The wise man used the visits to his surgery as an opportunity to teach the people of all colours who came to see him a bit of little-known Cape history. "If you go to Lion's Head near Table Mountain, try and find the shrine of Sheik Abdurahman Shah, who brought Islam to the Cape at the time of slavery. Many other Malay leaders are buried there. One day you'll see that the Rivonia prisoners will be freed from Robben Island, because they are protected by the founders of Islam here. Sheikh Madura was exiled in the 1700s here at the Cape, and died on Robben Island. What do you think happened to the souls of these people, far away from their birthplace? These are all our leaders who fought the Dutch. Many of the slaves were Muslim people from Malaysia and Bengal. Prince Abdullah Kadi Abu Salaam of Tidore was exiled to the Cape also about that time. He wrote a copy of the Koran from memory! This is a deep and holy history, missus. Your child is a part of all of this. Understand?"

"Doctor, I *want* to understand... Now *what* must I do?" Lizzie spoke like a child.

"Listen carefully...I am going to give you a bottle of *holy water* filled with small pieces of paper on which I have written prayers from the Koran. She must not eat any food and she must please stay away from pork...this child must *never* touch pork! She must drink only this water...four times a day. The water will heal her from inside...it will wash out the sad wind...but she needs many prayers after that."

"Thank you, Doctor. How much do I owe?"

"You can make a small donation, if you want to. But as I said, I am a holy man. I don't charge for spiritual services. It is my calling to work for the people who were brought to the Cape as slaves, as exiles and as prisoners against their will. It will take hundreds of years of work to cleanse the Cape spiritually. There will be many like me at the Cape for many many years to come until we are all free – spiritually free. When apartheid is gone and we are free, then I would most likely be dead. I don't think I'll see that day, as I am already 70 years old. Perhaps this child will see that day... perhaps..."

Lizzy seemed humbled. "Thank you, Doctor. May God bless you."

He called them back just as they were about to leave, "Before you go...remember to bath the child *separately* from the rest - in the orange blooms of the herb of wild *dagga* (cannabis) to sooth the restlessness and disease in her that will come from time to time. It helps to also use the wisdom from your Hottentot spirit guides. By the way, they were here too...but they spoke in clicks I don't understand..."

They left the shack sheepishly, Lizzy holding her daughter's hand tightly as if she was suddenly a very special child – some sort of visionary. For days and years since that day, they visited the wise Muslim man routinely. Tumelo was then, per instruction, bathed in wild dagga and separately to her siblings, as he advised. She drank countless bottles of holy water from wine bottles, which left her vomiting and sick for days on end. Her favourite past time was to watch the ants during this time of spiritual cleansing. She noticed how ants never stood still, only to feed or to greet – even then, they are moving. In the school's library, she found amongst the small collection of fifty books a book on ants. In the book, she read that ants were interesting insects; that there are something like 12,000 species. Known for their highly-organised colonies and nests, they are said to occupy almost every corner of the Earth. They share their food and work in a never-ending manner. Ants are also said to be the only group of insects that teach one another, helping each other, showing each other the way. As a child, she decided to learn something from the ants to protect her from the madness that was going on in South Africa at the time.

She also enjoyed more mirror games. She dressed up and called herself Jumaya, great-great-great-granddaughter of the Tamil woman Indira of Madras, from the Bay of Bengal. She'd cover her head with her granny's orange headscarf, with only her eyes showing, then she'd talk with tenth generation back great-grandmother Indira in her head, on the boat on her way to the Cape of Storms. She'd talk to Indira's spirit to help her find her way back home through the sad whistling Cape wind. She had to take Indira home. She had to take her home. Give her spirit rest. Release her from the evil of slavery. Take her home to her family, to her village. Take her home to the port from where she came. She wanted to walk into the sea for her. In her mind, Tumelo did a happy Indian dance for Indira, with her mother's old purple bedroom curtains wrapped like a long skirt around her waist, gold prize packet toy bangles on her ankles, and with wild yellow and orange daisies from the veld in her hair. She copied the idea from the colourful pictures of her father's *National Geographic* magazines of the people of Ceylon, as it was known then. They had no Indian music at home, only a small radio that was always tuned into Springbok Radio. She only heard Indian music on the cassette player that the local shopkeeper played in his shop. So she created the music in her head, and moved her young body like leaping flames in the mirror. The imaginative sounds of the flute, the harp, and percussion harmoniously took her into a trance-like state, to another home in the East that also became part of Africa, and a part of Tumelo.

Chapter 6
Find Me in the Sweet Smell of Tobacco

Tumelo went to a primary school on the outskirts of the Cape
Flats. The school, especially built for Coloured children
from families who were victims of forced removals in Cape
Town, had many children from the English-speaking Coloured
communities of Claremont, District Six, and Diep River. Some of
the children were English speaking, but they were forced to learn
in Afrikaans. Tumelo's first teacher was a huge, fair woman with
black straightened hair and scary eyes, Mrs. Fudge. A terror who
tormented every young soul, threatening to pull out their tongues,
and who literally beat the children until they wet themselves, Mrs.
Fudge could easily have gotten herself classified White, if she had
wanted. Perhaps this was the root of her frustration with the poor
Coloured children at her hands. They represented everything that
she hated in herself.

Even the school head feared her for her fearsome manner.
The children called her "bull frog", because she was so mean and
constantly angry, "blown up". She hated children who could not
sing. She hated children who were hungry and forgetful and whose
hair was dry and bushy. She arrived at school every day with rage
in her eyes. She came to school to beat children and to drive fear
into them. She marched around in tall high-heeled shoes with a
cane in her hand. She seemed angry with the world and with life.
She had no children of her own.

Tumelo feared her so much. In her class, Tumelo escaped
into daydreaming forever in class, longing for the conversations
with the interesting ants, and to dance with the lost spirit of
Granny Indira and to be in the caring, safe arms of Uncle Thaba,
who now more than often left for his "native land". She wanted

to talk to the ants and Granny Indira instead, and she wanted the teacher to explain the fearsome, confusing stories about the natives and their faraway, bizarre homelands and about the kramats of the princes and Muslim leaders at the Cape. There were many children at Tumelo's school who called themselves *slamse* (Muslims), derived from the word, "Islam". They did not know about the Muslim wise man, nor about the slaves and princes that came to the Cape by boat. Some looked like the people in the pictures of people from India, Ceylon, Java, and Malaysia in her father's *National Geographic* magazines. Many looked like Uncle Thaba, but they were classified "Coloured". The children looked down on the *slamse* children, though everybody was poor. There were names like Rafiek, Mymoena, Shariefa, Shafiek, Fatiema, Saliem, Hakim – and also Jumaya and Indira. The teachers beat the Muslim pupils for not saying the *Our Father* properly, and for not knowing the words of *Silent Night* at Christmas. Saliem often got a hiding for loudly singing the misguided words due to his hearing problem, "*Silent night. Holy night. All is come. All is bright. Blond young virgins. Mother and child.*" His enthusiastic, loud, misguided singing sent Mrs. Fudge into a ballistic spin. She would charge Saliem with a ruler and beat him hard over his face for singing about "young blond virgins". Nobody understood why and asked why, because the children did not understand the meaning of the word "virgin" in any case.

The children all got excited at Eid, the end of Ramadan, when the festival for the end of the fasting period was marked by Muslim children running around with snotty noses dressed in bright green, red, and blue silk ill-fitting big outfits, excitedly collecting money in the neighbourhood. It was a big event in the Cape Town community, because so many descendants of Muslim slaves lived there for at least 300 years, yet no teacher explained Eid and Ramadan to them. Mymoena and some children said they came from Constantia. Hakim and others said they came from District Six. Nobody talked about why they were no longer living there, and the teachers were not allowed to teach or talk about it. The *slamse* children were known to sell vegetables and fruit on street corners in the cold and the rain. The Christian children, like the teachers and their parents, despised the Muslim children, "Don't eat with the *slamse* children. They are dirty." Most of the children at school (Muslims and Christians) had empty eyes and bony frames. They could not remember their homework, they smelled of paraffin and fire smoke, and they begged for bread. Even the Muslim children begged for bacon and egg sandwiches from the children who brought lunch to school.

In her boredom, Tumelo spent her time watching the head lice parading through the paths in the children's hair, in and out they moved down the dandruff paths like the ants in her father's garden in the sun; just they did not stop to greet, like ants. They were too busy with their parasite activity feeding off the blood of hungry children. Later at university, she learnt the scientific name of these horrific parasites: *pediculus humanus capitis,* and she recited this long word over and over in her head, because they were so much part of her childhood.

A neighbour savoured these lice which she crushed with sulphur and fed as a medicine to those who suffered unexplained headaches. Another neighbour hunted down black cats, slaughtered them, and placed their blood-soaked heated skins on the foreheads of mysteriously ill patients to draw out the fever. People found innovative ways to survive the things that they did not understand.

Tumelo was fascinated by the fact that the lice resembled ants if one looks at them from the side through the magnifying glass that she found on Mrs. Fudge's table. The children's hair was infested with lice and nits, the glue-like small white eggs of the louse. She found an old book on lice at the charity shop. In there, she read that lice have lived on humans since 100,000 years ago, and that they are indeed our lifetime companion, which also reminds us of our common human ancestry, like the fleas on baboons. She detested the lice as she detested Mrs. Fudge. The lice came alive like nasty monster humans as she studied them under the microscope. The children's scalps and hair took on the form of dense forests. She watched through the microscope how the lice sucked and bit furiously into their scalps, like monsters devouring humans in horror movies. She imagined herself with dagger and shield in the forests fighting off the giant lice monsters. She saw Mrs. Fudge as one of these monsters. Mrs. Fudge smacked her regularly for daydreaming. She was fascinated with the activities of lice at school and of ants at home. They made life seem more bearable than the world of bizarre labels of "*Kaffirs*", "*Hotnotte*", and "*Muslims*", and the brutal behaviour of the frustrated Mrs. Fudge.

The children were not only bothered by lice, but also scratched themselves to death with a routine outbreak of scabies. Their sores leaked puss and blood. Their noses dripped with yellowish green thick mucus, which they wiped with their hands all over their faces and into their hair. Their eyes teared forever, as if they cried forever. They had small sores around their mouths and their eyes. Yellow puss flowed from some of the children's ears. Mrs. Fudge would be even angrier on these snotty winter days, and beat them over their sores on their legs, and she'd pull hard at their already infected painful ears.

Faeces and puddles of urine littered the toilet floor. In this misery and poverty, Tumelo drowned her mind in watching the lice, imagining them to be ants and imagining the ants to be humans.

Mrs. Fudge took delight in teaching with cane in hand. The Afrikaner-written reading book *Sus* and *Daan* was about a White family and their pets, a baboon (named *Kees*) and a turkey (named *Koeloe*) who picnic in their caravan in the bush. Tumelo and the children could not understand why the hell a baboon and turkey would go picnic with a White family in a bush. The horribly stupid Afrikaans book had sketches of children with pink skin and bright yellow hair. The children had never seen such hair and skin colour in their lives, nor such pets. It all seemed so daft. There were colourful drawings of their food on this strange picnic – cheese with holes, which you only see in books about mice and mouse traps, orange juice, bread, and cakes. The children's mouths watered as they paged through the book of the White family's picnic. In their hunger, they drooled over the pages and forgot about the story. Some fell asleep with hunger and listlessness in class.

Mrs. Fudge's chalkboard duster hit Tumelo like a missile on her head in the middle of a daydream. She marched up to Tumelo with her huge legs, her fat feet squeezed into her tiny high-heeled emerald green plastic shoes. She pulled her out of the desk by her ear until it felt as if her ear had dropped off her head right there and then. The next day Tumelo also had puss leaking from her ear. However, she felt alright about it, because it made her feel normal, like all the other children. Still, she continued to daydream. One day, Mrs. Fudge pulled Tumelo's hair almost out of her skull. Her scarlet ribbons fell on the floor; the bows untangled. An overwhelming fear gripped her being as Mrs. Fudge pulled and pulled her infected ear yet again to punish her for daring to daydream in class.

"Do you remember what we just read?"

"No, Miss..."

Mrs. Fudge hit the cane over the children's heads.

"What is the name of the turkey?!"

"Don't know Miss..."

"What is the name of the baboon?!"

"Don't know miss..."

Tumelo feared her, but she could not stop the daydreams. The fear in her heart got to be too much sometimes, and it sank into her bladder. When Mrs. Fudges shouted at Tumelo, she would be filled with so much fear that she lost instant control of her bladder. The warm urine would rush through her panties, down her legs, into her white socks and her black toughies. Soon, she'd be standing in fear in a puddle of her own warm pee. She'd go cold with more fear, as her ribbons floated in the pee on the floor., shapeless and wet. No more ribbons, just lifeless strings of red lying in fearsome urine. Then the children would laugh – all forty something of them. Mrs. Fudge would get hysterical at the sight of Tumelo wetting herself yet again, and she'd grab her long cane and hit her and hit her until her hands tired, until Tumelo fell down in shame in front of the class in her puddle of urine. When the pee dried, her ankles and legs itched, and the children teased her because she smelled of fish.

Mrs. Fudge was also fiercely in charge of the dental days, when the mobile clinic did their rounds at Coloured schools. Children were marched off screaming to the local clinic to have their teeth pulled out, returning toothless with huge pieces of toilet paper covering their faces. Everybody feared the mobile clinic and the marches to the White Afrikaner dentist, Dr. Jaap, who was reputed to be cruel along with his fat, frame-less White boere nurses who delighted in holding down screaming Coloured children. Dr. Jaap did not bother to administer sufficient anaesthetic before a tooth was extracted. His extraction team combed with psychopathic smiles and laughs through hundreds of Cape Flats schoolchildren who stood waiting in fear in long lines. Their Coloured teachers were made to stand on guard with canes in their hands. The teachers also feared Dr. Jaap, as he would insult them as "useless Coloured teachers" should any of the children escape. God forbid you tried to escape. You would not only face the wrath of the psychopath dentist and his team of nurses, but also the cane from Mrs. Fudge on your return to school.

Dr. Jaap was a huge White man who laughed with an evil pull of his face when he saw the frightful Coloured children. He would show them his needle and took delight in having them strapped down to have their teeth extracted. He did it with such relish, counting how many teeth he could get out in an hour. "Coloured people don't have teeth, *m-a-i-r-n*! Come let's remove the buggers!" he would joke as he approached another screaming child held down by the laughing nurses. Like Dr. Piet, his favourite dental treatment was to remove the four front teeth of each child. "You want to look like a *j-a-w-l-ie* Coloured, hey?" As he slowly pulled the teeth, the child would scream frantically in pain. "Aha!" he would say, "Now you can smile nicely, like the Cape coons. Like it, *he*?"

For all her peeing in class, Tumelo earned the nickname piss-pants. She thought of Mrs. Fudge as no different to the police who searched for natives, people who drove senseless fear into others. As her heart pounded and she felt her body losing control in deepest fear of the humiliating hidings that would follow in front of the class, she simply thought of Uncle Thaba's warm heartbeat. Then she would miss Uncle Thaba so badly. She worked out a strategy to survive Mrs. Fudge's beatings. Whenever Mrs. Fudge beat her in front of the class, she closed her eyes to be transported to the comforting world of the ants and to Uncle Thaba where she felt safe, blocking out the haunting sight of the children's toothless laughter. She simply learned to accept and live with the nickname piss-pants and with the notorious fishy smell. At night, her mother bathed her in water brewed in the unpleasant smelling herb, *kruidjie-roer-my-nie*, to sooth the open sores left by the beatings of the volatile Mrs.Fudge.

However, school was also fun. Tumelo had a friend Annie with whom she chased huge butterflies on lazy afternoons; the two girls picked wild daisies and decorated them in their hair. Because of her very indigenous looks, the children called Annie "the flat-footed Bushman" and refused to play with her. Annie looked like Uncle Thaba, and this was one of the reasons Tumelo chose her as her friend. Tumelo and Annie pretended that they were fairies in storybooks. Annie wore no shoes and had huge sores on her legs, and protected Tumelo from bullying at school. They stole honey from the neighbour's beehive for the two of them to eat, and often got stung by the bees in these adventures.

One Friday night, Tumelo overheard the hushed voices in their kitchen. Her parents were talking to a neighbour. It was already dark and after nine. She was already in bed.

She heard her father asking the visitor, "How did they catch Uncle Thaba?"

"We do not know if it was the police, but a man who witnessed the accident said that the van rode over him and reversed back over the body."

Her father sighed, his voice trembled, "Yes, they knew about him and they were looking for him for a long time. The van always came looking for Uncle Thaba. The captain used to ask us, where is that kaffir from Robben Island?! We used to pretend that we don't know about his whereabouts..."

"Do you think a neighbour squealed on him?"

"Yes, perhaps..."

"Did you see the body?"

"I arrived just before the ambulance came. He was already dead. It was messy..." Tumelo heard the late night visitor vomiting outside and coming back into the kitchen.

"Sorry about that. I am feeling sick."

"Why did they still have to reverse over him after knocking him over?"

"Don't know...His brain was squashed, and there was gray matter all over the road. They rode over his head. He was unrecognisable. But I recognised his duffel coat and the packet of humbugs in it. "

Tumelo's worst fear had come true. Her chest felt raw inside, as if it had been ripped open by some real physical pain. She sobbed herself to sleep. As she fell asleep, she saw Uncle Thaba suddenly appearing in the black darkness of her room, as if behind a screen of incense smoke. He smiled at her in a warm, reassuring way. He had on his favourite black warm coat, in which she could snuggle up away from the cold, harsh, and violent world of Mrs. Fudge and the police vans, where she could listen to his heartbeat. She could smell the cheap tobacco that he unwrapped from the orange coloured paper. He had the packet of humbugs in his hand that he bought for her that fateful night. She reached out for the comfort of his coat in the dark night and excitedly stretched out towards him, welcoming his warm, loving embrace. Her desperate reach took her nowhere. There was no Uncle Thaba. He had vanished into the darkness of the bedroom, into the mysterious cruelty of death. She called his name, but he did not answer.

She felt intuitive anger and fear in her rising to roaring levels in her throat, choking her vocal chords, forming a painful lump in her throat. Before she knew it, huge tears burst in painful, confused anger through her eyes, flowed uncontrollably over her cheeks into her mouth. Her lips trembled with deep anger. It felt as if her ribs were choking her heart. She struggled to breathe. Her head went dizzy. Her heart raced in the walls of her tiny chest. Her heart felt big, lumpy, and as if it had sunk down into the soles of her feet. It felt as if it about to shoot up into her throat, choking her to death. She realized that she would not see Uncle Thaba ever again. Her head ached with shock. She screamed hysterically and uncontrollably into the dark fearful night.

Chapter 7
Petals of Wild Daisies for Little Girls

If the wise man was right, Tumelo thought to herself, then Uncle Thaba would also be lost in the sad wind, trying to find his way home. She searched for Uncle Thaba in everything around her – in sweets, in flowers, in incense, but she could not find him. Her head ached and ached. Why did the boere take him away from me? Why did they hurt him so badly? She wanted her father to go pick up all of Uncle Thaba's little pieces in the road and to try and put them together to make him alive and whole again, because her father always fixed broken things.

However, her father said he could not fix Uncle Thaba, "Tumelo, nobody can bring Uncle Thaba back to life, not even the doctors."

So Tumelo decided to put Uncle Thaba's pieces together in her mind.

Every time Mrs. Fudge beat her in front of the class, she would close her eyes tightly, and call on Uncle Thaba's angelic protection. She reasoned that Mrs. Fudge's beatings could never be worse than the fear that Uncle Thaba had; it could never be more painful than his cruel and tragic death. As the beatings came, she would visualise Uncle Thaba pulling her closer, tucking her away under his protective armpit, and covering her with his warm coat. She would hear his comforting and reassuring voice. Even when she pissed her panties, she felt Uncle Thaba close to her, reassuring her of his presence. When the children teased, she knew there could be nothing worse than the humiliation Uncle Thaba suffered at the hands of the boere when he was alive.

Annie replaced Tumelo's loss of Uncle Thaba. They gathered white lilies from the veld and tried to catch frogs falling from the sky on rainy days. Annie did not seem to care about homework and teachers, only about buying cheap pink sausages and toffees from the nearby charity shop in the afternoons on their way from school. Annie seemed tough and wise. In the summer afternoons, they would head for the hills, dig holes in the dunes, and bury their feet in the cool white sand. They would press seashells against their ears to listen to the sound of the sea waves mysteriously locked in the shells. They would dig for roots of the edible wild plants, and watch the clouds gather and dream together of a new world where there would be no cruel people like those in the blue and gray vans looking for stupid books on people, and no teachers like Mrs. Fudge. They dreamed of a world in which there were no hungry snotty children, no dirty toilets, no giant psychopathic dentists in white coats that fed on frightful Coloured children's teeth, no hair lice, and no adults fearing other adults for stupid things. In this world, there were no funny men with huge fingers and private parts that stealthily crawled into little bodies.

"You like the stranger that calls you on your way from school very much?" Tumelo asked Annie.

"Not sure"

"You see this man often?"

"Well, always on my way from school. He waits for me in the path, hiding in the bushes, and then he tells me he does not want the kaffirs to catch me."

"Then what happens?"

"Then he says sweetly, come to uncle...come here my ugly Bushman child."

"Then I just go with him so that he can stop calling me ugly."

"And then?"

"Then he says, you are not only an ugly Bushman child, but you are also mad. What does one do with such a mad ugly child? Then I feel a bit sick, but I know that he'll give me a five pence and he'll call me pretty afterwards if I put him in a good mood. He'll also say I am not so mad, then, that my hair is beautiful and I am not a Bushman."

"Then is he happy?"

"Yes, very happy. Then he says, come to me my pretty clever girl. Here is five pence. Come with me to the tall reeds where we can watch the hippos bathing in the Vlei. If we are lucky, we may even find a tortoise for you to ride on. You are safe with me. Stay

away from the kaffir men in the village; they want to steal our
little girls. Then I go with him to the reeds..."

"When he hurts me and I want to cry, he goes 'shhh...the
snakes are sleeping...don't wake them; this helps with the madness
and will make you pretty from the inside out! You will get long
straight hair like Snow White and Cinderella, and you don't have
to play Guy Fawkes for money...'"

Annie begged Tumelo, "Twist your little finger into mine and
promise that you'll never tell anyone."

One of the highlights of their days as friends was the day
they watched *The Sound of Music* in the packed local community
hall. It cost only two and a half cents, and they ate oily Missaris
chips, red snowball cakes, and drank green Coloured soda fizzy
cool drinks. They became impatient about growing up, to one day
turn sixteen and fall in love, even in a country ruled by fear. On
Guy Fawkes Day, Annie would dress up like a Golliwog in the
books, with stolen black shoe polish smeared all over her body, and
decorate herself with rags and play the role of the tragic hero. She
would walk the dirt roads of the informal settlement, tin in hand,
begging for money from the already poor people, singing that they
must pity her because she, in her role as Guy Fawkes, has no hair.
Tumelo would be so proud of her confident, cheerful Guy Fawkes
friend who brought joy and happiness to the people, young and
old, in the neighbourhood. They would cheer her up, laugh at her
golliwog image, and at her hair.

Tumelo wished that she could be as brave as Annie, as confident
as Annie, as happy as Annie – who could even be happy about
absolutely nothing, even about people laughing at her hair. Tumelo
also waited excitedly for Annie to share her earnings from the Guy
Fawkes collection to buy them doughnuts and chocolates.

One autumn Friday Annie asked Tumelo to accompany her to
the tall grass in the school playground, far against the fence away
from the laughter of the children. She wanted to be where it was
quiet, she explained. Annie lay herself down in the tall cool green
grass, and asked Tumelo to measure her by marching along the
length of her small body.

"What was this about?" Tumelo begged to know.

"I am starting a *new life* on Monday. You are going to carry my
coffin at my funeral. Measure the size of my coffin, so that you will
not be in shock when you carry my coffin. I want you to prepare
yourself in your mind for my death. You were not prepared for

Uncle Thaba's death, but you'll be prepared for mine. I don't want you to cry or be shocked because I am going to a new, better world where all the children will have shoes to wear to school and books to read, and there are no Bushmen."

Tumelo went cold with shock. How could Annie *know* that she would die the coming Monday?

"My mother said it is bad luck to talk about coffins and death. Don't do it, Annie!" she shouted at her.

"I am not going away forever. I'll just be in another world and I promise to come play with you to show you that I am not *really* dead. You'll see. Promise me you won't cry. I am joining Uncle Thaba in another life."

Tumelo became angry as angry as the night of Uncle Thaba's passing. She bit her lip in frustration. She felt the anger well up behind the walls of her eyes, bursting into tears. It was a mixture of anger and fear. She felt that same choking pain in her throat and in her chest.

No, it could not be. Annie was certainly not going to die. Why would Annie die so young, so alive, and so happy?

That Friday afternoon Annie and Tumelo bought the pink sausages as usual and the sweet, milky toffees. Annie teased as usual, and told Tumelo that she would come around in the afternoon to fetch things that she would need for her journey in the new life.

In the late afternoon that Friday in April, before sunset, the dogs barked at a little girl standing at Tumelo's family's front gate. It was Annie calling. She had come as promised. How does one help someone starting a "new life", she wondered. How does one know that you are going to die, when you are still so healthy? She knew that Uncle Thaba did not come back again after that night when he floated into and out of the darkness of her room. Where did Uncle Thaba go? Why did he not come back? Would he now be safe from the blue and gray vans? What if those White policemen died and also went to heaven, would they still be chasing Uncle Thaba in heaven? Jesus and the angels were White in the pictures. Would they care to look after Uncle Thaba? Why were they White? How does one know that Uncle Thaba is safe, that his heart does not have to beat consumed with pain? Where do people go when they die?

Tumelo ran to her mom and blurted out, "Mom, Annie says she is going to die on Monday. Just like that!"

"Are you going mad? Or is Annie just as mad as you are? You must both go see the wise man. Nobody knows when they are going to die. Tell Annie not to be bad luck. Annie is not going to die. She's got an overactive imagination."

"Mommy, I don't want Annie to die...like Uncle Thaba did. Please, mommy, *don't* let it happen..."

Tumelo intuited that something was not right with life itself, at least not at that time in South Africa; that there was a kind of madness going on that could drive people to death in many different ways. There seemed to be many ways of dying.

Monday morning came as a normal blue day. Lizzy had convinced her that Annie was not going to die, and she was happy.

Tumelo wanted to avoid more visits to the wise man, so she stopped questioning her mother. She found out that strange things happened at the "surgery" of another wise man, whom they were now visiting regularly after the old one had passed away. This one was not a Muslim man, but a Christian man who offered magical healing of the body. He said he specialised in working with demon-possessed people. After Uncle Thaba's death, Tumelo's mother reckoned that she was perhaps possessed, so she took her to this new healer. There, Tumelo saw many things. Frogs were exorcised from people's bellies. Snakes were pulled out of anuses, vaginas, throats, and legs. Worms were pulled out of nostrils. A variety of demons could be pulled out of the human orifices, leaving the demon-possessed patient reeling on the floor, shouting blasphemous abuse. This wise man was very popular. He had a long wooden bench outside his surgery packed with people of all ages, all colours, and from all walks of life. This was the only time White people would come into the Coloured township, to see "the healer of the body". They would sit on the bench for hours chain smoking. It was the height of apartheid, but there were no "Whites-only" signs on these benches. Everybody sat on the same bench. When these White people came to see the wise man, they were equal to the Coloureds and Africans. The wise man treated everybody the same – he gave them no special treatment. They had to wait their turn, even if it took hours to see him. However, he did call the White male patient "*baas*" and the White female patient "*madam*". That was the only privilege they had at the surgery. Other than that, he treated their bodies and minds in the same way, beckoning for the demons to come out. At the surgery, everybody was the same. These demons only saw bodies and souls, he explained to the White patients. To the demons, bodies are the same, whether they are White or Black. Everyone is equalized in looking to find themselves and to get rid of the "confusion" at the Cape.

A range of cars were parked outside his "surgery" – Mercedes Benz, Volvos, Jaguars, including the poor Coloured hawker's horse and cart. People queued for cures from psychiatric disorders that nobody could name or diagnose, cancers of the womb and breast and even syphilis. Some explained that they were confused and lost, that they did not know *who* they were or *what* had happened to their family. Some were there for wanting to be accepted by their family, for wanting a better look and to be more "attractive" and "well-liked" in the apartheid world, for potions to get rid of a Coloured mistress or an adulterous White lover, or for aborting a "bastard" child. They were there to seek healing and a cure for whatever the crazy apartheid world dished up for them.

Whenever Tumelo's grandmother returned from the wise man, she would make a huge fire and boil a huge pot of water and *Hotnotskooigoed*. Then, she'd wash Tumelo three times per day, as instructed, in the enamel bath outside with all the Khoisan holy herbs the family could gather from the veld behind the reeds. The smell of the herbs would send Tumelo into a deep trance, and then she would meet all the lost ancestors in the dream world who all wanted to speak to her at the same time. She would wake in a cold sweat, hallucinating and vomiting. On Sundays, all the aunts would come to visit. They would gather around the huge green wooden kitchen table near the coal stove in their white painted corrugated iron house. They'd whisper about Tumelo, discussing her "visions". Her sisters would not play with her, and all the children would avoid her and call her "the mad one".

It was Monday morning. Annie's mother wailed and screamed, beating herself with a black scarf. She lost control, pulled her clothes off her body, and undressed herself in public. Her hands waved intermittently in desperation. She gasped and screamed again hysterically. Tumelo could see and hear Annie's mother from the classroom window. Tumelo froze at her desk. Her body went limp, numb, and cold. Tumelo swallowed the painful silence of their little secret. Her head ached so badly. She could not even cry, even if she desperately wanted to. Her eyes just could not do it. Her head wanted to burst open to seek relief from the incomprehensible pain.

Tumelo was angry with the angels, with Jesus, and with God. She never looked again at the pictures of angels that were hanging on the walls, with their huge wings, protecting little children standing at the edge of a cliff. They did not turn Annie into *Goldilocks* or *Snow White*, no matter how much she tried to please the stranger in the bush on her way from school.

Annie's funeral was on a rainy day. The Cape wind was howling, making wailing sounds like an elderly woman. Tumelo thought of Annie as also lost in the sad wind. She listened to hear her voice in the wind, calling for Tumelo to come play.

The teachers lined the children up and walked them in rows of two all along the long road to the red shack with the blue roof where Annie had lived with her mother. The school had made her a huge wreath of white lilies. Her body lay small and deep down in the white coffin. Tumelo touched her friend's face; it was beautifully black and ice cold, and her skin was taut. She ran her little fingers through Annie's short woolly hair, looking for lice. There were no lice. Annie's hair felt lifeless and damp, like wool left outside in the snow.

It was the first time Tumelo saw a dead body in a coffin. Her mother did not take her to Uncle Thaba's funeral, because his face was smashed in, they said. There was nothing to view or look at. Uncle Thaba's body was in pieces. At least she could look at Annie's face in a coffin. Even though her face was cold, pale, and tight, she could touch it, make sure it was her.

Annie looked so peaceful, so serene. Tumelo's fingers trembled as she touched her face. Her bottom lip trembled again like whenever she thought of Uncle Thaba. She felt that she was losing control. She felt that choking pain in her chest again, and she felt that bottomless painful pit in her stomach that nothing would ever be able to fill again. It looked as if Annie smiled at her friend. It was funny to see her so quietly dead with white pieces of cotton wool around her head. However, Tumelo had promised Annie that she would not cry, and she kept her promise.

Annie's mother stumbled forward and gave Tumelo a wild yellow daisy like the ones they pushed in their hair when they played in the sand dunes. The children sang, *There is a place for little children*. They had practised the hymn over and over again at school. Mrs. Fudge warned the children that she wanted them to sing "perfectly" at the funeral. After a short service outside the house in the rain with many noisy drunk relatives falling around and hungry thin dogs sniffing the children's clothes looking for food, the children walked the five kilometer walk to the cemetery. The children were very sad, but also excited to go to Annie's funeral, as it was an outing and there was the prospect of getting something to eat for the day. Mrs. Fudge had promised them that there would be cheese sandwiches with lettuce and tomatoes for the mourners. The hungry children could not wait for the funeral to be over, so that they could eat the sandwiches.

Annie was buried in a cheap, white, wooden coffin in the non-White section of the nearby cemetery, close to the forbidden Whites-only beach. Tumelo remembered at that moment (standing at Annie's graveside) how the two of them pressed the seashells from the Whites-only beach against their ears to deafen their longing to swim in the nearby forbidden sea.

"Tumelo, can you hear the sound of the waves?" Annie once asked.

"It is a Whites-only beach, but Tumelo we can go there with our minds. There are many things you can do with your mind, Tumelo...just try."

Now, Annie was finding a resting place in death near the forbidden beach where she so much longed to play.

As the small white coffin was lowered into the tiny deep dark grave, Annie's mother sobbed uncontrollably and fainted. Tumelo felt nauseous, her head wanting to burst with sadness; her legs trembled and wanted to give way. She wanted to comfort Annie's mother. She wanted to tell her that Annie was prepared to die and was excited to go to the "new world", wherever that was. However, it was Tumelo's secret with Annie. She could not tell anyone. They would have told her that the confusion had her again.

Each child was given a chance to fill the small deep grave with sand with a huge spade while the adults sang, deadening Annie's mother's heartbreaking sobs with *What a friend we have in Jesus*. The children sang out of tune, and were glad that Mrs. Fudge could not whip them that day. Annie's funeral had saved their legs just for that day. They placed wild daisies in an empty used apricot jam jar filled with sand and water on the little grave, without a cross, and without Annie's name on it. Just like that.

It was after four in the afternoon when the funeral ended. The autumn sun was setting, and the temperature dropped suddenly. The cemetery turned cold, dark and lonely. The gray clouds gathered. Tumelo panicked, and worried about leaving her friend alone in an unnamed cold deep dark sand hole without a blanket or warm socks and shoes. Her head ached and ached. She felt she had abandoned her friend. As they were marched off by Mrs. Fudge out of the cemetery, Tumelo kept turning around to see if Annie was climbing out of that terrible hole and walking home with them. She hoped and hoped in vain. Her head ached and ached as she tried to will Annie's return from death with her mind. She felt sick, because *how was life supposed to go on as if nothing out of the ordinary had happened?* The children's conversation was not very comforting as they walked back.

"Now the worms are coming to eat her down there."

"They'll come out of her stomach like snakes to eat her."

"Then she'll turn into a skeleton."

"Then she'll be a ghost."

"What goes to heaven? Her skeleton?"

"Fool! She is already in heaven. That is only her body."

"No, hell is on Earth. She is in heaven."

"Maybe she is already a ghost, walking with us and listening to what we are saying about her."

"What if she is not *really* dead?"

"Would we ever know?"

"What if she tries to crawl out of her grave tonight?"

"What if she was still breathing? Maybe they made a mistake."

"No, she was cold and dead. I felt her forehead."

"*Why* did she die?"

"Nobody knows why."

"She just did not wake up for school..."

Tumelo did not sleep that night. She worried about the worms that would come to eat Annie in her deep, cold, lonely grave. She heard the children talk at the funeral about the worms that are in graves. Perhaps she did wake the snakes behind the reeds, as the stranger had warned her not to do.

Chapter 8
Port Jackson Trees Weep Milk

Annie's spirit did visit as promised. She stood each night at the foot of Tumelo's bed. She would wake Tumelo with a whisper, "Come and play in the hills and behind the reeds, like we always did, Tumelo..." However, as Tumelo reached out for Annie, her presence would vanish in the loneliness of the dark. Tumelo was always excited and hopeful that she would find her, that she might catch her one day hiding underneath the bed or in the toy cupboard or in the cabin under the chicken feed. Tumelo would light a candle and search the room in vain. In time, after many such visitations and searching in vain for her friend, Tumelo accepted that Annie was gone forever and would never return to play with her in the hills.

Uncle Thaba's visitations seemed less dramatic. Tumelo would wake at the strike of the grandfather clock in the dining room at four in the morning, and there Uncle Thaba would be standing in the doorway, smiling.

"Uncle Thaba?"

"Yes, my child. It is me. Don't be scared."

"Where are you now?"

"In a beautiful place where there is only love and kindness, and where all people are the same."

"Is that *heaven?*"

"No. I can't tell you."

"Can I come with you?"

"No. You can't join me here. But I am with you every day."

Then he'd vanish suddenly after that.

The next day, Tumelo would feel strong and supported - ready to face the wrath of Mrs. Fudge's cane.

Her stray cat, Geoffrey, somehow understood her loss and he purred and caressed her with his head and licked her hair every night at bedtime. He knew about Mrs. Fudge and about the teasing children. He also knew about the devious ways of her math teacher, Mr. Van Jaarsveld, a man in his late fifties who fondled Tumelo with his huge cold damp hands whenever she took her math homework up to his table to mark. He had huge, inquisitive, knotty hard fingers.

Mr. Van Jaarsveld was quite a fearful sight – at over six foot tall, he looked like a scientist at work with rats in a laboratory. Tumelo feared that he would do experiments on her body, like they do with rats. Mr. Van Jaarsveld would reward her for good behaviour by calling her to his office for a private chat.

"Tumelo, you must come see me urgently in the office this afternoon after school. It is about your work."

"Yes, sir..."

When Tumelo got to his office, he would pour all the school's funds stored in a purple biscuit tin out on the table. There would be notes, silver coins and bronze coins.

"You can take as much as you want", Mr. Van Jaarsveld encouraged Tumelo, "as such a bright girl deserved the best."

In her shame, she would snatch the large shiny silver twenty-cent coins first. She knew that the one rand notes would make her mother suspicious, because where does a child get such a lot of money? So, she avoided the one rand notes. Once she had snatched the silver coins, she would run off out of the office, fearing that strange body smell on Mr. Van Jaarsveld, the sight of the front of his trousers that would bulge bigger, that familiar excited look in his eyes, the sweat on his forehead, his heavy breathing, and his huge strong nasty hairy hands.

"Hey, you little rascal!"

He would be too late. Tumelo knew when to escape, when his eyes went glossy as he stared at her legs as she deliberately bent over the table to reach the money. The other older girls at the school taught her this trick.

"You must be quick, Tumelo. And never hesitate. First, snatch as much as you can, then duck low out of his reach, and then sprint off."

"Wait for him to drool and stare at your legs, then run and run as fast as you can."

Mr. Van Jaarsveld drove a van that looked like an old ambulance of the 1920s, with no windows at the back. She chose not to tell on Mr. Van Jaarsveld. The truth was that she was scared, and she also liked the money. He tried his luck time and time again. He enjoyed just that moment of being alone in a dark room with a young girl. Just to stare and drool brought him satisfaction.

The school's pennies brought her many moments of sweetness in her loss. She bought humbugs and it took her mind off Uncle Thaba and Annie. She would buy herself some creamy *Sharp* toffees over the counter of the local shop where she used to go with Annie. She enjoyed tricking Mr. Van Jaarsveld, making him think that she would allow him to touch her, even just a little bit. Just listening to his heavy breathing gave her a lot of power and confidence. She got him to give her money to do the things that she missed doing with Annie. It helped her to deal with deep inexplicable loss.

"Hey, you little devil, when are you coming to my office again?"

She would smile at him teasingly, "Whenever you *want* me to, Mr. Van Jaarsveld."

He would get excited and lick his lips. There'd be a little foam at the side of his mouth, "This afternoon then, you little *bitch*!? In the office?"

She'd smile at him again, suggestively, as she swung around the pole that supported the fabricated building. "*Y-e-ssss*, Mr. Van Jaarsveld..."

His eyes would go misty – just the thought of what could possibly happen in that dark, dusty little office would excite him. Tumelo was acutely aware of his vulnerabilities. "Promise you'll be there. You little *devil*..."

As the days and weeks passed, and Annie did not come back to school or to meet with her behind the reeds to watch the flamingoes and pelicans making their nests, she retreated more into her own world, talking to the ants and to Geoffrey. She told them about the little girl whom the girls in the neighbourhood found in the bush on a Sunday afternoon when they went to look for butterflies behind the tall reeds where the stranger used to take Annie to watch the hippos. The little girl sat against a Port Jackson tree, with faeces and semen and blood-stained blue knickers, her eyes and mouth wide open, and a bottle, covered with sand, stuck deep into her bleeding vagina. She died soon after the girls found her.

A huge man had climbed violently in and out of her little body. He had thrust her small, delicate person and organs to pieces. Tumelo and the girls could not sleep for many nights after that.

"I'll never forget her face. She was still in her navy blue school uniform. She had two plaits of long hair. Her eyes stood wide open and still in her head, in shock. Her mouth was wide open, locked in shock", she told her cat. The cat purred and rubbed his head against hers.

She thought of Mr. Van Jaarsveld's stares and drools and five cents for sweets. After finding the dying little girl against the Port Jackson tree with its yellow blooms and cluster of colourfully patterned caterpillars infesting its green bark that day, Tumelo never went alone to Mr. Van Jaarsveld's office again. In her mind, she tried to mend the gaping wound between the little girl's legs; she tried to wash away the sand stuck in her, she tried to pull out the empty wine bottle lodged in her little bleeding vagina, and she softly closed her shocked little eyes for a decent burial. Tumelo's father often told her stories that he read about the Aboriginal Australian people in the *National Geographic* magazines – how they used the milk of the figs of the indigenous Port Jackson tree to cover wounds. That day, Tumelo saw these hard figs with their healing milk hanging above the little girl's head in the branches high up in the tree.

In her loneliness, Tumelo worked hard at school; she scooped school prizes, and she ran as fast as she could to avoid being caught by Mr. Van Jaarsveld. She liked the words of *Scarlet Ribbons* that Uncle Thaba often whistled to her. The song was about making the impossible for little girls possible, like the "new world" for which Annie had longed and prayed. There was hope in spite of the horror of the little girl found against the Port Jackson tree behind the reeds. Anything was possible. Life could be as bright as scarlet ribbons.

Her grandmother decided it was time to get a new wise man, one of "Uncle Thaba's people" from Transkei, as she put it, as the Muslim wise man and the Christian healer did not seem to help. This meant that Tumelo had to be taken to a *sangoma*, a Xhosa traditional healer who worked with the ancestors.

"This child does not speak much to other children. She talks to herself, and the ants. She has been troubled since her Xhosa ancestor passed on. He used to watch over her and she was a calm child. Since his death, she has changed. I think some evil force had taken hold of her," she told the sangoma.

Yes, Tumelo hardly spoke to other children after Annie's death. She fled to the reeds and hills instead, hoping to find Annie there, hiding playfully behind *fynbos*. She dreamed of running free on the white sand of the Whites-only beach not far away from their house. She pressed the seashells against her ears. Somehow, she could hear Annie's voice in the whistling swoosh-sound of the wind in the shells.

Tumelo's family was not visiting the beach any more, even on unbearably hot summer days. Her father, Richard, refused to since the family was chased off the Whites-only beach on New Years Day. He could not understand how the police could have the audacity to chase him and his children off the beach where he was born and grew up as a child. He felt humiliated as a father in front of his children when they chased them with Alsatian dogs off the beach that day. Tumelo remembered the biscuits and boiled egg sandwiches falling into the sand as they gathered their belongings hurriedly. *"Geen hotnotte, komberse en honde op hierdie strand nie!"* "No hotnots, blankets and dogs on this beach!" The policemen had whips and their Alsatian dogs were ready to bite the children. Richard did not know what to tell his children. He changed the subject on their way home and said, "My family had lived here for more than two hundred years... Lets go home and eat our picnic food at home."

Richard never talked about the beach again after that day. On that day, Tumelo saw her parents humiliated like children by White policemen who looked years younger than them. For the first time, she saw the fear in their eyes like the fear in Uncle Thaba's eyes. It stayed with her for the rest of her life.

On beautiful summer days in Cape Town, one could smell the sea breeze and hear the roaring waves crushing on the beach nearby Tumelo's home. However, Richard refused to take his children back to the beach. He had an alternative plan, he explained. The family would walk through the nearby bush to the marshland, where the hippos roamed.

Richard reasoned to himself, that it would be less painful for him, to see them swim in the mud and picnic in the bush in peace away from White policemen, than to go through that humiliation again. "You could play there in the mud and the shallow water. You can make the Vlei a beach in your minds. Imagine it is the sea, my children," he urged them. "With your imagination anything is possible..." He got the children to act normally, as if it was in fact a beach they were going to, to pack a picnic basket the night before, and a beach umbrella, swimming togs, and suntan lotion, along with little spades and plastic beach buckets. He'd wake his children at dawn and created the impression that it was the day for the beach, as he usually used to do. Once dressed and packed for a family day at the beach, they'd walk in a line holding hands, the smallest leading, following their parents quietly all along the long path through the thick bush of Rooikranz and Port Jackson trees and fynbos and thorns, to a spot he said was far away enough from the White people – where the White people could not *hear* them nor *see* them. The water was muddy and green, home to tadpoles, mosquitoes, and trout, and littered with broken glass wine bottles. However, the children felt free and safe as there were no White policeman who could humiliate their father, and like little baby hippos, they rolled their bodies whole day in the shallow water and mud to protect themselves from the scorching sun. They turned the mud into blue ocean waters in their minds, and the thorns in the bush became seashells, and the twigs and branches turned into soft white sand. From their picnic spot in the bush, they peeped through the reeds at the White people on their ski boats and sailing boats of different colours in the distance in the forbidden waters of the Vlei where they were not allowed to go. They could see the White children with their parents and hear their laughter on the boats, enjoying the water and the sun. They could smell the sea water of the forbidden beach nearby.

Chapter 9
The Rustle of the Wind in Fynbos

"The Whites just assume that all *so-called* Coloureds *want to look like that*, and extracted front teeth of *so-called* Coloured people for many, many years without giving people a *choice*. It is a colonial thing. Like with segregation and slavery, *so-called* Coloured people are not given choices about their bodies and health. That is one of the first things we must get rid of if we want to be free!" This was Mr. Torres talking to his students, Tumelo's first political teacher at high school. Tumelo was now 14 years old in the early seventies, and admired Mr. Torres from the first day she saw him. Mr. Torres was a handsome young man in his early twenties, of middle class Coloured background, with all his teeth intact. He looked like the South American revolutionary, Che Guevara, with his red beret and his long beard.

"But teacher, some girls and boys want the passion kiss to give better blow jobs!" a classmate defended mischievously. The children all smiled and looked around at one another in class. Those with the notorious passion gaps covered their mouths in embarrassment. By this time, Tumelo's teeth were replaced beautifully and she did not have to cover her mouth.

Mr. Torres was a perceptive and sensitive man. He covered for those with the gaps, "Nothing to be ashamed of...it is not your fault. Though it is a shame, *if* you are informed about the colonial roots of this phenomenon in this country and you still make the choice to allow White dentists to mess you around...but not if you were innocently caught and done an injustice to. Fight and resist this *imposed* 'Coloured' identity and look! What is this word *'Coloured'* anyway? You should not accept these racist categories of people..."

"Some of us have sadly become accustomed to the racist idea of *so-called* Coloureds as *savages,* and believe colonial myths of people and use unacceptable words, like *kaffirs* and *hotnots.* Let me give you a different perspective on this matter. I have read about a certain tribe, called the Bunun in Taiwan, who live in the mountainous regions and practice the extraction of their front teeth as a cultural *choice.* It is *their* culture and *their* choice, and that is very *different,* because nobody looks down on them for that reason. The same with certain tribes in Sudan and in many other African countries that remove teeth out of choice for good reason to do with culture and beliefs. While with *so-called* Coloureds under apartheid - things are very different. This is not about choice and a culture of being from the Malay Archipelago people (as some of you are) and of practising an ancient ritual; it is *imposed* by Whites as a culture to make people of a certain background *look* like *so-called* Coloureds; to make them fit in with the *so-called* coons, to make them look like fools. Get it?"

"Yes, but maybe some Coloured people come from Taiwan and Sudan...and that is where the culture comes from...and they therefore *choose* themselves to have the passion gap", another with a passion gap quipped.

"No, this is about an apartheid racist practice on people who the Afrikaners decided to categorise 'Coloured'. We are *not* Coloureds. We are *so-called Coloureds*; it is an *imposed* racist label and practice to divide people. *So-called* Coloured people have the passion gap and African people must carry pass books..." Mr. Torres was persistent about *so-called.*

That was Tumelo's potent moment of first love, and first true love, so she thought. This man spoke to her heart, her soul, her body, her dignity. "You have the most beautiful smile," he once remarked in passing, and on another occasion, "You have the most beautiful dimples."

And so, a beautiful and important friendship began for Tumelo. By the time she had reached 16, Mr. Torres picked her up regularly on weekdays and over weekends at her home for extra curricular reading and political lessons. They'd go to the Coloureds-only beach to discuss the revolution in South Africa and in the rest of the world. He introduced her to the music of Pete Segers' *Guantanamera,* recorded on a cassette that he played in his old blue Ford while they watched the waves and the local Coloured fishermen pulling in the nets of sardines. Mr. Torres planted in Tumelo a deep fascination with Cuba and a fancy for men who emulated Argentinian revolutionary Che Guevara and Cuban leader Fidel Castro. He would explain to her while they sat in his car watching the waves, "*Guantanamera* means girl from Guantanamo in Spanish. It is one of best-known songs in Cuba. We must go to Cuba one day to see how a revolution worked well for the poor people. Then he would sing for Tumelo on his guitar, "*Guantanamera Guajira Guantanamera... With the poor people of the earth I want to cast my lot ...*"

Mr. Torres was formidably sexy when he whistled parts of the chorus of *Guantanamera*. Tumelo almost fainted at least once or twice. He was gorgeous; he had a kind of raw sexuality coupled with a sharp intellect, a scruffy beard, and untidy eyebrows. When he whistled the popular sixties tune of *Elusive Butterfly*, his eyebrows gathered in a sexy way and his eyes darkened mysteriously like her father's. She learnt from early on to control romantic feelings in her body; not to let go of such things, but to restrict oneself only to the essentials of life's rules, to the do's and the don'ts. In an apartheid country ruled by thousands of don'ts, you simply oppress yourself. Keep yourself in. You know your place. Your body knows its place. It is something into which you are born.

Mr. Torres further taught her the ways of revolutionary rigidity and how to control passion. "In the revolution, there is no time for frivolities. Capitalism corrupts the mind and keeps you busy with the petty, superficial things in life that don't matter. Tumelo, we have serious work to do in South Africa. We have a Nazi and capitalist regime to overthrow."

Tumelo knew that he made sense, and she was quietly besotted by him. Tumelo suspected that Mr. Torres knew that she liked him. She imagined that he once came short of tasting her innocence, of tasting her young, wanting flesh when she had turned seventeen, not because he was into abusing young girls, but because she wanted to offer herself to him as a revolutionary sacrifice. Tumelo thought of Mr. Torres as a lover, as a potential partner, as a companero. She thought that it almost happened on the winter's day in July when she arrived at his quaint cottage in Wynberg soaking wet and cold, dripping from the rain. "Tumelo, you are cold and wet...come here".

He walked down the passage to his bedroom. She followed, anxiously hoping for a romantic encounter but also dreading its eventuality, as she was nervous about sleeping with her teacher.

However, she was deliberately pushing the boundaries to see how far things would go. She could hear the jealous girls at school whispering, "Tumelo has corrupted the revolution; she has tempted an innocent teacher to suck her breasts and to take her virginity. She has seduced him away from the revolution."

She ignored the scary thoughts of a possible scandal and walked towards him in his dark Spartan bedroom that smelled of stale apples. The wooden floor in the bedroom of the old cottage creaked with every step she took. She could hear the Cape rain beating down on the roof of his modest sparsely furnished place, located in a town that was once the hub of markets as the half-way point for travellers from the port of Simonstown on their way to the city of Cape Town. She scanned the book titles on the shelves in his bedroom. Amongst the many titles of *Fidel Castro, Che Guevara, Bakunin, The Spanish Civil War, The Ragged Trousered Philanthropist,* she found a book that grabbed her interest, the Bovilian woman writer's, Domitilla's, *Let Me Speak.* Her eyes also picked out the one that read, *Sex manners for men.* Tumelo blushed quietly. She was there to talk about revolution, but her eyes picked out this title. Her teacher actually read about sex, about the human body! She was fascinated, curious, seduced, and intrigued.

Mr. Torres pulled her towards him in a caring way, a brotherly way. She felt her skin go crazy. She felt warm and damp. It was pleasurable. He was penetrating Tumelo with his mind. Her body heat increased. Her pulse raced. However, she withdrew with ambivalent fear.

Instead, she realised, he looked at her in a gentle, caring big brother way, "Here, put this on. It should keep you warm." These words were like a bucket of cold water over her hot body. At first, she thought it was a towel. She looked down at the striped pyjamas cuddled in his dainty hands, and admired the hair on his forearms and on his hands. She caressed his forearms in her mind, imagining that she was stroking his hair on his chest, and in her mind she was also following with her finger the lines of his thick rough eyebrows. She imagined him gently stroking her hair, pulling her towards him and kissing her gently on her lips like in the movies – in that order in which romantic things are supposed to happen. Her mind wandered for a moment, lost in the smell of stale apples that mysteriously hung heavily in the room of the old dilapidated cottage. At that moment, she thought to herself that she could easily sleep with her teacher if she was forceful enough, just pushed things a bit, and let things get out of control. It takes a few seconds, a few body gestures. She just needed to look down in a shy way, touch her hair seductively, and step a little closer to him or put her index finger on his chest – like in the movies. That would disarm him and send them flying into maddening uncontrollable passion. She thought that she had that moment of power with Mr. Torres.

However, she did not. Mr. Torres had no intentions of sleeping with his student. He was too honourable. He stopped himself. He stopped them. He was too respectable to take up the offer from a lustful seventeen-year-old political activist. He tried to save the embarrassment for both of them.

"May I use your bathroom, sir?" Tumelo gestured anxiously at this sudden realisation.

Her face felt red and hot. Her heart raced.

He responded with sudden revolutionary discipline, "Certainly, you know where it is..."

She convinced herself that it was innocent enough to put on his pyjamas. They were warm and soft, taken from underneath his pillow and offered to her in his gently cusped small hairy hands. She imagined that he had just woken from an afternoon nap before she arrived. She closed the bathroom door – no, she wanted to deliberately leave it unlocked. Then she panicked; she locked it.

She studied the old broken lock, the peeling paint, and the poster of handsome Che Guevara smoking his cigar on the bathroom wall. It felt as if Che was watching her, checking out her intimate revolutionary behaviour. Handsome Che, as handsome as Mr. Torres, Tumelo thought. She stood in the bathroom naked, imagining every silent thought of Mr. Torres in the kitchen next door. She could hear him preparing coffee; she could hear the click of the cups and could smell the freshly ground coffee. He did everything so beautifully, with taste and tenderness. Then she heard the soft strumming of his guitar. He was singing along as he played, Jim Croce's *Have to say I love you in a song*.

She smiled to herself in the bathroom. She crossed her fingers and placed them on her chest. She looked again at Che's face on the wall. Yes, it seemed he was smiling too, as if approving of the imaginary romance with her communist teacher. She put the pyjamas on slowly, like a new outfit for Christmas. Every moment of the encounter was precious. She could feel the softness of the much worn item comforting the doubt in her as she pulled it across her skin, savouring every moment. As she put on the trousers, her intimate parts touched where his were. It was all in the nearness of the cloth – her dreams of the unity of their bodily parts coming true even if only in her mind. As she listened to the sound of the pouring rain outside, she begged him in her mind to abandon the guitar and to touch her gently. Her skin vibrated to the sounds of his deep masculine yet gentle voice, transporting her momentarily to an imaginative companero hideout in a forest in revolutionary South America, where the wind rustled amongst the leaves in the trees.

However, nothing dramatic happened that afternoon. They spent hours together, just drifting through song, not even talking politics or school work. In her imagination, he serenaded her, seduced her, and she drifted on clouds as he sang Bread's *I'd like to make it with you.*

Tumelo indulged all her seventeen-year-old fantasies in it all and enjoyed every minute of the seduction. The next day at school, she pretended that she did not know Mr. Torres more than the other girls did, that he was just her teacher at school. She giggled frivolously like the other girls when he passed them. She showed him her homework and allowed him to teach her with not one hint of familiarity at school.

"Sir, can I read Domitila's *Let Me Speak?* I promise to give it back to you." His hand stroked hers gently, and he gestured, "Of course, Tumelo, any time. Come around some time and we can talk about your reading programme." Domitila was a woman of the Bolivian mines, the courageous wife of a miner. The story is in her own voice of a life in imprisonment, of torture, and of leading the revolution by miners and peasants. It was a book of the time, published in 1978.

Tumelo imagined that the invitation to discuss Domitila Barrios De Chungara's courageous *Let me Speak* was another invitation for mutual seductive play through the pages of revolution and song. Her body was forming beautifully. However, very often Mr. Torres would remind her of the need to be serious, to let go of the sensual pleasures of life's indulgences, such as boyfriends. "You must work for the revolution. You must get boys out of your mind. These are all petty distractions. To be a revolutionary, is to be disciplined. Romances should be *for* the revolution not against it."

Mr. Torres encouraged Tumelo to keep her passions and lust checked and regulated. "We must meet often to talk revolution. You must conduct yourself like a revolutionary. We must free South Africa and transform it from an oppressed country to a liberated one." Tumelo had a sacred unspoken deal with Mr. Torres. She kept a dignified distance from him through the fire and passion, as part of this deal. Unbeknownst to him, she kept her virginity for him. She planned to give it to him one day when they had won the revolution in South Africa. But this never happened.

Tumelo once wrote to a comrade in Durban. "Intimacy is sacred. It belongs to the revolution. It belongs to freedom. My body is trapped in and to the revolution. It is a deal with the comrades."

Mr. Torres started to see her more regularly for more frequent reading sessions, guitar serenades, and discussions at his cosy cottage, with its vast library of interesting books and its unkempt front garden of creepers and tall wild weeds. After that intimate day with his pyjamas, they mutually avoided sensual things and romance. She swallowed hard as she suppressed her romantic feelings for him. All the feelings she had for him felt forbidden and wrong. She felt trapped in feelings of forbidden love. She kept on repeating to herself, " It has no place in the revolution. No place. No place." She tried to look unattractive. She wore no short skirts any longer, no tight jeans, no high heels, no low-cut dresses. She opted for long skirts and baggy trousers. She collected her long hair curls from the floor after she put a scissors through her hair and placed them in a plastic bag in the bin. She bought khaki coloured baggy trousers and shirts – military style. She thought of herself as a soldier, and she tried to behave like one. She longed to have an AK47. She imagined standing with an AK47 and blasting the boere's brains out at dawn as part of a firing squad. She thought of ten bullets for the task; one for each generation. She saw them falling over in a mass grave. After some months of intense reading of books such as *The Iron Heel* and *Ten Days that Shook the World,* Mr. Torres collected her on weekday nights to attend political meetings and reading groups. One day, Mr. Torres called her to his room to tell her something of great importance.

"You have now successfully graduated to the level of revolutionary cadre. This means that you are now ready to be introduced to the underground revolutionary leaders. But you have to swear secrecy and loyalty to my organisation and not get involved in any other political organisation." He picked her up the next Sunday at 2 p.m. at the corner of her street to take her to her first real revolutionaries' meeting. This was the first of many such Sundays that would follow. Tumelo was dressed in overalls, ready to be trained on how to handle an AK47. They did not speak that Sunday afternoon as Mr. Torres drove nervously, anxiously monitoring his rear view mirror to check if his car had been followed by the security police.

After a 30-minute drive through side streets, they reached a forest at the foot of the Hottentots Holland Mountains. They passed a huge farm on the left, and a few yards further they turned right into a dirt road lined with pine trees. The narrow dirt road crept discreetly into the mountains, virtually hidden from the public main road. One could easily miss it. They turned left some 100 yards up into a huge gate guarded by fierce Rottweiler bulldogs. This was the secret meeting place of the Cape Town underground Trotskyists, to where copied pages from banned books were smuggled from all over southern Africa and from abroad, particularly from leftist organisations in London. The meeting place was in a huge unused garage in the farmyard located in an unsuspecting Whites-only neighbourhood.

Tumelo was a little intimidated by the comrades in suits. It felt like a classroom. There were no AK47s; only a few other young students, older boys. She was disappointed. The senior comrades were mostly men, except for a couple of well-dressed women. One woman wore heavy make-up; her hair was neatly styled. These obviously brilliant women did not speak much; one seemed preoccupied with the needs of the men to have tea on time. These were men and women of substance, leaders in the community. However, the passive and subservient body language of the women in the meetings puzzled Tumelo. The loud presence of the men bothered her much the same. "They are all professors, brilliant comrades", Mr. Torres explained. "Oh, she is the first Black woman scientist of her generation in South Africa", Mr. Torres whispered as he pointed to one of the women who did not wear any make-up and looked quite stern and serious. "Everybody here is a person of great accomplishment in law, medicine, science...," he continued. "The South African revolution demands high standards of intellectual rigor and achievement." From that moment, Tumelo was inspired to be one of those women, but she wanted to do more with poor people, dirty her hands, wear her boots, deal with the boere. Whatever that meant.

Tumelo's school had a bad reputation in the local community. It was popularly dubbed "the maternity home", and more crudely, "the whore house". Stories abounded of teachers raping girls and of teachers taking the virginities of fourteen-year-olds in exchange for a pass mark in a subject. It was not unusual for a teacher to father the offspring of his student. At least two teachers married their schoolgirl sweethearts. The headmaster of the school, Mr. Hofman, was a huge, kind man, with narrow, perceptive eyes and thick glasses. He did not walk. He marched huge strides with arms swinging. He had fought in World War Two and could not stand noise. It reminded him of air raids during the war. When he heard the sound of a passing aeroplane, or the sound of the sirens of police helicopters monitoring the movements of township children protesting in the streets in 1976, he would fall to the ground, his body bouncing thunderously on the floor of his office or a classroom, usually in front of shocked children or visitors or parents. He would hold his head tight, clasp his ears, and bury his face in the ground, only to recover when the sound subsided. He was traumatised completely by the war, shouting loudly as he marched around the school with a long cane. He was always on the search for culprits, "whores", "paedophile teachers", drunkards, thieves, gangsters – whatever the "warts" were at the school – both teachers and students. And if he heard a noise, God forbid. He marched like a soldier until he sniffed the culprits out, and would proceed to cane both the unsuspecting teacher and his students. He marched the length and breadth of the school's vast field, sometimes for hours, deep in thought, doing the salute when a parent shouted to greet him. The school had no fence, or what there was of a fence, very little remained, and the parents led their livestock to graze on the school's field – sheep, cattle, and goats. When Mr. Hofman returned from his field march and private drill, he would rush into any class in the direction from where he heard a noise. Sometimes the teachers in these classrooms protested in vain that it was the class next door to theirs that was making the noise, but Mr. Hofman would ignore all protests. Such a teacher would also get a beating, while the noise next door continued unabated. The strange thing is that nobody got angry with Mr. Hofman. He was loved dearly by both the teachers and students, because they trusted him and knew he suffered from some disorder due to fighting in the war. He was shell-shocked. Often all was almost instantly forgiven. Mr. Hofman had a warm heart; he would laugh loudly when he was happy and he would cry openly and with wailing sounds when he was sad – and he would do this openly in front of the one thousand students and fifty something teachers. He spoke his mind and he called the students, "my children". Mr. Hofman returned disillusioned at having to face racism on the home front after fighting in the war. He was like the Black American soldiers who fought in the same war as Whites against Nazism and in the Vietnam War. The students knew his history and had great respect for Mr. Hofman, and forgave him for his odd political views at the time.

He protected his students fiercely from the security police, who often visited him to get the names of political teachers and students. Instead, he would serve them tea in the office and hoodwink them into thinking he would give them information, but then ended up telling them stories about his days as a soldier in the war, and how South Africa's problems would only be settled one day through fair conversation and power sharing. Mr. Hofman himself was a member of the dummy parliamentary Coloured Representative Council created by the apartheid government. This fooled the security police of the apartheid regime into thinking that he would betray his politically active students and teachers. He refused to talk to them behind closed doors, and would leave his office door open during such visits, much to the annoyance of the security branch. At the end of the long visit to his office, one could hear him shouting at the White male Afrikaner visitors with their huge, suspicious folders, "You want me to *betray* my children?! You want me to *sell out* on my people to the White man?! *No!* I regret, sir, I do not play that game! You are welcome to come have a cup of tea anytime, but my teachers are *my teachers* and my students are *my children! Leave my people alone!* I am God-fearing and peace loving!"

The enemy would leave sheepishly, confused, baffled, and shocked with their tails between their legs. However, they'd return repeatedly, hoping that Mr. Hofman might succumb one day, which he never did. During the many student protests, he denied the police access to the school, though they did manage to arrest one of the teachers at the school, ignoring Mr. Hofman's pleas, based on information that was provided through a spy network that reported that the teacher was a revolutionary who worked closely with Steve Biko, the Black Consciousness Leader. After this male teacher was confronted roughly on the playgrounds and bundled into a police van like a criminal, the school never saw that teacher again.

School was the last thing on the students' minds. They saw Mr. Hofman as a surrogate father, a keeper of their daily political activities.

Both White and Black anti-apartheid fighters were brutally murdered by the regime. The students realised that the struggle was simply not about Blacks fighting Whites, but about fighting the apartheid system.

When in August 1976, the students planned to march to the parade in the city to support their young comrades in Soweto, they cursed Vorster, then prime minister of the Nazi-inspired apartheid government. They cursed Afrikaans, the creole of the enslaved people at the Cape, formed from Dutch, Malay, Portuguese, French, Xhosa, Khoisan, German, and Arabic - a language the boere arrogantly made their language, and which by default came to be associated with colonial enforcement, slavery, and brutal apartheid oppression. Apartheid policies were written in Afrikaans. Rude White civil servants and powerful bureaucrats read the laws for the oppressed South Africans in Afrikaans (even if the people did not understand the language). Political interrogation took place in Afrikaans; many people were raped, killed and sodomised in Afrikaans; people were persecuted in Afrikaans; people were exploited, separated, and cursed in Afrikaans.

The students protested against the unqualified teachers who were focused on beating them the whole day, beating their bodies purple and blue. They cursed them because they took their frustrations with apartheid and its many demons out on the children's bodies. They cursed them because these teachers did not have a clue what to teach them. Some tried to teach in spite of their shortcomings, and others spent their time walking around with canes and doing crowd control like bouncers at nightclubs. The students did not understand the history, geography, math and science that they were supposed to learn from the alienating textbooks written by racist White males. External examination papers rewarded the "Coloured" students for rote-learning idioms, such as that when someone is very drunk, that person is "as drunk as a Coloured teacher"! The alcohol-smelling teacher would proceed to cane the class of forty rebellious youth, urging them to know their "fucking work" – including the embarrassing social "fact" about the teacher's drinking. This so-called fact easily could earn a "Coloured" candidate at least two marks in the external examination of his final year at school, which could mean the difference between a pass and a fail, and ultimately between getting a job and not getting one. It was therefore no wonder that some teachers often deserted the lesson for some unexplained reason, with the suspecting comforting flask of liquid underneath the arm and a depressing pathological expression on the face. Such a teacher would then seldom return to complete the lesson, and the students would go wild with boredom, brutalising each other with swear words, and insults about hair type, nose size, and skin colour. "You are a Bushman!", "A dog also shits hair!", "Don't keep yourself White; you have a flat face!" In the chaos, it was then not unusual for pornography magazines of White people fucking each other being shown around in the classroom. Nobody really noticed the absence of people of colour in such magazines, something which might have been viewed as bestiality, and in any case would have been illegal. Some of the Coloured children wanted to emulate the people in the magazines, and dreamed of becoming porn stars, of having "bees-lek hare" (sleek hair like a newborn calf), as there were no real career prospects if you were Coloured or African, or even Indian. If you were Black, you could become a teacher, a nurse, a postman, or a labourer. Most became labourers or remained unemployed. Black Africans in the Cape remained unemployed, because it was a "Coloured preferential area", meaning Coloureds got jobs first as labourers.

Some of the students gave up, hoping against all hope that they'd survive apartheid, that they'd get a good job, that some miracle will happen, and that the sky would open up one day and they'll be free. Many had dropped out. Others, who were determined to survive, resorted to copy verbatim the lies in the history books on how the land was empty when the Dutch arrived in 1652, how it was the destiny of Black people to be at the bottom of society as labourers, and for Whites to be in charge of them, that Coloureds were inherently lazy and prone to alcoholism, and that the Dutch and the English brought civilisation to Africa. These books told the students that White is beautiful and good and that Black is ugly and bad, that Africans stole cattle from Whites and were the culprits in causing conflict and war, that they were heartless thieves, that Whites were a pure, superior race, that Coloureds were a mixed breed of lazy idiots, that Indians were crafty, and that Whites brought civilization in the form of apartheid and separate development to South Africans. They stated that the ANC and PAC were terrorists, and that colonialism, segregation, and apartheid were good for South Africa. Students had to copy these lies word for word in cursive in thick, expensive hard cover books that their parents had to pay for with their hard-earned money. The students had to memorise all the lies and insults about the ancestors of their parents, the slaves they came from, about themselves, about their inferior beings, their inferior bodies, their inferior brain size and minds, and their inferior abilities that were only fitting for labourer work. The essay writing activity of these lies took laborious and painful hours and days, and formed a significant part of the psychological damage caused by apartheid education. Students guessed their way through examinations, rehearsing words and expressions in their heads, not having a clue as to what they really meant. Sadly, when the children in both primary and high school did not remember these "facts" of drunkenness and the supposed pathological laziness of Coloureds and the assumed inferiority of Black people, then some of the teachers would hit them blue. They were just passing time as the "keepers" in a mass prison, a kind of apartheid concentration camp and cruel mental institution. When Tumelo started to understand these things politically as a high school student, she forgave Mrs. Fudge for her beatings and cruelty; it was perhaps this teacher's only way of coping with the brutality she herself suffered as a human being.

However, many of the teachers passively resisted the lies that they were forced to teach. Some teachers tried to talk to their students about the liberation struggle leaders like Oliver Tambo, Steve Biko, Albert Luthuli, Walter Sisulu, Nelson Mandela, Winnie Mandela, Cissie Gool, Robert Subokwe, Neville Alexander, Bennie Kies, Victor Wessels, and Patrice Lumumba. Others were critical of the male-dominated histories of the struggle, and told them about the great women heroines in South African history: Masedibe Lilian Ngoyi, Sophia Williams, Dulcie September, Ellen Kuzwayo, Albertina Sisulu, Ruth First, Ray Alexander, Frances Baard, Florence Mkhize, Mary Burton, and Helen Joseph. As the students started to understand the history of South Africa, they forgave the drinking of the teachers. They forgave them trying to escape into the bottles of alcohol in the dark, untidy laboratories with the broken equipment. They forgave them for not having dignity. They even forgave them for having given up. They forgave them for all the madness for which their own young minds could not make sense. Black teachers were brutalised; stripped of their human dignity. They felt for them and with them.

However, there were still those who tried to trick the children into providing them with sexual favours. School was a bit of a madhouse, and at times like a circus, and a prison. One teacher routinely grabbed at Tumelo's breasts in front of other students as she exited his classroom. With a suggestive look in his eyes, he invited her once to join him in his car to go to the marshland in the bush, "to watch the pelicans and the flamingoes behind the reeds". Another wanted to know the size of her bra and pulled at her nipples. This all was done publicly and unashamedly.

Enlightened teachers tried desperately to get the students to learn about and listen to the political lyrics of Bob Marley, Bob Dylan, Miriam Makeba, Linton Kwesi Johnson, and Joan Baez. As an alternative to the enforced racist education, students spent afternoons teaching themselves in the local public library, stealthily tearing pages with important political facts from newspapers, encyclopedias, and magazines. They buried banned books distributed through the political underground in paraffin tins in unsuspecting backyards, and smuggled these banned books from friend to friend, neighbour to neighbour. They boasted about their knowledge in the classrooms and in student political meetings of political struggles in far away places, of the South African struggle as was seen through the eyes of a writer like Eddie Roux's *Time Longer than Rope*. They read a diverse range of books and perspectives: Peter Abrahams' *Mine Boy;* Sol Plaatje's *Native Life* articles written by Njabulo Ndebele, Ezekiel Mphahlele, Can Temba, and Todd Matshikiza in *Drum Magazine*. They read the works of Alex La Guma and Dennis Brutus, and they read Albert Luthuli's *Let my People Go*. They read Biko's writings in *The Black Review,* noting that "the most important weapon in the struggle is the mind of the oppressed."

Mr. Torres made copies of the newly published novel *Roots* written by Alex Haley and clandestinely distributed them amongst the students. Published in 1976 at the time of the student uprisings, they had all heard about this good book on slavery in America, and they wanted to have a class discussion on it. They read about how the slaves were chained to each other and to their beds in the dark dank holds, lying in their own excrement, and about the slave revolts on the slave ships and about slave auctions. They read about the first independent republic run by liberated enslaved people, Haiti, and about other parts of Africa associated with slavery, such as Senegal, the Gambia, and Nigeria. They learned about the intelligence of the slaves on the plantations, about the many languages they spoke, and the many African civilisations they came from, and how some of these freed slaves settled at the Cape and became "Coloureds". This was their first powerful and important introduction to how history can be learned in ways other than textbooks.

Tumelo found herself connecting with Uncle Thaba again through the characters and the stories of capture and escape from cruel White plantation owners. She read about how plantation slave masters raped teenage enslaved girls from Africa. It reminded her of the stories that she heard of Kruger and Kaiser Verwerp, born of rapes of their mother by a German farmer, and also the many stories she was told of how many Coloured children came about through the rape of domestic servants by White masters. Mr. Torres pointed out in his political education lessons that long before apartheid, slave women at the Cape often were raped too by their White masters. Tumelo discovered that slaves from Africa had their front teeth knocked out to make way for funnels through which they were force-fed to keep them alive on the ships when they resisted. Mr. Torres got his students to look at the notorious "passion gap" at the Cape in an entirely new and different way. He got them, through discussions, to draw parallels between what they read in an alternative history and their own experiences and lives.

The political teachers taught in a challenging environment. Some of the schoolgirls and schoolboys regularly worked as prostitutes at Cape Town Harbour – here they would go to entertain Chinese and Portuguese sailors in exchange for money to feed their poor families. If they were caught sleeping with Chinese sailors, they were only charged for prostitution as an illegal activity. If they were caught sleeping with Portuguese sailors, they were charged not only for prostituting, but for also contravening the Immorality Act, as the Chinese were classified as Black, and the Portuguese, Greeks, Italians and Japanese were classified as White on apartheid South African soil. The prostitutes had to be careful whom they slept with, to avoid being charged with the Immorality Act.

The girls who worked as prostitutes often came to share their fears at school: "If we sleep with the Chinese, then we don't risk being charged with immorality; but the Chinese are also reputed for dumping the bodies of prostitutes overboard ships in the deep murky water of Cape Town's docks. We fear being raped and murdered by Chinese sailors."

Both the boys and girls feared the violent Cape gangs who roamed the streets and who collected them at knife point from classrooms when teachers were not around - those that they knew and who "owed" them. They routinely gang raped them at the shebeens where they took them. The teachers had good reason to fear the gangs, as they often passed the school, armed with shiny long knives, threatening the girls with violent rape and the boys with sodomy. As they passed the school, the smell of cannabis drifted and lingered in the streets for hours afterwards. On such afternoons, the students were scared to walk home. The apartheid police, preoccupied with political activism and uprisings, offered no protection at such times. They also worked with the local gangs, collaborating on soliciting information about political activities and "political instigators", and to provoke unrest in order to trap unsuspecting student leaders and teachers. Once a Coloured child got trapped into a gang through poverty, there was only one way out – horizontal, in a coffin. The apartheid police knew this and used the gangs and *skollies* to undermine the revolution.

Chapter 10
Cape Fires in the Southeasterly Wind

It was September, 1976. The boring geography lesson on how clouds and thunderstorms are formed was disrupted by loud banging on the classroom door. "Come out, come out! March against apartheid! Defy your teachers! Leave the classroom now! The children in Soweto have been killed by the apartheid police! We are going to bring an end to apartheid today; the Nazi bastards are going to fall today! We are marching against the enemy today, each one of us! We are going to march apartheid dead; we are going to topple this oppressive system. Get out now!" The short, stubby unqualified male teacher stood hapless – cane in hand. The rowdy male students, who in their boredom spent most of their time reading pornography or drawing on cannabis in the notorious desks at the back of classroom number 17 at Forest High did not need any further invitation to heed the call to break out of the oppressive classrooms. The students simply ran out the door as if that in itself was freedom, pushing the shocked teacher out of the way. Some students spat on the floor in defiance of everything that they hated so much about the system.

"You bastard!" a shout came, bravely challenging Mr. Abdul and his cane for the first time. They were not sure *what* it was that they hated so much; they just knew that school was torture. "Mr. Abdul's *poes* (cunt)!" came a defiant shout. "Mr. Abdul, you are a *naai* (screw)!" came another. "No, they are all *naaiers* (fuckers), just like the *dieners* (police)!" shouted Elizabeth the daughter of the local shebeen owner, as if swearing brought great and the only relief. "Today, we are going to *moer* (fuck up) the teachers and the headmaster!" came an anonymous shout from somewhere in the mob that was now pushing towards the door with the might and

142

determination of youthful adrenalin. One student grabbed Mr. Abdul's cane from his hand and broke it in half, throwing the two pieces into his face, spitting at him and shouting "Fuck you, your bastard!" Mr. Abdul burst out crying. The 14 year olds stampeded him out of the way. They formed an angry mob of defiant youth. Mr. Abdul's lip trembled with anger, shame, and helplessness as he stumbled, trying to find his feet in the chaos. He tried to tuck and pull his creased suit into decency, trying to maintain the respectability of a proper teacher. Then he paused, and tried to make sense of it all, staring at the empty desks in front of him. The shouts of students increased; the senior students by then had taken over Mr. Hofman's office. They were taking charge of the school's phone, of the gates, and of all the keys. The senior students by then had already detained the janitor and his staff, as well. Mr. Hofman and his teachers had been locked up in the staffroom. Revolutionary shouts of defiance could be heard over the loudspeaker from streets away. The teachers had their power stripped from them in just one morning.

Later, the millions in the world would learn what was happening in Soweto and at many schools on the Cape Flats that morning. All the 1,200 students of Forest High gathered in the quad on that fateful and historic September morning. They were addressed by the leaders of the newly formed Student Representative Council (SRC). The chairperson happened to be Alfredo, a young revolutionary student who wore his hair in a ponytail, and had a very daring and fearlessly eccentric and outspoken manner. Alfredo feared no one, not even the huge cruel boere. He told the students that morning, "You have defied your teachers; now you can equally defy the apartheid system! There is no turning back! We are marching to the Grand Parade in Cape Town today to show our support for the students in Soweto. The apartheid police have brutally killed one of our young fighters, Hector Petersen. He is younger than many of you standing here today!" The students responded to his inflammatory speech with angry shouts and fists, swearing and cursing the apartheid government of John Voster. Alfredo was flanked by two fellow student leaders, lanky Arab-looking Shafiek, and stern Indonesian-looking Rafiq. Draped in red-and-black Yasser Arafat scarves, and looking serious and angry, they spoke about the vision of Steve Bantu Biko, the Black Consciousness leader of the Eastern Cape. "We have our own Martin Luther King that will lead us to freedom! Viva Steve Biko! Viva!" This was followed by "Long live the struggle! Long live!" "Down with apartheid! Down! Down with gutter education! Down! Down with Afrikaans – the language of the oppressor! Down! *Aluta Continua! El pueblo unido, jamás será vencido!!* A people united will never defeated!" - as if they were rising up against South Africa's own Pinochet. "*Venceremos!* We will overcome! The Struggle continues! *Aluta Continua!* Followed by a thunderous *Amandla Ngawethu! Power to the people!*" Something had happened in the months before as the students read about the struggles in Mozambique, Angola, Chile, Cuba, and America. The student leaders burst into a spontaneous singing of the American civil rights song "*Just like a tree that's standing by the water, we shall not be moved...Our parents are behind us, we shall not be moved...*" This was followed by, "*We shall overcome, We shall overcome one day, Oh, deep in my heart I do believe that we shall overcome some day...*" The mood was spontaneous, angry and somber.

The cadres that Mr. Torres had groomed through the reading groups on the farm were the leaders on that historic day. These were the songs he played over and over to them during "science lessons". The students were taking the revolution in their own hands. Alfredo continued: "We will rid ourselves from our history of enslavement and oppression. Like the Black people in America who rose up against slavery. Like them, we'll rise up against segregation. Freedom is in our hands! The time is now!" Many students were confused and too young to know what was happening. Their world was turned upside down that morning. Some of them mumbled along, trying to catch the words of the American civil rights songs, trying to form fists. Some senior students distributed pamphlets with the lyrics of the popular anti-slavery songs to help the uninitiated juniors along. This was the first mass political assembly of students at Forest High. Shafiek grabbed the microphone from Alfredo, and waved his red scarf high above his head, like a communist flag. He pointed the students in the direction of the school's gates, ordering the students to storm the gates of Forest High. "Forward we shall march to freedom! Forward we shall march! Forward!" As the students pushed forward, the young leaders erupted into jubilant singing of *Oh Freedom!* "We shall storm the gates like the Parisians stormed the Bastille in 1789!" came another announcement from Alfredo; he shouted amidst angry shouts from the mass of students. "Like Toussaint Louverture led the revolution in Haiti against the slave masters in 1791, we'll free ourselves! Like the slaves revolted at the Cape in the 1700s, we'll free ourselves! If the slaves could take their freedom in their own hands, then we can take ours too!" The students applauded Alfredo and Rafique for their brave orations and roared with cries of revolution, even if not all of them really knew then who Toussaint Louverture or Martin Luther King was. They just knew apartheid was *wrong*, and what was happening that morning was *right*.

"Take history in your own hands! Set yourselves free! Down with gutter education! Down!"

The teachers and Mr. Hofman huddled together in fear in the staff room, some chain smoking, others deep in thought. They could hear every single word of all the speeches and the freedom songs bellowing over the loud speaker. Some of these songs they knew well, and some sang along. The headlines that morning read "Soweto on fire!" Some read the news for the day; others engaged in superficial talk about sport, the weather and the latest fashion.

Mr. Peters, a neatly dressed middle-aged math teacher renowned for his cutting comments on current affairs and his notorious flask, laughed and nervously joked with the staff that the students were mad. "Listen colleagues, we have tried this in 1960 in support of the huge PAC march in Sharpeville against the pass laws, and what happened? The secret police came to hunt us out in this very staffroom, detained us, and transferred us to remote rural schools. Nothing came of it. Because there are spies everywhere. Ha! Think they can overthrow this military Nazi state?! Madness! We were not even *kids* like them, we were young *adults* and we failed to get it right! That happened almost twenty years ago. These children have no idea how mighty this army is; it is an established fact that the apartheid regime's army tanks can wipe out the resistance movement from Cape Town to Cairo in a matter of days! And they have Israel as allies, remember?! They are allies of South Africa against Mozambique, Angola...you name it! And where are our leaders today? On Robben Island – Mandela, Subokwe, Alexander, Kathrada, Sisulu. They are doing hard labour right now as we speak! Never see their families. The assassination of that Nazi Verwoerd did not even help! There is no hope for freedom in this country. Poor kids; they'll get the message and return back to class where they belong." He grabbed his blue Tupperware flask in frustration, and poured himself some black "tea" and went to sit in the corner, looking tired and disillusioned.

Mr. Hofman, got up from his chair to speak, trying to ignore some of the teachers drinking from their flasks. He pushed his spectacles in place, attempting to look very very severe, very respectable, and still very much in charge of his children and his teachers. "There is no other way for us Coloureds than *talking* to the enemy. At least we are not bad off like the Africans in Soweto. The police will not dare to shoot my children! They will not! I am going to go out there and tell them to leave my children alone!" Then he started to cry, wailing: "We are decent people! We are represented in government through the Coloured People's Representative Council! Even if some of you like Mr. Torres think it is a dummy political body, it is still at least a voice for us with the White man! I tell you, that is respectable and it works to talk to the enemy and you don't get locked up like the ANC leaders who are now prisoners on Robben Island! You see, we are not terrorists; we are a peace loving people. Now, it worries me that things are going the other way here at Forest High School...I suspect that we have been infiltrated by anarchists, dangerous terrorist-types that feed our children to the firing squad. Cowards!" He pulled himself together again, wiped his tears, and continued.

There were now rumbling noises amongst the teachers, noisy shifts and the irritable clearing of throats, angry whispers, signs of discontent, possibly perhaps division within the ranks of the teachers.

"I tell you!" he shouted, as he tried desperately to show that he was not going to allow himself to be intimidated by the irritable annoying body gestures from his staff. He proceeded to point his finger in an accusing manner to the group of young teachers smoking on the tattered and torn brown sofa in the corner of the staffroom, listening to sarcastic remarks about Mr. Hofman from Mr. Torres. "The *opstokers* (instigators) will be found out! There is no place for anarchists here at Forest High School! If you are an *opstoker*, then let me tell you, you are a coward – because you use children as cannon fodder! Cannon fodder! Look at that poor young boy in Soweto; he was used as cannon fodder! God, please help my children..." Then Mr. Hofman started to shake. The staff had witnessed this before on countless occasions when the political stress became too much for Mr. Hofman. He wailed, with his arms swinging, "My children! My poor innocent children!"

Mr. Abdul was (like many others) not politically informed, and tried to reason to himself through the events of the day while he sat huddled with his head down on the floor in a corner in the staffroom. He certainly knew that there was this thing called apartheid that regulated his life, that when he was a student the teachers hinted about the evil system, but many books were banned and they were scared to talk about politics and history. On every thirty-first of May, which was Republic Day in South Africa, marking the independence from Britain, his teachers hoisted the apartheid flag and got them to sing the national anthem. The sounds of *Uit die blou van onse hemel,* literally meaning "out of the blue of our sky" – referring to the beautiful vast African sky visible throughout the year in most parts of South Africa - the national anthem of the Nazi apartheid state, had an ironic poignant tone to it. There was something he could not really fathom; something that made him bitterly sad whenever he heard it, especially the line *"ons sal lewe ons sal sterwe, vir ons land Suid Afrika,"* meaning "we shall live and we shall die for our country South Africa." This line made him fear politics; even perhaps the sound of it. The word "politics" drove great fear into him and into many of the other teachers. Politics were forbidden. Politics against apartheid and its economy were banned. His teachers made him fear thinking, made him fear analysing, made him fear asking important questions even about being a "Coloured". The apartheid government had no mercy for people who became seriously involved in wanting to change things. He knew they hanged such people in Pretoria, those labelled as dangerous "terrorists", and that such people got sentenced to a life imprisonment on that much feared and harsh place called Robben Island. Once locked away on that island of hard rock and limestone, surrounded by a deep sea infested with hungry sharks, nobody would hear from you nor see your face again. When they hanged you in that feared place of capital punishment called Pretoria, nobody would hear from you again, nor even see your face again (he repeated this fearful thought in his mind). You do not even get a decent burial; yes, you never hear about such people again. Their names get recorded in black books and they have pauper graves – *persona non grata.* Children as young as 16 years of age were hanged in Pretoria for fighting apartheid.

Therefore, Mr. Abdul and many of the teachers at Forest High and other schools feared the *boere.* They feared Pretoria.

They feared the Island. They feared the local police chief with the notorious thick file of notes under his arm and the sight of his white Volkswagen Beetle. They feared John Voster Square, and the places of torture – South Africa's holocaust sites. However, inside himself that day, he felt torn, tormented – fighting the angry sounds of the rebellious students that thundered in his ears. He could not believe that these were the same seemingly passive students that he had beaten up daily just up to a few moments before, getting them to mindlessly memorise the dates of White colonial history: 1652 (the arrival of Jan Van Riebeeck), 1795 and 1803 (the arrival and settlement of the British settlers), 1899 (the Anglo Boer War), 1910 (the founding of the White South African Union – a truce between the English and the Afrikaners), and momentous 1948 (the coming to power of the White Afrikaner Nationalist Party in South Africa) - and all those other trivial dates of White colonial history in South Africa. They were important and significant dates in the school history textbooks, weren't they? He challenged his own mind with this question as he sat with his head between his knees, in the corner. It suddenly troubled him that the student leaders referred to the Bastille Day of 1789 when they spoke over the loudspeaker. They seemed to know more than him, more than what the apartheid school inspectors and books said he should teach them. He was just a page ahead of them everyday. It bothered him that they used their history lessons for the purposes of fighting the boere. He did not understand it. Mr. Abdul debated with himself. Cheeky, rowdy students! Arrogant twits! He had always believed that his job was about teaching the students about the "real facts" of South Africa's history. That in order to avoid the Island, John Voster Square, and Pretoria, these facts were to be underlined in the dull history textbooks and his job was also to get the rowdy, unmanageable students to remember the damn facts and to cane them until they could master them! That is how things worked when he was at school; it was mindless, but you did it to know your place in apartheid. In this way, he satisfied the school inspector and even the headmaster. So, yes, he reassured himself, it was about remembering the countless dates and names of the Dutch colonist Jan Van Riebeeck, the British colonist Sir George Grey, the British imperialist icon Cecil John Rhodes, and the Afrikaner icon Paul Kruger. They ought to *know* their history as "Coloureds", shouldn't they? If not, then they ought at least to appreciate the need to be interested in that history. If not, then they risked remaining rowdy, unmanageable, aimless, ignorant Coloureds. As these thoughts about decency ran through his confused mind, he pulled his jacket into place, re-buttoned it, and wiped the fluff from his tweed trousers.

He was telling himself many things that morning: "Must look decent. Must be a decent Coloured professional. Not like the drunken ones; not a hopeless, pathetic, alcoholic Coloured teacher." No, in his mind he wanted to be different. At that moment, he did not choose to speak to the rest of the staff. He only had labels in his mind for them: alcoholics, anarchists, communists, *hotnotte, and Boesmanne.* Mr. Abdul comforted himself with the self-assurance that he was trying to teach the Cape Coloured children decency, of becoming someone in this world – even if he was indeed still struggling to become a "someone", more than just a "Cape Malay", an "Other Coloured", as it said in his identity book.

By eleven o'clock that morning several schools in the area had joined the mass march through the Coloured township of Forest Hill in support of the students in Soweto. The police helicopters spotted a black wave of thousands of students as they headed for the parade in the city. The student leaders led the forced occupation of the closest railway station. The children pushed the ticket officers and railway police out of the way. They hijacked all the carriages, both the Whites-only and those for non-Whites. There was no colour bar that day. The students had taken over Cape Town. By the time the youth had reached Cape Town station and the Grand Parade, the full army had gathered on the parade on their trucks with rifles, whips, and fierce Alsatian dogs. They deceptively allowed the students to gather in their masses, as the students defiantly sang *"We shall not be moved!"* shouting the defiant, *"Amandla! Ngawethu!"* intermittently. There were thousands of schoolchildren in the parade that day. Within two minutes of gathering in their hundreds from schools all over Cape Town, the army with their rifles and whips and dogs moved closer on to the thousands of protesting children and youth. "You have two minutes to disperse!" came the announcement over the loudspeaker of the police in a flat Afrikaner English accent. However, before the students could even run, the police and army started to attack, pelting young bodies with whips and rubber bullets. They let the Alsatian dogs lose on screaming, frightful children, some as young as twelve years old. Youth were kicked to the ground, the dogs tearing out young flesh, whips aimed for young breasts and faces, leaving scars still shown to loved ones today as evidence of that heroic day when the youth of Cape Town took to the streets to fight apartheid. In the horror and fear of the moment, friends split, brothers and sisters split, and comrades split, each running for himself, herself. The police blocked the entrance to Cape Town station and cowardly cornered some of the youth in the back streets, sporadically shooting with live ammunition. This was a cruel, calculated move. The police had surprised the students.

Children jumped fences in White suburbs, and ran down unknown streets in White suburbs for miles on end through washing lines draped with wet clothing, more washing lines, more fierce dogs, more Alsatians, even jumping over cars, as adrenalin and more adrenalin pumped the fear through their arteries. African domestic workers in White suburbs hid some in servant's quarters. It was a frightful day. The country was shocked into reality.

Like many of her friends, Tumelo returned home bitterly disappointed, disillusioned, and frustrated. She was there marching for Uncle Thaba more than anyone or anything else, but this was cut short. She wanted to fight for his dignity as a human being. To the children, the police looked evil in their blue uniforms, like in pictures from Nazi Germany. Apartheid was a powerful military force; this, the children now realised. The apartheid regime did not see them as innocent young ones who needed protection. The children and their parents realised that day that the police would kill them without a thought. They realised that they were like child soldiers in a war, and that the struggle had to be carefully planned. There was a lot to be done. Apartheid was not going to be toppled in one day. As students, they got this message loud and clear.

It was a sombre, quiet, grey, wet day the following morning at Forest High. Mr. Hofman called an assembly of all the students and teachers. The student leaders protested at his office, demanding an opportunity to address the school. After some tough negotiation and resistance, Mr. Hofman finally gave in. Now the students were even more restless, more angry – urging their leaders with boisterous Mozambican and South American revolutionary chants of *"Aluta Continua!"* "The struggle continues!"

Mr. Hofman walked forward, stood on the small wooden podium, struggling to balance himself. "Enough is enough! Children, you have learned your lesson yesterday. There is no place for foolish anarchism at Forest High. There are *agent provocateurs* planted amongst you! Adults who are too cowardly to take up the struggle themselves, and who push the children to face the barrel of the gun; they do not want to face the bullets themselves! They are cowards, I am telling you! Your parents should be warned about them, this new danger in our schools. We need peaceful negotiation, decent talks like gentlemen – that will bring down this evil system; not marches, not protests in streets, not hijackings of trains – those are the ways of the anarchists! From today, I shall see that there is order at Forest High! Anarchy shall not succeed to reign here. I will make sure my children are safe. Is that clear, Shafiek, Rafik, and Alfredo?!"

He continued shouting and looked angrily in the direction of the student leaders. Then he continued, "There is no place for terrorism at my school! This is not a circus! This is a place of serious education, as our motto reads *'Forward and Upward!'*" His mouth foamed.

The student leaders ignored Mr. Hofman and what he said. With their faces covered with the scarves to avoid being identified by the security police who parked outside the school in white Volkswagen Beetles, they seized the opportunity to address the students. "Order, comrades! Order! We must be disciplined. The struggle commands discipline. We saw yesterday what it would take to take on the apartheid state. Many of our comrades have been beaten up so badly they could not make it to school today. Some are in the hospital; others are in hiding. The security police are now out to get our leaders. We must be brave and strong. We have to take one step back in order to take two steps forward, like in the Russian revolution of 1905. Do you understand?" "Yeah!!" they roared in agreement like young lions. The police in the Volkswagen Beetles sat through it all, taking copious notes of everything that was said over the school's loud speakers, and recording the names of the young orators.

The security police started to routinely come around to Forest High School and all other schools on the Cape Flats in the weeks and months that followed, paying regular visits to school heads for lists of names of the *opstokers*, the instigators - both teachers and students as the suspects. Mr. Hofman was now under increasing pressure to collaborate with them, but he still resisted. The Student Representative Councils at schools particularly were targeted for weeding out "communist activities" under the much feared Suppression of Communism Act in South Africa. People, children, and students living in the townships got used to the ubiquitous presence of the security police in Hitler's little white wagons, and did not take much notice of them. They became part of the daily life of living and fighting in the township under apartheid.

Within one week of that fateful day in Soweto, 176 people were killed, mostly schoolchildren. South Africa's apartheid regime came under international spotlight. Schools, post offices, libraries, and magistrates courts were set alight by children and Black people across the country in the angry protests that followed for weeks and months. Some towns looked like deserted ghost towns. There were boycotts not only at schools, but also at colleges and universities. African and Coloured youth were standing together as one, against the Afrikaner Nazi enemy.

Hector was not the only young victim. Police dockets in the Cape read: Noel Adriaanse, 13 years, shot through head; Lawrence Buba 14 years, shot; Shaheed Jacobs, 15 years, shot; Alfred Finch, 15 years, shot, Godfrey Khambule, 12 years shot, Dominic Letleka, 4 years, Sandra Pieters 12 years; an endless list of atrocities against the children of South Africa:

Run over by police car.

Shot in back at corner of Darling Street.

Shot through intestines.

The killings continued into Christmas and the rest of the Festive Season of 1976, spilling over violently into 1977. Thousands of youth of all colours fled South Africa to join the ANC underground, in its armed military wing *Umkhonto we Sizwe*, Spear of the Nation. The Soweto uprising had spread to the entire country within 15 months. A year later, the class of 1976 returned, and crossed the borders as armed guerrillas with AK47 rifles in hand. Within two years, 4,000 new recruits were trained in Libya, Angola, and Tanzania.

Through all of this, Tumelo had to grow up quickly and imagine herself as an adult with serious tasks ahead to help overthrow an evil system. She did not date, dress up, or play. She gave up her many friends, as they were all subject to suspicion (you were either for or against the struggle). She imagined herself to be a soldier and dressed in blue overalls. She gave up laughter, trivial teenage conversation, movies, disco, and even pop music. She thought of her body and mind as functional objects and matter to serve in favour of the revolution in South Africa.

Chapter 11
There's Rosemary;
That's for Remembrance

Two newcomers arrived at the school in early 1977. Mr. Benjamen, was a dark young man who wore dark sunglasses even on rainy days. He wore his hair in a huge afro and looked as if he hailed from East Africa, with his lean frame and black, red, and green coloured African shirts. He told the students that he worked for the then-banned and underground African National Congress. Ms. Nkosi was tall and dark and moved around the place like lightning in her traditional colourful Ndebele African fabrics and cloths; her eyes constantly surveyed the students and staff for possible spies. She seemed always in a hurry and had an impatience about her. Everybody spoke of her as "brilliant", and she seemed bored with the routine of school lessons. Word got around very quickly that Ms. Nkosi was a close friend of the feared and politically astute Black Consciousness leader, Steve Bantu Biko, and everybody understood then why she seemed constantly suspicious and on edge.

The two newcomers, who were appointed by Mr. Hofman to teach his children, did not hesitate to declare their ideological position in their very first encounter with the students. "We have joined the school as teachers to recruit cadres for the revolution in South Africa. We make no bones about this intention. We have nothing to lose in telling you the truth of why we are at this school."

By then, Mozambique had gained freedom under Samora Machel in 1975. The Peoples Movement for Liberation in Angola took power in the same year. At the time, activist students and teachers in South Africa were harassed and arrested under The Suppression of Communism Act out of fear of the revolution spreading further across into the country. Mr. Benjamen and Ms. Nkosi held open meetings with Shafiek, Rafiq, and Alfredo every lunch break and every afternoon to discuss the struggle and the options available for the course of struggle in South Africa. Sometimes Mr. Hofman would march in, pretending that he was looking for an errant teacher or child, and just walk out again, saluting as if he was still in the army. The teachers and students knew he was not serious with his threats, and spoke politics openly in his presence.

The school's library, where such political meetings took place, was poor in resources and was comprised of two large apartheid maps of South Africa and its "independent" homelands. There was also a torn world map hanging askew on the library wall, its labels hardly readable. This library had been started in the 1950s, but only had a set of encyclopaedias donated to the school in the 1960s and a huge Afrikaans dictionary explaining the meaning of racist words such as *Kleurlinge, Kaffirs,* and *Blankes* – the latter meaning "pure" and "blank" as in "unspoilt" - and the notorious shameful idiomatic expressions of Coloured teachers as "pathological alcoholics". The student leaders avoided reading the humiliating apartheid map with its demarcation of South Africa into four White-ruled provinces and its small spots of land, marked in black for the African homelands. The students instead turned their minds to pertinent political questions of the day.

New African freedom songs were sung at school assemblies and protest rallies in local civic halls. Many sounded like gospel music, such as *"We are marching in the light of God, We are marching in the light of God."* American gospel songs talking about freedom from slavery were popular: *"Oh freedom, Oh freedom, Oh freedom over me!"*

Tumelo spent her breaks in the library, where she overheard regular debates amongst the now leading three revolutionary teachers at the school about what the very best way forward would be for the revolution in South Africa.

Mr. Torres argued with Ms. Nkosi that gospel hymns were not going to help them out of their oppression. "The slaves in America sang songs forever on the plantations. That *alone* did not bring them their freedom. We must do something more serious than teaching the children to sing..."

"Such as take up AK 47s?" Ms. Nkosi challenged. She quietly summed up that Mr. Torres was very radical in theory, but not steeled for the armed struggle. "Be real. We are in schools, working with the children, preparing them for revolution. We must educate them for the revolution!"

"Who says taking up arms is *not* education?" she protested fiercely.

"We can't get the children to fight the army of the boers. That is political suicide! The most important thing is to get them to read and to understand how capitalism and racism work."

Within the first few weeks of her arrival, Ms. Nkosi had observed Mr. Torres' activities with the student with a keen interest. She was curious to find out how far his political commitment could be pushed. "The students said you gave them copies of *Roots* to read. They learned a lot about slavery and oppression in there, and found meaning in it for their own lives. But we certainly need more than handing out copies of *Roots!*"

Mr. Torres also had very definite views about religion and the church, which he often shared loudly. "*Roots* is just a start. They would have to ask the questions about the revolts, about radical powerful leaders like Toussaint Louverture and the revolution in Haiti. Then we are getting there. Gospel hymns are not the answer. How are we going to challenge racism, for example?"

However, for Ms. Nkosi, life and the struggle was much more of a rich tapestry. "I beg to differ. The Black gospel spirituals played very powerful roles in setting the slaves in America free. For example, *Swing Low, Sweet Chariot*. I teach the students that song. I tell them to sing it as if they are in the dark of night, to sing it like a revolutionary whisper. Because this was a song that sent the message from slave to slave that the coast was clear and that the time to escape had come. These were not just simple songs, they had powerful freedom meanings about the Underground Railroad that led to freedom. Did you know that about 100,000 people escaped slavery in America via the Underground Railroad? How many of these students know about Black women like Harriet Tubman who led this important revolutionary process for Black people?"

She then walked closely up to where Mr. Torres was sitting. The faint scent of her sandalwood perfume lingered over him in the dusty library with its many empty bookshelves. She teasingly hummed and sang softly into his ears, "*Swing low, sweet chariot,*

Coming for to carry me home, ...If you get there before I do, ...Tell all my friends I'm coming too.."

Mr. Torres blushed with discomfort at the nearness of her whisper in his ear and the political challenge she had dared to put to him in a most unusual way, which he did not know how to counter. However, Mr. Torres was determined to turn every argument to his advantage, "Yes, I have read all about it...but we can't escape apartheid in the way that the American slaves could escape the plantations. It is what we live. Where do we escape to? Into the sea? What we can teach the youth about the Underground Railroad is the use of secret codes that will become useful when they organise for the revolution. Our Underground Railroad will be something else – a network of powerful revolutionary activity across South Africa; of distributing banned reading material and using codes for their hiding places and titles. That is what we can learn from the slave resistance on the plantations...Our youth should know that race is a myth. Everyone is equal. There is only *one* humanity."

She hit back as she pulled her beautiful blue and yellow African turban into place with her elegant long fingers and long red nails. "But it is important for them to be *proud* to be *Black!*"

"Yes, but being proud to be Black must not mean a new sense of superiority or nationalism. There is nothing like a *pure* Black race or a *pure* White race."

"No, Mr. Torres, I see it a little different to you. Our children have been damaged like our ancestors since the days of slavery to think of their bodies and minds as inferior and of Whites as superior! This has caused *huge* damage in Coloured families on the Cape Flats. You know it yourself! Come on!" She teased and laughed at him.

"You mean *so-called* Coloured. We do not accept the racist terms that apartheid has given us."

"Yes, *so-called*. But I am a *Black conscious* person; there is really only *Black* and *White*. We should not complicate the revolutionary argument with so-called this and that."

Mr. Torres dismissed her teasing and spoke with a terse tone. "But the struggle is deeper. To learn about the new anatomy of equality of the body is also to learn about colonialism, slavery, and capitalism. Apartheid thrives and feeds on myths about bodies – yes – but *also* on capitalism, on exploitation. It is important to point out that people were not slaves as if born into it and made for it; they were people put into a certain economic relationship with others."

Ms. Nkosi remained persistent about the significance of race in the debate, "Agreed, and for that reason, our reality is that which Steve Biko writes about, not about the peasants in France or the workers in Russia some century or two ago, although there is some relevance in economic terms."

Mr. Torres conceded, "Yes, it is about the issues that Steve Biko addresses about being proud to be Black, but it is also more serious than that. Point is, this youth must realise that they have a huge task. The history of the country has to be rewritten, and they are important agents for that process. "

Ms. Nkosi snapped at this, "You mean the true history of this country still needs to be written..."

Mr. Torres knew that many teachers at Forest High had a bit of a drinking problem, and he played on it to make his case in the presence of the students. "We must teach them to think critically about their own identity as so-called Coloureds. Why should they choose not to drown themselves in alcohol? We must teach them that alcohol was used by Jan Van Riebeeck to enslave the so-called Coloured people at the Cape to make them dependent on the Dutch; to make them feel they are inferior and to encourage self loathing. The same in America, alcohol was part of the Slave Codes. Like the slaves at the Cape, people who were slaves had to have a pass and could not buy or own drink unless allowed by the slave master. But the African slaves *resisted* getting drunk. They *chose* not to become alcoholics. They had pride as enslaved African people and saw alcohol as a form of degradation and exploitation. They did not buy into the alcoholic culture as an escape into freedom. Like Van Riebeeck, the slave masters on the plantations promoted alcohol consumption during harvest time and holidays. Slaves were given large volumes of cheap wine, which they resisted, unlike so-called Coloured people who still choose to consume large volumes of this poisonous alcohol since the days of slavery at the Cape. "

Ms. Nkosi concurred, "Yes, it makes sense – because when slaves are drunk, they cannot organise a revolt, nor escape, nor be organised. Similarly, when Coloureds are drunk, they cannot organise a revolution."

Mr. Torres reiterated, "The youth of today who are the descendants of the slaves must understand that a sober critical mass is powerful because alcohol dependency of a people serves capitalism and racism; they need to keep Black people intoxicated. The plantation slaves did not become slaves of the bottle. We must free ourselves of the ghost of slave and slave master. Resisting alcohol is one way."

Ms. Nkosi suggested some further readings that she had access to through the Black Consciousness Movement to be distributed amongst the students. The teachers and the student leaders decided that the SRC should act as a reading and political cell which would recruit students to the course of liberation. This would be the strategy to recruit new cadres in politics and literature, to understand not only apartheid, but also the struggle of all oppressed and exploited people in the world at large.

Mr. Benjamen was not intimidated by Mr. Torres' frequent remarks on alcoholism and "so-called Coloureds". "Form art, film societies, and debating societies", he suggested, "to teach the youth that our revolution has much more in common with the liberation in Mozambique than with France of 1789 or with Russia of 1917." In fact, according to Mr. Benjamen, "South Africa's struggle had more in common with the Haitian revolution under Francois-Dominique Toussaint Louverture in 1791 than the fall of the Bastille in 1789." "It was about *perspective*", he added. "Let's teach them about the writings of Frantz Fanon and Amilcar Cabral, on how to *make* a revolution happen, on how to counter colonialism in all its forms, especially on a psychological level. We have to look at the *reality* of the South African struggle. We have to be *pragmatists*, not theorists. These are working class kids. Let's talk about that, and organize reading for the *laaities*, (youth) on what is *relevant* to their *own experiences and perspectives*. Perhaps we should ask *them* to set the agenda?"

Mr. Torres cleared his throat, rubbed his beard, as all great revolutionaries intellectual men of that time were expected to do, and responded with a kind of conviction which was not seen in many of his contemporaries. "We must guard against parochial nationalist thinking. The South African struggle is integral to the *internationalist* struggle, which means it is more than just about combating colonialism or racism for that matter. The core issues remain *class, race, and gender*. And I do concede that Fanon and Cabral are useful in locating the practical relevance of revolution and the liberation movements, but the struggle in South Africa is also about how we have to tackle global capitalism and imperialism in their many forms. We cannot afford a populist united front led by an elite Black middle class to whom freedom means something very different than to the worker in the mines and on the factory floor. We must prepare the youth to become revolutionary leaders in the trade union movement, in the mines, in the factories, in the classrooms, at university, in the schools..."

Ms. Nkosi interjected emphatically, "I disagree with both of you! You both seem sadly influenced by White liberal politics. Have you ever thought of the intellectual origin of all these ideas about class struggle that you have come to own – they come from European intellectual thought! I am strongly committed to a free *Azania*, a Black conscious Azania. We are Africans and must come up with our own ideas of freedom and our own terminologies. Only then will we be free! It starts with the mind – we must take forward the Africanist ideas put forward by Kwame Nkrumah of Ghana. "

Mr. Benjamen showed his displeasure, "Azania is not an African name; it comes from Roman times, from the Arabs and the Greeks...even the word 'Africa' is not from the people of the continent...lets not argue about polemics; lets talk struggle..."

Ms. Nkosi's preoccupation with Africa and the dismissal of the struggles in the wider world really irritated Mr. Torres. He had more interest in the class struggles in Russia, France, South America, and Cuba.

As a student, Tumelo witnessed many a debate like this in the empty room that was known as "the school library", continuing every break and every afternoon without fail. She started to gain confidence as she read more – banned ANC literature, banned PAC literature, banned English literature, inspirational works and novels such as Adam Smith's *The Wealth of Nations*, George Orwell's *Animal Farm*, *Marxism for Beginners*, *Trotsky for Beginners*, *Capitalism for Beginners*, *Socialism for Beginners*, *Communism for Beginners*, *Das Kapital*, *The Communist Manifesto*, Eskia Mphahlele's *Down Second Avenue*, Richard Rive's *Buckingham Palace*, Biko's *I write what I like*, Eddie Roux's *Time Longer than Rope*, the works of Njabulo Ndebele, Wally Serote's *To every birth its blood*, Bessie Head's *When Rain Clouds Gather*, and the international Trotskyist journals such as *The International Viewpoint*. She listened to the music of exiled musicians, such as Abdullah Ibrahim, Miriam Makeba, and Hugh Masekela, and to the lyrics written by the executed struggle hero that was hanged in Pretoria in the 1960s, Vuyisili Mini.

Mr. Torres co-ordinated the underground reading group at the school and distributed the books clandestinely to recruits amongst the young students. Code names were used like in the Underground Railroad on the slave plantations. "A friend of a friend sent you this book", meant that the book was smuggled from outside South Africa and was banned. The coded message meant that you had to read it in a secret place such as on the beach, on the mountains, or in the bush, and not talk about the content loosely to just anybody. The students devoured the political literature like locusts devour crops during a plague.

Soon, the reading circles were extended to hikes in the Cedarberg Mountains and to "film evenings" on Sundays in a school hall in the nearby former middle-class Coloured suburb of Newlands, where Tumelo's aunt had grown up. Newlands was a favourite gathering place for some Coloured teacher intellectuals and also for the Trotskyites. Here, the recruits from Forest High met weekly with other comrades for film viewing, debates and discussions on the liberation of slaves in America, on the oppressed in Nicaragua, Chile, Zimbabwe, Cuba, Palestine, and whatever popped up in current affairs in the newspapers and on the radio for that week. The students spread tips on how to tune into the banned Freedom Radio, for which South Africans could be jailed for up to eight years if caught. "This is radio freedom, the voice of the African National Congress and its military wing Umkhonto we Sizwe..."

The meetings in the now declared Whites-only Newlands were punctual and regularly held, and attended by revolutionary intellectuals of all colours and backgrounds – workers, professors, students, scholars, and teachers. Here, students also learned to recite Bertolt Brecht's *A Worker Reads History, about so many questions.* Or the students would amongst themselves discuss a bit of the relevance of Shakespeare, and the familiar syndrome found in: *Othello, the Moor of Venice...Even now, now, very now, an old black ram is tupping your white ewe...*Debates and discussion continued until late into the night, during summer and relentlessly cold and stormy winters. The next day, the students would all be back at school in their uniforms and in their desks - punctual and alert and determined to overthrow the system. They dismissed their textbooks and boycotted apolitical teachers and lessons, creating their own education and library instead.

From the reading and film groups, they were groomed to infiltrate trade unions, universities, schools, different political organizations, and civic bodies. Suspicious Afrikaner White men in long black coats sat in regularly and conspicuously on the intellectual discussions in Newlands. They participated enthusiastically with their notorious accents in talks on Shakespeare and the work of Bertolt Brecht. They posed as friendly, interested members of the audience who even dared to ask questions pertaining to the debates at hand, such as what is the difference between a two stage revolution and a permanent revolution? They enjoyed the tea and scones served afterwards by the wives of the Trotskyite comrades, and audaciously flirted with the women who attended the lectures, "And so what brings a lovely lady like you here on a cold wintry night to learn about this communism business? Are you a Trotskyist or a Leninist?"

Soon, Shafik and Alfredo were the leading young intellectuals in these sessions, presenting papers on topics such as "The National Question", "Whither South Africa?" and "The Balkanization of South Africa".

Schools on the Cape Flats and in other parts of the country erupted in anger with the announcement of the murder of the Black medical doctor and Black Counsciousness leader Steve Biko by the apartheid police on 12 September 1977. He was already the forty-fifth person who had died in police custody during detention without trial, which was introduced in 1963. There was sadness, anger, a mass meeting, and lengthy discussions on the appropriate and most effective ways in which to topple apartheid at Forest High as a cautious, yet undoubtedly angry response to his death. Mr. Torres argued that the brutal murder of Steve Biko by the apartheid regime showed that what the enemy feared most were ideas and questioning; that Steve Biko's death bore testimony to intellectual thought and questioning as the effective antidote for apartheid. He comforted the angry, questioning student leadership who gathered in their dozens in the school library to talk about the murder of Steve Biko, by explaining to them that ideas live on forever; that you can kill the person, but not the ideas, "Be rest assured that Steve Biko will live on forever in the minds of many South Africans! That is what really matters at the end of the day! The apartheid government did not kill the *ideas* of Steve Biko!"

"The most potent weapon in the hands of the oppressor is the mind of the oppressed." After the murder of Steve Biko, Ms. Nkosi withdrew from the regular political discussions in the library. She was visibly shattered. Her close friend had been murdered by the apartheid police. She called the students together in the library on the afternoon of hearing the sad news; her eyes were red and swollen. She was nursing her loss and read some quotations from his work, *"Apartheid is evil…Nothing can justify the arrogant assumption that a clique of foreigners has the right to decide on the lives of the majority."* She continued, *"In time, we shall be in a position to bestow on South Africa the greatest possible gift – a more human face. It is better to die for an idea that will live, than to live for an idea that will die."* Some of the students wept quietly, others clenched their fists tightly. The students observed a moment of silence and then quietly sang the poignant *Senzenina*, a Zulu song of freedom: *"What have we done? What have we done? Our sin is that we are poor, Our sin is that we are black. They are killing us. Let Africa return."* After which, they quietly dispersed to go home, with increased resolve and resilience to topple the racist regime.

When she arrived home, Tumelo went to lie on her bed and cried for Uncle Thaba, as a Black man who had lost his dignity, and as a human being fearing the pass laws. She saw Uncle Thaba in Steve Biko's face, large on the cover page of the local newspaper. She dreamed of Uncle Thaba standing on the other side of the Vlei on the water behind the reeds where they swam as children near the hippos and flamingoes. In the dream, he waved at her. The following day, she asked Mr. Torres, "How long do you think we'd have to walk this road to get to the other side?" He looked at her puzzled, because he did not know from where her question came. His answer seemed misguided and pedantic, "Freedom is a relative concept, Tumelo. A more appropriate angle to that question would be: freedom from *what*? Dogma is dangerous; avoid revolutionary rhetoric at all cost. It closes the mind to a variety of possibilities." Not waiting for her to explain, Mr. Torres pushed the play button on his cassette in the car, and proceeded to play the song of Pete Seeger's, *Little boxes.*

They did not discuss her question any further, and drove home in silence.

Ms. Nkosi did not speak much for weeks after Biko's death, and retreated in silence to her classroom at intervals and in the afternoon after school, knowing perhaps that the police were then also on her trail. Mr. Benjamen was philosophical and argued that

163

so many South Africans were already dying across the borders in their fight against the apartheid army, but conceded that Biko was an important martyr, "South Africa needs martyrs for the revolution; lives *have* to be sacrificed. In fact, South Africans are engaged in a military war with the enemy. Why are our students so shocked?" His militancy was apparent, "In fact, there are more lives than Biko's to be sacrificed, and we have to become resilient young soldiers of the revolution – only then would we do justice to the memory of the 69 people killed at Sharpeville in 1960, and all the children killed in 1976. Steve Biko is a symbol of resistance. We have to fight for Biko's memory."

South African society and its struggle were far too complex for a race struggle only, and many activists realised that. Mr. Benjamen always had an attentive audience, and the students erupted spontaneously with clenched fists raised above their heads, whenever he spoke, *"Amandla! Ngawethu!"*

The revolutionary teachers were not only South African. Ms. Jansen, a blond, leftist, bohemian-type recent arrival at Forest High hailed from Paris. She wore colourful rags like a 1960's hippie, and innocently sat wide-legged on a high chair in front of the class of bored adolescent boys and girls. She told them about Steve Biko's journalist friend, Donald Woods, and the anti-apartheid movement in London – a place she pointed out with a stick on the torn map of Europe in the library. There was no map of Africa. She hummed with eyes closed and played her guitar, singing American liberation songs for hours on end. The students gossiped that she smoked cannabis at school, but they soon grew to respect her even though she was White, as they discovered that she was a great teacher, and politically committed to end apartheid. What really freaked out the students and the teachers was that she spoke fluent Zulu, and insisted that the students break the apartheid laws to visit her at her home in the Whites-only suburb in the city centre. They never took the invitation seriously, because the police vans would have them picked up if they had done so. The boys masturbated at the back of the class while the unaware Ms. Jansen sat there singing, in a short dress, and playing her guitar with her eyes closed and with her legs wide open. One of the boys at the back daringly shouted, "Ms. Jansen has a big fat *poes* (fanny) and she is looking for a *naai (screw)*!" In the chaos and noise, Ms. Jansen threw her guitar on the table and stormed out of the classroom. She returned a few minutes later, still fuming, with a flabbergasted noisy Mr. Hofman on her heels. The students cowered, waiting for the wrath of his familiar long cane. However, instead, Mr. Hofman surprised them. He stood there and started to wail loudly. He sobbed, "Are we the people of Sodom and Gamorrah, only knowing about the evil tongue that insults women's anatomy? My lost children...my poor children... What have we done?! We must not look back, and turn into pillars of salt...We are paying for the sins of our fathers...!"

Then he suddenly stopped wailing, turned to Ms Jansen and nodded his head in respect, "Thank you, Lady..."

Then he left quietly, with his head bowed and his hands clasped like a spiritual man in prayer. The children and Ms. Jansen were now equally baffled.

Amongst poor people on the Cape Flats, the traditional obsession with the body and vulgarity of genitals did not only take on the form of swearing, but also as a compulsive need to be talking about the dis-ease within the various bodily organs. Men and women always had sad stories to tell about their various *dis-eased* (not at ease) anatomies. Social conversations easily drifted into discussion of bodily organs, and everyone seemed obsessed with diseases in their bodies, telling their own stories of this disease and that disease; nobody listened. The body was also spoken about in a very interesting way, almost as a form of reclamation. For example, instead of, "I have an infection in my chest", they'd say, "I *have* a chest", "I *have* a throat", "I *have* a stomach", "I *have* an eye", "I *have* a head", "I *have* a leg", "I *have* an arm", and "I *have* a heart." It was as if Coloured people had to *own* their bodies, *make it theirs*, *reclaim* it, even with dis-ease, and there are competing stories of ailments.

"I have sugar, high blood pressure, and osteoporosis."

"Is that *all* you've got?! I've got sugar, high blood pressure, osteoporosis, a weak heart, kidney stones, cancer, just had a stroke, liver disease..." Part of the process of claiming the body also involved claiming all its organs and all the diseases that exist.

Such a conversation can last hours, about everybody's body in the family, and also about ugliness and about beauty. Much of the swear words originate from the vocabulary of colonial Dutch slave masters, such as *hoer* for whore, *kak* for shit, curse words for mothers' genitals, insults about physical features, and so on.

Ms. Jansen somehow survived the verbal onslaught of the Coloured boys on her body. She offered to teach the students to speak Zulu and Xhosa, but they all found these foreign languages too difficult. Initially, many students did not appreciate her good teaching, because many believed that Whites chose to teach at Coloured and Black schools to benefit from "inconvenience pay". That is, they would be compensated for the inconvenience of having to sit in the same staffroom as their Coloured and Black colleagues, of having to drink from the same cups and taps, for using the same toilet without the "Whites-only" sign, and of having to teach Coloured and Black children. Most "Whities" at Coloured and Black schools were therefore perhaps misunderstood, and dismissively treated by both staff and students as "opportunistic mercenaries", as police spies, or as misguided hippies from England who needed to fund their drug and substance addiction habits. If they were against apartheid, they had to work really hard to prove this to the students.

When Ms. Jansen sort of matter-of-factly spoke about "Coloureds", then a defiant chorus would come from the boys and girls, "*so-called,* Ms. Jansen!" Ms. Jansen lost her temper one day as another chorus of *"so-called"* came her way, and shouted, "Fuck *so-called*!" The students went silent, shocked that an English hippie dared to take them on over the issue of their own identity. They were doing what Mr. Torres had taught them, that they were not "Coloureds", they were human beings; in fact they were "South Africans". "When anybody calls you a 'Coloured', you correct them and you raise your fingers to show inverted commas, you look them straight in the eye and you say defiantly *'so-called'!"* This is exactly how the students challenged Ms. Jansen that morning. They stared back in defiance at her. In response, she turned her back to write in a huge fat handwriting, the word, *"Freedom"* in white on the chalkboard. Still, they stared at her in anger.

One boy stood up and asked, "What the fuck does that mean to *you*, Ms. Jansen?! What do *you know* about *freedom* in South Africa, Ms. Jansen? You are a privileged White foreigner benefiting from inconvenience pay!" Ms. Jansen was not intimidated. She mumbled something deliberately in Xhosa, knowing full well that most Coloured students and teachers in Cape Town could not speak any Black African language. Even though the African townships were nearby, people were under constant police surveillance and did not integrate across segregated township boundaries. The

African world was far away for Coloured people under apartheid. Therefore, her fluency in Xhosa and Zulu was her trump card, a way in which she got the students to respect her.

Many Coloured people were dislocated from Africa. In most schools, there were maps of Europe, the United States of America, and of South Africa and South West Africa, but *not* of the African continent. Many Coloured families saw themselves as people originating from outside Africa, coming from Europe, Arabia, India, Malaysia, or from Indonesia, or from some obscure exotic islands in the Atlantic or Indian Oceans.

Not everyone was poor in Forest Hill. There were middle-class Coloureds and poor ones, with the latter group more inclined to use a swear word in each sentence.

The Harvey family was a large middle-class Cape Flats family whose children also attended Forest High. They stood out in the community because they were relatively wealthy and employed dozens of servants and "houseboys", often rural African women and men. Mr. Harvey was of the first "Coloureds" in Forest Hill to have bought a brand new Mercedes Benz in the 1970s. He looked like a handsome Spanish señor, and constantly and mischievously twisted his large moustache. With his greasy, sleek, wet, black hair wiped to the back, he could also pose as a stern-looking man with a gun on his hip. At that time in South Africa, he was a rare sight of opulence in his community. The Harvey family stood out in many ways. Everybody spoke and knew of their wealth, of Mr. Harvey' successful business as a builder, of his Mercedez Benz into which he squeezed all his thirteen children and his large Indonesian looking wife, dressed in their Sunday best when they went to church. He spoke with a loud voice, marched on the yard commanding all and sundry (including the dogs, chickens, and cats) and drove down the roads of Forest Hill in the style of an affluent man. He always drove at a slow pace down the avenues of the township, as if in a funeral procession in his gold-coloured Mercedez Benz, with its fine cream-coloured leather seats, while he smoked his cigars with his window down and his right arm leaning on the rolled down window. He was admired for his immaculate dress, his classy dark suits, and dark sunglasses, like a Mafia boss. The local White police were in awe of him and treated him with respect. They did not bother to question the many visitations to his property by the White business men. Sometimes the boere visited his yard in their gray vans to just check if everything was in order; that there was no breaking of the Immorality Act since Mr. Harvey had pretty young daughters. The children and local gangsters knew of him and feared his thunderous voice, his gun, his wealthy power, and his guts to shoot at any given instant. Many of his clients were wealthy White Europeans who came to settle in Cape Town. His huge residence with its many outside buildings was guarded by Rotweillers. A proud family man, he protected his Javanese looking six daughters like a hawk, and kept the wandering eyes of the visiting German male clients in check when they had grown into sultry looking young teenage girls. "Anybody who wants to fuck with my daughters will have their balls blown to pieces!" It was amusing to watch the huge confident White German men cowering at such threats from a Coloured man during apartheid. Mrs. Harvey would proudly invite her White visitors in for tea. "Come in for tea sirs, and you may even join us for dinner if you want to. We have plenty." The Harvey family wittingly made all White people visiting for business feel small and inferior. The daughters oozed confidence, and did not patronise any person visiting their father's empire – not even White people. Their house was large and sophisticated in the Western sense of the word: antique furniture, huge mirrors, souvenirs from all over the world, expensive Isfahan mats, original oil paintings on canvas, and antique crockery and cutlery. Mrs. Harvey had her own little black antique chair in the corner of the sitting room from where she could watch the neighbours passing by while she called on her numerous African servants to serve on her. They brought her tea and scones, oysters and olives, biscuits, and a variety of rich cheeses. She had a fine taste for food, comfort, and luxury. Mr. Harvey enjoyed indulging and spoiling his wife. He boasted with her at his arm, as his trophy wife at the Coloureds-only church in the white neighbourhood – dressed in expensive jewellery and fine silk and embroidered outfits that she brought back from their numerous holidays to the Cayman Islands, Antigua, Monserrat, Portofino, Monte Carlo, the Nile, London, and Paris. They brought back colourful stories and photographs of vacationing with White people abroad, and showed these off at their frequent dinners for their fellow parishioners and their friends. The male teachers of Forest High knew of the power and status of Mr. Harvey, and carefully stayed away from his daughters with their bronze African skins, their striking Filipino eyes, and their noticeable Irish freckles. They resembled the interesting genetic mixture of people from Africa, Asia, and Europe. Their father encouraged them to know that they came from the ancestors of the East, from the land of the princesses, from Javanese royalty who were brought to the Cape as enslaved and captured people of the Dutch East India Company in the seventeenth century.

Actually, the truth is, like most Coloured people, they really did not know where they came from because much of their family history was probably wiped out in the renaming process when slaves arrived at the Cape. The first act of colonization was to strip slaves of their names and to give them new Dutch names, making it difficult for them to pass on the full knowledge and truthfulness of who they were and where they came from. As time passed on, it eventually became a shame to remember that you came from enslaved people. So, like most people, as the years passed and generations died out, they imagined their own history, of how it was possibly comprised. Therefore, many Cape Coloured families perhaps took comfort in the fact that they could somehow try to trace their family origins through looking in the mirror and at pictures in the *National Geographic* magazines bought for five cents at township churches and community bazaars. However, perhaps there was truth in how Mr. Harvey told his story, of being descendant of the captured princes of the East.

Mrs. Harvey always carried with her a photograph of her great grandfather, an Indonesian-looking man, to prove that her roots were from the East, not from Africa. "You can still see the traces of royalty in our eyes, in our walk, in our long, thick, curly hair."

Mr. Harvey had a generous side for hungry children in the neighbourhood. He would get the servants to make sandwiches and colourful fizzy drinks of red, green, and orange sold in little glass bottles in cheap wooden cases from the Muslim man's truck on a Saturday. The children were called into the yard, where he arranged for them to sit and have a meal. They would feverishly bite into the sandwiches, which they only saw in magazines that they picked up from dump heaps in the veld. In their minds, this was "White people's food"; lettuce, cucumber, tomato, gherkin, and ham or chicken on thick slices of freshly-baked white bread. Mr. Harvey laughed heartily as the hungry children ate. On hot summer days, he would take delight in sitting on his veranda, the *stoep*, with a whip in his hand in the shade of their monstrous oak tree, twisting with the other hand the long ends of his generous moustache, interrogating all those who passed by. "Hey, you! What are you doing for a living? Don't behave like the hotnots, the vagrants, the no-good-for-nothings, the skollies. Get yourself a job!" "And you! What happened to your teeth? When are you going to get yourself some dentures?!" "Seems you people want to stay hotnots with no pride or dignity! You want to be like gam!" "Pull up your trousers and pull yourself together; that is why the White people look down on you...because you are like *skollies*, hooligans, gangsters!" "Why must I give you money? I know what you are going to do with it! You are going to the *smokkie* (the shebeen) and get drunk on cheap rotten wine and *dagga.*" His monologue of interrogations would go on and on while his barefooted servants respectfully served him.

The African women servants moved quietly through the large house and on the big yard with their babies tied and wrapped with colourful woollen blankets to their backs, obeying the commands of the daughters and the silent, penetrating stares of the affectionate but stern Mrs. Harvey. They shifted their heavy bodies through the house, doing the ironing, the loads of washing, polishing endlessly for everything to shine, peeling loads of vegetables, preparing whole sheep, turkeys, and chicken for the usual Sunday feast when about 20 regular guests came to share in the family's rare opulence on the Cape Flats. After Sunday lunch, their appetites sated, the regular guests would line up in comfortable chairs in the shade of the oak tree for their Sunday siesta. They would laugh heartily in the heat of the afternoon, sharing jokes and stories, the tears streaming down their cheeks.

The African servants and their babies lived as part of the extended family on the huge yard with the many outside buildings. Nobody knew where their husbands were or where they lived, nor if they were married at all. However, that was South African life at the time, the silence and absence of the African man who was the key target during police raids for passes. Therefore, nobody asked.

Mr. Harvey created his own Empire, his very own villa on the Cape Flats. His family lived a good life in spite of apartheid. Everybody in the neighbourhood whispered with obvious and inevitable envy about the abundance of the Harvey family, about how they would proceed to wake at four o'clock for Sunday afternoon tea when the table would boast a range of at least one dozen mouth watering puddings and cakes, the most expensive nuts and Belgian dark chocolates, pitted dates, caviar, wild salmon, and oysters. It was a known ritual, and one could view the feast from the road through the large windows from no less than three metres away.

The daughters would rush to the door to echo their father's sentiments, prompting the beggars to leave them in peace on a Sunday. "When are you people going to come right?!" After some relentless interrogation about work and laziness and teasing, he would finally call his daughters to feed them. The beggars knew of his big heart, and would beg with persistence, ignoring the insults and stares of the daughters who always protectively lined up behind their proud father at the door.

When regular beggars knocked on the Harvey family's door wishing to share in the indulgences, the African servants would first tease them endlessly, calling them by their nicknames before giving them a plate of food. Many of these nicknames used for Coloureds on the Cape Flats originate from seventeenth century Cape slave society – *Donkie,* the Creole for Mule, *Perd,* the Creole for Horse, and *Beenkop,* the Creole for bonehead as a popular description for a thin Khoisan man. Their favourite word for the Coloured vagrants was *Beenkop.*

Tumelo's friends at school often visited the Harvey family, as they attended the same church that their families attended for decades before the forced removals. In their discussions at school, they learnt that Khoisan people were simply called *Beenkoppe* by the boere, because they believed them to be closer to flora, fauna, and wildlife than to the human species. This belief about the Khoisan people was enforced further by displays of Khoisan models amongst wild animals in the city's museum dioramas. For the boere, Khoisan people served as merely exotic entertainment value, reserved for game parks and nature reserves, such as with the aboriginal people in Australia, and the Native Americans in America. Tumelo once read with shock in a late-nineteenth century geography schoolbook used in England during Queen Victoria's reign - which she found at the local dirt dump near their home where artefacts, ornaments, and books from White homes were regularly dumped - that the Khoisan people, Aboriginal Australians, and Polynesians were a "dying race" of "savages" - her people, the "Hottentot" of the Cape, being "the worst of all savages" in the world.

White people from London and elsewhere, visiting apartheid South Africa, were therefore taken on tourist adventures to see "wildlife and Bushmen". Others were taken on township tours to be shown where the boere "kept" the Coloureds and Africans. Similarly, for a long time, many Coloureds saw African people – those who spoke Xhosa, Sotho, Zulu, and so on – as from "another country", like Uncle Thaba. This was some perception formed through decades of segregation through the bizarre homeland system making people believe they belonged to different separate "nations".

Mrs. Harvey did not give into beggars very easily. She was a woman of a few words and only gave an occasional frank stare to show her displeasure with anything that was going on around her. Her husband was loud and noisy and took delight in giving things to the less fortunate, but she stared and did not suffer fools gladly. Her striking, narrow, Indonesian-looking eyes were a sharp, unambiguous answer to an irritating or annoying question or a request about food and household resources. She had a cutting sense of humour and was particularly worried about South Africa's future should White rule and apartheid come to an end. Like many Coloured people, her biggest fear was that the much feared "*kaffirs*" would one day take over the country. At their regular dinners, the main conversation was about preferring to be ruled by "the devil that you know, than the one you don't know!" As hostess, she would crack up in a joke, talking about how she would never venture to fly in an aeroplane after the end of apartheid. "Did you hear that when the Black man takes over in South Africa one day, they will become our new pilots?!" Everybody would laugh heartily at such a supposed ridiculous and impossible thought. She would look around the dinner table at her guests again, laugh, and exclaim, "I ask you, have you ever heard that a Black man *can* fly a plane?! I have travelled the *world* in my days..." She would proceed, lifting her head up high, smiling in blissful memory of her travels in the seventies, "Look, let me tell you something. We could not sit together with Whites in the restaurants at home, *but* we flew with them in the *same* plane...oh, *yeeesss*... (she would stress the word to make the point) - only when we came *home*...(her eyes would suddenly go watery, almost depressingly and confusingly sad as she got reminded of the long life of humiliation that apartheid has caused her and her family for being Coloured). She would continue, "You see... only *then* was there trouble for us when we had to use *different* entrances at the airport." She would look down and fiddle with the lovely cream-coloured organdie placemats and linen napkins that she bought from Harrods in Knightsbridge, in London. She had already informed her guests that the fresh clean and pressed tablecloth was antique linen and the table napkins were vintage accessories, dating to the late 1800s in England. In her fiddling with the snooty accessories, she was subtly reminding them of her class, of her material standing in the Coloured community, that she was indeed superior. She would continue the tale of mind-boggling humiliation, "In fact, we could not *walk* through the main terminal building! We boarded the plane from *somewhere else*! Around the back, I think. *Not the same door!*... But we were allowed to go through the *same* aeroplane door when we boarded the plane and we sat *next* to the Whites. Oh *yesssss*, my dear, *yessss*.... And when we landed in Europe, we were just like the Whites. *Equal...yesssss*, dear. Equal..."

The room would go quiet. To make themselves feel better about their own inferiority at the hands of the Afrikaners, they'd order the African servants around, calling for water, ash trays, napkins –the most trivial of items.

Once recovered, she'd continue to talk, with her arms delicately folded, as with pride, she now observed her guests admiring her antique English crockery. She watched with a calculated snooty stare as they nervously lifted the cups, decorated in blue with hand painted landscapes of an English countryside and fine gold gilding. She quietly knew they felt privileged to be in her refined middle-class company and home. While she talked, her husband would puff away stylishly in gentile fashion, rocking in his leather armchair. His expensive Montecristo No.2 cigars made him nostalgic of his days of cruises on the Nile.

The two of them would get excited and talk in unison, "Oh, we have seen the *world* in our days. Tokyo, Sydney, New York, Barcelona...You name it, we've been there!" At this delicate point, she would take over the conversation, "And you know what?" she would pause, stylishly sipping her tea from her antique wares, "strange thing, the *boere* were friendly when they were in the plane with us, in the sky, you know...and even in the tourist buses overseas." She would suddenly look troubled and sad, almost ill like someone telling a tragic story of death and destruction, "But God forbid when you came back! The boere would already change towards you on the return flight in the sky! The other White European tourists would be friendly and continue their conversations with you, but not the South African Whites – They went *quiet* when they sat next to you on the return flight, giving you those *know-your-place* stares. You know what I mean?! How can people change like that?!"

Then she would cough and splutter as the telling of this humiliating story sends her slowly brewed Earl Grey tea down the wrong way in her throat. "You stay a *Coloured*, a *nothing* in their eyes. Even the air hostesses - they are the same. They smile and serve on you in the sky, but they all split with you and rush through the main terminal building when you land back at Cape Town airport. There was no apartheid in the sky...only on the ground..."

Then, deeply troubled, she tried to convince herself that everything was not that bad, "But as we know, those were *good* days, seeing the world, how people in other countries live together... feeling what it is like to be a *person*..."

Her visitors knew these stories too well. They heard them ad nauseum every time they visited, and they had heard them so many times from other well-to-do Coloureds who were lucky enough to travel to Europe, the States, or Australia. What was there to say to one another? Nothing; they had no comfort to share with one another. They just drowned themselves in quiet thoughts of self-loathing about their physical features, about the way they talked, about the play-White relatives who had abandoned them. The realisation of real South Africa at the end of such a day of indulgence, laughter, and nostalgia of a life abroad with White people was like bitter aloe on the tongue after a scrumptious meal. Mrs. Harvey would contain the psychological pain in her and would continue the conversation for them, express sentiments on their behalf, rescue them all from their quiet demons, and reassure them of their superiority, "I won't put my foot into a plane with a Black pilot! I am telling you he would fly into the nearest mountain!" They would all crack up in hysterical laughter as they wiped their free flowing bittersweet tears. They would feel good about themselves again and crack up laughing, commanding with glee the African servants to bring this and that.

After hearing all the stories of travel abroad from the Harvey family and others, Tumelo wondered how Ms. Jansen treated Coloureds on a return flight with her from London. Ms. Jansen had befriended Mr. Torres by then, and every lunch break she gave him Xhosa lessons. Tumelo disliked her for being different from the other "Whities" at the school, for being politically astute, for being street wise, for being fluent in Xhosa and Zulu, and for being so close to the unreachable Mr. Torres. He told Tumelo that Ms. Jansen was part of the anti-apartheid movement in Europe which was already founded in the late 1950s. Ms. Nkosi withdrew even more from the library, warning Mr. Torres about White liberals who played the role of *agent provocateurs*, spies planted to undo the revolutionary work at Forest High. Mr. Torres hit back at Ms. Nkosi about the dangers of limited racial thinking; that the struggle was non-racial, that it transcended categories of Black and White. Mr. Benjamen got on with Ms Jansen, and together they continued to establish an ANC network with the students.

John Voster's fall came in 1979 with the Information Scandal and the election of the far right and militaristic P.W Botha. The country tumbled into a militaristic state, with huge investments into national defence on the borders against the communist onslaught, which by then had already taken off in the liberation of southern Africa, through amongst others, the Cubans in Angola and the exodus of Black youth after 1976 into the armed wing of the ANC, *Umkhontho we Sizwe*. Mr. Benjamen reasoned that he had to recruit soldiers for the army, not intellectuals, and introduced them to the African militant chant, *"Bhasobha iNdoda eMnyame Verwoerd!"* – "Beware of the Black man, Verwoerd!" Mr. Torres, with Ms. Jansen, also had begun to teach the African students at a radical private college in the city.

A local Coloured married leftist ANC couple in their early thirties, Mary and Steven, who prompted the start of Student Representative Councils at schools on the Cape Flats, joined forces with Mr. Benjamen to recruit for the underground movement at Forest High and the surrounding schools. Mary was into the bare essentials and minimalist pleasures of life. She looked almost Eastern European, with dark depressing eyes, her hair combed back, flat and unimaginative into a black listless ponytail. She wore the same clothes every day, baggy tracksuit trousers and a blue shapeless hand-knitted jersey. Yet, she oozed earthy, raw, sex appeal, and the male students at Forest High confided that they found her incredibly sexy. One could easily imagine her with army boots and an AK47 in hand; she looked the part. She disrupted local mass meetings with her feisty revolutionary spirit, shouting *"Amandla Ngawethu! Power to the People!"* and she rarely smiled. She showed severe impatience with Coloured racism and ignorance.

Her husband, Steven, sported a beard and was already going bald at a very early age in life. He looked like a cross between Karl Marx on the paperback cover of *Das Kapital*, and the anarchist Bakunin - just slightly balder than both. Like Mary's, his deep-seated eyes were dark, penetrating, and severe. He was always casually dressed, but never wore jeans. They had a well-known style in the community as the formidable revolutionary couple. Steve was known to address gatherings calmly after Mary had thrown her fiery mischief in at a mass meeting. His philosophical, calculated, and insightful responses to Mary's well-timed provocative questions were well anticipated at mass gatherings in local churches and civic halls. The students took them seriously and listened; they had brought a freshness to political debates and discussions in Forest Hill. Often they almost simultaneously erupted into a public attack on the "arm chair" and "champagne and caviar socialist" Cape Trotskyites. On such occasions, Mary shouted emotionally at the masses gathered in the community halls: "There is a bloody revolution out there! South Africa is at war! Understand?! Our comrades are *dying* on the borders of this country as we are speaking! Armchair politicking will get us *nowhere!* Amandla!! Forward to the armed struggle! Forward! *Long live Umkhontho we Sizwe! Long Live!*" A thunderous echo of the revolutionary slogans would erupt from the masses of students, parents, and teachers who gathered at the political rallies.

At one mass meeting, Mr. Torres got up and interjected, "We must fight the common enemy, not our comrades!"

Mary challenged, "Then go to *where* the enemy is; take up the AK47s and storm the enemy!" Steven nodded his head in agreement, in support of the revolutionary passion of his long-term partner. They always seemed deeply in love with each other, as if their love was an important ingredient to make the revolution happen in South Africa. This revolutionary couple presented a formidable force to Mr. Torres' ideology and campaign for a "disciplined revolution", and a political vanguard party, as more and more Coloured working class youth joined the ranks of the ANC.

Rafik and Alfredo were invited to the meetings to challenge their teachers. Ms. Nkosi brought in a Black Consciousness young student philosopher recruit. Ahmed was a Palestinian-looking young man who addressed the Coloured community at one such a mass meeting on the "Three Race Nations" theory and its relevance in South Africa – the Caucasoid, Mongoloid, and Negroid – as he put it. However, his lecture met with boos from the Trotskyite left. Ms. Nkosi struggled to defend Ahmed, but failed to convince the audience. Mr. Torres saw in this moment the opportunity to speak about the myth of race as created by the economic exploitation of Black people worldwide since the days of slavery at the Cape under Van Riebeeck and plantation slavery by the English in the Caribbean. "Let us not buy into the race myth that justified slavery, exploitation and oppression! We cannot explain race and in fact racism without explaining and understanding economic relations of power. Let's not mislead our youth with propaganda on the existence of races! All of us should by now be familiar with the research on the evolution of the human species. We all belong to one family, *Homo sapiens sapiens*. We need to read up on archaeology. Physical difference is a superficial phenomenon. It is that which makes us different, and attractive to each other; hair texture, pigmentation, stature and the colour of our eyes." Mr. Torres' argument was the most cogent and convincing that evening, and invited nods from the audience who was in total awe of his eloquence.

After Mr. Torres had spoken, the Black Consciousness activists stormed out of the mass meeting, angry with the armchair politician who had deflated them. Mary and Steven thought the intellectual discourse on "race" irrelevant to the times, and suggested that the audience ponder rather on the question of making the revolution happen in the streets and on the pavements.

Tumelo's world had opened up intellectually as she was being groomed to help make the South African revolution happen. She tried to suppress the memories of Annie and Uncle Thaba. She tried to forget the rituals taught to her by the Muslim wise man and the Xhosa *sangomas* and about the cleansing qualities of the seventh wave in the Indian Ocean. In earnestly trying to be an intellectual for the revolution, she forgot completely about the ancient healing and protective powers of the herb rosemary that her grandmother taught her about - *rosmarinus officinalis* – meaning "dew of the sea", its oils her mother rubbed routinely into her scalp as a child. It was popularly believed to improve memory, and to be a symbol of remembrance for the dead, as in Shakespeare's Hamlet, Act 4, Scene V, when Ophelia in her painful madness and bereavement remarks, *"There's rosemary, that's for remembrance."*

Her thoughts of her own possible insanity and of the other supernatural realms that did not scientifically exist, did not seem to fit into what was becoming of "revolutionary conduct". They were misplaced, simply foolish thoughts at the time of revolution, when she could not explore the height of what she thought was necessary madness in her and in others to bring about change. She buried these forbidden thoughts, fantasies, desires, rituals, ancient ancestral wisdom, and the associated memories of those who had passed on in the deep corners of her bodily organs; got them to absorb her real being for some other time in her life's journey. She was still entranced by Mr. Torres, and his eloquence and intellectual challenging manner at knife-edge tense political mass meetings that made her knees weak with desire for him. She was already a young woman, out of school, organising mass meetings and uprisings, and they continued to meet alone in the cosiness of the library of his cottage.

He read revolutionary poetry to her written and sung by the Chilean communist Victor Jara. Her read to her of the tragic story of this folk singer who was tortured and murdered in the notorious stadium of Chile in the coup that ousted Salvador Allende in September 1973. Mr. Torres recounted with deep sadness how the Chilean dictatorship broke Victor Jara's hands to stop him from playing revolutionary songs. As Mr. Torres rhythmically spoke about Victor Jara's broken hands, he strummed his guitar and sang Victor Jara's last song in the *Estadio Chile*. *"Canto, Que Mal Me Sales! (How imperfect you are!)"*. He chose to say the words, trying to get the Spanish pronunciations right for her. She was captivated by the protruding veins on his hands, and the way he softly strummed the chords of his guitar. He repeated Victor Jara's last words in the stadium where he was tortured and murdered with 5000 others. : *"What I now see, I have never seen..."*

Chapter 12
The Wailing and Squawking
Calls of Seagulls

Mr. Hofman decided to appoint Tumelo as a young teacher straight out of her last year in school at Forest High, at the age of just over 17. Mr. Torres was ecstatic that she had joined the staff, even as a teenager. By then, a few more young teachers in their early twenties had joined the staff, so she did not feel all that out of place. Most notable was a White male named Mr. Magee, a tall American, the son of famous film actors in Hollywood. Mr. Hofman laughingly and dramatically introduced a bewildered Mr. Magee on his first day at the school, making reference to the Irish American character in the song-and-dance 1942 Hollywood musical film, Yankee Doodle Dandy. Mr. Torres sarcastically mumbled about the thoughtless and spontaneous association coming from a Coloured South African, because they were themselves stereotyped by the boere as song-and-dance characters, "coons", and abused for White people's annual New Years' entertainment in the streets of Cape Town.

However, it was always difficult to read Mr. Hofman's true intentions; it could have been that he wanted to mock White racism towards Coloured people by pointing out similar stereotypes. Over six feet tall, with twinkling small eyes, and brown curly hair, Mr. Magee wore the same clothes every day – a brown blazer and a brown pair of trousers, worn out at the elbows and knees. Tumelo noticed that Mr. Magee had been watching her intensely for a few days during break time. She could feel him staring at her from behind and this often made her feel uneasy, as he was at least ten years older than her, and he was - well, White.

One morning, before school started, he just walked up to her and blurted out in a heavy American accent, "Hey, you look like a youngster? You're a *teacher* already? What is your name?" This was the first time in her life that she had come face to face with a White American man, as in having a conversation. It was, for her, an odd encounter.

She did not give her name. "So *what* are you doing in South Africa?" she responded. "I was curious, and bored, - honest." "And how did you end up choosing *this* school? You know it is one of the roughest on the Cape Flats?" Mr. Magee was upfront and in-your-face honest, "Well, by accident actually. My spending money had dried up and someone recommended that I approach the Coloured Affairs Department for a teaching job, as they needed teachers badly. The White inspector told me that it was good to choose a Coloured or African school as Whites teaching at these township schools got inconvenience pay. Quite frankly, I needed the money."

"Did you have to be *qualified* in education?" she enquired gently, like a naïve child.

"No, my friend said everything goes if you are White in South Africa, everything works in your favour; you win all the time, it is a land of milk and honey. You simply have to know something to be able to teach at a Coloured school on the Cape Flats. To be White in South Africa, they say, is like living on the dole in England, lots of benefits..."

With this startling confession, he scooped further mouthfuls of strawberry yoghurt from a pink carton as he answered her in a brutally honest manner. He wiped the messy yoghurt from his lips, with his sleeve. Tumelo noticed his hands, his long, lean knotty fingers,

"You wear interesting clothes. Where do you buy them?"

Mr. Magee grinned. She noticed his big teeth in his large smile. His American accent was boastful, "I don't *buy* clothes! I choose them from the wardrobes of the film actors in Hollywood!"

Then he mumbled modestly, staring down into the large yoghurt carton, "My parents are wealthy film producers..." He gulped more spoonfuls of strawberry yoghurt, as if he had not really declared anything significant. Tumelo was stunned, since she could hardly afford to see movies at the local film theatre for Coloureds, called for good reason, the "flea bioscope". Television came to South Africa shortly before that, and Tumelo watched the

American miniseries, *Rich Man Poor Man*, about the lives of the Jordache brothers, at a neighbour's house. The television went on at six o'clock in the evenings, opening with the Afrikaner Anthem and the apartheid flag. All the children in the neighbourhood would descend on the small modest home up their street. While the children and youngsters crowded the small lounge, the family protectively ate their dinner in the kitchen behind a locked door. Here, they also watched the soap opera series of the oil magnate JR and the wealthy Texas Ewing family in *Dallas*. Along with the Western movies, *Magnificent Seven* and *Billy the Kid,* this was the closest they got to forming a visual sense in their minds of America and its people. All the teenage girls in Tumelo's street copied Charlene Tilton's sleek hairstyle – the actress who played Lucy Ewing, JR's granddaughter. This meant lots of painful swirls and uncomfortable nights. Even the male teachers at Forest High got into the *Dallas* hairstyles. Mr. Abdul often turned up in the morning in class, with the very telling cut of the swirl across his forehead – then he looked a little bit like Uncle Jack. The rest that Tumelo learned about America, she found in books about Martin Luther King, and by watching the film *The Grapes of Wrath* with Mr. Torres at school. The students found inspiration to survive poverty and despair in this 1940 film about the story of an Oklahoma family, the Joads, who became migrant workers in California after they had lost their farm during the Great Depression in the 1930s. They also watched films about racism in America, such as about an interracial romance and the White upper middle class family's response to a Black boyfriend in *Guess Who's Coming to Dinner.* When Tumelo thought of America, she thought of the huge class division that existed between the rich and the poor, the similarities in race segregation as in apartheid, and the genocide of the Native Americans. Therefore, she could not contain the shock of coming face to face with this friendly wealthy White American man, Mr. Magee. To show him how shocked she was, she reacted to his wardrobe stories, "*Wow!* Just like that? You wear the wardrobes of *film stars*?! I was always a Robert De Nero fan. We watched *The Godfather, Part II* at the local 'flea bioscope'."

"*Flea* bioscope?!"

"Yes, it says it all, doesn't it?"

"And what do the children think of these movies?"

"They like them."

The conversation between Tumelo and Mr. Magee started to flow.

"Many of the boys wanted to behave like Mafia gangsters after seeing that film! They walked around the playground, twisted their mouths in a half smile, and narrowed their eyes like Robert De Nero and made threats to their gang rivals in the style of Mafia chief, Don Vito Corleone. The boys with sleek black hair copied the hairstyle of Al Pacino, while those with "kinky" hair looked on enviously wishing for 'bees-lek hare'." Mr. Magee tried to impress her more. He took off his jacket and showed her the label on the inside of its collar; his slender knotty fingers underlining the words on the label. He read the words aloud as if she could not read them herself, *"For Robert De Nero..."*

Her mouth hung open. Mr. Magee looked at her and studied the amazed expression on her face. "Yep? I have many more at home in my wardrobe. I can show them to you, if you don't believe me."

"No, I won't come to your place for that..." He shrugged his shoulders in a dismissive matter of fact way and put the jacket on again, as if he did not notice her rejection.

She was still curious about this boastful American man, "Your family must be rich then?"

"Yah, but we are *Irish* American. We also know discrimination, well sort of..." "But you are still *rich*..." Tumelo insisted and emphasised.

Mr. Magee raised his eyebrows and looked down at her, suddenly a little less friendly and more provocative, "Ever heard of the slogans in England and in America that said, *'No Irish, no Blacks, and no dogs'*, and *'Help wanted..no Irish need apply'*?"

Tumelo did not give up, driving her point home, "Yah, I've heard about that, but you are *still* White and privileged in South Africa."

He insisted, "Heard about the *Irish stereotype*?" She remembered some of the things Ms. Jansen spoke about when she discussed the word "stereotype" with them, "Yes, like with Coloureds – the cheating alcoholic, many children, violent, dumb, and not to be trusted..."

"Oh, so you *do* know..." Then he suddenly cheered up and smiled, "But, hey it was not all that bad! We had a number of famous Irishmen as U.S. presidents...John F. Kennedy was one of them. Did you know that?" He hurriedly scooped the last spoonfuls of strawberry yoghurt while he was talking. She was quiet.

"Do you ever watch telly?"

"You mean as in te-le-vi-sion?" Tumelo dragged out the newly acquired word in her Coloured Afrikaans accent.

He smiled, "Yep...You like what they show you here on telly?" He paused and squeezed the yoghurt carton and walked to the bin in the corner of the room. She watched him from behind; his swaggering walk was like a movie star in the American Westerns. He combed his long knotty fingers through his hair. It all seemed like deliberate theatre as he targeted the carton to fall slow motion into the bin, swinging himself on one leg. She noticed his pointy, narrow brown shoes, like Steve McQueen's boots.

Tumelo was standing, leaning against the window, her arms folded as she answered him, "Yes, South African television is run by the South African Broadcasting Corporation, the Afrikaners. They decide our culture for us, what news we are shown, what music we should listen to. South Africans are forced to watch *boere orkes* or listen to Afrikaner *liedjies*. Many things are banned here in any case. So not much variety or choice."

She was a little annoyed that Mr. Magee could ask her such an obvious question.

"What is *boere orkes*?"

"Afrikaner orchestra, played by many fat boere men, men pulling accordions." "Oh, it sounds like Irish folk and dance music in pubs..."

"Probably..." "And that other word, did you say *liedjies*?"

"Afrikaans for tunes..."

"So the Afrikaners have their own music and culture?" "Yes... we don't like it; it's not very nice, but we have to watch it for countless hours on television. Only White people on the TV with White music. Sometimes we see Black actors, but in stupid roles as fools or as savages in the jungle..."

"And radio?"

"Well there is Springbok Radio as the main propaganda station. And there is also Radio Bantu, Radio Lebowa, Radio Setswana, Radio Tsonga, Radio Venda, Radio Port Natal, Radio Good Hope – radio stations for different tribal groups."

"And what do Coloured people listen to?"

"You mean *so-called*...they listen mostly to Radio Good Hope and Radio 5, and we have just heard there is Radio 702 in Johannesburg that one can tune into."

He ignored her use of so-called, pretended he did not hear. "That is not all, surely...I also hear there is *Radio Freedom*, huh?"

She tried to ignore this question from him, tried to downplay it. "Oh yes..."

He copied the voice of Oliver Tambo, *"This is Radio Freedom, the voice of the African National Congress and its military wing Umkhonto we Sizwe...* Heard it?"

Mr. Magee smiled at Tumelo, narrowing his small penetrating eyes. "You know you could be jailed for five to eight years if you are caught listening to Freedom Radio? Did you know that?"

She shrugged him off, pretended she did not hear him this time. She did not readily trust him, and retorted, "We listen to Pink Floyd's *Another Brick in the Wall* on Radio 5."

Mr. Magee then fiddled impatiently with his car keys in his pockets, "I've seen some political pamphlets around in the classrooms ...you reckon I should read them? Which ones do you think are the good ones? Azania, ANC, Communism...which ones would you recommend?"

She had managed to escape the intensity of his stares, "Yes, I think you should read all of them – they are enlightening; they keep us informed of what is going on in this country; about the facts. It is a good alternative to the *Cape Herald,* which is the chief paper aimed at so-called Coloureds, with stories of rape and violence and with pictures of half-naked girls posing in bikini's for lustful male readers. Some of the girls here at school have already made those pages..."

"*Really...?*"

Tumelo wanted him to know more, "Did you know that there is a supplement in the Afrikaner newspaper *Rapport* for so-called Coloureds? It is called the *'Rapport-Extra'.* They publish White news in support of apartheid, with White faces and adverts for White homes, White death notices in the main classified section, and Coloured faces and Coloured news and pictures of Coloured beauty queens in bikinis, adverts of hair straightener, and cheap white wine, called Virginia, complete with tales of murder and rape in the *Extra* ! Don't you think that is really ridiculous?"

Mr. Magee chuckled and shouted in amazement, "You are fooling! Bizarre!"

They started to have regular conversations in the weeks that followed.

"You think there is a lot of poverty in South Africa?"

"Poverty *and* racism – that is our problem, a combination of the two."

"Do you know that Americans and Europeans know *more* than what you people here know of what goes on in South Africa? Will you believe me if I tell you that?!"

"Probably, because you get all the news and information we don't get. You also have more books to read."

"Hey, but let me tell you I did not know this country was *this* mad...I am thinking of the outrageous ways of Mr. Hofman, for instance...!"

Tumelo became protective, "What do you mean? Mr. Hofman calling you Yankee Doodle Dandy? Don't read too much into that. He is like that. He is harmless. He loves the students and looks after them as much as he can manage to...though he has his political limitations..."

"No, you know what?! It is more serious than that. I was so shocked that Mr. Hofman did not even bother to ask me for my papers. He seemed to think that because I was White, I was *automatically* qualified, and I got the salary including inconvenience pay! What do you make of that?!"

"Geewiz...and you accepted!"

"Yah, but I am not that bad. I can still teach the children something. I have a Masters degree in African History from Columbia University, and I care about equality, human rights, and children. But, quite frankly, I am not sure about some of the other White teachers here. Some of them seem strange and not fit to teach children...what do you think?"

"Ms. Jansen is quite good – not to be underestimated. She can teach you Xhosa, though she is from Paris."

"Really? Uhm...that is pretty impressive...And the one who is always biting her nails and foaming at the mouth, and who is *always* and *always* late?"

"Oh, that is Miss Paddy. They say she brings her bottle and cannabis to school and shouts at the children whole day. She is always losing their English essays and tells them to fuck off when they question her too much about the work."

"And what about that young German boy who is teaching science?"

"Oh, that is Mr. Klaus. He told the students he is nineteen years old. He can't speak Afrikaans, but he has been hired to teach science to the Afrikaans-speaking children. The students say he talks to himself in German most of the time while he just sits on his chair rocking backwards and forwards in front of the class. And when the class gets too rowdy, he starts throwing the duster at the children and he goes wild and they all run out. Then he walks out too and goes to sit in his car. He is just here to pick up some money and to pass time."

"Bloody fucking crazy...and the older White woman who wears that despicable see-through white skirt and the sloppy big green jersey? What about her? Is she perhaps any good?"

"Oh, that is Ms. Wills. The children say she is on LSD. She apparently told them so. She shakes all the time, and hardly comes to school. She has been hired to teach mathematics. Teachers come and go all the time...that is perhaps why Mr. Hofman hired me, although I am young – at least he knows me."

"But there must be *some* White teacher who *cares* – besides Ms. Jansen. What about the physical education teacher who is always with the boys? They seem fond of him...?"

"That is Mr. Raap. He has a seedy reputation, literally and figuratively."

"A paedophile?"

"He is always inviting the young boys to his house to have striptease parties and to swim naked in his huge swimming pool. He knows that the boys are in awe of being in a Whites-only neighbourhood. So he cunningly exploits that desire."

"Really?! That is shocking...Seems then I am one of the few decent White teachers at a Coloured school..." he smiled.

"Well, we don't *know* you yet! There is a good White history teacher, an Englishman from Kenya. He is very respectable and decent. I trust him."

"And we earn more than the Coloured teachers with the same qualifications?!"

"Yep...*plus* inconvenience pay that you get to have to suffer and share a toilet, classroom and staffroom with us..."

Mr. Magee looked embarrassed, but kept the conversation going, "Sounds like South America, where children get abused, sodomised, drugged...This reminds me of schools in Nicaragua under the Somoza dictatorship... "

And one day, she put on a brave face and finally asked him, "What would make you think you would find excitement in this doomed country? You should not even be *talking* to me because you are a White man, you know that!"

Mr. Magee then decided to tell her a little more of his adventures in Africa. "Well, I have been travelling from far north on the continent, gradually down through Central Africa and then into Southern Africa. And, gee, it has been a *fascinating* experience."

"You mean seeing wild animals and a vast landscape?"

"No...I am talking about African women...I have never seen beautiful women like those in my life before!"

"But women are the same everywhere, is it not so?"

"No, there are women of all physical *sorts* in Africa! Have you ever travelled in Africa?"

"No, we can't – only to South West Africa or to Lesotho or Swaziland. We can't move much around here, not even into African townships..."

"What a pity...you are being deprived of so much. In Africa, I saw a variety of differently shaped women! Nubian beauties in the North – tall, lean, and dark. As I travelled further south, women became darker and more voluptuous. The more south I travelled, the more fascinated I became with their body shapes and interesting differences – the huge heavy bottoms, the elongated breasts and heavy legs, the shorter hair, the shorter bodies! Ooh..."

He continued, starry-eyed, as he described with obvious captivation, "Further south into southern Africa, I saw women of all shades of yellow, brown, and black. I was especially fascinated by their fleshiness, the further I travelled towards the South Pole. And you know *what*?! Cape Town is like an oasis of different kinds of women from all over Africa and the world coming together! Now *that* was an even bigger surprise for me. Have you ever noticed the *different* kinds of people here?"

"No, not really. It is just normal for me..."

Tumelo was taken aback by his frank and direct sexual manner. She had never encountered anything like it before. This was her first conversation with a White man about politics, which seemed to move straight into a conversation about the sensual allure of Black women and their sexual magnetism. However, being young and unworldly, instead of reprimanding or challenging him for his voyeurism, she told him naively, "We do not travel much out of the township, so we only see mostly so-called Coloureds..."

Mr. Magee thought Tumelo was lying, "Come on! You're joking! Ridiculous!"

"This is the land of *apartheid*, you should know! My uncle was a Xhosa man, but he died when I was still very young. That was my last encounter with an African man from the township."

He looked at her open-mouthed, "I don't believe what you are telling me...and your contact with *White* people?!"

"Well, unfortunately, we only get to know most of them as opportunistic teachers, and as cruel masters and madams. I know that my aunt's master is White, and he drops her off on Friday afternoons in our street, and my mother worked for White madams since the age of eleven. But that is all. You know we are not *supposed* to mix with Whites nor with Blacks..."

Mr. Magee's mouth was still hanging open, "And do you communicate with *Indian* people?!"

"Well, they mostly live in Durban and Johannesburg. There is an Indian township close by, but nobody goes there, as they are second-class and we are third-class; the African people are fourth-class. You sort of have to know your *place* in this country. It is like segregation you had in your country isn't it? Very similar. Why are you *so* shocked by segregation *here*?"

"Yep, you are right. So where do *you* fit into all of this that is going on in this country?" He looked her up and down. "I like your hair, the black curls..." He gently touched her hair with his long inquisitive fingers. Though Tumelo felt uncomfortable, she was polite and did not push his hand away.

"Well, I am a mixture of many people in my genes – mostly African from the aboriginal Khoisan and African people, and from slave women from Malaysia and India, a German woman, a Frenchman, and an Englishman who came to fight in the Anglo-Boer War at the turn of the century. I am a little bit of the United Nations." At this, Tumelo laughed and Mr. Magee laughed as well. The tension between them mellowed a little.

"Well, I am only a potato famine Irishman turned American. Boring, hey?"

They both laughed again, still a bit nervous about each other.

Then she pushed his hand lightly away from her hair. "As comrades, we avoid emphasising differences to do with hair and the shape of the body in South Africa, because things like that have been used by the Nazi regime to wipe out the Jews, and is used by the apartheid government today to segregate our people, to put them into physical-type categories. We are all *human beings*."

He sighed, "Same as in the States and in Australia, I suppose. Hey, but you *African* women *are* beautiful! This continent is fascinating!"

She blushed at his persistence and looked down in embarrassment. "You sound like a tourist..."

"No, *come on*...look around you. The children at this school could be from the Bushmen in the Karoo, from Africans in the Congo, from the Xhosas, the Zulus, the Setswanas, the Sothos, the Indians, from Zimbabwe, Namibia, Egypt, Sudan, Algeria, Nigeria, Uganda, Morocco, Ethiopia, Arabia. Or from Indonesia, Malaysia, China, Japan, India, Aboriginal Australia. Or from Palestine, Israel, Mexico, Cuba, Chile, Nicaragua, Venezuela, Brazil, Peru, Argentina. And even from Turkey, Greece, Italy, Spain. And sorry to disappoint you but some don't even *look* Black or Coloured at all – they could be from Scandinavia, England, Scotland, Ireland, France, Germany, Denmark...Have you noticed? The whole bloody world is in the Coloured people...*think about it!*"

"*So-called Coloured people, Mr. Magee*...I just know we have all been dumped together in a township after the forced removals from White areas, in a kind of mad country where things don't make sense...A whole mixture of the world and from other parts of Africa came here for the past 300 years and more."

Mr. Magee was still curious, "Apartheid is not so long ago. So people *must* have slept together? Don't you think? I mean this colour bar thing is a joke! Huh! I heard that even the boers have Black blood in them...that means that *many of them are actually Coloureds?!*"

"Yes, but there was segregation and the colour bar before that...introduced by the English...!"

"Well the Irish and the Scots also suffered under the English... we can empathise...though not entirely, of course... "

Mr. Magee watched Tumelo's movements closely. He once heard her talking about political training that the students needed at school, the way she was trained. He was curious about that. So, after a few weeks, he attempted to pick up the conversation with her one afternoon in the staff room.

"You said *political*? Do you mean you are being trained *politically*?" He smiled curiously, his small eyes sparkled showing that he *knew* she slipped something she should not have.

Then he hesitated, "No, forget about it. We'll talk about it again when you are more relaxed."

Tumelo immediately had her guard up. Was this man a spy? She was not supposed to trust any White person. "No, there is nothing to talk about..."

Then he walked up to her, pointed at his chest and looked her in the eyes and asked, "You think I am a *spy*?!" He seemed to have read her mind. He leaned forward and stared into her eyes, searching for a sign of trust.

She pulled back and walked away. At this point, she sensed someone watching her from behind and she instinctively turned around.

Mr. Torres was sitting on the couch on the opposite side of the staffroom, reading a newspaper. She felt she had betrayed him, and they did not speak for some weeks after. She avoided talking to Mr. Torres, and he avoided her.

Mr. Magee drove a huge silver Ford, reminiscent of America of the 1960s and he sported dark sunglasses, John Travolta style, as in the musical *Grease*. One of the frivolous male students teased him when he walked in the corridors, by mimicking John Travolta with a black hat and cigarette in the mouth. The student serenaded him while he moved his hips sensually towards Mr. Magee, *"You're the One that I Want ooh ooh ooh..."* Mr. Magee found him irritating, and made no secret of it. He was not going to be anybody's Yankee Doodle Dandy.

Tumelo found out through their many conversations in the months that followed since their first encounter that Mr. Magee was amazingly knowledgeable. He knew much about what was going on in Mozambique and in Zimbabwe at the time. He knew a lot about Samora Machel and Robert Mugabe and the independence struggles in Africa. He spoke informatively about world politics, about Nicaragua, Chile, Cuba, the Vietnam War, and even about African literature and African music. They started to bond as friends and she started to trust him slightly more, consciously trying to ignore the fact that he was a White man.

However, she found him at times still too inquisitive and too interfering, like a loud-mouthed and forward middle-class

American. "So what do the students think of being taught by a *kid* they had just been a fellow student with a few months earlier?"

Mr. Torres had also warned her when they started to talk again that she must not readily confide in Mr. Magee, as he could be a plant of the FBI, who was perhaps trying to bring about an end to apartheid but on imperialism's terms. It would not necessarily mean an end to poverty, only a change in the faces in government and in civil policy, he explained, "Black people will run the country, but poverty will remain for the majority of people."

Mr. Torres' information on the secret strategies of the FBI sounded convincing, so she had reason to be a little careful with Mr. Magee.

Noticing her withdrawal from him in the recent weeks, Mr. Magee walked up to her in the school's corridor and asked her directly out of the blue, "Do you think Mr. Torres may be in *love* with you?" He looked her straight in the eye, as he always did. Without blushing, he waited eagerly for an answer, his hands in his pockets.

As always, she avoided his penetrating stare. "No, we are just comrades..."

At this, he moved closer towards her, "So he is *politically* involved with you, but not *romantically*? Have I got it right?"

She tried to walk away from him and his interrogation about Mr. Torres, "No, we just share the same vision for South Africa."

He stepped a little closer, "Do you go to his house a lot?"

"Of course, I do.We are serious people. There is a lot of work to be done for the revolution in South Africa."

Mr. Magee was still restless and persisted, "What do you do there *alone* with him? You are still a youngster. Sorry, I know I am pushing, but I am *curious...*"

She did not hide her irritation with his forwardness, of him prying into her private life. "We are not into frivolities! We are not adventurists!"

Yes, she thought to herself, perhaps he was an FBI plant as Mr. Magee warned. This was perhaps his way of trying to get information on Mr. Torres. She knew then that word was out in the underground movement that the British Secret Service, MI5, was spying on Coloured Trotskyite teachers in South Africa; they warned the South African apartheid government in the 1960s that these teachers were "dangerous" and "red" communists who posed a similar threat of subversion in southern Africa as the militants. That meant that Mr. Torres was certainly perhaps under MI5 surveillance, as he matched the profile of a communist teacher.

Mr. Magee noticed Tumelo's increasing annoyance with his inquisitive political questions. At times of such questioning, she wanted to turn around like a poisonous serpent and unexpectedly strike at him, so that he would never again venture to question her about her visits to Mr. Torres' cottage. Noticing her quiet anger, he once stood in front of her and put his hands up above his head in a gesture of innocent defence, like in a kind of theatrical hands-up in a Western movie, "Oh, sorry for intruding...I just think he might *like* you..."

His eyes smiled at Tumelo, almost begging for reconciliation. She did not know what to make of it.

She insisted, "I don't think so. He is a very *principled* man."

Mr. Magee was still not giving up, his American accent was heavy and loud, "Tumelo, has he *ever ever* made a pass at you? Please tell me."

"Nope..."

"Has *any man* ever made a pass at you?"

She did not answer Mr. Magee, and walked away from him that day, vowing to herself never to talk to him again.

They met up again a few days later, when he stopped her as she passed him in the corridor one afternoon after school. She was wearing her blue denim dungarees and new tackies that day, and her hair was wild and uncombed; it was the way she liked to look.

He stopped her in her tracks and put his hand on her shoulder, far below his tall body. She looked up at the over six foot tall White man. "Can *I* make a pass at you? I think you are so *beautiful*. I like you...especially because I think you are not aware of your beauty..."

She thought he was patronising and insincere, trying to drag a Black woman to bed as part of his tourism in Africa. She tried to wriggle herself away from him in the dark corridor, and snapped, "You *know* it is *forbidden* for me to be with you, and you are *much* older than me. My mother is waiting..."

"I'll go with you to your mom. I want to tell her how much I like you. Would you mind if I do that?"

She melted, and winked at him. "OK. Help us with the groceries then. My mother and I are going shopping this afternoon. Give us a lift to Wynberg. She'll be pleased to have a White man as a driver".

From that day on, Mr. Magee offered to give Tumelo and her mother a lift in his huge blue Ford to Wynberg every Friday afternoon after school whenever she asked.

Her mother was very pleased. She sat proudly with huge dark sunglasses and an orange sun hat in the passenger seat in front, and told Tumelo tersely to sit at the back. "A White man has never been my chauffeur before, my child. I am going to enjoy *every* minute of this." When she got out of the car, Mr. Magee jumped out to open the door for her. Lizzy stepped out like a regal African queen, with her head up high. Mr. Magee thoroughly charmed her. His kindness towards Lizzy had the desired effect. It made her like him just a little more.

She was surprised at her own feelings of sudden enchantment with the gentle lanky White giant. For the first time, she started to notice how handsome he was.

Tumelo was never instantly attracted to White men. As a young woman, her natural chemistry came with encounters with dark men like Uncle Thaba; men with black, smooth skin, with dry, short hair, and who smoked cheap tobacco. She found them familiar enough to trust and to be comfortable with, warm and humorous beings, with whom she could easily bond with on a very deep level without giving too much of herself. She shared a deep resonance with such men, like the first boy she fell in love with when she was at primary school, Angelo, the one who never laughed when she peed in her pants, and who helped her to dry up the floor during break.

However, something else was starting to happen with her now. As Mr. Magee gently became a part of her family routine and generously showed his humanity towards her family, she found that she did not think of him as "White" any more. She watched every move of his soft piercing eyes and the intelligent movement of his mouth as he spoke. This was an attraction to watch out for; the one that *grows* into love, something unforgettable and permanent. Tumelo started to consciously fight her feelings for Mr. Magee, because they were forbidden and she believed that she would get hurt in the end. Above all, she did not want him to *ever* suspect that she had felt some attraction to him. Unaware of her feelings, he often reached out to touch her with his slender, delicate fingers. At such times, she reluctantly shied away from his touch. She knew that if she had succumbed, she would have fallen for him fatally, because he had managed to soften her heart through his kindness and his humanity.

Any woman knows intuitively that it is not colour, nor looks, nor class that makes you fall more than hopelessly in love with a man, beyond the initial attraction that may or may not be there. It is one simple thing that makes a man win a woman for a lifetime - kindness. It is instinctive, in the way that the ancestor of all humans, chimpanzee females, fall in love with the male of her species that is gentle with her, and that shares with her. She was tempted to resist his kindness, as a natural defence, as not to lose herself in his ordinariness, in his humanity.

Mr. Magee also gave her a lift when she visited Mr. Torres for the regular reading appointment at his cottage. He suggested once that she go with him instead, as Mr. Torres "seemed unconscious of the finer enjoyable things in life". "He is so serious, Tumelo. Has he ever tried to take you to bed?"

She shrugged him off, "No, I am still a virgin."

After such times of more persistent questioning, she would withdraw from Mr. Magee again, not trusting him all over again. The personal questions would start the vicious cycle of mistrust. She was also quietly disgusted that Mr. Magee could even *contemplate* such a thought.

On one occasion, Mr. Magee offered to show her the Whites-only beach nearby where he went windsurfing. The song of 10cc, *I am not in love,* was playing on the car radio. The tide was low. They sat quietly, watching the seagulls feeding on the leftovers littered by the bathers on the White beach sand. The summer sun was setting in glorious orange on the horizon across the ocean. They watched the White people walk their dogs on the beach. Mr. Magee put his hand softly on Tumelo's shoulder, turned to her, pulled the curls gently out of her face, "Hey, I really *really* like you. I think you are *gorgeous,* especially when you have your hair so wild, and you wear this red tartan shirt and these blue jeans."

"We should not be here in your car together. This is a Whites-only beach. The police vans are going to start to make their rounds at sunset. Take me home; let's get out of here. The bathers saw us and they'll go home to phone the police."

Mr. Magee seemed unperturbed about the police vans and the Immorality Act, "Can we go to the movies together one night to watch the musical *Fame*? It is playing at the flea bioscope, so there should not be a problem with us being seen there together?"

"Why *Fame*?!" she snapped, frowning and pushing his hand off her shoulder.

"It is about young Black people's motivation for success at New York's multiracial High School for the Performing Arts. You'll enjoy it...it is something worthwhile for you to see. Tumelo, you can come with me to New York. We can get out of this apartheid prison and be free...free to kiss, free to hold hands, free to walk on the beach...think about it..."

She did not look his way. She watched a dog barking the ever-increasing seagulls away as the sky turned a deep orange.

She pulled further away from him, leaning towards the armrest on the inside of the car door, her voice feisty and emphatic, "*No*, I am going *nowhere!* I am staying in South Africa for the revolution. I'll go to New York one day perhaps, *after* freedom, *not* before. Even if that means when I am an old woman; it takes as long as it takes to be free..."

He sighed and slammed his hand on the steering wheel in frustration, his head leaning between his fists on the steering wheel "You are like a stubborn rural Italian village girl protecting your virginity at all cost!"

She was shocked, "Well, whatever turns you on...thing is, I *don't* trust White men, especially not *foreign White American men...*"

"Can I kiss you? Just *softly* on your lips. Nobody will catch us, because it is getting dark and we'll be able to spot the headlights of the police vans when they come...it takes a few seconds, just one gentle kiss...that is all I am asking for, not your virginity or anything like that...I promise...come, Tumelo, lets give love a chance..."

Her human instinct wanted her to succumb. Her nipples hardened slightly and her lips quivered, her mouth turned moist and sweet inside. She avoided his soft seductive eyes, the sight of his fingers, the things that make her so weak for him in his gentleness and kindness with her. However, a commanding revolutionary voice whispered in her subconscious. Thoughts of revolutionary discipline ran through her head, like a set of uncompromising rules: Don't trust anybody, especially not a White foreigner. He could be a spy planted by the FBI. Remember the atrocities of Vietnam? Remember Martin Luther King, Remember Chile?

Remember Victor Jara? Remember Steve Biko? Remember Uncle Thaba. Remember? Her temperature cooled. At that intensely difficult human moment, she hoped that Mr. Magee did not smell the natural desire in her for him. She squeezed her legs tightly together, and fastened the top buttons of her shirt hastily to discourage Mr. Magee.

As the sky darkened, the harsh wailing and squawking calls of the seagulls could be heard as they scavenged the last bit of litter left on the almost deserted beach.

Tumelo tried to negotiate a way out of her own fire for Mr. Magee, "Ok" she said to him, as she pulled away from him, "don't *touch* me. Let's make a deal. I'll go see *Fame* with you. A deal then?"

He kissed her on her forehead, gently held her chin in his hand, looked softly into her eyes and then hesitantly pulled his face away from her. "Yes, Tumelo, that is a deal...thank you for trusting me just a little bit."

The orange sky by then had disappeared completely behind the horizon, and the faint barking of dogs could be heard. The flock of seagulls had flown back to their nests in the rocks. Mr. Magee drove off at high speed, and they headed home.

The next day they went to see *Fame* at the flea bioscope. This was Mr. Magee's first visit to a Coloured cinema. They sat next to each other, but did not hold hands. Mr. Magee sang along with the lyrics as the theme song played in the opening scene, *I'm going to learn how to fly. High...!"*

On her way back in the car from the cinema, he turned to her, "Enjoyed that?" She gave a non-committal nod.

"You *too* can be famous one day. You can go to Hollywood and become a film star; or, as I said, you could make New York your home. See how free and brilliant those kids are in America – Black and White. You can choose a new life where you don't have to endure apartheid. Come to New York with me...please try to consider it, at least...I have written letters to my parents about you and how much I like you. I am sincere in my intentions with you."

"No. I can't go."

Mr. Magee's parents visited Forest High a few months later as he had promised. Mr. Magee proudly introduced Tumelo to them, and they were excited to meet her and confirmed that they knew all about her from the letters Mr. Magee had written. "Our son wrote so much to us about you..."

It became known to everybody at the school and in the neighbourhood that Mr. Magee was now visiting Tumelo's home regularly. Her mother adored him for his pleasantness, his openness, and his sincere nature. She never saw him as "White", she said. To her, he was simply a decent young man, a "gentleman" whom she could trust in the house around her daughters. The neighbours somehow did not report his visits to the police, as they may have thought of him as an "inconvenienced" White teacher doing home visits, nothing more.

Lizzy joked once with him. "If it had not been for apartheid, then I would have *liked* you as a future son-in-law." With this, she kissed him gently on his forehead. His eyes twinkled up and he rubbed his head slightly against hers like a cat stroking himself up against the face of its owner when in a hugely affectionate mood.

However, Lizzy's fickle attitude sometimes confused Tumelo; it made her nervous. At times, her mother got uptight about a possible serious relationship that might develop between them. This fear became particularly noticeable the more frequently Mr. Magee visited and the more relaxed the family became with his regular visits. He was no longer drinking his coffee with them from a cup and saucer, but from a chipped and much-used coffee mug from the kitchen cupboard. He was no longer just knocking on the door; he was familiar enough with their home to turn the door handle and welcome himself in. Their dogs wagged their tails when they saw him at the gate and when his car pulled up; they jumped up at him to lick his face as he entered their yard. Their cats comforted themselves against his trousers, leaving him covered with hair and flea powder. The grandchildren competed for his attention, fighting to sit on his lap as he sat on his favourite chair in the sun-soaked dining room.

In spite of the strong familiarity that had grown between Tumelo and Mr. Magee in the daily intimate routine of her family home, they still did not hold hands. She still tried to escape his strong fixed gaze as he sat on his favourite chair watching her movements around the house.

One day, Tumelo's mother called her to sit next to her on the bench underneath the huge fig tree in their back yard. Her mother's invitation to talk about Mr. Magee came as a surprise.

It was a hot day, and as they sat down, a dozen large black birds with yellow beaks flew out of the tree. Lizzy picked a huge juicy fig a little high up in the tree, breaking a few branches in its path. She bit into the fleshy fig, with its juicy, red, sweet insides and thick, tasty, blueish skin as she spoke. She did not peel the fig; she just bit into it. She fixed her eyes down on her pink colourful floral apron as she started to speak.

"Tumelo, I want you to understand where I am coming from; I don't think any White man is ever *genuinely* interested in a Coloured girl. It is not that I don't like Mr. Magee; in fact, I like him too much, and that worries me. He is almost too good to be true. He is the first White man that has made me forget about colour. I am very fond of him. I often forget he is White and that bothers me. Also, I am worried that the neighbours may start to notice that he is too familiar with us and will inform the police."

She slid her hand underneath the top end of her white bra. The thick off-colour straps of her bra were hanging from her fleshy shoulders now visible at the sleeves of her blue top. She pulled out a crumpled white handkerchief from her bra, patterned with a bouquet of flowers. She slowly wiped the fig juice dripping from the side of her mouth with her handkerchief, waiting for Tumelo's response.

"But I am *not* serious about him."

"Yah, but I am just imagining what *could* happen...; you know love is a strange thing you can't stop or control...if it is there, it is there...and once you sleep with him...then, my child, it is over... You are still a *virgin*. I know that. I don't want you to get hurt. He will never be able to marry you, and you'll become like all the other abandoned Coloured girls who can never speak of the father of their child. Remember it is a *crime* in South Africa to be a Coloured girl in love with a White man. You know you can get jailed for this? I know we never speak about this possibility, but we'll have to start to face the reality of the life we live under apartheid. I feel sorry for Mr. Magee...and we don't want you to flee the country and live in another part of the world – we have already lost your sister that way. We'll be heartbroken to lose you too...I don't know when I'll ever see that child again...you must understand where I am coming from..."

The figs were overripe, and some spoiled ones were strewn on the ground. Tumelo watched the ants feasting on them.

This was the first time Lizzy spoke to one of her four daughters about love and apartheid, and about her absent daughter who fled with her White Spanish lover to get married in Madrid. They did not see her for seven years, until she returned with her daughter and pretended to enter apartheid South Africa as a "single woman". It was illegal for them to be together as mother and child in South Africa, but they defied the law by entering the apartheid country together, though they soon returned to live in Europe.

While Lizzy was talking, Tumelo kept on watching the ants. Lizzy was drying her tears with the end of her apron at the mention of the enforced absence of Tumelo's sister. At that point of grief, she forgot that she had a handkerchief. She got up hurriedly to hide her pain from her daughter and fetched a broom and a dustpan a few yards away. She started to sweep the spoiled figs into a heap and into the dustpan.

"He'll disappear to Los Angeles, and you would sit with his baby and without a career or a future. No, my girl, don't go with him. I have given it careful thought. I like him, but I don't trust White people enough myself...we are too used to this apartheid life...best that way...I am sorry to upset you..."

"Mother, why are you talking about things I am not even *thinking* about?"

"No. I don't want the same to happen to you as with Aunty Sally. You know the story?"

"Which story?"

"We still don't know who the father of your cousin is...it is a big secret. Aunty Sally never talks...and nobody asks."

"Which child?"

"Henry, the first born. They say he is the love child of her master, the English millionaire, Mr. Wigmore-Dean. When she gave birth to Henry, Mr. Wigmore-Dean said she had lied that they ever slept together. And he was quite condescending and rude about it. Then we saw his true colours!"

"Didn't you see? He looks like Mr. Wigmore-Dean!"

"No. I've never seen Mr. Wigmore-Dean because he never stops his Jaguar at the house, only at the corner of the street, and then Aunt Sally walks the little distance home."

"Yah, he is scared Grandma will see him...same face as Henry... no mistake! Spitting image, I am telling you! Same posture, same eyes, nose, and even his hair and skin colour. He even *walks* like him – and yet he has never seen him."

"Has Henry never met Mr. Wigmore-Dean?"

"No. I think his wife knows about her husband's secret child with their Coloured servant. So Aunty Sally only takes other children there when she works over weekends."

"And does Henry ever ask who his father is?"

"She would get very angry when he did ask. She would say, your father died long ago in a car accident when you were a baby...I don't want to speak about him. And little Henry would say, mommy the children call me *Whitie* and *boere* and they say I don't look like the family...they say I *am* a White man's child."

Henry was crudely nicknamed by the adults in the neighbourhood as *witvoet,* as having one black foot and one white foot.

Though Mr. Wigmore-Dean dropped Sally at home every Friday afternoon in his dark blue luxurious Jaguar car, he never asked to meet his son. He would speed away even before his long time servant would suggest such. The family often talked about her many expensive gifts from Mr. Wigmore-Dean – gold and diamond jewelry, French perfumes, exclusive boutique fashions, and various styles of lingerie.

Everybody avoided Aunt Sally over weekends when she often was known to be moody and sad. She sat and sipped her soothing gin and tonic and listened to her favourite vinyl single record of Patsy Cline's *I Fall to Pieces,* which she played over and over again until the needle went blunt, and she'd sing along aloud. Henry bore a strong resemblance to his White father, even in his manner.

"So what did Mrs. Wigmore-Dean say about all of this?"

"Oh, she was angry. She hated Aunty Sally. But she was ill with cervical cancer and she blamed Aunty Sally for it. Yes, Aunty Sally was once fighting with her in the Wigmore-Dean's big queen-sized bed. They punched each other. It started when she called Aunty Sally 'you Coloured rotten whore; you gave me cervical cancer!'"

"So the affair was serious then?"

"Yes, very. Mr. Wigmore-Dean slept regularly with Aunt Sally in the servant quarters on his big Clifton estate with its tennis court and Olympic-sized swimming pool. And when Mrs. Wigmore-Dean went to hospital for cancer treatment, then they slept together in the queen-sized bed in the main bedroom. Aunt Sally behaved like the madam then. She boasted with us how she ordered Mr. Wigmore-Dean around in the house like a houseboy when the Mrs. was not around. 'When his wife is away, he is like putty in my hands', she used to boast."

Lizzy laughed and continued, "Yes, he had to shop for her regularly, and she demanded the best. She did not accept any cheap gifts from him; he had to get her the best Italian leather bags to match with every outfit, the best rubies and the best diamonds. He had to keep her happy, otherwise she would have taken Henry to the house to stay there...to spite him."

"But it sounds as if he loved her. She was so much a part of him..."

Then Lizzy's tone changed. She stopped laughing. "Not really. If he did in fact love her, he would have got divorced and he would have sold up in South Africa and taken your aunt to live with him in England. But he did not! See, you can never trust a wealthy White Englishman. He would never be seen with a Coloured woman in public! There are many stories like these. It is an old thing. Goes back a long way, this thing."

Her mother spoke while she swept the floor. She sighed, looked up at Tumelo again thoughtfully, "Be careful, my child. You'll get hurt. You stay Black and inferior in a White man's eyes. Remember that. It is an ancient thing. Will take centuries before Whites see Coloureds and Blacks as equal. I won't live to see freedom. Perhaps your children will..."

Mr. Magee took pride in being daring in his friendship with Tumelo. Mr. Torres noticed her increasing intimacy with Mr. Magee and warned her again. "Do not trust him. The FBI comes in many forms. He could be superficial like all other wealthy White Americans. They are simply adventurous, and sometimes they are just fishing for information on people in the revolutions in Africa."

"You mean he could also be into looking for exotic women like the others?"

"Yah, you must remember that for many White men, Black women are simply part of an adventure, part of an anthropological expedition of 'the other' in a jungle... "

"You mean like not viewed as equal?"

"Yah, as curiosities, like objects to be studied, to be touched, and to be explored. Be careful of his attentions. I see he is also visiting you at home and driving you and your mother around... you should not allow him so much into your private life. You don't know him well enough."

201

Then she remembered how when the first time they met, Mr. Magee described women in Africa to her. Yah, perhaps Mr. Torres was right.

Mr. Magee and Mr. Torres continued to keep a safe distance from each other. They did debate about human rights in Cuba and the atrocities of the Vietnam War, but not much more than that, except about interesting hiking trails in the beautiful Cape mountains. Their relationship was polite and distant. Mr. Magee could disarm his colleagues with uncomfortable questions. Mr. Torres did not always like his intellectual style.

The peaceful atmosphere at Forest High did not last long. Within a few months, the Cape Flats schools were catapulted into a long school boycott against gutter education and unqualified teachers. The four years of planning, reading, and political recruitment into the underground ANC had paid off. The *Free Mandela* campaign had started, though Nelson Mandela's face was still banned.

Marxist scholars who had studied in London at places like Sussex, Leeds, SOAS, Cambridge, Birkbeck, and the London School of Economics were all active in the anti-apartheid movement in England, and had returned to teach history, philosophy, politics, and sociology at the White liberal University of Cape Town (UCT). Only a small exclusive middle-class group of Coloured students made it through the permit system for admission to the prestigious UCT. However, the University of the Western Cape (UWC) became the political university of the Coloured working class. It became an attractive place for notable Black writers and scholars.

The masses of youth at schools were tired of singing freedom songs, the same ones repeatedly. The teachers were tired of sitting in the staff rooms for hours, waiting for instructions from the student leaders, tired of the political debates in staff meetings. Teachers at Forest High grew tired of Mr. Hofman and his tirade of tears and accusations, tired of being accused of being possible spies if they seemed too quiet, or too preoccupied, tired of being insulted as "unqualified and uneducated", tired of being snubbed by Mr. Torres and his leftist and communist colleagues and the student leaders, tired of doing nothing from eight in the morning till three in the afternoon. To help them cope, some resorted to escaping into shopping sprees or impromptu visits to the local *shebeens*, where they drank beer and smoked cannabis with the schoolgirls and slept with them.

Many schoolgirls at Forest High fell pregnant at this time. Some were simply gang-raped by bored boys at the school, or by the gangsters in the township who preyed on them as they aimlessly walked the streets while their parents were at work, or invariably on strike or at mass meetings until late at night. Some girls were raped by their corrupt teachers. Nobody reported such crimes. It was simply not a priority at the time. The police were not interested in civic crimes as they focused on political surveillance. Everybody had hoped that these bad things would go away one day, like impenetrable mist that evaporates mid-morning when the bright sun eventually comes out.

On occasion, a toothless mother and some supportive women from the neighbourhood, still in their nightgowns and morning slippers with their hair in colourful rollers would visit the school in the early morning to complain loudly at Mr. Hofman's office about a teenage daughter's unexplained pregnancy, "Your teachers must have their *piele* (dicks) cut off! Your teachers must go *naai* (screw) their own daughters! Mr. Hofman what are you doing to do about the restless *piele* of the *naaiers* at your school?!" they chastised.

Mr. Hofman usually pleaded ignorance of the sexual activity at his school. "All the teachers here, madam, are honourable men and women. They are gentlemen and ladies." He persistently called every man "sir" and every woman "madam", regardless of race, class or background.

"No, Mr. Headmaster, your teachers are child - *naaiers* (fuckers) ! You don't know what is happening right under your nose here. The whole community is talking. They call your school *the maternity house*. Did you know that?! One of the teachers has been climbing up my child. I am going to report it..."

The emotional mother's supporters would interject violently with arms swinging in desperation, "Don't be a fool! The police won't help us!. They *also* climb up our girls! At least we can talk to Mr. Hofman. We can't talk to the police..." After such deeply despairing encounters, Mr. Hofman confronted his staff time and time again crying loudly, the tears streaming down his cheeks, "There are not only cowards at this school who use my children as cannon fodder. There are also *rapists* at this school! Gentlemen, what are you *doing* to *my* children? I *never* touched a child in any indecent way in my entire life!" This was true. The schoolgirls trusted him and liked him. They always felt safe and protected with him. The system left him feeling helpless, like a fool. When the gangsters heard of a pregnancy at the school, they would trap the teachers at the shebeens and beat them up. They did not take kindly to rivalry of any sort.

Chapter 13
Earthy Smells for My Revolution

Like the schools, there were universities for different "races" in South Africa. If you were Black, you were forced to attend the university for your "tribe" or "race". If you wanted to study at a White university, you had to obtain a first grade pass, an aggregate score of 60%, and you had to apply for special permission from the government to do so. For instance, you had to show that your course of study was not offered at the university for your specific "race". The apartheid government created five university colleges for Black students: Ngoye for Zulus, Turfloop for the Tswana and Sotho, Fort Hare for Xhosas, Belville (UWC) for Coloureds, and Durban-Westville for Indians, all located in poor and deprived areas.

Located on the Rhodes Estate on the slopes of Devil's Peak of Table Mountain, and founded in 1829 as the first White, English, male South African college, stands the University of Cape Town (UCT) the oldest university in South Africa. Sometimes, the Cape blanket of fog covered Table Mountain as far as the university building, which made it impossible to see the prestigious institution against the mountain from far out on the low-lying areas of the Cape Flats and the False Bay coast. It was known as South Africa's own "Oxford", because many of its teaching staff came from the leading UK universities.

On a perfect summer's day, the Cape skies would be blue and one clearly could see the university steeped high on the mountain's slopes, several dozen miles away, even from Forest High. Many students at Coloured and African schools avoided pinning their dreams on ever gaining entrance to the elitist White institution. It was as far out of their reach as when on a foggy day in Cape Town, view of the university buildings disappeared from sight under the notorious Cape blanket.

Many Coloured people hoped that they would reach there through some miracle. Tumelo was one of them, and she passed the test to gain entrance.

To get to UCT from Forest Hill, Tumelo had to take the seven o'clock Coloureds-only bus to Wynberg, and then board the non-Whites third-class coach of the train to Newlands Station. From there, she took the eight o'clock multi-racial UCT bus that travelled the five kilometre journey to the Whites-only institution.

Nestled below a dramatically huge monument of Cecil John Rhodes, dedicated to his contribution to the British Empire, UCT's colonial architecture was intimidating. The imposing monument of Cecil John Rhodes on horseback above the university buildings overlooked the vast Cape Peninsula stretched out before him. His gigantic posture is designed to create the impression of facing northeast in the direction of North Africa, towards Cairo, and was aimed to capture his dramatic vision to conquer the whole of Africa, from the Cape to Cairo. The memorial consists of 49 steps, each one representing a year in the life of Cecil John Rhodes. It reads, "To the spirit and life work of Cecil John Rhodes who loved and served South Africa." The university's faculty buildings are covered with creeper plants, which are a dark green in summer, a golden brown in autumn, a leafless grey in winter, and a bright light green in spring. The students learnt to watch these colours as a measure of their progress in the academic year. By the time the leaves turned brown and grey, then they knew whether they'd pass or fail that year, as their major tests and assignments coincided with autumn and winter. Student recruitment officers for the university reassured Tumelo that there was no apartheid or race prejudice at UCT, as the institution was known for its "long tradition of anti-apartheid activity and liberalism since 1960".

At that time, 20 years later, UCT boasted world-renowned people as alumni, though all White. Amongst them were the socialist and feminist Enid Charles, who spoke out against the racist eugenics movement, Professor Christiaan Barnard who performed the world's first heart transplant, virologist Max Theiler, who was awarded the Nobel Prize in Medicine for developing a vaccine against yellow fever, the world-renowned playwright Athol Fugard, and the anti-apartheid journalist Donald Woods.

The morning trips on the "multi-racial" UCT bus were a little uncomfortable and intimidating. Tumelo found that she was about one of three Black students on the bus every morning. The bus, filled to the brim with 60 odd students, of mostly loud, athletic, young White men in navy blue and khaki shorts and beach tongs (even in winter) was in itself a rather odd space for any Black student to be. These young men who indulged in loud conversations about fighting the "terrorists" on the border were evidently recent returns, barely perhaps 18 years old, from military conscription in fighting the communist Cubans, Russians, and the ANC on the Angolan border, or the PAC in neighbouring countries like Lesotho. The apartheid government forced all young White men to perform military service as soon as they turned 16. As a White boy child, you could only escape conscription if you were medically unfit or if you could claim a "race classification error", that you were not "White" but actually "Coloured". However, one did not hear any of such appeals. During conscription, these young White boys were brutalised and drilled into killing Blacks and communists, and they were made to fear ever becoming a *kaffir boetie* (friend of a "kaffir") - this formed part of their daily drill and their mantra.

In her regular trips over three years as an undergraduate, she observed that very few White students approached a Coloured or a Black student for a conversation on the bus. Whites spoke only to each other; and the Coloured and Black students sat quietly with their heads down, buried in their course books. The White students on the bus were fully aware that Tumelo and her friends were there on special permits – permission by the apartheid government for Coloureds and Africans to attend the Whites-only university, and not the University of the Western Cape (UWC). In spite of its anti-apartheid protests and notable White liberal and radical alumni, most of the White students and professors tended to treat the Black students dismissively, as if they were see-through objects. Tumelo found that UCT was very racist, and therefore decidedly alienating for any Coloured or Black student. Virtually a "Whites-only" place, it was steeped up high on the slopes of the Devils Peak mountain almost condescendingly overlooking the Cape Flats, from which it was completely alienated.

The UCT was part of the White residential world. The majority of White students never had any contact with the millions of people of the Cape Flats (the nearest township was only about ten kilometres away).Through its medical school, where they specialised in studying tuberculosis and other typical "Coloured diseases", the White students mainly made contact only with Coloured people as hospital patients, domestic servants or gardeners.

"Watch the colour of the leaves on the building, students", the intimidating White male lecturers usually warned on the first day of a first-year undergraduate course. "Watch how they change colour as the weeks and months go by. And start to worry when they fall down to the ground towards mid-year to warn you of your possible fall at this place of *world excellence*! This is not a place for mediocrity!" Black and Coloured students did not really exist in the eyes of such lecturers at UCT. Discrimination at UCT took various forms: not remembering their names in small classes, not allowing them to participate in debates and discussions, ignoring their hands when they had questions to ask, awarding them the lowest marks, failing them in tests, not looking their way when lecturing, not offering them academic support, ignoring them in small tutorial groups of not more than eight students, penalising them for radical political analyses in essays – treating them as the invisible, mediocre, silent, anonymous mass. Black students huddled together in the libraries and on the train and bus in the mornings and in the evenings to support one another – morally and psychologically. One particular lecturer was especially keen on sorting Black students from White students. Professor Kohl was a middle-aged, tall, stern German woman who wore a cream coat, brown leather gloves, and a pearl necklace. She was dressed more appropriately for the theatre than for a lecture, as most of her colleagues wore jeans and tattered shirts, and did not seem to bother to comb their hair. Professor Kohl of the science faculty did not hide her taste for class and her discomfort with - if not her outright dislike of- Black students.

When Tumelo registered for Professor Kohl's course, there was already one Coloured student who was the daughter of one of the cleaners at the university who had failed the course the two previous years. Twenty-year-old Norma struck a depressed and lonely figure, who walked with her back bent and her head down. She started a friendship with Tumelo, and her first conversation was spine chilling, "I am relieved that there are now a group of five of us..., and that I am no longer on my own with 'the dragon'."

"What do you mean?!" Tumelo asked.

"Dragon has been keeping me here for two years. I have been the only Coloured student in her class. The White students don't talk to me and dragon awards me fractions of one as a mark, not whole numbers."

"What do you mean by *fractions*?"

"As in one eighth out of 20, while the White students get whole numbers from 12 upwards."

"That is not possible! It does not make mathematical sense."

"I know it sounds impossible; *nobody* wants to believe me... she does not even call me by my name. She sees right through me...you'll see for yourself...my mother keeps on telling me to try harder, as she can hardly afford the fees. I've done well at school, that is how I got into this place, but since coming here, I have not moved in this course run by the boere. No matter how hard I try, Dragon still marks me down. I tell you, even if I should copy a White student's work word for word, which I did once, Dragon still failed me and gave me a fraction and awarded the White student 70% for the same work!" "So why did you not complain, report her to the authorities?"

"Dragon is a racist, and there is nobody to complain to... complaints about racism are not encouraged."

What Norma described made sense. The student body rallied around campaigns against apartheid, but not against racism suffered right under their noses. It was an interesting contradiction.

"Perhaps now that we are more than one, we'll be able to make a noise and perhaps bring it to the attention of the student body", Norma hoped.

Coming from one of the poorest areas on the Cape Flats, Norma was not only Black, she was also poor – which doubled her struggle at White, snooty UCT, which favoured middle-class Coloureds who came from the more prestigious schools. Norma had attended a school similar to Forest Hill, in one of the poorest Cape Flats townships. She was determined to get her degree from the "ivory tower" where her mother was a cleaner.

It was not long before Tumelo herself experienced the "dragon" in Professor Kohl. Her methods of making Tumelo and others feel decidedly unwelcome and inferior were cunning and calculated. On a typical day, Professor Kohl would pretend to struggle to remember their faces and their names, or that they were ever one of her 20 students, even though the minority of students was Black. This kind of pretentious memory loss happened interestingly and consistently over a period of three years, and only in her relationship with Black students. As Norma had described her methods, Professor Kohl only looked at the White students while teaching, and looked past the small group of Black students as if they did not exist. German Dragon was the irony of liberal UCT, with its large Jewish staff and student mass, its anti-apartheid protests, student activities, and newspapers. Professor Kohl referred to the Black students anonymously as "the people with the big hair" – to her, they had no names, no faces, no identity. They were not individuals; they were to her a homogeneous nameless mass. She gave them dismissive looks when she handed their scripts back, all marked down to a ridiculous fraction of the number one. And she spoke with an affected dragging foreign German accent to rub it in as she called out the marks for the Black students, something reminiscent of the Nazis. Only one Coloured girl scored 12 out of 20 and above – she was quite fair, had blond hair and light eyes, and could easily reclassify herself as White if ever she wanted to. She had a relatively easy time at UCT with all her courses.

Professor Kohl even encouraged the Black students "to try remedial classes". The students' complaints to the science department fell on deaf ears, with one of the students complicating the matter a little bit when she caught one of the professors in a compromising position with the secretary on the office table. The students grew despondent and frustrated, as there was no race equality complaint office, although there was a well-established student union run and staffed by White students who defended UCT's anti-racist tradition and ignored all complaints that gave evidence to the contrary. Nonetheless, the Black students pushed through with their resilience to survive UCT and kept active in the broader struggles against apartheid. Instead, they used the classes to intimidate Professor Dragon; they distributed political pamphlets on racism and apartheid openly in class and placed stacks on her table under her nose. They snubbed her by turning their backs on her while she lectured, holding loud conversations about organising anti-racist political rallies. They caused chaos in her class, treating *her* instead as *persona non grata*. Their tactic was to *deliberately* make *her* feel unwelcome and misplaced. By some mysterious explanation, all of the Black students managed to pass the full course at the end of each of the three years, even though the cumulative mark she awarded them did not add up to a pass mark for any one of them. It seemed that their strategy of alienation and intimidation had worked, or perhaps her seniors were aware of her racism and had her marks moderated. However, similar racism must have been going on quietly in many other courses as well, as the drop-out rate amongst Black students at UCT was notoriously high. Some struggled to cope with the vast gap between the low level of education in most Coloured schools and the often superior academic teaching and research levels at UCT. Lecturers and professors came from London, Oxford, and Cambridge, and the Black students were simply challenged to deliver the goods for them as if it was an equal world. However, Tumelo and her friends were also fortunate to benefit from some of the academics that were active members of the anti-apartheid movement in London; unfortunately, they were few and far in between.

One of the highlights for Tumelo was the day she attended the T.B. Memorial lecture by the world renowned historian Howard Zinn in the Jameson Hall in July, 1982. His lecture was titled "Students and Youth Against Racism". Howard Zinn opened his lecture by saying that the name of South Africa immediately aroused powerful emotions among all people in the world concerned with human freedom. He spoke about the parallels with regard to racism in South Africa and in the United States, and about the Freedom Charter founded by the Congress of the People in 1955. Large numbers of White students were now being detained and charged for anti-apartheid political activity under the Riotous Assemblies Act.

While at UCT, Tumelo got her political education through left-wing Black political, civic, and trade union networks from the streets of the Cape Flats that operated in the campus libraries and the surrounding bush on the slopes of Devils Peak mountain.

Tumelo was now seeing less of Mr. Torres and the academic Trotskyite Fellowship. Mr. Magee had returned to Los Angeles to work as a full-time human rights academic. He wrote her a few letters and sent her some friendly post cards. By then, she had also left home to join the revolution on the streets, and to join ranks with her comrades in the trade unions and in various leftist organisations. Olive-skinned Tessa recruited her at UCT to work with the women in the trade unions. They had met in a psychology tutorial course. Tessa was much older and wore her black curly hair long and bushy. Routinely dressed in a blue tracksuit trousers, she wore black army boots and a tight top that accentuated her large breasts and nipples. Tessa was street-wise and a serious lefty with a crude and daring manner. With her attractive thick uninterrupted Frida Kahlo eyebrows, she successfully lured a number of young Coloured and liberal White male students to her underground reading group. Women also found her sexually compelling, and Tessa used this to her political advantage in her recruitment campaigns amongst the students.

One could smell the sweat from her armpits and her bodily odour when in close conversation with her, even on a cold day. According to Tessa and the Anarchists of the Cape Flats, the world of communism was one in which you did not indulge in "petty bourgeoisie pleasures", and swearing was an essential part of one's "revolutionary vocabulary". "Nickers, toilet paper, and underarm deodorant are all petty bourgeoisie creations to serve capitalism. Who said we *needed* these things, as the body was of the earth? Who created these artificial costs? Allow the hair in your armpits to grow wild and sweaty like the sweet wild smell of horses, as that makes you an authentic African. And don't use shampoo and conditioner; only sunlight soap – because revolutionaries are from and of the earth! And another thing, a true revolutionary does not wash her *pussy* every day!" She intimidated young women recruits with what constituted "genuine revolutionary conduct" at a first induction meeting at the student commune. "To be a true revolutionary, you must *smell* like the people! You must not become bourgeois armchair politicians with the Trotskyites, smelling of costly French perfume!" Tumelo used her discretion with Tessa's unsolicited advice on personal hygiene and her misguided information on poor people and their assumed compulsive need to *smell*.

In spite of Tessa's odd ideas about "revolutionary conduct" and her occasional indulging of the body in "earthly smells" to prove one's commitment to the workers' struggle, Tessa and Tumelo got on very well. Tessa arranged for Tumelo to work in a Woman's Refuge with Coloured and Black women who were destitute or abandoned on the Cape Flats. In her political work with these women, Tumelo discovered that some of them (as young as 15) were seasoned sex workers who serviced the White men and foreign sailors in the city. Tessa and Tumelo decided to launch a political education campaign with the sex workers. Tessa's advice on intimate hygiene did not go down well with them, either. They noised militantly with her, "Sister!, it is *important* for us to wash our *pussies* and our arm pits. We'll be out of business, if we don't! If you don't wash yours, that is your problem, but don't interfere with our wares in this trade where our pussies provide much needed bread on the table! We've got to look after our *business!*"

Tessa and Tumelo organised literature for them to read on feminism and women's struggles, held discussions with them at the commune, and got them to question unemployment and gender issues in South Africa. As Tessa said to Tumelo in one of their many discussions, "The important point is to get them to act on their *class* position, and to get them to *engage* in the class struggle as *exploited* women, not so much as *Black* women."

The women were not keen on analysing too much. "Tumelo, are you *crazy?* We are enjoying this. The wealthy White men are crazy for us! They pay good money for a Coloured prostitute. They say our forbidden flesh tastes sweet." Tumelo did not have any luck at first. Then she decided to try to invite them to one of the commune's reading groups that were held in Forest Hill. However, the street-wise women saw in the visits to the reading groups opportunities to do business with the comrades. For them, the reading groups were simply another potential financial opportunity to put bread on the table for their families. In the end, after all their efforts, Tumelo and Tessa were devastated to discover that their recent recruits were enjoying rather adventurous romping with some of the comrades, though they soon discovered that the lustful comrades did not have money.

The women challenged Tumelo in private, "Hey, the comrades have been asking us for free fucking fucks! They still owe us money for the last two weeks. They want us to do their dishes and to fuck non-stop. What do they *think?* That is not good economics for a woman!" they scolded.

"See, that is why we rather work on the road and wait for the White men in the Mercedes Benz cars. They pay at least and don't expect us to do their dishes or to have non-stop sex whole night. Its simple politics and *rational economics. That* is what your revolution should be about!"

Working-class Coloured women are reputed to be feisty; daring often to take on men with knives and swearing in public. Petula had the familiar edge of a notorious rough woman. Most femicide incidents in South Africa are said to be amongst working-class Coloured couples. Some violent men are known to murder their wives through the most spine chilling means: scooping their eyes out of their skulls, stabbing them more than a dozen times, slitting their throats, and shooting them through the head. It was not just a matter of verbal abuse such as "you are grossly obese", but some Coloured men could indulge in self-loathing through insulting their partners, "Why is your arse so huge?! Your Bushman arse! Ugly thing!"

"Look at your long Bushman breasts! I'd be ashamed to walk with you in the streets!"

"Goodness me, you have thick Bushman lips! Ugly bitch!"

"Your have flat, ugly Bushmen feet!!"

"You have a flat, big, ugly Bushman face!"

The biggest insults are those about a Coloured woman's private parts. Like the fate of Sarah Baartman, some Coloured women would often find their own husbands and sex partners describing them in derogatory ways in public, about their vaginas, their buttocks, and their breasts.

"Your *Bushman poes!*"

"You are a *hotnot jars jintoe, a lustful hotnot whore!* That is *why* I've got to fucking beat you up! Understand?!"

When the police arrived after such domestic disputes, the woman would deny that there was anything the matter, while her husband stood next to her kissing her forehead. They would both change like quicksilver, in a kind of co-dependence on emotional, verbal, and physical violence and self loathing.

Drunken brawls and shouts of *Bushmen whores* and *Hottentot drunkards* would overflow into the street with neighbours, friends, and family joining in with shoes, spades, knives, axes, and bats. The blood would flow after the ritualistic indulgence in Friday fish and chips. The police and ambulance would arrive hours later – if at all. Then, the next morning all would seem to be forgotten. The couple that started all the drama would sometimes copulate in public as a display of their contradictory undying love for each other. Afterwards, the man would serenade her loudly with Ray Charles' *Crying Time.* The seemingly remorseful husband would sob while he serenaded his wife, still nursing her bruises and broken heart of the night before. They'd fall into each other's arms and dance in a tight embrace outside in front of their little shack to Percy Sledge's *When a man loves a woman*, tripping drunk over the escaping, hungry, thin cats and the dogs. Everything would be forgotten.

There is a long history to this tradition of violence and sexual vulgarity amongst the working-class Coloureds as a previous-slave community that goes back a long time. Enslaved people at the Cape did not enjoy sexual freedom, and could not be sexually free with their wives or partners. They were also at the sexual service of their White masters and the visiting European sailors at the Cape. Between 7,000 and 9,000 slaves lived in the slave lodge in Cape Town for over 132 years. Enslaved people, who became today's poor Cape Coloured people, were hanged, broken on the wheel, quartered, had their flesh torn away by red-hot pincers, were impaled with a stake driven up their anuses, and left to die in public. Runaway enslaved people were flogged and would have their ears, tips of their noses, and right hand cut off. Enslaved people were regularly mutilated and verbally and emotionally or psychologically abused. Punishment for murder could entail being chained to a stake and being burnt to death. The remains of an executed enslaved person often were left on display for the eagles to devour as a warning to others.

In this ancient history of body violence, the streetwise women naturally had their blades sharpened for the communist-inspired comrades, whom, it turned out, they figured out were "exploitative". Some comrades had refused to pay them after a marathon night of loud sex. They were angry because this meant that they could have made much more money standing on the road to be picked up by the White men instead of servicing their fellow Coloured friends at the commune. Petula protested with her body language and hands gesturing very graphically about the story that she was telling Tumelo and Tessa, "You see, with the White men on the road, it is quick and easy business because these men are afraid they'll get caught by the police. They pick us up; we lie down flat on the back seat so that the cops can't see us, and then we go to a park or to some deserted dark mountain pass close by to *pomp* (pump). If we want to make a lot of money in one night, we give the White boss a quick blow job or an anal to make him come quickly out of fear of being caught by the boere. He then pays quickly without argument. Everything is over within less than 10 minutes, and we get ready for the next guy. But with these comrades, they first expect you to clean the house, cook some food, then you must get into his bed for the whole fucking night, under *his* rules and conditions! When you wake up, he's got his arm tightly around your neck in a grip so that you can't escape. Then he has the audacity to want one for the road before you go. And after all those hours of servicing him which involves several blow jobs and hectic screwing, he then argues with you about bloody payment! Scandalous men they are! We do not care about their revolution and their moral preaching, because they have no respect for us and our time. No, we don't want to come to the reading groups anymore. Besides, it is time consuming and we lose out big time on business. Good luck with your revolution with the 'comrades'!" Petula shouted at Tumelo, slamming the door furiously in her face.

Tumelo ran after her into the toilet to reason with her to give the comrades a chance and to work for the revolution. Petula looked her up and down, then scratched in her bag. Taking her time, she took her little plastic pink framed mirror and make-up bag out of her shocking red plastic handbag, and painted her lips with thick blood red lipstick in slow deliberate strokes. Then she took out her comb and removed the swirl stocking from her head, and brushed her short coarse dry hair, pulling it hard down to flatten it straight. She pulled up her black mini skirt a little higher just to cover her crotch, to show off her black fishnet stockings. Tumelo noticed that she looked so much like Annie. As she caught Tumelo's admiring stares at her indigenous looks, she swung around on her high red plastic stiletto shoes, and remarked with disarming feminine confidence and a cheeky broad smile, "The White men *lust* for women like me...I get a *lot* of *business*!" She then walked off swaggering with her jacket flung over her shoulder, like a South African Naomi Campbell on a catwalk.

Tessa reprimanded the comrades as "hypocrites" for exploiting the sex workers. The comrades, of course, denied any sexual activities with the new recruits. "They have been trying to seduce us; you know what *women* are like...you two are idealists..."

Tessa and Tumelo were equally livid. "What do you mean by *what women are like...?!*" Some heated discussion in the weekly reading groups about the status and treatment of women by the comrades, and reading and debate about values, attitudes to and power over bodies, gender politics, and the revolution followed for weeks on end.

Still, Tessa and Tumelo did not give up on working with these brave wise women. They still managed to get some to attend meetings where they introduced them to the lyrics of songs by Marianne Faithful, Billie Holiday, Joan Armatrading, Tracy Chapman, and Nina Simone. After several weeks, they grew tired, as the women were often fickle in their dealings, having had the double pressure to earn their keep on the road, and eventually after some months Tessa and Tumelo gave up on working with the sex workers.

Tessa's motto was that they organize and allow things to happen organically, without a self-appointed political "vanguard". In their many hours of reading in the bush, Tessa once told Tumelo, "The great anarchist thinker, Bakunin, said: 'the urge to destroy is also a creative urge'. We must allow for spontaneous upheaval, for revolutionary creativity, like in the Paris Communes of 1871 and Spain in 1936. Lenin destroyed the Russian revolution of 1917. History has shown that revolutionary politicians become too easily preoccupied with seizure of power, they want to speak and govern on *behalf* of the people, as the people's vanguard. I tell you, watch the ANC guys when freedom comes. I am telling you – we'll come to see that struggle for individual power at the expense of the people!"

Tumelo enjoyed the many hours of reading and discussion with the enchanting, bright, brave and risky Tessa at river streams in the Cape mountains and in the forests, amongst the Proteas. Sometimes they met amongst the large vineyards and amongst the pine trees and discussed banned literature on how to overthrow the apartheid system. They strategised for revolution for hours, reflecting on where they may have gone wrong in the work with the women, while they fed on overripe grapes and nutty pine kernels in the beauty of the Cape vineyards and forests amid the unsuspecting dangerous Cape Cobra snakes that sometimes slithered across the hot sand paths and perched on the rocks in the sun.

The Women's Refuge was not a cosy place. Many things happened there in secret. A number of the girls were depressed and suicidal. They were not at the means to receive psychotherapy for the trauma suffered as a result of drug addiction, alcoholism, rape, incest, and sexual abuse. Tumelo befriended Amber, a dark Coloured woman of slight build with an Afro at Blossom House. Amber was recruited by the ANC and invited Tumelo to stay with her at her partner's house for the weekend to talk politics and to plan some things. It was only with the sight of a blue plastic bucket, the kettles of hot water that she kept boiling in her room, and the many towels that it dawned upon Tumelo that something else was happening. Amber seemed angry, delirious, and mad with emotional and physical pain. Tumelo stared at the wildness in Amber's eyes, at the blood soaked towels on the bed, the bucket, the many wet newspapers. Amber wept feverishly and started to shake uncontrollably, "We are due to escape over the border within a few days to join the ANC underground. We are going to take up arms against the boere. We want AK47s. You have no choice in this." She grabbed on to Tumelo in pain, almost choking her in her tight grip to cope with the pain, "Help me, comrade...please...!" In Tumelo's mind's eye, she saw the police, the feared vans, the deaths in detention, and the hundreds of missing bodies. As Amber lay on the bed writhing with near-death pain with her legs wide open, her uterine blood splashed in Tumelo's face, dripping from her eye over her cheek. The room smelt of raw liver hot out of a recently slaughtered pig's carcass. Tumelo's heart raced and her hands were trembling and sweating. She grabbed the cheap blue coarse toilet roll on the bed, tore a piece, and used it to dry the blood from her face. Amber seemed in a trance.

"The child's blood..." Tumelo thought.

Amber whispered, "There is urgent work to be done in this country...urgent work...very urgent work..."

Shortly after her body rejected what was not to be, Amber fell into a deep depressive state and cried bitterly, because she realised she was not going to see her family for a long time. She cried raw, deep, painful sobs as her head rested against Tumelo's breasts. As her body jerked with every sob, Tumelo's heart beat louder and sounded into her ears. She did not utter a single word of judgement to Amber. Tumelo cleaned her up with comforting warm water, dried her traumatised body gently, and dressed her in her soft pink winter pyjamas. She tucked Amber into bed and laid her hand gently on her back, rubbing it with soft sympathetic strokes. Tumelo did not know what to tell her or what to promise her. Jimmy Cliff's *Many Rivers to Cross* was playing on the radio. It was a kind of little funeral. There was nothing to promise and nothing to say; not knowing where life was taking them, not knowing whether they would survive somehow and see the light at the end of the tunnel some day. The incident left Tumelo vomiting at the university's toilets for days. She vomited for South Africa and its insanity. A few days later, Amber and her partner successfully skipped the country, crossing through Botswana's border to work for the ANC underground. Tumelo would not see her or hear from her for another decade or more.

After Amber's sudden departure, Tumelo hit a deep depression and grieving process, completely out of the blue. In this bizarre and unspeakable search for what she had lost, she cheated her way into anatomy classes with the medical students at the University of Cape Town's medical school. She befriended the assistant to the anatomy professors, Mr. Hendricks, a small, dark Coloured man in white overalls. He had black, wide eyes that looked as if he was in a constant state of shock, like the eyes of a fresh corpse, of someone who had passed on from a violent death. He mechanically worked through the dozens of corpses in the anatomy room. "So you are an arts student at the university, but you actually want to study *bodies*? Strange..."

"Yes, I am interested in bodies..."

"Now, how am I supposed to explain the presence of a Coloured student at this mortuary to these White professors?! They say they are liberals, but they will notice your presence instantly and very soon they'll be asking me about you. There is only a handful of Coloured students here at the medical school and the lecturers know them all. So, miss, you'll be sticking out like a sore thumb..."

"I have a permit to study here. I can show them my student card."

"No, that does not help. You'll *still* stand out like a sore thumb. Just have some story if they should spot you; otherwise I'll be in trouble with these White people. You know what things are like in this boere-country."

"Well, I am studying archaeology and we have to deal with the question of race...so anatomy lessons are relevant..."

"OK, you've convinced me...sort of, but not entirely...(sigh)... Which body shall we look at first?"

"A Black man's...one that has died in an accident."

"Not sure if we work with mutilated bodies. Let me show you the bodies that the students and the professors are working with at the moment."

"That is fine..."

The anatomy building was cold and eerie. The sad whistle of the wind outside could be heard, and the strong smell of ether filled the passageway to the huge steel doors where the corpses and carcasses were "filed". He took Tumelo into the cold mortuary. Bodies were lying on steel tables covered with white sheets. Each body had a tag with a number on. There were jars on the shelves filled with body organs – lungs, hearts, livers, brains, and kidneys. He removed the sheet from one body: the corpse of a Black man who must have died in his fifties. He looked too healthy to have died of disease. He had a label on his big toe, like all the others, NZ 347267. Tumelo remembered these numbers. She saw many corpses and many numbers. All were stacked in drawers marked with labels. Their skins looked like the shaven skins of pigs. Some had their ribs exposed, with their skins peeled back. Mr. Hendricks noticed her keen interest in the body of the Black man in his fifties.

"Oh, that one is for the students to study the formation of muscle." He pulled out corpse after corpse from the huge drawers. One was of a 10-year-old Khoisan looking girl, like Annie. He did not comment on her body as she lay there peacefully, almost undisturbed. Tumelo noticed a long cut from her chest right down to her pubic area.

"Most of these people were homeless Coloured or Black people or vagrants with no family. I'll show you something interesting."

The UCT was renowned for its world excellence in Medicine. It was here that the world famous heart surgeon, Chris Barnard, performed the world's first human to human heart transplant in 1967. Chris Barnard was rumoured to be a racist himself, with a secret Coloured family that lived on the Cape Flats.

The "surprise" Mr. Hendricks had for Tumelo, it turned out, was pieces of human anatomy in jars – eyes, tongues, ears – of that sort. An even "better surprise", as Mr. Hendricks put it, was the full-bodied womb of a Black pregnant mother who died at full term. There the baby was lying, quiet, and serene, with her thumb in her mouth, "You can open it like a lid. See?" remarked Mr. Hendricks with much excitement, smiling enthusiastically. Tumelo looked away. Then, for the first time, she noticed a soft smile on the face of the anatomy man, and a softening of his eyes as he gently opened the womb of the corpse (which was cut horizontally in half) using the navel of the mother's corpse as a handle, as if he did not want to wake the unborn little African girl from her deep slumber. Tumelo's heart went into a spasm, almost involuntarily so. She thought of Amber's abortion, of Annie's corpse, and of Uncle Thaba's body that she never got to view or touch to say farewell.

What happened to his body when he died in cold blood on that winter's Friday night? It was now 15 years later when his memory came to visit her unexpectedly at UCT. The swoosh sound of the wind tucked at the corners of the tall gray anatomy building in the cold dark shadow of Devil's Peak. She heard Uncle Thaba's voice in the wind – his lost soul trying to find its way home, trying to get home before the van ran into him. She heard Amber's baby's voice trying to find her mother who had disappeared into the ANC underground movement. Her mind was tormented with the deep loss. What had happened to Uncle Thaba's body parts? What was his number on his body tag in the mortuary? Another number – like a number in his passbook? Did they cover him to be warm, protected from the cold as he lay there cold dead? Did they really bury Uncle Thaba? What if they brought him to the medical school? Perhaps he was amongst one of the corpses? Perhaps Dr. Chris Barnard was studying the spasms of fear in his heart? Or perhaps the surgeons were studying the shock in his eyes after the boere reversed over his already dead body? No, perhaps he was too mutilated, perhaps just a pulp of blood, broken bones and muscle. No, he could not have been there. It was too long ago, but the loss and bereavement still felt so raw. She wanted to find Uncle Thaba and put his broken pieces together.

She did not know what drove her to go to the mortuary that day. She did not know what had triggered it all. She found nothing at the mortuary, because she was not even sure what she was searching for, in any case. Mr. Hendricks looked at her and noticed her change of mood. "Young lady, why do you suddenly look so sad? I have shown you what you wanted to see. Come on. Don't be sad..."

The strong icy wind tucked at her as she walked down the steep road from UCT's medical school that led to the train station at the bottom of the hill. She boarded the Coloureds-only carriage on the train. She felt empty. A sense of deep bottomless loss overcame her. She forgot to get off at her destination. She had lost sense of time and place and could not recall how she had found her way home that night.

Chapter 14
The Letter on the Rock on Devil's Peak

While studying at UCT, Tumelo was exposed to the intellectual thoughts of anarchist communist groups, which promoted the ideas of Peter Kropoktin and Mikhael Bakunin, emphasising the power that lay in mass control through communes, such as the Paris Commune of 1871, and in Russia of 1905 and 1917, and Spain in 1936. Cadres were trained to identify fascists, Stalinists, spies, *agents provocateurs*, and all other organized agents which undermined the revolution in South Africa. Tessa and her friends at the commune were ideologically close to the London-based anarchist communist movements.

Banned literature was distributed to students clandestinely from Mozambique, Zambia, Zimbabwe, the USSR, Nicaragua, Palestine, Cuba, New York, Sweden, Denmark, Finland, Chile, Spain, Greece, London, and France. Debates centered around whether South Africa needed a two-stage revolution or a permanent revolution; whether the country needed workers' militias or parliamentary reform. Which programme was the most relevant for the South African revolution?

The security police targeted youth and those inspired to work with civic and religious groups. Thousands of South Africans were jailed in the 1980s – parents, children, students, teachers, workers, priests, sport activists, artists, writers, journalists - anybody who threatened the state in some way.

It was at this time that Tumelo became friendly with a communist, Adiel Khan, who had his own international network of communist activists and, amongst others, entertained Greek communist pilots and air-hostesses at his home. Their "social visits" entailed smuggling banned literature into the country on their flights into South Africa. Conversations late into the night under clandestine conditions were filled with the intellectual names of notable South African and American revolutionaries such as the Chilean Pablo Neruda and Salvador Allende. White South African revolutionaries like Joe Slovo, Bram Fischer and Ruth First were household names. In these circles, revolution knew no colour and transcended boundaries.

While eating moussaka, the South Africans of all colours and the Greek pilots sang to Mikis Theodorakis' 1975 recording of Pablo Neruda's *Canto General,* holding hands with their eyes closed, stamping their feet to the beats of the sounds blasting out of the speakers of Adiel's old record player. Adiel, an atheist, was very handsome, and had many women chasing him, but he seemed uninterested in romance. His house was a library of hundreds of books and vinyl records. He was intellectually fiercely formidable and independent, and challenged Tumelo to question even the anarchists. His perspectives on current affairs were fresh and authentic. He hated dogma of all sorts, and refrained from sectarian judgment of leftist ideologies that were not particularly in line with his. Adiel was fascinated with all cultures, all religions, ideas, and belief systems. He detested discrimination of all sorts, and read avidly on all histories of all countries and continents in the world. He could speak on psychology, archaeology, security studies, sexuality and feminism, religion, African literature, Shakespeare, pedagogy, politics, history, sociology, philosophy, geography, music, law, and poetry. He organised many lectures and debates in Newlands for youth on various topics. His razor-sharp intellect intimidated many of various leftist political persuasions.

At this time, Tumelo was also seeing Don, a White ANC militant student of about 20, who was tall, lanky, and lean with a bush of spiky black hair. Don and his brother wore the same worn navy uniforms every day; they never changed their clothing. Tumelo was not very diplomatic about their dress code with their first encounter, "Why are you dressed like *that* on campus, like someone doing conscription? Is it deliberate or is it some fetish?"

"Hey, sista, we've just done our conscription in the navy...now we wear this as casual wear to tell the boere to *fuck off!*. They need to get the message that they don't control us White *laaities* (boys). We are going to blow their brains out with AK 47s, I say..."

Don's manner was strikingly casual and daring. He was unnervingly fluent in Xhosa, like Ms. Jansen and many of the White lefties at UCT.

"Can I give you a lift home?" Don offered after their first encounter.

"Alright, but it is in the *Coloured township*...and it is almost dark...I don't know if you want to travel that way this time of the day...but sure, I won't say no for a lift, if it can save me some bus fare."

Don spoke Rastafarian–style, cool and dreamy. "That is fine. I work in Black and Coloured townships all the time. It is the way of the struggle, sister."

They walked the long road downhill from UCT to the parking lot at the bottom end of the campus, where his rusty red Volkswagen Beetle was parked. Smoking cannabis openly in public while they were walking, he eventually asked the important question on their first meeting as he politely opened the car's door for her. "So, are you a *comrade*, sister?"

"Well, there are many types of comrades. Which one? Which ideology?"

He giggled sarcastically, "ANC, Stalinists, Leninists, Pan African Congress, Black Consciousness, Workerists, Trotskyists... which one? Take your pick...it is a *free* country...I say..."

"Well, I started off as a Trotskyist, and ended up with both the Workerists and the ANC."

"And the BC?"

"No, ...the struggle as we all know it is not just about *colour*. It is *also* about *capitalism*."

He smiled as he drew deep on his cannabis joint. "No, the race struggle is still important, as a *strategy*, but let's talk more at some other time. I've got to go meet with some workers; we are organising a strike in the Eastern Cape. Can we meet again amongst the books in Jagger library some time in the coming days? For nothing really, just a comradely chat..." At that moment, he appeared militant, rough, and irresistible.

Tumelo got into his car. He pulled away at high speed and went speeding down the road that winds its way into the town. His window was turned down and Bob Marley's *One Love* was blasting on his car radio. His head was virtually outside the window as he puffed on the cannabis, risking being pulled off by the cops for speeding, for smoking cannabis, and for being with a Coloured woman. Tumelo gestured with her hand that he must stop the car.

She was businesslike, "OK. Just stop here in this road! I'll walk the rest of the way. Thanks for the lift."

He then pulled off to the left of the road at high speed. "Hey sista, what's the matter?! Scared of the boere, hey? Don't worry sister, I'll fuck them up...I am a revolutionary *gangsta*!"

She responded angrily, "I don't *want* any *unnecessary* attention!"

"Still a paranoid Trotskyist, hey? Spies everywhere kind of thing, hey?" He chuckled and drew again deep on the joint of cannabis, narrowing his eyes. Tumelo felt weak and stupid.

"Thanks for the lift. I have to run..." She felt like a coward. She jumped out of his car, ran for the overcrowded bus heading for the township and did not look back.

He shouted and raised a clenched fist as he hung out of his car window hooting loudly, as his car passed her with petrol fumes bellowing, consuming her lungs. "See you amongst the books tomorrow after lectures at about fourish? *Amandla*, sista!"

Although Don struck her as reckless, she could not resist turning up for the appointment the following Friday. It turned out that Don was the son of a millionaire, whom he described as "one of the major English capitalists" in South Africa – in the league of the Oppenheimer family. She became curious about him.

They met regularly amongst the bookshelves in the main library and as time passed, they got to know a lot about each other. He was her only White friend at UCT, and only because he befriended her and forced his company. The comrades at UCT were suspicious of many friendly Whites, warning that they may be spies posing as comrades.

Tessa was quite upset about Tumelo's White friend, and she showed this in her swearing and her attitude. She did not hide her discontent, "If it is not politics he is interested in; then he is after your *body*. I was watching him studying your ass while you stood in the queue in the cafeteria the other day when you were not looking. White men just want to fuck a Black ass. He sees a *fuck* in you; nothing more serious."

Tumelo decided to put Don's political commitment to the test. "Are you not *uncomfortable* about all the wealth that your family has in this apartheid country where 87% of the land was robbed from the Black people? How can 8% of the people in this country own almost 90% of the land? The land question is going to become a serious question in South Africa one day! And don't you feel *ashamed* that you are benefiting from all of this?"

Don was not startled, nor did he blush. "See, sista, that is *why* I have joined the ANC underground to topple the capitalists..."

"You mean you are willing to fight the war against your *own family?*"

"If it comes to that, yep, sista! I've got my own AK47, I say. I am a soldier of the workers' revolution. No Mickey Mouse stuff, girl. Why do you think I am so fluent in Xhosa? I work with the comrades underground in the rural villages. Serious stuff, comrade. You Coloureds can't speak Xhosa or Zulu. You need to be able to speak the language of *da* people! if you want to be part of the revolution in South Africa. Come with me to work in Transkei, and I'll teach you a few things about what is going on in this fucking mad place. Leave Cape Town! It is a holiday resort for armchair politicians."

"What do you mean? The struggle is here too. It is *everywhere*... we are all in it in our various spaces...Coloured people are also exploited, are also homeless, are also *African*..."

"Yes, but the Trotskyites are fucking things up here. The middle class Unity Movement are Coloureds who can't even swear like the Coloured masses....they speak Oxford and Cambridge English. You must be able to speak the fucking language of the people if you want the revolution to work. It is about class; they pontificate in their armchairs in their mansions in the townships, with no fucking clue of the *real* South Africa. They all have university degrees as doctors, teachers, and lawyers and they look down on the poor Coloureds, calling them 'vulgar'...and what is that other obscene condescending word they use to describe the poor Coloureds? "

"You mean the *lumpen proletariat*...well, I see sense in what Franz Fanon says in 'The Wretched of the Earth' about the crucial role of poor brutalised people in revolution – though I'd work with prostitutes, but not that easily with gangsters...I've learnt to respect streetwise people, especially women..."

"Well, we share something in common then...the *laaities* on the street *know* what is going on; don't underestimate the wisdom of a pavement vagrant or a homeless bloke...they may be desperate, but not ignorant."

"You know a lot about street politics for a *posh Whitie*..."

"You know what they call your middle-class friends? *Posh naaiers*! Posh fuckers!" He chuckled and coughed.

"Let's stop this mudslinging...we are supposed to talk as comrades..."

"Sarcasm will get you nowhere...it is about class *identity*, not class *origin*..."

"Well, I think it is important to work in practical ways and in many kinds of ways with people. I feel that whilst recognising the value of street wisdom, it is also important to educate people through reading. I had a reading group with the prostitutes in the township..."

"Playing the 'vanguard' of the lumpen proletariat, hey?"

"I work with the anarchists..."

"Hey they have not also worked things out..."

"What do you mean?"

"The South African revolution will only come through a populist united front under the independent leadership of the trade union movement, and we must be where the people are in the rural villages and the Homelands – that is where the real South Africa and apartheid is; not petty apartheid such as segregation laws and stuff or the Immorality Act, but real bloody *shit* man, like not being able to work the land to feed your *fucking* family, not seeing your husband because he works on the mines in Jo'burg, and does not have a penny to send home, children dying of hunger like flies, and you have to deal with African chiefs who are lackies of the boere ...this is the real stuff man. The Cape is a *playground*, sista...!"

"And how *exactly* is this revolution that you are talking about going to happen?"

"My brother was working with other lefties to infiltrate and influence the ANC. They are all members of the South African Communist Party, and they are advocating for a populist united front in which the workers retain their independence and fly their own flag."

Don and Tumelo's regular clandestine political conversations took place in the Jagger library, amongst the Latin books in the late afternoons, after most students had already gone home. They stood talking, while they pretended to stand and read the books on the shelves. Neither of them understood Latin, so the books acted as a prop in their little theatre. When debates between them got too fiery, they would declare a truce and not meet for several

227

days until one of them would leave a cryptic note for the other on an agreed space on a desk on the top floor of the library, where the less interesting and little used books were shelved. Don and Tumelo had studied the library well, and discussed and agreed on the "no-go zones" and the "safe zones".

Don started to pick Tumelo up at night in the township and took her for secret visits to the upmarket apartments of his wealthy relatives. Here, he stored banned literature smuggled in by the ANC, which he had hidden under the floorboards of the unsuspecting homes and their owners, "Nobody would suspect these wealthy Whities of communism and terrorism! The boere are too fucking stupid to work this one out, I say! So this is a safe house, right under the boere's noses! Wicked plan, hey? Hehehe!"

When the two of them were together, they were best friends. They read, fought, laughed, danced, and celebrated. They rolled like two best buddies on the floor to the reggae sounds of Bob Marley, Peter Tosh, and UB40. He started to call her "Tumi" affectionately, because he was so much taller than her. Don ate frugally like a typical White leftie: brown bread, black coffee, humus, celery sticks and carrots.

"Don, why do you eat so little, like a White leftie?"

"Ah, I don't think about food, sista...there's too much fucking going on in this mad country to be thinking of food...besides I like a good joint...the grass of *da people*...I am preparing myself for the bush, for fighting with the real people who don't have much to eat. Why are you so worried about fucking *food*? You sure have enough on your bones? You won't last on a hunger strike, Tumi!"

"Good food is important, especially if you can *afford* it. Why do you want to *romanticize* poverty? Don't insult poor people...This is where the White lefties get things wrong...The poor people do not want to be *patronised*; they *know* that you are rich and that you can and should eat properly. They also know that you have old money stacked away somewhere in Europe that you can always fall back on to."

Don did not answer this time.

Don carried more ANC literature than university reading books with him in his haversack on campus. He walked around with several badly copied copies of the 1955 Freedom Charter and together they distributed these in toilets and lecture halls. Sometimes they fought over what the best way was to distribute pamphlets, which to distribute and which not to distribute. Tumelo felt that they should not favour only the ANC. Don fought with her, with his joint in his mouth, "It's a fucking war, man! Even amongst the people themselves. We must back one strong winner, and that is Oliver Tambo's ANC! Comrade Tambo is our man! Viva Tambo! Viva!"

"No! The people should study all options against apartheid and decide for themselves, even if they choose the ANC in the end! What happened to your critical views on a vanguard party?!"

"The ANC is not a vanguard party; they are *the fucking people themselves*...in their fucking masses!"

After such fiery fights (and there were many), Don would try to reconcile with Tumelo by offering her his predictable lunch of humus and stale brown bread, unappetisingly wrapped in a flimsy yellow plastic shopping sack, and they'd go sit in the bushes high up in the Devil's Peak mountain above the statue of Cecil John Rhodes. He'd take out his guitar to placate her, and they'd sing reggae songs into the late afternoon, including the favourite Bob Marley's *No Woman no cry*.

Tumelo grew tired of Don's persistent cannabis smoking and asked him once, "Why are all you rich White *laaities* on drugs? Is it a White middle-class hippie hobby? A favourite past time? I find it disgusting, because why is it so important for you people to get *high*? You already have so much to get high about. The lumpen proletariat gets high because it takes their mind off poverty...what do you have to take your mind off from?"

Don was cool, "Because *White laaities* in South Africa are fucking seriously and really seriously *messed* up...Aaargh, man, are you going to give me that Coloured leftie middle-class Karl Marx stuff of drugs (like religion) as the *opium of the people*?!"

Then he pulled her roughly towards him like a good pal to make a point of principle and comradely loyalty, "I'll do grass, sista, but this bro' will *never* take hard drugs; the White world will not get the better of him! Don't go to the dark side, the soppy side of life and rules...the depressing middle class shit..."

The security police operated and posed as male and female White "students" at UCT, so Don and Tumelo had mutually agreed rules: they walked past each other as if strangers in public on campus after their hot debates in the library and in the bush behind Rhodes Memorial. They did not know whom to trust any more.

As their fear grew, they somehow started to feel increasingly attracted to each other, almost like brother and sister, rather than as lovers. They started to sleep together secretly in his untidy bed after reading sessions at candle light in his darkened cottage, to create the impression there was no one home. Don's bed was covered with his dog's hair and smelled of flea powder. He wrapped himself naked around her affectionately, but each time they just kissed and fondled, without penetration, before falling asleep – like a ritual to show mutual trust as comrades without going all the way. However, the constant fear, the increasing tension as the South African revolution sped up and the political intimacy led inevitably to a more serious bond.

One night, while lying in his arms, with him reading aloud to her from Albert Luthuli's *Let my People go,* they were unexpectedly overcome with the gravitational natural force of human passion. They abandoned the book, threw it on the floor, and Don climbed on top of her. It was the first time Tumelo came close to penetration with a man. They wanted each other so much, but at that moment, her body went cold and frightened and she resisted her comrade and close friend. They restrained themselves with thoughts of the feared Immorality Act. They both burst out crying, only allowing their naked bodies to ride over each other like 12 twelve-year olds playing doctor. That night, Don ejaculated feverishly on her stomach, after which they both cried and cuddled each other in the fear of the night at candlelight, falling asleep soon after to dream of a new world of freedom. The next morning, they left the cottage early before sunrise to avoid being spotted by neighbours spying for the Immorality Act.

Soon after this night of gentleness and poignancy, the police were on Don's trail, doing the normal surveillance around his home. Did someone see Tumelo at his house? Was there a spy in the library? Was there a spy monitoring their walks up Devil's Peak. They never used a phone, so they must have been tailed by car. Was it someone who posed as a comrade interested in the pamphlets? Was it someone hiding behind the *fynbos* and posing as a hiker on the slopes of the mountain? They had always tried to keep a low profile.

They decided on a new plan. In the weeks and months that followed, they met no longer in the apartment where the banned literature was stored, as this was now too risky; only in the bush in the mountain – and only when they spotted no hikers there.

Don walked around with binoculars in his rucksack. They would bunk classes just to catch up on their political readings and to have their regular discussions, in order to keep up to date with the most current events and to distribute the latest pamphlets. They changed their meeting days every week. One week it would be on a Tuesday, followed by a Thursday, and then perhaps a Monday, and sometimes they would skip a week, so as to not create the impression of a regular predictable pattern.

Don's last note to Tumelo was written on a rock at their spot in the mountain, when he did not turn up as arranged. "The captain is on us...painfully yours, forever." She did not hear from him again, as they never made phone calls. Then she decided to do a last check at their safe zone spot in Jagger Library. There, she saw the little folded note. Don had left Cape Town to join his brother in the ANC underground movement in Transkei.

They would not see each other until two years later at the launch of the country's most powerful and revolutionary United Democratic Front (UDF) in the huge Coloured township of Mitchell's Plain in 1983. There were 1,000 delegates representing 575 organisations at the launch. Within a year, 600 organisations had joined with an estimated membership of three million people. It was a strongly supported "inter-racial" movement, which included the poor, the vagrants, and the workers. It had a strong Coloured leadership, including of the militant trade unions. On this day, the clergyman, Alan Boesak, emerged as a powerful orator and revolutionary. Nobody looked down on him as a "Coloured" or a "hotnot" or a "Boesman". He was accepted as the leader of the people of South Africa in all their colours, faiths, and political persuasions. This was a significant moment of departure from apartheid and labelling in South Africa, and also for the revolution in terms of its broad anti-racist united front, though ideological factional fighting remained.

By this time, extreme caution had set in with Tumelo about pursuing anything romantic with Don, as the personal lives of the young cadres were not only monitored by the security police, but also by the various unforgiving ideologically-linked comrades on the Cape Flats.

At this historic mass rally, the Trotskyists were on stage singing the Communist Manifesto anthem *L'Internationale*, composed by French communist songwriter and worker Eugene

Edine Pottier of the Paris Commune of 1871. The launch of UDF was an electrifying experience in Mitchell's Plain.

He was dressed in a faded jeans, a black fleecy top, and with a red woollen cap pulled low down just above his eye brows, and Tumelo melted all over again when she saw Don. However, their first words to each other after all this time were not romantic at all. They jumped immediately into a conversation about politics and ideology, as if they were back at their spot in Jagger Library. Don was now sporting a beard, seemed more mature, and was no longer wearing his notorious navy conscription uniform.

Their conversation was short, as it was quickly drowned out by the chanting of the masses of the people. Don teased her, "Hey, Tumi, isn't it strange and ironic that the middle-class Trotskyists are here today with the masses?"

"But *this* is what we were both working for all along Don... this united front, the coming together of all forces to topple the apartheid regime. We must celebrate!"

"You are right, my sweet..." He chuckled, kissed her gently on the forehead, and they spontaneously embraced. The fire was still there, but they knew they had to let go.

In their parting, Don feverishly grabbed her hand and let go of it slowly, after which he turned to walk away from her. He kept turning around and waved her kisses, his other hand holding his fist up high as a symbol of revolutionary resilience. He eventually disappeared into the thunderous mass of jubilant chanting workers. She would not see Don again until 20 years later – in a free South Africa.

Chapter 15
No Time – for Now - to Notice the Beauty in Cape Vineyards

Since his student protest days at Forest High, Alfredo became known for his endearingly eccentric ways after his release from jail. Everybody spoke about how he survived the brutal beatings and psychological torture he suffered there at the hands of a gang of huge burly boere police who left him for dead, drowning in his blood on the floor of a cell. He had grown into a brave young hero who was well-read and groomed by Adiel Khan, and widely admired by the women comrades for trying to take on the boere single handedly.

One summer's night he asked Tumi out to a fund-raising dance to fight apartheid. However, his plan was to turn the dance into a political rally at around ten o'clock. At the scheduled time, he took over the microphone, chanting slogans, giving political speeches, pointing out one by one in a slow, determined speech the traitors who worked with the security police. The dance turned into a brawl, with the reactionary Coloured patrons marching out and the comrades staying. Cocktails flew into unsuspecting faces, the band packed up angrily, women started pulling each other's hair, fights broke out in the women's toilets, and the men hit each other with wine bottles. The security guards were beaten up as well in the process. Tumelo and Alfredo eventually had to flee the dance themselves.

"Why did you do that?" she asked him, flabbergasted and shocked.

"Because we need to sort out the *traitors* amongst us. They sold out. We know who they are...they must know that we know who they are..."

Alfredo was a young man who fought the enemy tooth and claw at every single opportunity he got. With his passionate revolutionary spirit, he was the one for whom Tumelo fell deeply. He had swept her off her feet by reading Shakespeare's sonnet 116 to her on bended knee, after he told her of his stories of how he battled the boere and survived them in jail.

Love is not love Which alters when it alteration finds, ...Love alters not with his brief hours and weeks...but bears it out even to the edge of doom...

They danced the whole night to Tracy Chapman's *Talking about Revolution* and to the repeated playing of Eddy Grant's *I Love to Truck,* which unfortunately happened to be the DJ's favourite. It was a potent combination: the music, the conversation, and the poetry.

In the months and years that followed, they spent most of their time together organising meetings, campaigning, and writing pamphlets until the early hours of the morning. They distributed the pamphlets in their hundreds to schools, civic organisations, factories, universities, mosques, churches, and trade unions within hours of planning and writing them.

Theirs was a speedy romance. They got married very quickly on a Friday autumn afternoon in April. It was a cold day and the sky was bright blue. Brown leaves were already falling off the trees, and the days were becoming colder and shorter.

At the time of their wedding, the struggle had advanced to a full civil war. The community newspapers were flooded with reports on consumer boycotts, rent boycotts, transport boycotts, rallies, marches, and stay-aways. There were hundreds of organizations – civil, religious, political, educational, workerists – operating in hundreds of towns, both rural and urban. There were street committees, alternative structures of local government, alternative education programmes, people's courts, and vigilante structures. The country was in the grip of revolution, like never seen before.

Long after Tumelo had left UCT, the campus became more radical as the work of the United Democratic Front spread to campuses all over the country. The White student activists started to present a serious challenge to the apartheid government. Many of the White students no longer accepted conscription. The End

Conscription Campaign started in 1983, though it took another 10 years though for the end of conscription to be announced by the dying apartheid government. White students were now also *sjambokked* (whipped), detained, harassed, in receipt of death threats, and they were assaulted and tortured. Students were shot at indiscriminately on campus, regardless of colour, and even White women students were now brutally beaten up by the riot police in the Jagger library and were detained and locked up in prison.

Tumelo and her friends had triumphantly survived the racist White lecturers such as Dragon, the White buses, the Whites-only student residences, and the imagined possession of the spirits of these racist professors in glasses at frequently held student seances. They entered schools in the Coloured townships as recently graduated teachers in 1985. Tumelo returned to Forest High as a qualified teacher. Mr. Hofman had retired and was no longer at the school. He passed away a few years later, having suffered an unfortunate and tragic death.

In 1985, the ANC had made a call from Lusaka to make the apartheid system more and more unworkable, and the country less governable. That same year, school boycotts erupted across the country. The school students were burning tires and building roadblocks. They were doing the military African liberation dance that the police feared, the *toyi-toyi*, and they were chanting:

"*Amandla Ngawethu*! (Strength to the People!). Victory is certain!"

"The struggle continues! Amandla!"

"Botha hear the young lions roar! Freedom or death – victory is certain!"

By the end of 1985, there had been more than 390 strikes involving 240,000 workers. Within two months of teaching, the newly appointed headmaster called Tumelo in to question her about her political activity, and the police started to monitor her movements. Within a few days, her students had managed to rally together some forty-odd working-class youngsters from the Cape Flats in the campaign against apartheid. They raised their own funds and used the money to buy reading materials and newspapers, to make photocopies, and to organize picnics in the mountains, which they turned into debating sessions and community development strategy workshops on values, democracy, and education. Besides working long days and nights during the week at Forest Hill to educate the youth and adult learners for the revolution, Tumelo was also working in the African and other Coloured townships over weekends with a close friend, fellow teacher, and comrade, Cynthia. The two of them held workshops with the teachers in the townships, tirelessly teaching the youth about the myth of race and the history of apartheid. They got the students to make their own posters for rallies, taught them how to organise at school, and how to challenge and question the system. They worked with about 100 youth at a time, and formed close bonds with the teachers in the African townships through joint teaching programmes.

When the State of Emergency was declared in June 1985, the students united and marched from school to school against apartheid. There was now no turning back as there had been in 1976. Everybody was united in one thing: apartheid had to be overthrown urgently. After the declaration of the State of Emergency by the Botha regime, the troops moved into the townships. The army occupied the streets with their huge trucks and machine guns. All meetings were banned. No more than two people could meet at a time. When three people met, it was called a crowd, and therefore it was illegal under the State of Emergency. The army patrolled streets and marched into homes in the townships, searching houses and imprisoning people at random – mothers, fathers, sisters, brothers, sons, daughters, grannies, and grandpas. The students and teachers were banned from entering schools because the schools became revolutionary cells. The army guarded the locked school gates with their trucks and machine guns. The boere had become desperate in their plight to defend the apartheid monster. Thousands of youth, children, parents, and students were picked up by the army and detained for months and even years without trial. More than 25,000 people were arrested and detained without trial. Teachers became the main targets of the killing squads, especially in the militant Eastern Cape. Some of Tumelo's students were detained and jailed. Others, including teachers like herself and Cynthia, were forced into hiding for months. Captain Adolf's visit, file under the arm, driving a white Volkswagen with two other privately dressed police officers, meant only one thing. You simply never returned. Tumelo was subjected to psychological torture, with regular calls at various times of the night and day. These ranged from death threats, to intimidation about her movements, and to the harm that would be done to her bodily organs such as her kidneys and also to Alfredo's baby, which she was carrying, if the two of them did not stop their political activities.

Captain Adolf visited the school to arrest Tumelo, but she was tipped off by the ANC comrades and escaped him. Tumelo and Alfredo split for security reasons, and they moved from safe house to safe house, each going their own way, living with various elderly couples whose names they were not allowed to know, nor were any conversations allowed while they stayed. These various elderly couples fed them, bought painkillers for Tumelo's persistent kidney infections, and kept them under lock and key. On any day a stranger would arrive as a "messenger" and order them to pack hurriedly, as the police had information on their whereabouts. They'd be moved in the night to a new location – again to another quiet reserved mysterious elderly couple. So, they'd move town to town, spending a few nights here and a few nights there.

Tumelo eventually ended up in a derelict building on a deserted beach in the wilds of the Cape. She was relieved to find Alfredo there. Not visible from the road, the beach could only be reached by jeep or on foot. They stayed there with student leaders in the local community and continued the political education - until an arranged messenger brought the news that it was perhaps all right to risk returning to the township. The security police could not catch Tumelo, but they eventually caught up with Cynthia and detained her. She was put for some time during her stay in solitary confinement in Pollsmoor Prison (where Nelson Mandela was also held for some time).

This was the time of the notorious necklace killings, of which both the police and vigilante groups from the township were guilty. A necklace killing would involve putting a tire around your neck, dousing you with petrol, and setting you alight. The psychological torture of those the police could not catch was often brutal as well. An empty coffin was delivered to the mother of a young priest who was leading the anti-apartheid struggle, and there are many untold horror stories of a similar kind. Many were still tortured and assassinated. The UDF leadership had been detained, murdered, and kidnapped, or abducted. Many militant and more radical activists simply disappeared. People, especially youth, were interrogated and brutally tortured. Some were fed rat poison, and others were beaten to death or drowned.

While she was in hiding, Tumelo's family got calls from the security police in the early hours of the morning: "We know your daughter's movements. We know everything about her. We know about the pain right now at this moment in her left kidney and the medication that she is taking for it. We know her doctor. We'll poison her body. You'll see. She'll suffer for a very long time. You'll never see that child that your daughter is carrying grow up; we will burn *both* of them to ashes." The caller introduced himself some times as "Captain Adolf", and sometimes it sounded like *boere* women police officers. The voices would alternate and so would the timing of the calls – sometimes just after midnight, or at one or two in the morning, but always in the very early hours, and always at the time of deep slumber.

During this time, Captain Adolf eventually caught Alfredo, and he was imprisoned at Victor Verster in rural Paarl, known for its beautiful surrounds of acres of Cape vineyards, situated about 50 kilometres from Cape Town.

When Cynthia was released, she and Tumelo resumed their work relentlessly in the African townships.

The children who had been in prison for weeks and some for months already did not know why they were there, except that they were playing in the street when the army trucks came. Their mothers and fathers also did not know they were in jail. The apartheid police were accountable to nobody, only to the regime and Botha, "the big crocodile", as he was called. Every night the children cried in their cells for their mothers, wailing loudly and begging for toys to be brought to the cells with which they could play.

South Africa did not celebrate Christmas for a few years, calling that time of year "a black Christmas", as too many were dying in detention and were killed by the apartheid police and the army – children, youth, adults. Suspected spies and collaborators with the enemy were simply tortured and killed.

Those released returned home often as severely broken and disturbed people, yet still very resilient to overthrow the apartheid regime. Some of the women were raped in prison, and some of the men were sodomised. Many went on hunger strikes, and many were murdered in their prison cells. Many were still in solitary confinement, subjected to torture, rape, and death randomly on a daily basis. Nelson Mandela would stay another four years in Victor Verster Prison.

When Alfredo was released from Victor Verster Prison on Christmas Eve, Tumelo prepared for their first born with a celebration party for all the comrades who had been released from detention with him.

Tumelo was moved into theatre at twelve-thirty on the afternoon in early January 1986 during the State of Emergency. After some hours of labour, the obstetrician decided that Tumelo should have a Caesarian section. Unbeknownst to her, a young White gentleman with an army-style haircut and a flat Afrikaans accent met Alfredo in the waiting room to introduce himself:

"Are you the father?"

"Yes"

"Congratulations! Well, I am the hospital's doc-terr who has been called in to help with the delivery of your baby. Normal procedure. Nothing to pair-nick about."

While Alfredo got dressed in his theatre frock and face mask, the doctor went into the theatre and introduced himself quietly to the White theatre staff, including to the obstetrician, "Hello, I am Dr. Elviro. I am the patient's general practitioner. She has requested that I be present at the birth, to assist with the delivery." Tumelo was already under and unaware of her appointed "Dr. Elviro".

The theatre team did not ask further questions, as this was standard practice at private hospitals when patients invited their general practitioners, although they found it odd that Tumelo had not informed the hospital ahead of time. However, nobody really cared about following procedures even at private hospitals at that time of civil war in South Africa; it was during the State of Emergency.

Shortly after giving birth to a healthy boy, Tumelo was in severe pain and shots of morphine could not help. She screamed endlessly. It felt as if some operation instrument was left in her insides, or as if her insides were filled with acid that was eating at her. While in hospital, she had nightmares of the numerous phone calls and death threats, of Afrikaner men in army uniforms storming into the ward, ripping her baby from her breasts and threatening to burn both of them by the brutal necklace method. Dr Elviro instructed the nurses to treat her for "post-natal psychosis", as mothers often are plagued by paranoia shortly after birth. The nurses administered morphine and tranquillisers.

Tumelo returned as a nervous wreck from hospital, and could not get herself to open the windows or the curtains for months after the birth of her son, in fear that the security police would carry out their threats. The hospital could not locate Dr. Elviro on the register of medical practitioners for payment. No further questions were asked; Tumelo and Alfredo were left to live with their fears and suspicions.

For 10 long years after Dr. Elviro's encounter, Tumelo struggled to urinate without feeling immense pain. Her bladder and kidneys were constantly infected. Her abdomen remained hard and bloated. She lived on painkillers and antibiotics. After the birth, the early morning phone calls had stopped. Tumelo remained an active campaigner, and her work remained widely supported by the students, fellow teachers, parents, and fellow community activists.

The State of Emergency lasted for four years, as it was renewed by Botha every year following 1985. The calls increased for the unbanning of the ANC, the unbanning of Nelson Mandela, and the many others who were still in prison. The army remained in the streets, still randomly searching houses and imprisoning youth.

It emerged through the Truth and Reconciliation hearings, years later, that a police captain, Eugene de Kock, was said to have ordered the deaths of many activists at *Vlakplaas* - a farm near Pretoria used by the death squads since the seventies. The notorious stocky captain with his short, bulky, black hair, flat, passionless mouth, and calculating narrow eyes, wore notable large, framed, dark, square sunglasses. He used tactics like sending a booby trap cassette to an ANC activist – a young father and husband, which blew off his head. Children and schoolteachers were mercilessly shot by the death squads, execution-style. Some were drugged, shot, and burnt to ash. The death squads did not discriminate - professionals and ordinary people were killed cold-bloodedly. Bodies were buried secretly, or burnt or dumped in rivers. Activists were hunted down, were killed, and were bombed as far into Swaziland and Lesotho. Trade union offices and churches were relentlessly bombed by the police and the army over the next few years. Many of these attacks were allegedly ordered by Botha himself – today, a free man.

Chapter 16
Hair for the Nests of
Migrating Black Swallows

By late 1989, thousands of teachers of all colours had joined the leftist factions working within the ANC structures. Botha had resigned, and de Klerk (the former apartheid Minister of Education) was elected president. A Whites-only general election was held in 1989; de Klerk led the campaign for reforms towards a "new South Africa". He had called off the last State of Emergency by the end of 1989. Mass rallies and marches now were permitted. Talks were started between the Afrikaner capitalists and the ANC leadership in Lusaka and Dakar. Mandela by then had urged the ANC to negotiate. Walter Sisulu and other Rivonia triallists had been released. The Harare Declaration of August 1989 had called for "a new constitutional order", based on the Freedom Charter of 1955. On 2 February 1990, with the opening of parliament, Mandela's release and that of other political prisoners was announced, and the ANC, PAC and SACP were unbanned. The 30-year-old ban on the ANC was lifted. Apartheid's official end was being announced 40 years after its evil commencement in 1948.

Nelson Mandela was released on 11 February 1990 after 27 years in jail. He was already 71 years old, and walked hand-in-hand with his then-wife, Winnie, who was incarcerated and severely tortured for most of her life under apartheid. People danced in the streets of the entire country on that day. Mandela addressed a crowd of 50,000 people on the Grand Parade where the protesting children had gathered in 1976. The priest who had a coffin delivered to his mother's house with his name on it had also survived. He was standing just behind the freed Mandela on the Grand Parade. In his speech, Mandela encouraged, "Our struggle has reached a decisive moment. Our march to freedom is irreversible. Now is the time to intensify the struggle on all fronts. To relax now would be a mistake which future generations would not forgive!"

In 1991, the Group Areas Act was scrapped and the first major negotiation meeting of the Convention for a Democratic South Africa (CODESA) was held. Its main aims were to discuss the future constitution and negotiations for the economy, and to prepare the path for power sharing between the ANC and NP. Right-wing racist Whites such as the founder of the Afrikaanse Weerstandse Beweging (AWB), Eugene Terre'blanche (his surname meaning "white earth" in French), were up in arms, attacking the negotiations and talks with the enemy, and calling de Klerk a traitor of "his people", the Afrikaner nation. Yet, de Klerk himself came from a deeply racist, nationalist family, and he had held several positions as a cabinet Minister in Botha's military regime. A Whites-only referendum was held in 1992 to get approval for continued apartheid reforms.

As former Minister of National Education, de Klerk formed and maintained apartheid universities, and people like Captain Adolf may have worked in his political interests. However, as the political pressure increased and civil war erupted, de Klerk took a surprise sudden turn towards becoming the leader of *verligte* ("enlightened") Afrikaners, against the *"groot krokodil"* (huge crocodile) Botha. P.W. Botha was forced to step down as the leader of the National Party and as State President, after the revolution in South Africa dealt him a stroke from which he did not recover. The relationship between de Klerk and Mandela was not entirely rosy, as de Klerk still played the White baas in the relationship and in discussions, which Mandela did not take kindly to; however, they managed to have the important discussions for negotiation. For this, in 1992, de Klerk and Mandela were jointly awarded the Prince Asturia Award by Spain, and then in 1993 the Nobel Peace Prize, for playing "crucial" roles in ending apartheid. The Trostkyist and other left-wing factions and trade union movements were severely critical of the negotiations and talks, but Mandela and the ANC had won the confidence of the masses and the world in the peace talks for a new South Africa. This was a significant turning point.

The ANC exiles started to return to South Africa, 40,000 in total. Tumelo was then almost 30 years of age, still pushing with Alfredo, in their own way, to decisively topple the racist evil system, which was by then declared by the world as a crime against humanity. South Africa had come a long way from the brutalising racist system since the days of Uncle Thaba, Kaiser, and Kruger, though their people were still not yet free.

It was during the period 1990 until 1993 that the battles between the ANC and boere Nationalist Party intensified in the Western Cape, and the priest who was close to Archbishop Desmond Tutu and Tumelo started to work closely together with the youth and the local community to wrench local power from the racist National Party. Tumelo gave birth to a gentle boy in 1992, who fortunately was not affected by her induced physiological traumas with the security police some years before, but he too was still not yet a citizen of South Africa. Giving into international and civil war pressure, the ANC and the Nationalist Party were in negotiation talks, preparing for South Africa's first democratic elections.

However, things did not go smoothly. In the campaign period leading up to the elections, working class and poor rural Coloured voters were fed alcohol by Coloured and White Afrikaner politicians at political rallies and on the day of the election, in line with an ancient tradition of Jan Van Riebeeck's tot system of the 1650's. The NP went on a fear mongering door to door "Stop the Comrades" racist campaign, and distributed something like 75,000 glossy comic books amongst fearful Coloureds on the Cape Flats. They warned that Africans would flood across the railway tracks and take the homes of Coloured people once the ANC had gained power. They also warned that they would not only take their homes, but also their jobs and daughters! The Coloured NP supporters openly fuelled ancient Coloured racism against the *"kaffirs"* in their election campaign with the poorest and most insecure of the Coloured working class. They fed on the fear and confusion of a brutalised people with a brittle identity who had lost their family names and who did not know from where or from whom they came.

Coloured supporters of the NP reasoned, "We don't vote for *kaffirs, Muslims* and *Bushmen.* We vote for the White people. Rather the devil you know than the one you don't!" Some of these sad Coloured people spoke of the Coloured Western Cape ANC political leader, Alan Boesak, as a *hotnot* and *Bushman* who should "go straighten his hair". Coloured ANC supporters who broke up NP mass rallies in townships were told to "fuck off and go comb your kinky *Bushman* hair!" The *boere* sat on the stage with their fellow Coloured politician leaders, laughing at the various commotions, high dramas, and drunken brawls about hair and facial features. The television showed disturbing images of how they called their former oppressors and slave masters proudly *"baas" (boss),* how toothless, alcoholic Coloured women placed their wet lips on FW de Klerk's forehead, even though his wife, Marike, was a known racist who referred to Coloureds as a "no people", a "leftover" people. She snubbed even Nelson Mandela when he jointly received the Nobel Prize with her husband for bringing peace to South Africa. Notable Coloured politician leaders who ardently supported the boere were reputed to be alcoholics, and sported the notorious swirl mark on their foreheads.

In April 1994, South Africa went to the polls to vote in its first democratic South Africa. When Tumelo and Alfredo cast their vote for the ANC on 27 April 1994, it was one of the most exciting days in their lives. Her grandmother was voting for the first time. She was already 94 years old, and like many other Black and Coloured senior citizens, she slept with her identity book underneath her pillow, scared she may not have it to vote. Lizzy and Richard, her parents, were both almost 70 years old when they voted for the first time in their lives. Tumelo was by then already a mother of two and in her early 30s.

However, when the results were counted, it transpired that many Coloured people voted in their thousands for the old racist White master and their swirl stocking collaborators, while the large majority of the country voted ANC. Captain Adolf's boere cronies were still in charge at the local police station and in cahoots with the local corrupt Coloureds.

In the 1994 election, the National Party (NP) led by de Klerk, came second with a little over one-fifth of the total vote, and won power at a regional level in the Western Cape. Nelson Mandela was elected president, and de Klerk became deputy president in the new government of national unity.

After mass resignations through retirement packages offered to the most experienced and of the best teachers at Coloured schools in the Western Cape, before the provincial government of the NP took over, Tumelo was pushed unceremoniously out of the school along with other anti-apartheid activist teachers. The local ANC priest was also under increasing political pressure to leave his church.

A local NP supporter and priest, Mr Minnaar, a lean and mean looking man who wore ankle length pencil-narrow piped trousers, particularly delighted in sorting out anti-apartheid activists at the schools in the neighbourhood. He had the habit of grinding his teeth while he spoke, drove around to schools with the police, and there were rumours of him as a much-feared domestic tyrant at home. He called Tumelo and her comrades "venomous elements" to South African society, and with a cynical expression on his face and his finger wagging, he'd get up in mass meetings, "There are a lot of you I'd like to see the back of one day! I'll make sure of that alright!" Everyday at school was made a living hell for the ANC-aligned political activist teachers. It was perhaps something similar to Arthur Miller's *The Crucible,* based on the witch-hunt and framing of communists through vicious means. There were everyday smear campaigns against activist teachers like Alfredo and Tumelo.

Mass rallies were organised and supported by the NP to instigate anger and mischief against such teachers. Hatred and rumour of the "evil ones" spread like wildfire amongst staff factions and groupings. The students were told that Tumelo was one such "demon-possessed" teacher, and that her evil power resided in her "bushy wild hair" and gave her "unnatural power" over the minds of people, and that the students should try and cut her hair if they wanted to get rid of the "evil spell and hold" on the school. Believing these mischievous tales, a small group of Christian Fundamentalist girl students fell at her feet in the courtyard during one break, speaking in tongues and beckoning for the political demons to leave her body.

On her last day at the school, Tumelo gathered all the letters of thanks and memorabilia that students and parents had given her over the years, amongst them, pictures of her posing with student leaders in workshops and in reading groups in the African townships when she worked there with Cynthia on the anti-racist theme of "the origins of people".

She took a walk into the square where the students had gathered for years and where she herself had stood as a 14-year old in 1976, listening to the political orations of a daring Alfredo, and where she had dreamy conversations in the wintry sun with Mr.

Magee and Mr. Torres, about what freedom in South Africa may one day look like. It was now between 14 and 20 years later. She recollected highlights of revolutionary moments with Mr. Hofman, and found herself transported back to 1976 and the revolutionary 1980s, vividly remembering every moment of the struggle in her life there at Forest Hill. A number of her past students had gone on to play leadership roles in the ongoing battle against apartheid as university and college students, and as trade unionists and civic leaders. It was in that square where she organised and addressed political mass rallies against apartheid, where they sang *"We shall overcome"*, and shouted with balled fists *"Amandla Ngawethu!"* Like with many other comrades during that time, her departure from the school was quiet, without a public announcement – swift and clinical, the way judgement is served in a short trial.

The seagulls flew down on to the tarmac to scavenge the breadcrumbs left by the students during break, noising and fighting over the breadcrumbs. Tumelo cut a few inches off the ends of her curls, tied the hair into a bundle, and placed it in a corner in the courtyard. The newly arrived swarm of twittering black swallows flew down to collect her hair.

Chapter 17
Watch the Ants Feed to the Rhythm of Ngqothwane

The rain started to pour heavily. "Ok, you should find your way, madam." The dark man rushed back to the small shelter a few metres away, cutting off any more questions from an obviously confused visitor - a nuisance in such inclement weather. Tumelo rolled up her window, confused. Why a students' reunion at *Valkenberg*? As she turned the car to the right, the car's headlights shone on the prefabricated room ahead, with a huge black number painted on its light green wall: Room 485. Through the pouring rain on her windscreen, she could make out a few figures standing inside. Black figures moved inside, walking up and down. There were balloons, like for a children's party. Colourful balloons – green ones, blue ones, orange ones, black ones, yellow ones, white ones, and red ones. The rain poured down unabatedly. She could hear the music playing. Tracy Chapman? Yes, it was Tracy Chapman's *A' talking bout Revolution.*

She carefully stepped out of the car, overwhelmed. She did not want to bang on the door and announce her arrival too loudly, so she remained in the car for a little while. Loud shouts interrupted her almost catatonic train of thought. "Ms Kok!" The students had spotted her as they looked through the window to see if their guests had arrived. Yasmeen, now a grown woman and mother in her late twenties, came out running with a a soaking black umbrella to greet her at the car. She turned down the window to greet her.

"We were worried about the weather, and since it was short notice, that you would not pitch!" she shouted, the rain dripping from the dented umbrella she was holding.

They walked back together arm-in-arm under the miserable Cape wetness to room 485. As she stepped in, Tumelo recognised some of the faces of 1985. They were all visibly older now. Adults. Some already mothers and fathers, with young children on their laps, and some hanging on to them. The reunion turned out to be a gathering of about 10 student leaders of 1985. The other teacher who was there, Mr. Bailey, was a fellow hard working and popular history teacher who had suffered a nervous breakdown at Forest High, at the time of the bitter battles between the NP, the Trotskyists, and the ANC. He was a UDF and ANC activist, and when things became too much, he simply collapsed and was forced to retire on chronic anti-depressant medication. Mr. Bailey still seemed nervous, shaky, and emotional, but was relieved that he was not the only one who honoured the invitation from the former students. He sat quietly with his lean lanky legs folded, and took out a cigarette. He was still chain-smoking *Gauloise* cigarettes. He lit the cigarette, sighed again, looked down, and stared at his shoes. His hands were shaking.

Tumelo remembered the long conversations the two of them had as teachers, when they tried to work out ways in which to focus the despondent youth; how they tried to convince them to just try and survive just *another* day to fight apartheid. Many children never made it to school; many struggled to stay in school. They had many stories of why they could not make it to school regularly. Some spoke of the African *tokkelosh* (the African leprechaun) that chained them to their beds, that stole their time, that raped their mother or their little sister during the night, that beat up their father or brother. In countering his teacher's disbelief in the famed vicious African *tokkelosh*, one student vividly described to Tumelo that he had once himself caught his neighbour feeding her *tokkelosh* traditional Irish Stew of mutton, carrots, and peas. He described the *tokkelosh* as hairy, strong, and small, fully dressed in a polka dot three-piece suit, and chained like a dog on a leash. He told how the neighbour had to feed and clothe the *tokkelosh,* and also arrange sexual favours with Coloured women for his gratuitous sexual appetite, for which in return, the *tokkelosh* stole money for his madam and kept poverty at bay.

There were numerous fascinating stories from students to smile about for many years later. As Tumelo sat on the white plastic chair, her eyes caught a row of ants that were finding their way to and from the sugar bowl on the table, crossing the floor into a small, sandy hole in the corner of the depressing room. They seemed, as always, at peace, collectively happy, co-existing with each other. Nobody was eating the sandwiches and treats arranged on the table. Some crisps were sprawled on the makeshift pine table covered with newsprint. A few Coke bottles were left unopened, the gas escaping.

It turned out, as Yasmeen announced, that the party was in honour of their teachers who had with them "survived the apartheid regime". As feisty as always, she urged everybody to dance and to eat and to celebrate freedom to the knock knock rhythms of Miriam Makebe's *Qongqothwane*.

Chapter 18
The Praying Mantis

South Africans were ready to celebrate the freedom of their bodies and of their minds. Black South Africans were walking in parks and sitting on benches in parks feeding squirrels for the first time in their lives. Their children were putting their toes in the seawater of once forbidden beaches. They were spending holidays in previous Whites-only resorts.

It was all bizarre and strange, like being released from a Nazi mental institution and not knowing what to do with your new-found freedom. Tumelo and Alfredo wrapped themselves into their own worlds. Alfredo played Beethoven's *Concerto No.5* frequently on the piano in their mutual moments of nostalgia, in the absence of the adrenalin of the many years of struggle and fighting that kept them going. Beethoven's last concerto composed during Napoleon Bonaparte's reign in Europe, and also known as *The Emperor,* helped them to silently come to terms with their new identities as free human beings – yet misplaced and dislocated from themselves, because the revolution perhaps culminated in a negotiated settlement, an unnatural end. Alfredo could play piano by ear for hours while he stared up at the 1820 portrait of Ludwig Von Beethoven placed on their wall in their home above the piano.

However, as karma would have it, there was still unfinished business with Don, whom Tumelo ran into at a local fishing harbour where she used to go with Alfredo to watch the turbulent waves. He was wearing the same style of clothes – faded denim jeans and casual top. They were still, as in the old days, ecstatic to see each other. Don still looked the same, only slightly older.

"Fancy, finding you here after 20 fucking years, mermaid?!" Still fond of swearing, he appeared as cool as she had always known him. They hugged and laughed.

"And to think it is now a *new* South Africa! We are not forbidden to be together any more sista!"

"You married? Its been a long time?"

"Four *laaities*, sista...unbelievable...and you?"

"Two...and divorced...after almost 20 years together...Afredo and I painfully lost each other when the freedom we fought for so hard had come."

"I am very sorry...must be deeply wrenching for you both..."

"Yeah, and for the children...In spite of our problems, we shared something very strong and special in fighting apartheid, but we were perhaps not strong enough to see freedom through and to enjoy its rewards together..."

At this, Don looked away from Tumelo to avoid seeing the obvious pain in her eyes. He had married a Jewish White woman, a fellow wealthy law student from UCT. He looked down at the foam of the waves that was forming on the harbour deck. He threw his cigar stub to the ground, the foam quickly dissolving the ash. She noticed the faint lines on his face, the only evidence that 20 long years had passed by since she had last seen him.

He cleared his throat, "Tumelo, I wanted to tell you something all these years...what happened to us was not right... The *boere* bastards deprived us of having normal lives...I'm sorry for all that happened to both of us..."

She looked in the direction of the deep green ocean, watching the dolphins frolicking, and the seagulls flying low above the huge rolling waves. The seagulls squawked and flew down to feed on the small crabs and sardines that fell from the fishing nets of the boats onto the smelly concrete landing.

Then Don's mood changed, and they both giggled as tears filled their eyes. He put his arm around her, "But, hey, we must toast to some red wine! It is all over, sista – though only fucking 20 years later!"

He was still the same mischievous, charming Don.

"Do you remember our song up there in the madness of Devil's Peak? Remember?"

"Of course, I do...I am not *that* old!"

They laughed and hugged in the chilly Spring Cape breeze and sang softly together their Bob Marley favourite at the harbour light as they watched the boats rock gently, and the fishermen shouting the price of freshly caught fish, "...*no woman no cry...*"

Smiling, they slowly let go of each other, both relieved to be free to be, though their paths would never cross again.

A few years later, Tumelo met the dark African man with the ancient warmth of Uncle Thaba that she was seeking. His name was Themba, meaning "trust" in Africa. They met on Robben Island when Tumelo visited there to retrace the footprints of Uncle Thaba. Robben Island by then had been established as a tourist destination and world heritage site, telling the story of its place for the incarceration of Nelson Mandela and other Black leaders, of defeated African chiefs, of princes, of banished women, of long suffering lepers, of African "criminals".

Tumelo and Themba, who was an entomologist, had common special interests in penguins and ants. Unlike the comrades, he could speak about a wide range of subjects, from how the heart pumps blood, to the similarity between the anatomy of pigs and humans, and about the chemicals involved when certain insects mate.

"Did you know", he told her once, "that after mating, there is danger for some male insects?"

Tumelo was amazed, "No...how?"

"Did you know that the Praying Mantis females sometimes eat their mates, starting with the head? "

"How bizarre!"

"That's not the end of the story. The male mantis actually continues mating even though his head is gone!"

"You may fear I may be a praying mantis then?"

He did not answer.

They fell instantly for each other, as the Robben Island ferry glided through the deep Cape waters in the five kilometre trip to the world famous island. Though theirs was a brief affair, she rode with him on the wind of change without fear. He was the conversation with her soul, the depths of who she really was and wanted to be. In their silent embraces on a wind swept Cape beach, he wrapped her under his coat. He held her chin gently with his long dark fingers and they kissed for hours, his tongue wrapping and massaging hers gently for long moments; she had never been kissed passionately like that before, and believed she never would be again.

She stroked his ebony dark forearms, while he gently stroked her hair. It felt like forever and a day. She rested her head on his warm chest and listened to his every heartbeat. Nothing could simply compare to that night with her African man under the pitch dark sky of the southern cross stars, he for whom she waited for so long. She lay in his arms quietly, on the green grass of the mountain slopes, inhaling the allure of his skin that smelled of sandalwood incense and tobacco.

Themba and Tumelo shared an unspeakable deep mysterious ancient energy of understanding and healing. There were no fights and tensions, just a simple, beautiful, highly evolved serene togetherness that did not depend on regular physical penetration. Sadly, two years later, Themba succumbed to AIDS, after contracting HIV through a blood transfusion after a motor car accident. However, even the news of his death left a serene calmness, and she felt him closer to her than ever before. The magic with Themba ended amicably and with necessary beauty. Then she remembered his favourite story of the Khoisan people's sacred Praying Mantis, and she smiled to herself.

Chapter 19
Take Me Home to the Fynbos on Pink Flamingo Wings

Tumelo landed at Heathrow Airport on a bitterly cold English winter evening as the African wife of an EU citizen, on the anniversary of the day of the emancipation of slaves at the Cape. Seated next to a window, as the plane touched down, one could spot the small lights in this dark dim congested island, populated by some 60-odd million people from all over the world. This was to become Tumelo's new home out of Africa. It was a long walk from the plane to the signs that say "Baggage", and further down was "Passports", which further split into "EU passports" and "Non-EU passports". Tumelo found herself at the end of a very long queue of Indian women in saris, Muslim men in scarves, and Muslim women with veils just showing their eyes who had complaining, jet-lagged, fatigued children hanging on to them. In the same queue were South African White Afrikaners, men and women in colourful African attire from Ghana, Nigeria, Ethiopia, and Zimbabwe, in addition to Arab men who looked wealthy and impatient with being subjected to a line up with the poor in the world. The queue snaked some distance, with unfriendly, terse, security personnel and immigration officials manning the procedure.

Tumelo waited for about 40 minutes before it was her turn. "Next!" the unfriendly White official shouted in her direction. As she approached his desk, he looked her up and down in a suspicious way while he flipped through the pages of her South African passport. "What are you coming to *do* here?"

"I am a spouse of an EU citizen."

"You know that you can't lived off *benefits* here?! You read the conditions of your visa?!" Tumelo refused to answer. It was as if she had slipped back into a time warp. She had earlier read the ominous sign posted alongside the queue, "No assault on personnel will be tolerated." Somebody had warned her that in England, words have different meanings and nuances, and you have to be careful. "Assault" in Cape Town may mean an axe in your forehead or a knife stab in your heart, but in England, it could be something as mild as a few assertive words or gestures. She had landed in sensitive empire country, the motherland. It was the start of an interesting new journey and new chapter in her life.

The nasty immigration officer stamped her passport with a loud sigh and then proceeded, "OK, go over to that little room on the right where you see '*X-rays*'."

A huge, White, unfriendly nurse sat behind the desk in a cold office with a few chairs of the kind usually found in the dusty civil service offices of the 1960s. Tumelo filled out some forms about her medical history, and some moments later after handing them to the nurse, the doctor entered.

"Come through with me to the X-ray room." She noticed that names were not acknowledged. She was anonymous from the moment she landed at Heathrow. In South Africa, being addressed by your name was very important – a sign of respect.

"Take off your clothes and put on the gown hanging behind the door. Pregnant?"

"No."

"Come with me; we want to check for disease. You are from Cape Town, I notice. We need to check out your lungs for tuberculosis."

After the X-rays were done, she waited some time in the waiting room for the results. The doctor came back, "Go back to the immigration desk."

When she arrived a few months earlier for a previous visit to Europe, she was interrogated as if she was an intended suicide bomber. Picked out from the crowd with a colleague, Janice, who was travelling with her, they noticed that Afrikaner White South Africans who had travelled with them on the same South African Airways flight were let through immigration without a hint of suspicion or questioning.

Janice and Tumelo knew each other from the days of being in Dragon's class at UCT. For free Black South Africans, Heathrow

Airport was like a bolt of lightning from the sky, a shocking suction back into racism. They were horrified that Europe had not progressed far since the days of Professor Kohl, especially because London was the founding place of the anti-apartheid movement and the world famous Trafalgar Square of South Africa House where the statue of Nelson Mandela was planned to be erected.

"Hey, you two!! We want to question you together!" The tall immigration police officer gave them searching looks. He was standing a few yards away from them behind the immigration desk and instructed the officials (Sikh men) staffing the queue to keep them one side for "further questions".

Having put to rest the ghost of apartheid and its humiliation based on their colour, their first instinctive response was to chuckle, because it seemed like a surreal comedy. The last time they had experienced this kind of treatment was with the *boere* under apartheid. They used to shout at them and their mothers and fathers, "Hey you!! Get out of the shop. Go around the corner where you belong. You can't buy things in a shop. There is a little window for *you people* at the back! No dogs, Coloureds, or Blacks allowed *in* the shop!" When they boarded the wrong carriage on the train, they shouted once at Tumelo's mother, "Baboons that side to the back! This is Whites-only! Know your place!" When someone stole something, Blacks and Coloureds present were searched first.

Tumelo learned very quickly within those moments at Heathrow Airport that racism was not only a South African thing, but it was quite present in many parts of the world. In Denmark, she was mistaken for a Muslim woman, and snubbed in shops. When Tumelo entered a shop in Melbourne in Australia in 2000, she had a similar experience. When she went into a shopping centre, she was followed by one of the White attendants in the shop. She turned around and asked her, "Why are you following me? I don't need any help?" The shop assistant studied her suspiciously, then looked at her bags, at her pockets, and at her hands. She, most likely a descendant of the working class in England who was sent to Australia for petty crime such as stealing food, clearly had been ordered by the management to follow Tumelo because she was Black like the Aboriginal Australian people, and people like Tumelo are therefore assumed and thought to be "natural thieves", as if it is in the bloodline.

With her new-found freedom as a citizen of a free South Africa and as a permanent resident in Britain, Tumelo had to discover painfully this new truth about the world. You are viewed as either a thief, a terrorist, or up to mischief of some sort when you are Black in the colonial world. Her son, with his cornrow hairstyle, was stopped and searched for knives and suspected of crime by police in England almost on a weekly basis. His White friends had it easier. It was simply assumed by the White police that he has either already committed a crime, and if not, he was certainly on his way to do so. For some people and places, the world had certainly not moved on since the deeply racist days of Uncle Thabo.

"What are you laughing about?!" The immigration police officer shouted at Tumelo and Janice as if speaking to naughty children.

"Just laughing..." Janice quipped still amused and bursting with the humour that she saw in the situation. The official looked slowly through their passports, page after page. He frowned as if he finally had *something* on them. "Hey- you two – why are your surnames the same?!"

"Because they *happen* to be the same. We can't help it. Like you get people with the same surname anywhere in the world..."

"Are you *Muslim*...?!" At this, he pushed his head forward into their faces, almost toppling himself right over the counter.

Janice burst out laughing again at the absurdity, then a little louder. "No, we are not! People in Cape Town are *from all over the world* and can look and act like *anything*. Have you ever been to Cape Town?"

The brighter and beautiful side of Cape Town is like Rio de Janeiro, a place of festivals, food, long nights with strangers around fires having a *braai* (barbecue) and laughter. In spite of his aggression, Janice therefore extended a warm Cape Town smile his way.

He did not return the favour. Instead, the White Englishman became agitated with her perceived frivolity. To him, she was playing the fool, "It is no *joke* lady! Nothing *funny* about it. What do you *do*?! Why are you *here*! Stop treating this as a joke!"

What the White Englishman did not understand, is that a Capetonian Coloured person is hard to crack emotionally and psychologically.

"We are here to teach *your* teachers in the UK about things we know that *you people* don't know." Janice quipped.

"Coming to *teach* people *here?*" he asked with outright prejudice and curiosity.

He gave the paperwork of official invitations one dismissive look. He then proceeded to call another police officer: "I think I've got something with *these two...*"

A stern-looking White woman walked up to them as if marching in a military parade, frowning as if she was about to capture terrorists. "*Passports?!*"

They handed theirs over to her with their paperwork.

"What do you *do!?*"

Tumelo became impatient and sarcastic. It felt like some crazy provocation strategy. "We have *just* told your colleague that we are *professionals* on an exchange visit with the UK. Read the paperwork. We teach. We educate, on racism actually..."

"What do you *teach and train* people in?"

"Racism, human rights, civilisation, and development..." Tumelo snubbed.

"*Why* are you *here?!*"

"We have just *told* you!" Janice was now also becoming annoyed.

"My patience is running out with you two...why are you *here?!*" the English woman demanded again foolishly.

"We have just told you! And besides we are from the *Commonwealth* ...from Nelson Mandela's country, from *South Africa...*" Tumelo tried in desperation.

"No...we are not *sure* about *you two...*"

Janice turned to Tumelo and whispered, "Sister – I am afraid. This is about our *colour*...Gawd, unbelievable...Look all the White South Africans walked through with their green South African passports, without a hassle, without a suspicious stare. I cannot believe this? *England?!* In *England?!* Gawd – we had forgotten about this in South Africa. Thought we left Professor Dragon behind 20 years ago! Maybe she reincarnated and came to fucking Heathrow!"

When they eventually were let through, they were sweating. Janice was no longer laughing. Tumelo's blood pressure had shot up. She felt nauseous and sick, like after a search and interrogation under apartheid. The immigration officials at Heathrow had

touched a raw nerve. The two of them went into the toilets at
Heathrow. They looked at themselves in the mirror. They looked
at their hair, still as big and curly as in the days of Professor
Kohl. They stroked their complexions with their hands. They
had zoomed back into a time, into a horror movie of the past
that they had almost forgotten about or thought the world had
put to final rest. Janice turned to Tumelo and they both sighed
simultaneously, a deep, familiar, ancestral sigh.

Tumelo had met Janice for the first time on the UCT bus in
the early 1980s when they were sometimes the only two Black
passengers. They had marched together and made placards
together for the struggle. A few months before their travel to
Europe, Janice's mother, who was ecstatic at being free, died of a
heart attack.

The encounter at Heathrow brought back vivid memories of
how Janice's mother spoke to both of them as they sat on a spring
day in a previously Whites-only park in Cape Town, enjoying
the birds and the colourful Cape spring blooms. She seemed the
happiest woman in the world as they sat chatting on the bench
in the park feeding squirrels, "To think that I worked as a child
domestic in the White madam's house, and here we are today a
free people! Who would have thought that one day I'd be sitting
with you in the *White madam's park* on the *White madam's bench?!*
Now, you two, promise me something. When I die, bury me in the
White madam's cemetery next to her grave! Even better, bury me
in the *same hole* – if you can find one! That would be first prize!
This *Coloured madam* wants her *sweet revenge!*" She laughed
outlandishly as she joked about the White madam and told them
how happy she was even when freedom only came in her life when
she was already well over 70 years old. This was Tumelo's last
conversation with Janice's mother.

When she died so suddenly after this conversation, Janice
fulfilled her mother's wish. Her funeral service was held on a
rainy day in a former Whites-only church. As the coffin descended
slowly into the former Whites-only grave in the former Whites-
only cemetery, the sky opened up. The silvery white bulky clouds
parted. The sun shone through, and a faint rainbow formed in the
horizon in the direction of the sea. Janice was holding Tumelo's
hand tightly as they buried her mother and fulfilled her wish. And
in her painful and still lonely moment of grief and final goodbye
to her mother on that day, Janice turned to Tumelo and smiled;

the tears streamed down her face running into the raindrops that pearled from her full ebony-coloured face.

At Heathrow, Janice turned to Tumelo, "I want to take a shower. I feel violated..."

There was graffiti scribbled on the plastic toilet holder in red ink *"Save the world! Kill a Muslim!"*

After settling in England in the months that followed, Tumelo felt that she had certainly zoomed back into being a Black person in the 1970s and 1980s in South Africa, not with similar severity, but with more nuanced racism. On her daily trips on the tube in London Tumelo was shocked to see how seats next to Muslim and Black people were left deliberately unoccupied. Often, Whites wouldn't take up the seat no matter how packed the train is. In South Africa, she was part of a majority. In England, she was now a "BME" person – Black Minority Ethnic. It felt as if she was having a very nasty dream from which she struggled to wake, a nightmare, just to wake up to find it was not over. It was as if the White nurses and doctors were staring over into her cot to welcome her into this next apartheid hell, while she lay there as a newborn baby stripped of everything.

She came to meet many brave and strong African and Caribbean women who had done their time, like many ethnic minority women, in the notorious Black-populated mental institutions in England. A Black friend from South Africa confided, "I just snapped one day, and found myself in this hospital ward with other Black women...it happens to most of us...your brain can't take racism and discrimination any more...not in this day and age...with Mandela smiling at you in Westminster opposite the Houses of Parliament!"

Her work took her to listen to hundreds of stories like her own in London. One woman told her. "I arrived here in London as a qualified Black teacher. In the end, I was told that I should look for something else. I ended up as a bus driver. I was told to forget who I was in Africa; I was just not up to 'standard', they told me. I have been driving the red buses here in London for some years now, although I feel wasted as a qualified teacher."

In her various travels in London, Tumelo met African Caribbean people who had survived deep mental trauma. Like Tumelo, they do not want to be victims. They do not want to give that kind of credit to the empire. In listening to all these stories, many memories of her life in South Africa came flooding back.

Stories of her ancestors came flooding back. Just when she thought it was all over – the struggle had started again. Just when she thought her looks and background did not matter at all, she was transported back into another bizarre, mad place.

In July 2007, three bombs hit the underground trains in London. A fourth bomb exploded on a big red London double-decker bus an hour later. The bombings left 52 commuters and four suicide bombers dead. The bombings were notably on the fourth anniversary of the Bradford Riots in West Yorkshire, as a result of tensions between the Anti-Nazi League and the far-right National Front. The riot, which involved about 1,000 young people, left more than 300 people injured including 120 police with damage of nearly £30 million. It was later reported that the Asian men were given "excessive" prison sentences, and that the judicial system failed to consider the fear that people feel for White racists in the UK. It was reported that 200 racists arrived from Belgium on the morning of the riots. Other racists arrived by train and car to attack the Asian community.

Tumelo then understood the interrogations at Heathrow, as the July 7 bombings were blamed on the international terrorist organisation Al Qaeda, meaning *The Base* in Arabic. Al Qaeda and its leader Osama bin Laden was also held responsible for the 9/11 attacks on New York in 2001. Tumelo was now caught up in this new war with the body, in which her own body now was associated with what "the global enemy looked like".

Asian-looking young people with backpacks are particularly suspect in the UK. Everybody stares suspiciously at suitcases and grocery bags. London, like New York, is gripped in fear. White men and women in business suits, with sweat forming crystals on their brows, brave the underground tube in London every morning in silent fear.

Two weeks after the fateful bombings another tragedy hit London. It shook the world's nerves when 27-year-old Jean Charles de Menezes of Gonzaga in Brazil was shot dead in cold blood as a suspected suicide bomber on the underground at Stockwell. Jean Charles de Menezes could so easily have been a Coloured young man from South Africa, living in and working in London (like so many do). The neatly dressed young electrician and son of a bricklayer, far away from home and family - like so many thousands of Londoners - was held down by police and shot seven times in the head at close range. His face flashed for two years after the incident on posters and the front pages of national newspapers – a familiar face of a mixed race young man, like a cousin or nephew of Tumelo's on the Cape Flats. It turned out that he was not carrying explosives, nor was he in any way connected to the bombings. It was said that he "looked out of place", and somebody even falsely imagined that "he had a bomb belt with wires coming out". Some eyewitnesses also claimed he "was dressed like a terrorist". However, he was simply and neatly dressed in light denim jeans and a top, as it was a hot summer's day in London. In recent news reports, it turned out that the police officers *knew* he was not a bomber some time before he was killed. More disturbingly, CCTV cameras revealed that de Menezes was picking up a morning paper and walking calmly through Stockwell tube station moments before he was gunned down as a terrorist. He was not running and jumping over ticket barriers, as originally reported by the police who shot him. Jean Charles de Menezes was simply an ethnic minority Londoner, a "Coloured", like millions of his kind in the world. Ironically, he could so easily have been a young Barack Obama or a Hugo Chavez, who interestingly look like "Coloured" men from the Cape Flats. In England, his fatal misfortune was that he "looked" like a "suicide bomber".

In London, Tumelo met a man from Chile who had endured torture in the stadium where Victor Jara was murdered. He showed her his amputated fingers, and she was reminded of the days with Mr. Torres and his guitar. She met Cubans who lived under Fidel Castro and who danced with her into the night to *Guantanamera*. She met Bolivians who had worked in the coal mines that she read about in *Let me Speak*. She met Nicaraguans, Venezuelans, and hundreds of compatriots from the African continent. She met Sudanese women who had fled from mutilation of their genitalia. She listened to heart-wrenching stories of women from Sierra Leone who fled during the civil war, and who have never really recovered from the trauma of losing place and identity. She met a Bosnian man who lost his father in the massacre of Muslims in the genocide, and who changed his name to a Christian name to get work in prejudiced England.

Disturbingly, she met a young, Black, Nigerian woman, who worked at a recruitment agency, at which she was instructed by her White bosses to not short-list "difficult surnames we can't pronounce". She met Serbs, and Croats, Greeks and Turks, Indians and Pakistanis – the world in its beautiful diversity of also conflict and tension. She had come to enjoy the warmth and dignity of African Caribbean people, the quick minds of the poetic Nigerians, the cuisine of the Moroccans, the charm of the Egyptians, the philosophical company of the Nepalese, the spontaneous laughter of the Italians, the passionate rhythmic dance of the Spanish, the fine cuisine of the French, the passion for truth of the Scotsmen, and the determination of the industrious Poles. They were all simply just people, people from the common race of humanity.

However, she also had some close shavings with "spoilers" of this common humanity, right-wing Afrikaners who made England their home by supporting the BNP campaigns and designing their websites and racist pamphlets after fleeing South Africa after the 1994 elections. Two Afrikaner men, likely followers of Eugene Terre'blanche, once sat opposite her on the tube, loudly discussing in Afrikaans "the problem with immigrants in Europe" and "getting rid of the kaffirs and Muslims". The two men, dressed in Hawaiian shirts and khaki shorts, followed her when she disembarked. One bore an uncanny resemblance to Captain Adolf.

At Piccadilly Circus one evening, she went into Garfunkels Restaurant to enjoy a black coffee. It was warm and cosy inside as she listened to *Mr. Bojangles* playing on the radio. Tumelo hummed along to herself as she watched people passing by in their warm coats and scarves of many colours. The large shop window was damp with the breath of the customers inside. She cleared a piece of window with the sleeve of her jersey to peep through. The young Polish waitress, struggling with English, brought her the menu. A copy of the conservative *Evening Standard* lay on the table. She flipped through the pages.

One double spread page was dedicated to "fighting terrorism". Another article read "London's migrants cost £50 million per year...people are sponsored to enter Britain..."

She watched people passing by – all anonymous and indifferent. Spotting her, an elderly, friendly, seemingly homeless White man with his many plastic bags stuffed with his only personal belongings pushed his face against the window into her face. He pressed his nose flat like a clown on the glass. He smiled at her; his teeth were brown and uneven. Some of his teeth were rotten down to the gums. She studied the hairs in his large round nostrils. Unshaven, he waved a copy of *The Big Issue* at her; his gesture was warm, brief, friendly, and clown-like. He walked on again and waved at Tumelo, as if they were old friends in a deja vu encounter. He disappeared into the subway of the Piccadilly underground.

Three Black Muslim women wearing scarves passed by the shop window, walking huddled together. Visibly awkward and uncomfortable in the crowd, their heads pointed down on the road towards their shoes, as they seemed accustomed to finding their way in London without having to look up.

Two windscreen cleaners ran up and down the road at the traffic lights. One, a huge, scruffy White man wearing a baseball hat, walked bravely with cigarette in the mouth running between cars, giving them an unsolicited service. Some paid him, others bluntly ignored him. His partner, a Black man of similar description and desperation ran up and down alongside him, begging from the indifferent motorists. Tumelo watched the red buses come and go.

She walked back to the square, up the steps of the green statue to take a closer look at Eros, a figure from Greek mythology with mermaids and small water fountains around its base. Eros from Ateros – God of requited love, of love returned, love that must be answered for it to prosper.

Chapter 20
The Dance Behind Reeds

In the houses of many homes of older Cape Coloured people who were born in the 1930s and before, pictures of Queen Elizabeth, Prince Philip, and Princess Diana adorn the walls of lounges and dining rooms, as part of the "family album". In drawers and in glass cabinets, there are silver jubilee memorabilia of Queen Elizabeth ll, coronation spoons of Betty and of the Queen Mother, marriage mugs of Prince Charles and Princess Diana, bookmarks and key rings, photos of Windsor Castle, of King George V, and of Prince Philip. The British royal family was in the past an important part of the identity of many older generation Cape Coloured people who curated their homes as if they were part of this "family". It was part of saying, "I am a decent Coloured", or "I come from this family", or "I have my roots with this family".

An African Caribbean friend in London whose mother worships the queen and the royal family related, "When my mother cooks Caribbean food here in London, she closes all the windows so that the neighbours don't get the *whiff* of our African flavours." She added, "As if that is not enough, my mother further *wraps* the leftovers in *dozens* of plastic bags, so that the neighbours can't pick up our African roots. So, even though my mother longs for her food from home, it is a *major* ritual for us as a family to be able to eat the food we long for..."

Sipping from her glass of white wine, the queen peeped over the rim of her glass as she spoke with Tumelo. She seemed a simple ordinary, friendly, elderly lady. What was the fuss all about the queen? Tumelo wondered.

At the palace, she also met a Black designer from Senegal who had made a name for herself, "I am good enough for cocktails at

Buckingham Palace, but do you know that when I was called by a White client who wanted to see me on a referral in upmarket Sloane Square, where Princess Diana liked to shop, I had a nasty encounter. I rang the doorbell of this house. The wealthy woman opened the door, was surprised to see that the famous designer was a *Black* woman, and abruptly ordered me to go around to the back door. I refused and walked away."

Tumelo was indeed not alone at Buckingham Palace. She knew that all her ancestors were there honouring a long awaited karmic visit. The sound of the African orchestra drummed and rattled the walls of the palace. They arrived without invitation, and invaded the palace as regal as queens and princes, and as kings and queens in their own right. The music instruments formed an instrumental ensemble of harmonic African and Indian sounds, of stringed instruments, plucked and strummed, of flutes, of the oboe, of clarinets, of bassoons, of trumpets, of trombones, of horns, of tubas, of drums big and small, of percussionists, of bells, of rattles, and violins. The ancestors were all there in their diverse entirety. There were the Khoisan ancestors scantily dressed like Gandhi and burning rosemary and *buchu* and the orange blooms of wild dagga in abalone shell; great great granny Indira was dancing trance-like on the red carpet to the flute, to the harp and drums, shaking her belly in ancient rhythms, with the elephants following her. Her enslaved Muslim great-grandmothers walked in gently with their black veils, walking with their heads bowed, even her impoverished great-grandfather from England entered like Oliver Twist, cap in hand. Annie was there, with wild daisies decorated in her hair, and with shoes on her feet, and a case for her schoolbooks. Uncle Thaba was there, a free man with all his pieces together and without a pass, and without his shackles from Robben Island. Lena and Robert walked in, draped in honeysuckle branches, loving openly. Themba walked in with a crowd of jubilant children, women and men who had become the haunting face of Aids. The little boy from the Karoo walked in with his playing sticks without a limp.

The crowd was escorting a special queen from Africa. Delicately fully covered in purple cloths, carried on the back of an African elephant, and with brass bangles on her feet, she waved her ostrich feathers as she entered. She had returned with all her pieces in place since her painful death and parade at Piccadilly in England 200 years earlier. The scent of *buchu* and wild *dagga* orange blooms invaded the corridors of the palace, as a band of African drummers serenaded the African queen in. An African shaman, a trance-healer, danced until he went into a state of trance. The Muslim wise man was there cleansing the palace with his incense sticks. The palace was infused with the cleansing of sacred roots, herbs, water and precious oils.

For as Tumelo and her siblings splashed and laughed in the mosquito-infested green muddy waters, making it a sea in their minds, the hippos far behind the reeds in the deeper waters hid their little ears in shame, while the pink flamingoes danced amongst the reeds, with their heads poignantly bowed, and the pelicans took flight.

Yes, anything is possible.

Post Script

President Nelson Mandela established the Truth and Reconciliation Commission (TRC) after the legal abolition of apartheid. South Africa chose the path of "truth and reconciliation" instead of the post-Nazi Nuremberg Trials in Germany.

A close intellectual friend and comrade of Mr. Torres and Adiel (who was a member of the ANC) was appointed by President Nelson Mandela as the Minister of Justice. He promoted the TRC as an important legal process to allow for South Africans to come to terms with their past and to move forward as a "reconciled nation".

The TRC was set up in Cape Town through the Promotion of National Unity and Reconciliation Act, No 34 of 1995. The Commission called for witnesses of gross human rights violations committed between 1960 and 1994 and for Winnie Mandela and the liberation movements to appear for atrocities committed. Perpetrators could apply for amnesty.

F.W.de Klerk apologised to the Commission for the harm caused by apartheid. P.W. Botha mocked the TRC as a "circus" and never apologised.

The Commission handed in its final report in 1998. Many people in South Africa feel that the work of the TRC is incomplete, as the deep horrors of colonialism and apartheid and the everyday unspeakable psychological damage done to the victims of apartheid and to those who sacrificed their lives and families for the struggle have not yet been talked about openly.

Eve survived as a mental health patient, to see the release of Nelson Mandela in 1990, but died peacefully in her sleep in 1993, a year before the first democratic elections in 1994. Eve's parents and grandparents had natural deaths during the height of apartheid in the 1950s and 1960s.

The driver who knocked down Uncle Thaba was never found. His sons became leading human rights lawyers in the Eastern Cape.

Andrew Thunderstorm married an African woman, a fellow medical doctor at Baragwanath Hospital. They both became active in the campaign for anti-retrovirals for pregnant women in South Africa under Mbeki's government.

Mrs. Thunderstorm returned to England, to live in the remote countryside where she campaigns actively against the British Nationalist Party (BNP).

Dr. Piet is still making dentures. His African helper resigned from his job during the student uprisings in 1976. Some twenty years later, he graduated as the respected Dr. Sifiso Mseleku, an orthodontist, from the University of the Western Cape (UWC). His patients are from the "Coloured" community and as a practice policy, he does not do extractions of front teeth.

Lena grew old enough to witness how the relatives and descendants of Robert, of Aunty Maggie and Uncle Jack, and even of Kruger and Kaiser, became staunch right-wing racist Afrikaners in later years in South Africa.

Mrs. Fudge retired as a matron of a school hostel in the Northern Cape, where she still lives.

The Harvey family traced their roots to ordinary people in Indonesia. One of their African servants became a leading and well-respected local ANC politician. The Harvey couple remains much admired members of their church and community and has converted to the ANC.

Tumelo never saw Mr. Torres again. He had mellowed and lived with his long time partner in a cottage on the coast, where he spent his time building boats.

Mr. Magee phoned Tumelo a few times from his new home in Kuala Lumpur and sent her some cards, letters and also his latest books on the emerging imperialist power of China in Africa. He was a freelance writer and happily married to a fellow White American.

Norma became a leading and successful schoolmistress, and a couple of her classmates became leading provincial political Ministers.

Nobody heard about Dragon again.

Petula graduated from UWC with a PhD in the field of feminism, and directs a women's organisation fighting sexual and domestic violence on the Cape Flats.

Tessa married, had a family, and lives a low profile life on the coast as an avant garde artist.

Dr. Elvira was never traced.

Captain Adolf and other right-wing South African racists joined the British National Party in Europe.

Ahmed was appointed as a key minister in South Africa's cabinet in 2004. He no longer promotes the "Four Races Theory".

Alfredo and his comrades became key government officials in the New South Africa.

Ms. Nkosi and Mr. Benjamen remained committed teachers and post-apartheid activists for global justice.

Themba was one of close to 5 million people in South Africa who sadly succumbed to AIDS.

The k-word rightfully is banned, though still widely used like the h-word. The racist label "Cape Coons" has been replaced by the now widely accepted term "Cape Minstrels".

A new generation of black African ANC Youth emerged during President Mbeki's reign under the leadership of the notorious Julius Malema.

The AWB founder and leader, Eugene Terre'blanche, was brutally murdered by two African males over the Easter weekend in 2010. One of the murderers was an African child of 15 years old. Police were investigating reports of alleged sodomy and a wage dispute.

Most South Africans are today proud to be Black, Khoisan, and South African. White people all over the world are also increasingly researching and embracing their African roots. A book published in 1984 during the height of apartheid by a White academic, H.F. Heese, listed the names of more than 1,000 Europeans who married people of colour in the Cape Colony between 1652 and 1795. They gave birth to huge "Afrikaner" families who most likely claimed "purity" and supported apartheid.

South Africans are still traumatised by the large-scale psychological damage done by apartheid, and many are urged to write their stories. Tabloid newspapers, such as *The Voice*, have filled the gap to provide a form of escapism for marginalised and mostly poorly-educated Cape Coloured communities, through the local in-your-face language of the people.

Both world statesman Nelson Mandela and world renowned Archbishop Desmond Tutu discovered respectively through their recent DNA tests done in 2006 and 2010 that they come from the indigenous San people, like most Cape Coloured people. The most powerful and influential political leaders in the world today also come from a similar history of a mixed heritage: President

Barack Obama of the United States of America and President Hugo Chavez of Venezuela. The DNA tests show that all human beings come from one common ancestor who lived in Africa. We are one human family, and the term "Cape Coloured" is therefore not useful.

Today South Africa is one of the wealthiest countries in the world, in both mineral resources and production. It is very advanced in industries and technology, and has one of the most progressive constitutions and equality policies in the world. However, land ownership is still predominantly White. There are a few Black millionaires, and the majority of the poor are Black and Coloured.

South Africa made world history not only in 1994, but will also do so in 2010, when it hosts the first World Cup in Football on the African continent. The people of South Africa will be welcoming the world to its beautiful shores and landscape steeped in a painful, yet triumphant history of a diverse and immensely proud people of the world who have magically survived.

Big voluptuous bodies and images of African beauty are now celebrated.

Today, no children in South Africa have to hide behind reeds with their parents in shame of their skin colour.

Printed in Great Britain
by Amazon

44577657R00162